To my Son
with love,

Amy Tan

The Perez Legacy

The Perez Legacy

❖

Redemption

Judith Tanielian

To order additional copies of this book, contact:
Xlibris LLC
1-888-795-4274
www.Xlibris.com
Orders@Xlibris.com
649863

CONTENTS

Dedication 7

Acknowledgments 9

Prologue 11

Chapter One: Eduardo's Early Life 17

Chapter Two: Life in California 31

Chapter Three: The Gang 45

Chapter Four: Villa Perez 56

Chapter Five: Crime at the Villa 64

Chapter Six: A Revelation 71

Chapter Seven: Philip's Reverie 74

Chapter Eight: Hunting and Healing 100

Chapter Nine: The Cousins and Angie 116

Chapter Ten: A New Beginning 120

Chapter Eleven: The Contract 131

Chapter Twelve: Lessons 138

Chapter Thirteen: The Sting 145

Chapter Fourteen: Etiquette 150

Chapter Fifteen: Revenge 157

Chapter Sixteen: Thanksgiving 164

Chapter Seventeen: The Christmas Party 171

Chapter Eighteen: A Friend Poses a Puzzle 178

Chapter Nineteen: Kristen and Andrew's Wedding 185

Chapter Twenty: The Vacation 191

Chapter Twenty-One: The Lessons Continue 201

Chapter Twenty-Two: College 220

Chapter Twenty-Three: The Internship 228

Chapter Twenty-Four: A Painful Diagnosis 241

Chapter Twenty-Five: The Legacy 253

Epilogue 259

DEDICATION

My sister, Jeannene Tanielian, was the consummate story teller and her ability to relate vivid word pictures entertained me for hours as a young child. Our bicycles became horses that took us on wonderful adventures. As we grew older I lived her life vicariously in many ways as she generously shared stories of travel that took her to many wonderful places. Jeannene and I had talked of writing a book together but, before we were able to accomplish that, she was taken from us.

Jeannene, this story is for you.

ACKNOWLEDGMENTS

This book was not created in isolation, and so I am compelled to acknowledge and thank those people who contributed to the completion of this work.

My husband, Dr. Aram Tanielian, was a driving force in the completion of this book. He held me accountable to my proclamation that I could do this. He listened to each chapter as the plot developed and then listened again when the last chapter was complete. He encouraged me and provided honest feedback and valuable suggestions. Thank you, Aram. I love you.

Our family friend, Basil Pius, a writer in his own right and a college English teacher, read my third draft. Basil corrected my grammar and punctuation, advised me about revisions, and encouraged me to publish. I am indebted to you, Basil, for the hours you spent on my manuscript.

Libby Smith, a retired teacher and an actress, provided invaluable criticism after reading my manuscript. When she wrote in the margin, "I don't buy this," my heart sank. After spending weeks reworking things, I have a better story and I am a happier person. I have you to thank for that, Libby.

I would also like to thank Charles Dylan Cox for the technical advice he offered with such a willing heart.

PROLOGUE

The Palos Verdes Peninsula
October 12, 1990

"Your cognac, Uncle Philip." Eduardo set the drink's tray on a side table of inlaid wood. Philip Perez took the glass proffered, holding it against the fading light to better study the color and clarity of its contents. His hand trembled with the effort. Tilting the glass sideways and then upright, the older man watched amber tears slide down the smooth inside edge of the crystal, revealing the viscosity of the liquor, an indication of its character. "Tears and character," he said almost to himself.

"Uncle?" Eduardo questioned.

"A fine nectar," Philip replied in breathy tones, looking up at the younger man. "Do you remember your lessons, Eduardo, color, clarity, and viscosity? The eye must appraise the liquor before the tongue can fully appreciate it."

A guarded smile smoothed lines of tension on Eduardo's face as he met his uncle's gaze. There was great strength in the older man's intensely dark eyes and penetrating stare. His hair, although still black, had been severely thinned by chemotherapy. His smile revealed straight even teeth in a hollow-cheeked face, and a light five o'clock shadow covered the prominent chin and jawline. Eduardo's smile spread slightly as he noted Philip's navy cashmere blend jacket, still a favorite after so many years.

The young man reached to light a lamp on the table between the two overstuffed leather chairs where Perez enjoyed holding court. "No, leave it off," Philip instructed. "Maria lay wood in the fireplace, and firelight will be sufficient." The older man knew his deeply held feelings would flow more easily in the shadowed comfort of his favorite room, and tonight he had much to discuss with Eduardo. The words came with difficulty, and Eduardo wondered if Philip had the strength to share what was on his heart. The tremor of his hand was conspicuous. Eduardo's own hand slid from the lamp to the older man's arm, resting on the cashmere sleeve, once tailored to a muscular frame, now hanging limp and deflated.

Setting his drink down, Philip placed his own hand over Eduardo's and patted it paternalistically. He both anticipated and dreaded the conversation that lay before them. "Did you bring a glass for yourself?" Then eyeing the tray with the decanter and a second glass already poured, he said, "Ah, yes. Good." He removed his hand and motioned to the fireplace before them.

Once the kindling caught, Eduardo sank into the chair reserved for him, setting his hands on the wide armrests. The leather was smooth and cool beneath his sweaty palms. Involuntarily, a chill passed through his body. Eduardo usually enjoyed such moments as this, but tonight a sense of foreboding hung heavily in the room. He reached for his glass, wanting to chug the whole thing, not from a desire for the liquor but for the hope of relaxation it might bring to his body. Dutifully, he held it to the firelight, examining the liquid amber before tilting the glass to observe the sheet of fluid break into tears and slide back into the body of cognac. Holding the glass to his nose, he inhaled briefly then more deeply, trying to appreciate the underlying fruity tones. Cautiously, he sipped and stifled a cough as the liquor burned his lips and throat. The overriding sensation was one of having just imbibed kerosene.

Philip smiled again. "It is an acquired taste, but if you sip slowly, it will most likely not end up on the Tabriz." His eyes, so dark they appeared black, now twinkled with mischief; and in that moment, Eduardo realized that Philip knew about a surreptitious tasting years ago when the boy's curiosity overcame his better judgment. A large swig had quickly ended on the carpet in a bout of choking and coughing.

Eduardo bowed his, head chuckling in embarrassment. "Are there no secrets in this house?" he pled.

"I hope not," was the reply, "at least not after this evening." Philip Perez was not in the habit of sharing deeply personal information or his best liquor with Eduardo; but his life was ending, and there were things he must say, things to which both he and Eduardo must agree. His thoughts went back over twenty years to a day he could not forget, and familiar old bonds of anguish began to wrap around his soul, bonds that had not troubled him for years. They began their tightening, choking hold, drawing him down into an emotional pit from the depths of which he would see no light. A soft moan broke the silence of the room.

"Are you all right?" the young man asked, his concern evident.

Eduardo's question broke through the darkness enveloping Philip. "Yes," he said, turning to the young man, "I am all right." But the eyes no longer twinkled. Sunken into their sockets with the progression of disease, there was pain, but Philip offered a weak smile. All right, Eduardo was unconvinced. The disease had taken its toll, but he sensed there was a deeper pain that he did not understand. Recognizing the concern on Eduardo's face, Philip deftly shifted the focus of the conversation to the young man.

"Are you still angry with me, Eduardo?" he asked, his broad brow furrowed in concern.

"Angry?" The question had indeed shifted the conversation and caught the young man off guard.

Though Eduardo's face was turned toward him, the lengthening shadows obscured his expression, and Philip could not discern his companion's thoughts. "Yes, angry," he repeated. "I have not been easy on you."

Eduardo stared deep into the flames fluttering atop the logs before them. "No," he said, "no, there is no anger, only gratitude." The words did not come quickly, but they were deeply considered and sincere. He raised his glass to his lips and took a second sip.

Appreciation for the cognac still eluded him, but he swallowed, feeling warmth in the back of his throat after it slid down. *Gratitude and love,* he thought, for truly he had come to love this man who sat beside him.

Philip laughed. "Gratitude at last. You were quite angry in the beginning, Eduardo, and for a very long time." Though fearing in some sphere of his being that the boy was only being polite, in his gut, he sensed the truth in Eduardo's words.

Eduardo drew a deep breath. He heard the fear in his uncle Philip's voice, and in spite of the man's chuckle, the anxiety gripping his own soul deepened. There were few things this young man feared, but tonight the dark shadows gathering in the study could almost be touched, and his gut tightened in anticipation of something he could not name.

Eduardo's eyes drifted over the shadowed room, eventually resting on the outline of a hand-carved desk that sat before a large window. Ornate woodwork at the corners continued down the legs and across the front, concealing a small drawer that, when unlocked, pulled as smoothly from the desk as a well-oiled knife from its sheath. Eduardo had found the desk two years prior half hidden beneath piles of hides in a smelly leather shop outside Mexico City. A sightseeing interlude had been unexpectedly interrupted by the discovery and acquisition of the desk. There had been little to recommend it with layers of peeling paint and a sticky drawer, but an eye trained for detail was drawn to the artfully joined pieces of wood and the unmistakable craftsmanship of a once beautiful piece of furniture. *Another lesson successfully put into practice,* he thought. The desk's careful restoration took weeks and was personally attended to by Eduardo. After removing coats of paint, he had stained and buffed the dark wood until it attained a smoothness that begged to be caressed. Philip was especially

fond of the gift and spent many hours there writing in his journals. Other
pieces in the room had been carefully chosen by Eduardo as well, and he
knew the restrained elegance of this cozy den brought pleasure to his uncle.
He played his toe around a floral design on the Tabriz carpet. The rug had
cost Philip a small fortune, but its densely knotted wool and silk made it an
investment worth every cent.

Eduardo smiled in reverie and gently swirled the contents of his glass
before taking another sip. Uncle Philip was correct about the anger, although
Eduardo did not think of it as anger. What this unwilling foster child
experienced in the first few weeks of his life at Villa Perez was something
more akin to rage. Unconsciously, he massaged an old scar on his left
forearm, an action that was habitual and borne of anxiety.

"What was the worst of it?" Philip probed, having been lost in his own
reverie for a few moments.

The smile deepened on Eduardo's face as the warmth of the cognac
spread through his body, easing the grip fear had put on him. "The music,
Uncle Philip, the music angered me the most. It was foreign to my ears, to
my whole being." The boy chuckled. "It required a contemplative spirit, and
you yourself know that I was not a contemplative child. I hated the music
long after I could name each concerto, each composer."

"You show appreciation for classical works now, Eduardo. I hear the
music coming from your room in the evening, and it is not the irritating
cacophony of sounds you once embraced." This was said with a knowing
smile.

Eduardo could not suppress a laugh. "You will not be satisfied until you
have won my very soul," he joked. "Yes, have it your way. I appreciate the
music of the masters." Then eyeing Philip in mock seriousness, he said, "But
I will always love the electric guitar."

"I think the wardrobe brought you no pleasure either," Philip offered.
The vision of Eduardo, petulant in his first suit, raised a hearty chuckle
ending in a bout of coughing.

"A glass of water, Uncle?"

"Another cognac!" This was followed by more chuckling and coughing.

"I will call Dr. Montoya," Eduardo said, rising. "We have already
overstepped his instructions with the first glass—"

"Forget Montoya," Philip interrupted. "He knows the prognosis.
Nothing will change it. Good company and a hearty laugh are the medicine
I need now, and you can provide me both."

Eduardo hesitated only slightly before pouring the cognac. The fear
was returning. What would he do without this man? Oh, he would survive.

He was prepared psychologically and intellectually to take his place in this world, but he could not imagine his world without Philip Perez. In tones barely above a whisper, his fear found a voice. "I will miss you greatly, Uncle."

"And I you, Eduardo." Tears slid down the older man's cheeks.

CHAPTER ONE

Eduardo's Early Life

San Jenaro, Mexico
June 1984

A pivotal event occurred in Eduardo's life when he was fourteen. It was the kind of event by which one marks time for the rest of their life by saying "before" or "after" such and such happened. Few events occurred in the little Mexican village north of Guadalajara that stood out from the day-to-day routine of things, but this night was the precursor to one of those events for Eduardo.

The night air was still and humid. The sweet scent of jasmine growing under the bedroom window mingled with a metallic odor, a hint of impending lightning. Eduardo did not know if it was the crash of thunder that awakened him or the sound of angry voices in the living room. Anger was an emotion his grandfather rarely displayed, and the old man did not tolerate shouting in his house; but tonight his voice rose with fury. Eduardo lay quietly listening to conversation that projected in pieces through the thin wall separating the living room from the house's only bedroom.

". . . only if they . . . the boy . . ." And a hand hit the table.

"Fool . . ." That was Tia Juanita's voice.

". . . your promise . . .," It was Grandfather again. "You have never liked . . . don't understand . . ."

"His father and grandparents were spoiled rich people. The boy is just like them. He will get in the way," Tia Juanita said in a voice growing loud enough for Eduardo to catch each word.

"That was the agreement," sounded Grandfather's voice, stronger than Eduardo had ever heard it. "That was the agreement. You know I am not well. I have not been well since Lupe . . ." Here, he choked. "The periods of depression are more frequent and severe. The boy would suffer greatly if I had another spell."

"We would all suffer if that happened again," Juanita said. Loud footsteps echoed across the living room floor. The front door opened and slammed shut in perfect synchronization with the second clap of thunder. Grandfather entered the bedroom, slammed the door equally hard, and crawled into bed next to Eduardo. The boy lay quietly, listening as Grandfather's breathing settled into a steady rhythm and his tense body relaxed. He knew his grandfather was not well, and this caused Eduardo anxiety. The old man suffered from bouts of depression, and when Eduardo was an infant, Grandfather had had a heart attack. The boy ran the pieces of conversation through his mind and was convinced that Grandfather and Tia Juanita had been talking about him. Tia Juanita always said he got in the way no matter how hard he tried to please her. Now it seemed he would get in the way again; but in the way of what? He wished she would treat him as kindly as she treated her grandsons. Grandfather had paid the coyotes to take four of them across the border into California. Now that they were gone, Tia was even more cross with Eduardo. When Eduardo talked with Grandfather about it, the old man said she missed her grandsons and that was why she was cross. The grandsons sent her money each month, but the money had not changed her attitude for the better. If Eduardo had understood jealousy, he would have understood Tia Juanita; but his heart was as kind as his grandfather's, and jealousy was not an emotion he indulged in. Although Grandfather was not rich, he made sure Eduardo had proper clothes, enough to eat, and a few toys and pieces of sporting equipment. That and Grandfather's love sustained Eduardo in contentment. The boy did not understand that Juanita used a different yardstick for measuring her happiness and contentment.

The morning broke fresh and clear. Grandfather left the little house, saying he would be back later. Eduardo arose to get ready for school. In the bathroom, he studied his face in an old mirror that had lost some of its silver backing over the years. His skin was much fairer than that of his grandfather or the rest of the family. His grandmother had died long ago, and there were no pictures of her. His parents died when he was too young to remember them. Maybe he resembled one of them. He moved within inches of the mirror. At fourteen, Eduardo's chin and upper lip sprouted silky hair that matched in color the wavy black mass atop his head. He rubbed his jawline, bewildered and yet somehow proud of the new definition his jaw and nose were developing. No longer the soft face of a little boy; perhaps this was the face of his father. He studied his broad tanned brow, blinked the snapping black eyes staring back at him, and the corners of his mouth curled up ever so slightly in approval of the young man he saw.

He knew father and mother died in an accident, but that was all he knew. Once, when he was five or six, he asked Tia Juanita where his parents were.

"Humpf'" she snorted. She turned to face Eduardo, and the contempt in her eyes was unmistakable. "Trying to be something she was not meant to be, your mother was, living like a princess in that big house, wearing dresses that cost as many pesos as my husband made in six months in the fields." Tia Juanita's remarks were met with puzzlement. "Your mother was too good to live here with us," Tia said as if explaining her hatred. "She married into a wealthy family. It was only natural that someone would eventually give her the evil eye." Juanita's own eyes narrowed as she continued. "They all died except you: your father, his wealthy parents, and her." The last word was spit from Juanita's mouth as a short cruel laugh raised itself from her chest, almost choking her next words. "You were too ugly for anyone's jealousy, and so you lived." She watched unmoved as tears welled in Eduardo's eyes. He ran to the bathroom, shutting the door so Tia Juanita could not watch him cry. Curled into the corner next to the toilet, he sobbed until his tears were spent. Before leaving the bathroom, he cautioned a look in Grandfather's old crackled mirror. He saw the tear-stained face of a small child, but he never saw what Tia Juanita described as ugly. He did not know why Tia lied, but in his heart, he knew she had. There was no evil eye, and he was not ugly.

Eduardo cleared his mind of the reverie and walked out of the house with an empty stomach. It was the last day of school for the year. The anticipation Eduardo usually felt at the beginning of summer was missing today. In its place was apprehension stemming from last night's events and Grandfather's early departure this morning with little more than "I'll be back."

The morning air was already getting dusty from the trucks rumbling down Camino Destileria, transporting their loads of agave hearts to the tequila factory a half mile from Grandfather's house. Eduardo stepped out on the porch and brushed a coating of the red powder from Grandfather's rocking chair, coughing as it settled on his clothes, his hair, and his face. This was where Grandfather sat most evenings after dinner. The chair had been Grandmother's when she was alive, and Grandfather said sitting in it made him feel closer to her.

Descending three wooden stairs to the dirt yard, he searched the road for any sign of his grandfather. For as long as he could remember, he had lived with this quiet man who spoke little, but whose words carried great wisdom. When his grandfather was not busy doing yard work or making repairs on the house, he could usually be found in the rocking chair reading his Bible. In the evening, Grandfather read to Eduardo; and when the light was gone, he quoted passages from memory. Eduardo sat on a small stool at Grandfather's feet and leaned against the porch railing. He was happy to be next to this gentle old man who by the end of the day smelled of sweat and grass and wood shavings.

"Do you understand the meaning?" Grandfather would ask.

Eduardo always assured his grandfather he understood the verses, but in truth, he rarely listened. His mind transported him to soccer fields where in his imagination he scored one goal after another to the cheers of adoring fans. Eduardo did not understand his grandfather's devotion to God. Hadn't God taken Grandfather's only child, Eduardo's mother, in a horrible accident? If God did not protect people from bad things, perhaps he was better ignored. But Eduardo did not want to disappoint his grandfather; and so he pretended to understand, pretended interest, pretended devotion to a God he neither trusted nor understood.

"You see how I have memorized so much of God's Word," Grandfather would say. "You must hide his words in your heart too, Eduardo." And then Grandfather would give the boy verses to memorize.

Grandfather's house was small like the others along Camino Destileria. Over the years, the houses bordering the dirt road had been painted in various colors, the fronts often mismatched with the sides and backs. Large peeling patches revealed colors of bygone years, and here and there, the wood showed through. Roofs were shingled with tin that had lost its sheen under a patina of oxidation and a hearty coating of dust. It was a colorful collage emitting energy and joy in spite of its shabbiness. The yards, unbroken by fences, provided playing fields for various children's games and meeting areas for families and neighbors who gathered in the cool of the evening to share the day's happenings. It was a place of community.

A large avocado tree stood in front of Grandfather's house, offering shade and fruit in the summer. Eduardo plucked an avocado and joined a group of friends headed for school. Another truck sped by, raising clouds of dust in its wake. After the agave was crushed and steamed into sweet liquid, it was fermented, bottled, and hauled away in the back of eighteen-wheelers to warehouses. The roads were not constructed to accommodate the trucks, and in the rainy season, large potholes developed that would be filled with gravel once the rain stopped.

The distillery was the largest industry in the area, and it was assumed that the children of the community would all take jobs in the fields or the factory when their formal education ended. Most children completed eighth grade, but few went beyond. The nearest high school was twenty miles away and required an expenditure of time and money that few families could afford. This was Eduardo's last day of his last year of school, and he would not be one of the lucky few who travelled to the high school. Tia Juanita told him he would work in the factory, starting with menial tasks such as cleaning floors and toilets. He was strong, so maybe he would also help unload trucks or haul loads of pinas to the washing station. Eventually, he would be trained to crush the pinas or oversee the fermenting process. The days were long, and the heat inside the buildings drew energy from the workers as they labored to draw the sweet liquid from the agave.

Unknown to Eduardo, one of the trucks leaving the factory after dumping its load had picked up Grandfather and was taking him forty miles to the outskirts of Guadalajara where he would catch another bus to the Banco Nationale. He only hoped that when his business was complete luck would place another truck headed toward the distillery in his path; otherwise, he would be forced to wait, perhaps hours, for the bus back home.

Passing the town's adobe church at the south end of Via Redencion, Eduardo and his friends turned into the schoolyard. Eduardo paused and looked up at the wooden cross arising from the crest of the church's simple campanario and wondered if Grandfather was inside praying.

*   *   *

Little was ever accomplished on the last day of school. The children were rowdy, and the teachers were distracted. The day passed, and the bell rang for the last time until September. Outside, another cloud of dust rose in the wake of a battered farm truck on its way to the tequila factory. Eduardo fanned the air around his face and continued his slow shuffle home. The air was hot, and dust stuck to his clothes and exposed skin. The truck had carried hundreds of loads of pinas, and the fermenting remains on the bottom and sides of the bed gave off a sick sweet smell that drew flies like a garbage truck. Eduardo's head was bowed, his hands thrust into the pockets of faded jeans that were growing short. He did not see Grandfather in the passenger's seat of the truck. His thoughts turned to the days ahead. He would not see his friends this summer. They would be working too. Only Juan would go to high school in the fall. The rest would work in the factory or the fields. Tia Juanita told Eduardo last week that if he did not want to work in the factory, he could go out into the fields and learn to harvest the hearts of the agave. It was good money. Her husband, Tio Umberto, harvested the pinas before he died. Eduardo shuddered.

It was dangerous work. When Uncle Umberto had accidently hacked off the toes of his right foot, the foot became infected. He was sick for several months, and then he died.

Absentmindedly, Eduardo kicked a clod of dirt thirty yards down the path where it exploded on Espie Morales's backside. She shrieked and picked up a rock, slinging it in his general direction. Her aim was bad, but he ran laughing the few remaining yards to Grandfather's house. He hadn't meant to hit anyone, but if someone had to be in the way, he was glad it was bossy old Esperanza. Eduardo crossed the road and noticed the farm truck pulling away from his house. Grandfather had gotten out and was climbing the steps of the porch.

The boy bounded up the front steps and stopped short of the screened front door. Tia Juanita's voice punctuated the air in measured staccato. *She must be telling Grandfather once again how to run his household*, Eduardo thought. Talk about bossy.

"I have been waiting here to try and talk some sense into you one last time. This is a stupid waste of money, you strong-willed old fool." She spat out. "You will have nothing left for yourself. He will go up north and forget about you. He will only create trouble for my grandsons. How can they work and babysit him too?"

"You are the strong-willed one," Grandfather replied in a voice that was calm yet firm. "I will send him to California, and your grandsons will look out for him as they would for any family member."

"I can't reason with a foolish old man," Juanita yelled, plodding to the front door and slamming the screen as she departed. "You!" she hissed, bumping into Eduardo with her bulky frame. "You little snoop. How long have you been eavesdropping?" She thumped Eduardo's head and stomped down the steps.

Eduardo sucked in his breath, watching to see if the stairs would collapse under her weight. Turning, he saw Grandfather holding the door open for him. "Wretched woman," Grandfather said. "With all the help I've given her . . ."

"What is she talking about, Grandfather?" Eduardo asked fearfully. He had heard enough of the conversation to know the answer without asking, but he did not want to believe it was true.

"Sit down, Eduardo," Grandfather said, moving to the tiny kitchen and pulling out a chair.

"I love you, Grandfather," the boy said. "I love you and I love living here with you."

The old man bowed his head, and his lips moved silently. Eduardo knew he was praying. When he had finished, he looked up at the boy. "What do you want to do in life?" the old man asked, his eyes piercing the boys, searching for something, some sign of hope for the future.

Eduardo's eyebrows came together as he thought deeply about Grandfather's question.

"Well," he said, "Tia Juanita said I will work in the factory or in the agave fields like the rest of the men and boys in the village."

"I am not asking you what Juanita wants," Grandfather said with gentleness in his voice. "I am asking what you want." The eyes did not waiver.

The boy was rarely asked about his own wishes. "Well," he finally said, "if I could do anything, I would play soccer." He began laughing at the absurdity of the thought and was glad Tia Juanita was not there to mock him.

"Ah, yes," Grandfather said. "I too wanted to be a soccer player." A smile spread across his face. "I practiced and practiced, but it was not to be."

"You, Grandfather?" Eduardo rolled this around in his mind. He was grateful that Grandfather was not laughing at him, even though he fought back a smile at the thought of the old man running down a soccer field.

"I was once young too," Grandfather said with a twinkle in his eye.

Eduardo looked down, ashamed of his thoughts.

"It is OK, Eduardo," Grandfather said, placing his hand on top of the boy's own hand. "It is hard for the young to understand that the elderly have not always been old." When Grandfather revealed his own plan for Eduardo, panic griped the boy's heart. As much as he despised the thought of spending his life in the factory or in the fields, at least he would live in Grandfather's house. He would come home to this familiar place each evening and sit with Grandfather on the porch. He would play a game of soccer with his friends after dinner. But Grandfather was sending him to California. Grandfather was sending him to live with his cousins and go to high school in California.

"I could take the bus to school, Grandfather. I could go here," Eduardo pled.

Grandfather's eyes welled with tears. He patted the boy's leg. "This is better," was all he would say. "This is better."

*　　*　　*

The following day, Eduardo and his grandfather boarded a bus for Guadalajara. Eduardo had no memory of any place but the village where he lived, San Jenaro. "You will go to school and learn English in California. You will learn many other things. Maybe you will become a doctor or an engineer," Grandfather said, looking off into the distance as if he could visualize Eduardo's future. "Or maybe a soccer player," he said with a smile. "Maybe when you are a successful man, you will send for me, and we will live together in America."

Eduardo was not convinced. It would take years to finish school, and in the meantime, he would be forced to live with his cousins. Grandfather was old. Eduardo was not sure he would even see Grandfather again.

The bus bumped along the dusty road out of San Jenaro. The air was stale with the closeness of bodies and the ripe barnyard odor from chickens in crates and a little goat in the back of the bus. Grandfather opened the window but closed it quickly after they were plastered with dust and inhaled a lungful of exhaust fumes. Several families sat in clusters throughout the vehicle: sleeping old people, bored parents, whining children, and crying babies. The chickens and goat disembarked with their owners a half hour out of town, somewhat clearing the air and making more space.

Grandfather had an old shopping bag filled with tortillas, cheese and fruit, and a bottle of water that they shared at noon just before the bus entered Guadalajara. The water was warm, and the cheese had gotten oily. The tortillas were drying out, and only the oranges were appealing;' but they ate every bite before the bus arrived at the depot and disgorged its passengers.

The bus station was crowded. "Grab your bag," Grandfather told Eduardo, "and, follow me." The old man headed for a doorway. Eduardo lifted his suitcase and followed as quickly as possible. Once outside, Grandfather directed Eduardo to a line of people. "We'll get a taxi," he said. "I think we have time for a little tour of the city before we have to head for the airport." He smiled at the boy whose head was turning back and forth, taking in sights he was unaccustomed to. After a five-minute wait, they stowed their bags in the trunk of a cab and climbed into the backseat. "My grandson has never been in Guadalajara," Grandfather told the driver. "We would like a little tour, and then we need to go to the airport."

The driver was a friendly man, and as they drove through various districts, he explained the history of the city. The most imposing structure was the Cathedral Centro and Plaza de los Laurales. The cathedral had twin spires and an arched roof between them. They drove past the Teatro Degoliado, the Palacio Municipal, and the Parque Alcalde, and saw other parks and statuary, some with fountains.

"Do you have enough time to stop at the Mercado Libertad?" the driver asked. "Perhaps the boy would like to see the shops."

Grandfather said they had enough time for a short stop at the large market. It was grander than anything Eduardo had ever seen. "It would be fun to shop here," Grandfather said, "but we have to get to the airport."

They drove past the business district on the way to the airport. "Guadalajara is becoming very modern," the driver said. It was obvious he was proud of his city. There were so many tall buildings with huge glass windows. The architecture was very different from the old section of town. These buildings were sleek and modern in design. People crowded the streets in each section of the city, but here people dressed in suits and expensive dresses rushed about with determination on their faces.

Soon the taxi pulled into the Guadalajara International Airport and dropped them at the curb in front of the larger of two terminals. Long quays of people stood at ticket counters, dragging loaded carts of luggage behind them or hurriedly pushing their way through crowds to the terminal gates. Eduardo hung tightly to Grandfather's jacket with one hand and kept a death grip on his small suitcase with the other.

It was late afternoon when the flight was called for Tijuana. Grandfather and Eduardo crowded into the line at the gate. Eduardo reached for his grandfather's hand. His grip began to turn the old man's hand blue.

"It's OK, Eduardo," his grandfather soothed. "There is nothing to be afraid of. Do you know I was afraid the first time I flew in an airplane?"

"You have flown in an airplane?" Eduardo asked. He was finding out new things about his grandfather today. "Where were you going?"

The old man looked off in the distance and did not speak. Eduardo wondered if he had heard the question. He was about to repeat it when his grandfather spoke. "Lupe and I were going to your grandfather's hacienda."

"You are my grandfather," Eduardo declared in confusion.

"Everyone has two grandfathers," the old man replied.

"You knew my . . . my father's father?" the boy asked, taking a minute to sort it out.

The old man looked down at the boy and smiled gently. "Yes, yes, I knew him. He was a good man."

"Tickets please," a young woman at the gate said, interrupting the conversation; and in the excitement of his new adventure, Eduardo forgot the conversation.

In less than three hours, the airplane landed in Tijuana. Darkness had settled, and Grandfather said they would go directly to a hotel. It was a short bus ride into the business district of the town where Grandfather found an establishment with a restaurant. Stale cigarette smoke hung like a cloud in the lobby and mixed with the odor of unwashed bodies and cheap cologne. The walls, showing signs of ancient whitewash, were covered with graffiti and stains.

After carrying their bags to their room, Grandfather guided Eduardo back downstairs into the hotel's restaurant. Here the smell of carnitas, pollo, beans, and rice bathed in their lovely sauces and spices filled the air and overcame the unpleasantness of the lobby. Eduardo's mouth watered, and his stomach began to growl. He studied the menu, both confused and delighted by the number of choices available. The waitress came and took Grandfather's order. She looked expectantly at Eduardo.

"We need to order," Grandfather said chuckling. "If we take much longer, we'll be ordering breakfast."

"Can I have anything I want?" Eduardo asked.

"Anything," Grandfather assured him.

"Carnitas, beans, rice, tortillas, churros, and soda," Eduardo pronounced.

*   *   *

Their room was directly above the dining area, and fortunately, the smells from the kitchen rather than the lobby wafted through the floorboards. They were less appealing, though, with an overstuffed stomach. Muffled conversations of late-night diners interrupted their thoughts as they dressed for bed.

Eduardo looked around the unfamiliar room and longed to be at home. "I do not want to go," he said for the thousandth time.

"I know, my son, I know," Grandfather replied. "But you understand why I am sending you, do you not?"

Eduardo sat on the edge of the bed, studying a small cockroach as it crawled across the wooden floor. "Yes," he said. "You want me to have a good education and become an important person so you can be proud of me."

"It is not just for me," Grandfather said. "It is not just for you, either. It is my obligation to your parents to see that you do well in life. The old man stepped to the chair where his satchel lay. "Here, I have something for you," he said. Reaching inside, he removed a small soft cloth and revealed the contents. "You will take this with you to California and always keep it safe. This was your mother's. It was the cross your father gave her for her fifteenth birthday. It was all that was left . . ." He choked. "Take special care of it. It will help you feel close to me and to your parents."

Eduardo cupped his hand to receive the cross and chain. He turned it round and round, studying the workmanship. A smooth dark gold cross with small rectangular cut gems: diamond, ruby, emerald, and sapphire set at intervals in the gold. The back was smooth and had an inscription. Eduardo strained to read the letters, but they were faint and worn. He slipped the chain around his neck and looked in the mirror on the wall. "It is a girl's chain and cross, Grandfather."

"Yes," his grandfather agreed. "I know you will not want to wear it, but you can look at it and think of your parents . . . and me."

"It would look very nice on a girl. It is very pretty," the boy said, removing the cross and wrapping it back in the cloth. He carefully placed it in his jacket pocket.

The old man was almost asleep when a trembling-voiced question aroused him. "Was she pretty"?

"Ummm?"

"Was she pretty? Was my mother pretty?"

"Very," Grandfather replied.

A small tear ran down Eduardo's cheek. "I miss her."

"I miss her too," said the old man. He was weary, and sleep beckoned; but he turned and wrapped an arm lovingly around the boy and pulled him close.

* * *

The two travelers rose and dressed before the sun was up. "They said it is important to cross the border when traffic is heaviest," the old man explained to the sleepy-eyed boy. "There will be many trucks crossing this morning. We are to meet the person who will take you across at the open air market. He will have a white truck with Guerrero Brother's Vegetables painted on the side."

The truck was easy to find, even in the pale light of dawn. The old man handed a thick envelope to the bearded driver. When the man opened it, Eduardo saw a wad of bills. It was more money than he had ever seen in his life. Where did Grandfather get it?

The man shuffled the bills, nodded his head, and stared at Eduardo. "Once you're inside the truck," he said, "no talkin'. Comprender?"

Eduardo turned to his grandfather for one last embrace. He swiped at the tears spilling down his cheeks and tried to speak, but sobs choked back the words. He did not have a camera, so he would have to hold this memory of Grandfather's face in his heart.

"You are a good boy, Eduardo, just like your father," Grandfather said. Tears coursed their way down the old man's cheeks, and Eduardo was helpless to stop the flow of his own tears. He threw his arms around the old man and felt the brush of Grandfather's hand against his jacket pocket. "Take care, Eduardo, and do not lose this," the old man whispered, patting the pocket. "Make me proud. Make your father and your beautiful mother proud. Take care, my son, and never ever forget I love you."

With that, Eduardo was hoisted into the back of the truck. "Move to the back. You'll have to stand behind the load. We've got a couple crates of rotten onions back there." The driver laughed. "Nothing keeps the border guards away like rotten onions. You'll get used to it or not." He laughed again. "There's a bottle of water, and if you gotta piss, there's an empty to do it in. Don't mix 'em up in the dark."

"Will I ever see you again?" Eduardo asked, stepping backward, not wanting to take his eyes off his grandfather.

"If God wills it," his grandfather replied.

There was enough room in the corner for Eduardo to stand. He placed his suitcase on end, hoping it would hold his weight, and carefully sat, leaning against the truck wall for support. Crates of produce were moved in front of him, and in less than twenty minutes, the door was rolled down. It was pitch black, but Eduardo could hear grandfather's voice outside.

"His cousin Martin will meet him outside the warehouse on Los Feliz Street," the old man said. "Please make sure he doesn't go with anyone else."

The driver turned to Grandfather. "Am I transportin' a baby?" His finger shot out at the old man. "Here's how it works. I take him to the warehouse, drop my load, and the kid gets out. If his contact is there, he leaves. If his contact isn't there, too bad."

"Please," the old man said softly. Eduardo could not see his grandfather pass another roll of bills to the driver.

The driver shoved the roll in his pocket. "I'll tell you what, if his contact isn't there, I'll drop him at McDonald's two blocks down on Figueroa Street. I might even buy him lunch." The man laughed, patting the roll in his pocket. A fist rapped on the side of the truck near where Eduardo was wedged, and a voice yelled, "Remember, no talking."

Eduardo stretched his legs, and finding the bottles, he wedged them between his feet. The trip would take less than two hours, but in this cramped space with the stench of spoiled onions, it would seem much longer. The truck lurched forward, gears grinding. Eduardo's stomach lurched with it. They twisted and turned through the streets of the town with the boy swaying on his suitcase, getting dizzy and praying the road would straighten out soon. The truck lurched again, slamming his head against the back of the truck. He lost consciousness and slithered down in a heap, wedged between crates and his suitcase.

Metal ground against metal as the door of the truck rolled up on its tracks. The sound raised Eduardo into consciousness. His head hurt, and he struggled to get his breath in the heated, fetid air. Where was he? Men's voices at the back of the truck shook him fully alert. His legs were cramped, and he struggled to straighten them. He kicked the water bottle, and it rolled in the small space.

"What was that?" he heard in English. "Who's back there?"

"It's nothing," the driver said, his voice betraying anger. "The load shifted over some bumps in the road."

"Unload it," was the reply.

"That will take hours. My vegetables will be no good by the time I get to the market."

"Unload it or they'll rot right here."

"I am alone. My back is bad."

"Jones," said the voice, "have Victor bring the forklift over here and help this guy."

Eduardo could hear the voices, but he didn't speak enough English to understand everything they were saying. He felt dizzy and nauseated. The onions made his stomach retch. He was going to vomit. He buried his face against his arm and swallowed hard. He knew he was already in trouble with the driver, and he didn't want to make it any worse. The forklift driver positioned his vehicle and began removing stacks of crated vegetables. Two border agents climbed into the back of the truck and began pulling crates forward, inspecting as they went. The air was hot and foul.

"What the . . ." One of the agents ran to the door of the truck, leaned over, and retched. The second agent joined him quickly.

"Onions," said the first agent. "Rotting onions. My wife stashed a sack of onions in the back of the pantry, and they rotted. It took us two days to figure out what it was, but I'll never forget that smell. No way could anyone be in there. Put the stuff back," he instructed the forklift driver. Turning to the trucker, he snarled. "Looks like your load has already spoiled. I shouldn't let you even bring that crap in here. As soon as Victor gets those crates loaded, get out of here before I change my mind."

Within ten minutes, they pulled out of the border crossing and were on the highway headed for San Diego. The air was hot, and Eduardo felt his stomach rebel against the stench of the onions. He pulled his jacket over his face to try and quell the rising bile. It was no use. He retched again and again until his stomach was empty and his sides ached. He spit, trying to clear his mouth. He felt for the water bottle with his foot but couldn't find it. He closed his eyes, wishing he was unconscious again.

*   *   *

As the truck's cargo was unloaded on the dock of a warehouse somewhere in the industrial section of San Diego, Eduardo stepped out into the light. He breathed in deep draughts of the warm air, tinged with diesel fuel, but he could not escape the stench of rotten onions or the vomit that stained his pants and jacket. The onions had been disposed of, and the truck was being hosed out. Eduardo wished he could stand in the spray and wash himself. He took his jacket off and rolled it into a tight wad, inside out. The roof of the warehouse shaded the dock, and he scanned the street as he stood there. The door of a dilapidated pickup truck opened half a block away; and an older version of Eduardo's cousin, Martin, walked his direction. A once smooth, boyish face sported a few days growth of beard and a scowl. The eyes were hard and fastened on Eduardo.

"You the cousin?" the driver asked.

"Martin," was the answer. "Almost left. Been waiting over an hour."

"Just the usual trouble," the driver said. "Had to stop for inspection and got inspected a little more than I'd hoped for."

Turning to Eduardo, Martin snapped, "You must be Little Eduardo. What the heck did you roll in? You smell like a garbage dump." Inclining his head toward the pickup, he said, "Get in the back. You're not riding inside smelling like that."

"Rotten onions," the driver said.

"Huh?"

"Rotten onions, keeps the border guards from searching the truck too closely."

"Thanks a lot," Martin said. "It'll take days to get the smell off him."

"At least he's here," the driver smiled.

"Yeah, right. Another big thanks. Now I've got a babysitting job." Martin walked to the truck, grabbed a McDonald's bag from the cab, and threw it in back.

"Here, kid, eat up."

Eduardo reached a filthy hand in and pulled out a cold limp French fry.

CHAPTER TWO

Life in California

Wilmington, California
Summer of 1984

The drive to Los Angeles took three hours. Martin wove in and out of traffic, and Eduardo slipped from one side of the truck bed to the other until he found a handhold. His cousin's apartment was in Wilmington, south of Los Angeles. The area surrounding the apartment was depressed with grates on store windows and trash littering the sidewalks. Their place sat above a Laundromat, and the entrance was up a flight of wooden stairs on the side of the structure. The building had been white at one time, but the sun and salt air had slowly peeled the paint away in great chunks, leaving the wood exposed. Martin tossed a large plastic bag at Eduardo. "Stick your clothes in here and take a quick shower." He pointed to the bathroom. "Don't take all day. There's four other people livin' here, and someone might have to take a piss." Eduardo longed for the sheltering arms of his grandfather. He had never been close to his cousins. On the contrary, they had always treated him with distain, and the reason eluded him.

"You're gonna do our laundry," Martin told Eduardo after the shower. "We're gonna take these clothes downstairs, and I'll show ya how to wash them. Ya better not forget what I show you, cuz I'm only tellin' ya once." He took the boy into the Laundromat and instructed him to throw his clothes into a washer. "Put this much soap in," Martin said as he measured the liquid into a cup. "Shut the door and put two quarters in this slot. It'll take about twenty minutes. When the machine stops, put the clothes in one of those dryers over there. It takes dimes. Don't ever wash a small load like this again. It wastes soap and money. We're only washing a small load because I don't know if that smell's gonna come out, and I don't wanna stink up everybody else's clothes. As soon as the clothes are dry, take them out.

People don't like ya leaving your clothes in the machines after they stop. You paying attention?"

"Yeah, I got it," Eduardo said. He didn't bother to tell Martin that he'd been helping his grandfather with the laundry for years. He could have told Martin a few things about separating colors from white clothes and scrubbing greasy stains before throwing them into the machine, but he let it pass.

"Well, Niña, welcome to California," Martin spat. "I think we'll have you do the cookin' and cleanin' too."

"I'm not a girl," Eduardo said defensively.

"Maybe not, little guy," Martin said, roughing up the boy's hair, "but you're gonna do the girl's work."

Eduardo shrugged his cousin away.

"See ya upstairs," Martin said, tossing the boy a few dimes.

*   *   *

The cousins left the apartment early each morning and went to an area where day laborers waited for job offers. It was always physical labor, ditch digging, moving, farm work for minimum wage and sometimes less. Late in the morning if they hadn't gotten work for the day, they were willing to take less just to bring something home. Some of the big bosses knew that and would wait until ten or eleven o'clock to send their drivers by looking for workers. On those days when the cousins worked late, they might not get home until nine or ten at night. Sometimes they were too tired to even eat.

"I met a longshoreman the other day," Ramon said one evening as they group sat down to tacos. "Do ya know how much those guys make an hour?" When they shrugged their shoulders with disinterest, he answered his own question. "Seventeen bucks an hour, and they get time and a half when they work more than eight hours or if they work holidays."

"Everybody gets time and a half and holiday pay except day laborers," said Julio, "But it's not like we can go down to the docks and get hired."

"We need to become citizens," Carlos said. "Maybe we could get fake ID."

"I'm gonna find me a girl," Ramon said. "If you marry a citizen, you can become a citizen."

"I'd rather get fake ID," Carlos said. "I'm havin' too much fun Saturday nights to be tied down to some woman and a bunch of kids. Besides, if you have to take care of a wife, you won't have money to send to Abuela."

"Just because you're married doesn't mean you have to be tied down." Ramon laughed. "Besides, if you get citizenship, you can get a job that pays enough for a wife and an abuela too."

"You could deal drugs," Julio said, smirking. "Those guys really rake it in."

"If I hear you even talk about that again, I'll kill you, Little Brother. That applies to all of you," Martin said, turning to the others.

The days grew boring for Eduardo very quickly, and he was both anxious and fearful for the beginning of school. His English improved when Martin advised him to watch English programs on the television, and while he was anxious to try his new vocabulary out, he was fearful that he would make a mistake and be laughed at. His mornings started at six o'clock when he rose to make breakfast. After the cousins left, he cleaned the apartment. By nine o'clock, there was nothing to do but watch television, and the novelty wore off after a few weeks. Eduardo didn't always know when the men would return home, but dinner was expected when they did arrive. Sometimes they straggled in one or two at a, time depending on whether they found work in the same place or not. On weekends, they slept in. On Saturday nights, the cousins went out drinking with friends, and again, Eduardo was left alone. Sunday mornings, the cousins were hung over. Martin was mean when he was drunk, so Eduardo tried to be as quiet as possible. He was told not to go out by himself unless it was to do laundry. Not that they cared about him. They just didn't want him getting into trouble and drawing attention from neighbors or police. Eduardo was used to being active. He longed to play soccer or run or do anything that would get him out of doors. In spite of the warning to stay inside, he eventually ventured out onto the street. At first, he watched from inside the Laundromat while washing and drying clothes, but it wasn't long before he wandered to the sidewalk in front of the building and then to the convenience store next door. He didn't go farther than the block where he lived, but it felt so good to be outside. His ten-minute escapades gradually increased until they became an hour. You couldn't spend an hour standing in front of a Laundromat, so he walked completely around the block. There was nothing interesting on the backside, just a fenced parking lot. The action was at the store fronts. He was always careful to go out when he knew the cousins would be gone, knowing he would be punished if they discovered him on the street. He stood on the sidewalk one Friday afternoon, watching the cars go by. The washers and dryers inside the Laundromat spun in unsynchronized percussion as loads too large tossed and spun the clothes of a dozen families who spilled out onto the street. Toddlers in strollers were kept occupied with Cheetos and Sippy cups of juice or soda. Older kids rode trikes, bikes, or skateboards up and down the sidewalk. Eduardo squatted against the wall and watched a kid his size jumping the curb and flipping his skateboard in the air.

"Can I try?" Eduardo asked, standing up as the boy zipped by him.

The kid spun his skateboard and stopped. "You ever done this before?" the boy asked.

"No," Eduardo responded hesitantly.

"Do you live around here?"

"Upstairs with my cousins."

"Where's your parents?"

"Dead."

"Really," the kid said taking a new interest in Eduardo. "That's tough," he said without much feeling. "I can teach ya a couple of things, but then I gotta go." He threw the skateboard down on the ground close to the Laundromat wall. "Hop on," he said. "Try the right foot in front then switch. The first thing you gotta do is figure out which foot you like in front."

Eduardo did as he was told, settling on the left foot after several switches.

"OK, get your balance and push with your right foot," the kid continued. "Then bring your right foot up and glide.

It was easy enough with one foot on the ground, but it was a strange sensation, when he brought his right foot up on the board and tried to balance while rolling. He arms flailed about as counter weights, while his brain tried to correct for the motion. The kid had made it look easier than it was.

"Diego," the boy said, extending his hand.

"Eduardo. Thanks. That was kind fun."

"Gotta go," Diego said, picking his equipment up. He took a few steps and then turned back to face Eduardo. "Wanna come down to the skate park?" Eduardo looked back up toward the apartment windows and then back at the kid. "It's just two blocks down," the boy said, sensing Eduardo's hesitation.

The cousins probably wouldn't be home until after dark. "Sure," Eduardo said.

The skateboard area occupied a small corner of in the neighborhood park and consisted of two wooden ramps spaced about fifteen feet apart. A dozen boys competed to see who could reach the highest spot on the ramps, skating back and forth and turning as they lost momentum at the top. Children played on nearby swings, and a group of older boys and young men loitered on a picnic table. Eduardo missed the look and slight tilt of the head that Diego sent to the guy in the center of the group gathered at the rickety wooden table. Sitting down on the grass, Eduardo watched the skateboarders, and for the first time in his life, he felt a twinge of envy.

"Got your own board, kid?"

Eduardo looked up to see a young man who had moved away from the group at the table.

"No," he said and looked away. A slight feeling of uneasiness made his stomach queasy. He hoped if he ignored the guy, he might rejoin his friends.

Instead, the man squatted in the grass next to Eduardo. "Nick's down the street sells pretty good boards."

"Cuanto?" Eduardo asked. He had $20.00, which grandfather gave him in case he needed food or something else.

"Oh, fifty bucks will get you a really good board plus trucks, wheels, and bearings."

"I don't want a truck," Eduardo said. "I'd like a skateboard, though."

The guy threw his head back and laughed. When he finally stopped, he extended his hand. "I'm Miguel. You don't know nothin' 'bout skateboards, do you? Trucks attach to the bottom of the skateboard and the wheels fit on the trucks. If you're gonna get a skateboard, you need two trucks, four wheels, and bearings."

"Oh," Eduardo said, hanging his head once more, this time in embarrassment. "I don't have fifty bucks."

"Too bad, kid," Miguel said. "You new to the neighborhood?"

"Yeah," Eduardo replied.

"Your whole family come up?"

Eduardo turned to face Miguel. Was it written all over him: fresh from Mexico? "My cousins," he said. "My grandfather sent me to live with them and go to school."

"Well, lucky you." Miguel smiled. "You should be able to pick up some spending money in your spare time."

"Really? You think I could get a job? I work hard. I used to help Grandfather." For the first time in several days, Eduardo felt a surge of excitement.

"I could probably find ya something," Miguel told him. "When are ya free?"

"Most of the day, but I gotta be home when my cousins come home."

"I think we can work somethin' out," Miguel said, his smile broadening. "Do ya know your way around the neighborhood?"

"No, but I learn real fast."

Rising, Miguel laughed. He patted Eduardo on the shoulder. "Meet Diego here tomorrow afternoon at three o'clock."

"OK," Eduardo replied.

"Don't tell your cousins you got a job just yet, Eduardo. I mean if it don't work out or something . . ."

"Yeah, sure." No harm there. If the cousins knew he had a job that didn't work out, they'd just make fun of him.

The sun was setting. Eduardo found Diego and said goodbye before making his way back to the apartment. He didn't see Miguel give Diego a thumbs-up. Hope was rising in his heart for the first time since he left his grandfather's house. Maybe California wouldn't be so bad after all.

*   *   *

Eduardo hurried through his chores Saturday morning. By three, the cousins had left the house, and he rushed out of the apartment to the park. Diego sat where Eduardo had last seen Miguel. On the table beside him was a small brown sack.

"Hey," Diego said, jumping off the table. "Ready to go to work?"

"Yeah. What are we doin'?"

"Just runnin' a couple of errands, then I'm gonna show you around the neighborhood. You just come along with me this afternoon an' watch what I do. When I think you can manage on your own, well, you'll start raking in the dineros."

"OK, I'm ready. Where do we go first?"

"Gotta wait for a guy right here," Diego said, looking at his watch. "If he's not here in the next five minutes though, he's going to be out of luck, 'cause I'm not waiting 'round like some jerk."

Eduardo frowned. "But if someone's coming, don't ya gotta wait 'til they get here?"

"Not in this game, Eduardo," Diego said. "If he's late, I can find a dozen other guys happy to take this stuff off my hands." He patted the sack.

"What's in it?" Eduardo asked.

Diego turned to him and smiled. "Guess."

"I don't know," Eduardo said, thinking he knew but not quite able to believe that his new friend was involved in delivering something illegal.

Diego stared at the boy. "You really can't guess?" he asked.

"Well, yeah," Eduardo said, starting to fidget. "I can guess, but if it's what I think it is, it's illegal."

Diego roared with laughter. "Look at you. Are you legal?"

Eduardo's pupils dilated. How did this kid know? Before he could say anything, a Volkswagen Jetta pulled up to the curb, and the young man at the wheel gave three short honks on the horn.

"Come on," Diego said. "Just watch and listen." The transaction was short with few words said. The brown paper sack was exchanged for a wad of bills. "Simple, verdad?" he said, counting out the money.

"Yeah, looked easy," Eduardo replied.

"And," Diego said holding up the cash, "part of this is mine, payment for runnin' errands and makin' deliveries."

Eduardo felt torn. Part of him wanted to run back to the apartment, turn on the TV, and learn a few new English words to practice on Martin and the others tonight. But the other part of him, the part that wanted a new skateboard, won out. He reasoned that he personally wouldn't be using the drugs. And if he wasn't using them, was it really so bad? He wasn't forcing anyone to use them. And he really needed the money if he was going to get a skateboard. It was probably just pot anyway. He knew some older boys in San Jenaro who smoked marijuana, and they were OK. He felt as if he was on a different planet than the little village where he had been raised, and he tried to convince himself that the same rules did not apply here. But Grandfather's face flashed in his mind, and he heard Grandfather's words, "Make us proud of you." His stomach cramped, and his palms got sweaty. He turned toward the apartment as a cold chill convulsed him.

"You don't look so good," observed Diego. "You scared? 'Cause if you're gonna be a little girl, we don't want nothin' to do with you."

"I'm not a little girl, and I'm not scared," Eduardo retorted as anger pushed all thoughts of Grandfather out of his mind. The boys spent the next few hours exploring the neighborhood. Diego pointed out apartment houses, shops, and one more park where Eduardo might be asked to make deliveries. When it was time to go home, Diego grabbed Eduardo's arm. "Hey, don't talk about this to anyone . . . ANYONE," he said, "Miguel's orders."

"Yeah, sure," Eduardo said, pulling his arm free. "You don't have to worry about me. If my cousins knew I was doin' this, they'd kill me."

"OK, then. See you tomorrow. Same time, same place."

"Yeah," Eduardo said. "See ya."

*   *   *

The weekend went by quickly. Sunday morning, the cousins were hung over, and if Eduardo knew their habits, they would be in bed until early afternoon. At ten, he met Diego at the park. Church bells rang nearby, and Eduardo felt a twinge of homesickness. In San Jenaro, he would be walking to church with Grandfather at this hour. If he was honest with himself, he also felt a twinge of guilt; he knew Grandfather would want him at church instead of doing what he was doing. He hadn't stepped his foot inside a church since he'd been in the United States. He shuddered as if to shake himself free from his thoughts, and spotted Diego walking his way. By Monday afternoon, Diego turned Eduardo loose to make his first deliveries, and by the end of the second week, Eduardo held more money in his hands than he had ever possessed. Diego had taken Eduardo to Miguel's "office," the backroom of a local garage and body shop to collect their earnings.

"Good job, kid," Miguel said as he sat at his desk and counted money. He dropped a small stack of bills into Eduardo's hands. "You keep workin' like this, and soon you'll have a car instead of a skateboard." He looked at the boy and winked. "I take care of my guys, and you're one of my guys now."

A car? That thought had not crossed Eduardo's mind. He hadn't thought past the skateboard. A car, and maybe a boom box and some new shoes; he began looking in shop windows as he followed Diego to the skateboard shop. There was a whole lot of stuff in those windows that appealed to a fourteen-year-old boy.

*   *   *

Eduardo hid the skateboard behind a bush whose branches were wedged against the side of the Laundromat and went upstairs to make dinner. After the cousins had eaten, Eduardo cleaned up the kitchen and watched TV. Later, he crawled into his sleeping bag. Sleep would not come, and he heard his grandfather's voice.

Who may ascend the mountain of the LORD?
Who may stand in his Holy Place?
The one who has innocent hands and a pure heart;

Innocent hands and a pure heart, innocent hands and a pure heart, innocent hands and a pure heart, it ran like a loop though his head. Eduardo tried to push the voice away, but it got louder and louder. He got up and turned on the television and flipped through the nickel ads, checking out the prices of used cars.

*   *   *

It seemed Ramon was making good on his plan to find a girlfriend. "Meet Angie," he said one Saturday afternoon. Ramon was handsome, and Eduardo knew that if he wanted a girlfriend, he wouldn't have any trouble finding one. He was taller than his three brothers and had the same curly black hair and dark brown eyes, but Ramon had a moustache, which gave him a dashing and slightly mysterious look. He also knew how to talk to the girls, handing out compliments the girls knew were in excess but which also seemed to fill some need deep inside them.

"Hi, Eduardo," Angie said, extending her hand. Then turning to Ramon, she quipped, "He's cute. I thought you said—" She stopped herself before she completed the sentence.

Eduardo looked at her quizzically and then said, "Hi."

"I'm making dinner for Ramon tonight. He said you usually do the cooking. Wanna help me?"

"Sure," Eduardo replied, grateful for any relief in the kitchen.

"I'll show you how to make Angie's salsa. We're having nachos tonight." She tossed him her car keys. "I've got a red Chevy Impala downstairs. Would you get the two grocery bags out of the back for me?"

Eduardo caught the keys and headed for the door, but not before he saw Ramon mouth the word Impala behind Angie's back. This girl seemed nice, and he hoped Ramon was not planning to just use her for his citizenship. He found the car behind the Laundromat. It was old but well cared for. He opened the door, and the interior smelled of flowers. Eduardo lifted the bags out of the backseat and returned to the apartment.

"Just unload them on the table, Eduardo," Angie instructed. "There's not enough room on this tiny counter."

Eduardo again did as he was instructed. Tomatoes, peppers, cilantro, onions, chips, jalapeños, hamburger, spice mix, and cheese were set out on the table. Before many minutes had passed, Angie had him washing and chopping the vegetables. She talked as she worked. How long had he been in the United States? Did he like school? What did he want to be? Did he have a girlfriend? Where were his parents? He thought the questions would never end, and yet he kind of liked it. She seemed genuinely interested in him, and even though she wasn't especially pretty, she was nice. He really hoped now that Ramon liked her and wouldn't take advantage of her.

"OK, let's set this on the table," she said when the meat was done. There wasn't enough room for everyone at the table, so they filled their plates and sat in the living room.

"Angie's studying to work in a dentist's office," Ramon told the others, "Whadda ya call what you're gonna do?" he asked her.

"I'm going to be a dental hygienist," Angie said.

"I think you should be a cook," Ramon continued.

"Does that mean you like the nachos?" she asked.

"Best I've ever had," Ramon said and winked at the others.

"They're really good, Angie. After helpin' you, I think I could make 'em myself."

"Good for you, Eduardo. A woman always likes a man who can help around the kitchen." She nudged Ramon in the ribs.

*   *   *

During the first month he worked for Miguel, Eduardo made more than the fifty dollars it cost for his skateboard, and to him, it felt like a thousand. He kept the money and the skateboard hidden from his cousins. He was becoming skilled on the board and occasionally took risks, resulting in bumps and scrapes. That is to say nothing of the risks he was taking, making six to ten deliveries a day. So far, he had not been discovered by undercover narcotics officers or uniformed cops. Arrest was an outcome he chose to push to the back of his mind like the voice of his grandfather, which was becoming more and more faint. The adrenaline rush that accompanied his covert activity was becoming an addiction in itself, although he was not sophisticated enough to realize this fact.

*   *   *

"This kid is useful," Miguel said to Diego one day, handing him a "bonus" for finding the new recruit. "Keep 'im in line, and don't let him start usin'. If you keep doin' this, I'll have to make ya one of my lieutenants." When the delivery boys started buying their own product, they became sloppy and were a threat to the whole gang or "the business," as Miguel liked to call it. The user/dealers had to be dealt with severely and often brutally or risk exposing the whole group, including Miguel. The gang itself, Los Reyes of Wilmington, was small; only ten months ago, Miguel moved down from the valley with the blessing of his "godfather" and of course a cut of the profits. He brought two trusted friends with him, and they quickly recruited six others from the community, including Diego. It was a small group, but it was growing. Diego showed a lot of initiative, both recruiting and dealing drugs. In fact, within a few months' time, he had developed a large cliental in the local schools. Unlike Eduardo, it wasn't so much the money that drew Diego to Los Reyes. It was the feeling of belonging with someone who wielded power, power and prestige among the other guys in the neighborhood. With no father in the house and a mother who worked sixteen hours a day, Diego was on his own. Miguel had become his surrogate father, and the others his brothers. This was a feeling Diego had never experienced, and it was intoxicating. So much so that Diego would do anything to prove his loyalty to the members of Los Reyes. He had only been called on once, so far, to do this. It was at his initiation into the gang. "Ya gotta be strong to be one of us," Miguel cautioned him. "We hafta know ya wouldn't betray the gang."

"I wouldn't," Diego assured his mentor.

"Ya gotta prove it," Miguel said.

The proof was a forty-five-minute beating that Diego was expected to endure without making a sound louder than a gasp or low moan. In enduring it without complaint, he demonstrated his loyalty as well as his ability to adhere to a code of silence. The concussion he received kept him off his skateboard for the next several days, not because of any doctor's advice but because he was so dizzy he couldn't have stayed on the board even if he wanted to. Waves of nausea kept him from eating, and even though it had been ninety degrees outside, he covered his bruised arms and legs with jeans and a jacket. He was expected to continue his deliveries, and he did. He was now a man, a member of Los Reyes. He was a hardened warrior.

Once he recovered, there was a new aura about him. It wasn't that he stood more erect or walked with a determined step. He still slouched, and the oversized jeans worn with the waist below his buttocks gave him a look of having just soiled his diaper. There was a resolute look in his eyes, a look that became steely and menacing if he was displeased. It was not a look his clients or new recruits usually saw unless they failed to make good on payment or stepped out of line.

When school started, Eduardo assumed that the deliveries would slow down. There were classes and homework after all. His English was improving, but classes were an effort, and he had to pay close attention. "Man, I've got homework," he told Diego after the first day of school. "I gotta get home."

"Ya think work stops just 'cause school started?" Diego snorted. "Ya think Miguel is gonna go for that? He has obligations, and he needs the cash flow."

"Well, find somebody else," Eduardo replied. "Like I said, I gotta get home."

They had just reached the chain-link fence that bordered the school property. Diego grabbed Eduardo's arm and slammed him into the fence.

"Listen, little man, and listen close," Diego said "No one defies Miguel. You're part of this operation now, and you're not walkin' out." Diego jerked

Eduardo's shirt until the boy's face was within inches of his own. "Now what are you gonna do?" he hissed.

"Go home," spat an angry Eduardo. "You can't force me to work, and right now I got other stuff to do."

Diego slammed the boy into the gate post. "You'll do exactly as you are told or suffer the consequences," he said.

Eduardo heard or felt a crack, and a stab of pain shot through his side as Diego punched him. He struggled to catch his breath, splinting his side with his free hand. A crowd of curious kids began gathering around them, cheering as if they were at a gladiatorial exhibition. Diego's grip tightened on Eduardo's arm, and he half ushered him, half dragged him off the school property.

When they were a block away, Eduardo had regained his ability to speak. "Leave me alone, man," he said, pulling away from Diego.

Diego pinned Eduardo against the wall of the nearest building and lifted the boy's shirt. He ran his hand along Eduardo's side. "I didn't crack no ribs," he said. "But you're getting' a heck of a bruise."

"Leave me alone," Eduardo repeated, pulling away from Diego. "What kinda friend are you anyway?"

"The best friend you got," Diego replied. "Whether you believe it or not, I'm lookin' out for you."

"By cracking my ribs?"

"Sorry 'bout that, and they're not cracked. At least I don't think so. Look, Miguel depends on us. He pays us decent, and well, if we quit or slow down, he'll see it as bein' disloyal. Loyalty is important to the guys."

"Working after school starts and takin' a beating weren't part of the deal," Eduardo snapped.

"You don't exactly have a written contract." Diego laughed. "Come on," he said, putting his arm around the boy. "Let's get you home and get some ice on that bruise."

*   *   *

Diego helped a sullen Eduardo to the couch and put a bag of frozen peas on the bruise. "Look," a conciliatory Diego said, "you gotta learn some discipline. I don't want ya getting too big for your pants. Just cool down, and it'll all work out, you'll see."

Eduardo eyed him suspiciously; after all, the kid had just about fractured one of his ribs. "Why should I believe anything you say?" Eduardo asked.

"Because I'm your friend, and as your friend, I gotta keep you in line." Diego smiled.

"Nobody's gotta keep me in line," Eduardo retorted, his eyes narrowing. "Like you said, I don't have no contract. I can do whatever I want. If I don't wanna work for Miguel, he can just find somebody else."

Diego's eyes became steel, and his face went pale. "Listen," he said in a voice that was quiet and serious, "don't say stuff like that. Like I said, loyalty is very important to Miguel. You can't just walk away. So don't talk like that. If somebody walks away, there's a risk they might go to the police, and Miguel won't allow that."

Eduardo's eyes met Diego's. Suddenly, he realized, like a parrot in the jungle, he had been tempted by the bait and never suspected the net that was about to fall on him. His heart began to race. His breathing sped up. There was no escape, and the realization had just hit him like a ton of bricks. A primal moan escaped his lips.

"It's OK, man," Diego said. "I was a little hesitant at first too, but look at me now. I been doin' this for six months, and what I got to show for it is a big fat roll of cash and a new group of brothers. I got the best skateboard in the park, the best Nikes, and next week, I'm getting' a bike. That'll shave some time off my deliveries. Hey, I bet you've got enough for a bike. You haven't even bought a new pair of shoes yet. A bike would save you some time for your homework."

It was true. Eduardo probably had enough for a new bike because he never spent his money. If he got shoes like Diego's, his cousins would want to know where he got the money, and how would he explain a bike? As if reading his mind, Diego offered a suggestion. "Your cousins wouldn't even have to know. You could just lock it up outside and make sure not to ride it when they're around."

"Can I go with you?" Eduardo asked. "I mean when you get your bike?"

Diego smiled and shook his head. "Tomorrow," he said getting up to leave. He patted Eduardo on the arm and smiled. "It's back to normal for us tomorrow." He walked to the door and let himself out.

Eduardo sat in the empty apartment and stared at the floor. "Oh, Grandfather," he whispered, "what have I done?"

* * *

The following day, the two boys went to Casey's Bike Shop. Even though the store was fairly small, there was a large array of bikes in a multitude of sizes. "What are you looking for?" the owner asked. "Bikes," Diego replied as if the guy was crazy.

*   *   *

"I figured that out already," Casey said. "What I'm asking is what are you going to use them for?"

Eduardo and Diego shot each other a look of fear. "Whadda ya wanna know for?" Diego asked.

"'Cause I wanna help you find the right bike," the owner replied, a bit miffed. "Are you riding them to school, are you racing, are you going mountain-biking? I have bikes for different things. I need to know how much you want to spend too. Some of these bikes are pretty expensive."

"We're just gonna ride to school and around town," Diego said. "Sorry, I didn't mean to be rude."

"That's OK," Casey told him. "I think I got the thing for you right over here, a couple of three speeds. Not too expensive, nice looking, and they're well built.

The boys looked the bikes over. "How much?" Diego asked.

"Seventy-five each," Casey replied.

"Can we try them out?"

"Take them out in the back alley," Casey said. "Mike is back there working on a couple of bikes. He'll keep an eye on you. Don't try to run off or you'll be sorry."

"We won't," Eduardo said, speaking up for the first time.

"Up and down the alley a few times should tell you whether or not you like them. I'll be waiting in here."

Eduardo had a small bike in San Jenaro. He had outgrown it by the time he left for California. He hoped he remembered how to ride. Diego was already zipping up and down the alley, doing wheelies and coming to abrupt stops. "Come on, slow poke," he yelled from the far end of the alley. Eduardo climbed on the bike and began a wobbly ride toward his friend.

"You're no better on a bike than you are on a skateboard," Diego yelled at him, laughing.

The boys wheeled the bikes inside, paid cash, and rode proudly down the block.

CHAPTER THREE

The Gang

Wilmington, California
October 1984

"Here, make yourself useful, kid," Miguel told Eduardo one Saturday afternoon when they were all hanging out at the skate park. He tossed Eduardo a tightly wrapped package.

"I'm not a kid," Eduardo answered. A new bitterness had entered his voice. He had money, and he had things, but none of it made him happy. His cousins treated him like an imposition they had to endure, and he felt enslaved to Miguel. He was aching to be his own person. "I just turned fifteen, and that is almost a man."

"OK, little man," Miguel laughed, "are you man enough to join Los Reyes? I mean like be a real member?"

Eduardo took a deep breath and shifted his gaze from Miguel to a distant object. Had anyone asked him what he was looking at, he could not have answered for what he saw was not in front on him but lay within himself. He tried to analyze what he was feeling. He wanted to belong to someone, to something, and he did not belong with his cousins nor did he feel he belonged to any group at school. There was a restless longing inside him that he could not identify. What he didn't understand was that he longed for significance, significance and purpose. In addition to his need to belong to someone or something, he needed to feel his life had meaning.

Miguel eyed the boy suspiciously, and his expression turned hostile. "Ya gotta problem with these guys," he asked with a sweeping gesture that took in the men standing behind him. Though Miguel's face bristled with two or three days of beard, he kept his scalp shaved to reveal a tattoo of a snake crawling through a skull on the back of his head. When he turned toward his guys, the snake eyed the boy menacingly.

"No . . . no," Eduardo stammered. "It's just, I . . . well."

"'Cause if you do, we gotta real problem." Miguel's fist bobbed with controlled strokes inches from the boy's face. "Not everybody's invited to join. It's a privilege."

"Yeah, a privilege," one of the other guys said with a menacing laugh.

"Yeah, OK, I want to join," Eduardo said, remembering Diego's words of warning and hoping to avoid a bloody nose or worse.

Miguel withdrew his fist. "I hope you're not just sayin' that, kid, 'cause this is serious business. When you're one of us, we'll take care of you. Won't we, Diego?"

"Yeah, Miguel, we'll take care of him," Diego said, wincing at the memory of the beating he took when he joined the gang.

"We gotta set up the initiation," Miguel said, smiling at the group. "Yeah, you're gonna have to prove your loyalty to us. We don't want no babies who squeal the first time they're in a fight or who rat us out if they get picked up by the cops." He slapped Eduardo on the shoulder, nearly knocking the boy off balance, and pointed to the package. "So we'll let you know when we got things set up, OK?"

"Yeah, sure," Eduardo said, mustering a weak smile. After receiving directions to the drop, he got ready to leave. The delivery was to an apartment a few blocks from Miguel's office. "I'm not takin' my bike over there," he said. "It'll only take me ten minutes to get there on foot." He wheeled the bike into the shop, propped it up on the kick stand, and stepped out into the street. He didn't enjoy the thought of going into the particular apartment complex where the delivery was to be made. It was run-down, and people were always yelling inside. The last time he was there, some paramedics wheeled a body out on a stretcher. People who didn't even live there walked into the building to shoot up in the hall. He had even seen a guy running out of the building, waving a gun. He shoved the drugs in his pocket and headed toward Anaheim Street.

"Hey," a woman's voice called from a passing car a few minutes later. "Eduardo!"

Eduardo groaned. It was Ramon's girlfriend, Angie.

"What are you doin' here? Want a ride?"

"Hi, Angie, I'm just goin' a few streets over to work on a project with a classmate."

She eyed him suspiciously. This was not an area of town where many kids lived. "I'm on my way to the apartment. Want to come along and help me carry in the groceries? I've got a huge watermelon."

Dang! Eduardo liked Angie. She was the only one who seemed to care about him. He was always happy to spend time with her, and he never failed to help with her grocery bundles when she came over to cook for Ramon. In fact, he was glad to eat her cooking instead of his own. He hesitated. "OK, but I can't stay. I really gotta get my project finished."

"Ramon's lucky to have a nice cousin like you," Angie said once they were on their way. "His brothers are OK, but I can always count on you for help. Oh no," she moaned.

"What, Angie?" Eduardo asked, thinking something horrible had happened.

"I forgot the cake pan at home. It'll just take a minute to go back and get it."

Eduardo moaned inside. He had to get to the apartment on Cordova. "Uh, Angie, I really gotta get to my friend's house. Maybe you should just let me out here."

"It'll only take an extra minute," she assured him. "Anyway, you should see where I live. It's such a pretty part of Wilmington."

Eduardo watched the blocks slip by. Angie turned left and then right. They passed through the business section of town and entered a neighborhood of little bungalows with barred windows and fenced yards. "Are we close?" Eduardo asked.

"Almost there," Angie said. They continued on and turned into a tree-lined street named Lakme. The houses were not barred, and the beautifully landscaped yards were not fenced. Eduardo looked in wonder as Angie pulled up in front of an adobe bungalow with palm trees and colorful flowers in the yard.

"Is this your house?" he asked

"This is it," Angie said. "You like it?"

"It's beautiful."

"Come in and see it. You can meet my folks," she said, bounding out of the car.

Eduardo ran to catch up with her. "Angie, I really gotta go."

"I know. I'll just be a minute." She put a key in the lock and swung the door open. "Mom, Dad, we've got a visitor."

"We're in the kitchen," a woman's voice said. Angie led Eduardo through a living room furnished with plump cream-colored couches and the largest television set he had ever seen. Through the dining room was the kitchen where her parents sat at a small table, enjoying coffee and cookies.

"Mom, Dad, this is Ramon's cousin, Eduardo. Eduardo, these are my parents, Señor and Señora Dominguez," Angie said.

"Hello," they both said in unison. Any other time, Eduardo would have been glad to sit and chat with these people, but he was nearly in a panic.

"Hello," he said in return, shaking Angie's dad's hand.

"Sit, sit," her mother said, rising and pulling a chair out for the boy. "Would you like a cookie or maybe a piece of cake?"

"Give him a soda," the father instructed. "These kids like soda." Angie was rummaging around in the cupboard for the cake pan she had forgotten.

"Uh, I really can't stay," Eduardo said. "I gotta help Angie unload the groceries and then run over to a friend's house to finish a school project. He was expectin' me a half hour ago."

"Well, you can take a cookie with you," Mrs. Dominguez said.

"Found it," Angie said, standing up with the funniest shaped cake pan Eduardo had ever seen. "OK, I promised Eduardo I'd get him back to his school work. Maybe he could come and have a real visit some other time."

"Bring the boys over for dinner Sunday," Señora Dominguez suggested.

Fifteen minutes later, the groceries were unloaded, and Angie was happily opening jars and setting pots on the stove. "Tell me about your project," she said as she worked. His cousins never asked about his schoolwork, and now when someone showed a little interest, he had to lie.

"Uhh, well, it's about the history of California," he said.

"Oh, yeah? I loved studying history. How far back are you going?"

"To the Native Americans, before the Spanish." He hoped she would stop asking questions before he tripped on his own lies. "Gotta go," Eduardo said, setting the last bag on the table and heading for the front door.

"Behave yourself and don't be late for dinner. It's going to be good. And, Eduardo," she said, craning her neck to see him, "next time, see if your friend can come over here. I don't like that neighborhood."

A surge of guilt coursed through Eduardo's veins. Angie was the only woman he could remember who showed any concern for him. Tia Juanita didn't really care about him. In fact, he was sure that she had always wished he would just disappear. *The way Angie treats me must be kind of like how a mother treats her kids*, he thought. His sense of guilt increased to the point that he physically shook his shoulder to try and rid himself of the uncomfortable feeling, but it wouldn't leave. He knew what he was doing was wrong. His cousins didn't really care about him, but they would be furious if they found out about his connection with the gang. If he got into trouble, it would mean trouble for them. Somehow though, he felt that Angie did care about him. That thought bothered him a great deal. He left the apartment feeling torn about what he would do next. He patted his jacket pocket where the drugs had been out of sight. He was late, and some customers got pretty angry when you were late. He raced off on his skateboard. The drop went fine, and Eduardo returned to Miguel's office to leave the money.

"You're late," Miguel said. "Did the drop go OK?"

"I saw some cops near the apartment," Eduardo lied. "I had to hide across the street 'til they left."

Miguel eyed the boy suspiciously. "Took ya long enough. What would ya do if you were caught?" he asked.

Eduardo stared at Miguel and mulled the question over in his mind.

"Think, kid," Miguel pressed. "What would ya do? You gotta have a plan, an idea in case ya do get caught."

"I would tell 'em I didn't know drugs were in the package," Eduardo said, believing this was the right answer.

"No way," Miguel retorted. "Ya really think the cops would believe that? The next thing they would ask you is who gave ya the package. What would ya say then?" He grabbed Eduardo's shoulder and looked hard and long at the boy.

Eduardo winced as Miguel's fingers dug into his shoulder, compressing the tissue until it bruised. The reaction did not go unnoticed by the gangster. "Look at you," he said, "ya can't even take a little pinch without making a baby face. Well, listen to me. Those cops would do anything they could to find out who gave ya the drugs, and I wouldn't be very happy if ya told 'em."

"I would never tell 'em," Eduardo promised.

"Easy to say, kid, but me and the boys are gonna make sure you're tough enough to keep certain information to yourself. Meet us at this address at seven this evening," he said, pressing a paper into Eduardo's pocket.

"I don't know if my cousins will let me go out."

"Be there."

* * *

Eduardo kept his money stashed in an old envelope at the foot of his sleeping bag. Even though he had spent a large sum on his new bike, there was still more money than Angie expected to find when she tidied up the apartment. The cousins had returned home and were enjoying beers in the living room while Angie made the beds and shook out Eduardo's sleeping bag. When the envelope and its contents spilled on the carpet, her first thought was that Eduardo's grandfather had given him money for his trip. But this was a lot of money.

"Ramon," Angie called from the bedroom. "Ramon, come here a minute."

By the time Eduardo returned to the apartment, all four cousins were waiting with the envelope prominently displayed on the kitchen table.

"What's this, Cousin?" Martin asked. "Where'd ya get all this cash?"

"Hey, that's mine," Eduardo said, reaching for the money.

"Yeah, we know it's yours," said Julio, slamming his fist down on Eduardo's hand. "What we wanna know is where ya got it. Are ya stealin'?"

"No way," Eduardo said, looking from one to the other. His hands began sweating, and he thought his heart might pound out of his chest. They were going to find him out, and he didn't know what would happen next.

Martin slammed his own fist down on the table. "Where'd ya get this, Little Cousin? The truth."

"I got a job after school," Eduardo stammered. "I didn't think you'd mind if I finished my chores first."

"A job," Carlos scoffed. "Maybe we should find a job like this. We work for $6.00 dollars an hour in the hot sun, and none of us has a stack of bills like this."

"What are ya doin'?" Martin demanded again. "Who gave you the job, and what are ya doin'?"

"Eduardo," Angie cut in, "what were you doing today when I picked you up over on Anaheim and Cordova? You weren't really doing a school project were you?"

"Cordova Avenue?" Ramon yelled. "What were you doin' over there? That's crack head alley."

"Eduardo," Angie said, "please tell me you're not taking drugs."

"I'd never do something stupid like that," Eduardo said. He might not be the smartest kid at school, but he was smart enough not to take drugs.

"Then what are you doing?" Angie pled. "Please, Eduardo, you've got to tell us."

Eduardo hung his head. He couldn't look Angie in the eye. Facing her was like facing Grandfather, and he could never let Grandfather know what he had done.

Martin stood and grabbed Eduardo by the shirt. "You're dealin'," he pronounced. Looking around at the others, he repeated himself, "He's dealin'."

"No," Angie said. "Eduardo, please tell him it's not true."

Eduardo stood mute. His gaze did not leave the floor. It had happened. He knew when he entered the apartment that something had changed. He was not going to get out of this, and he was afraid of what was going to happen next.

"Who ya workin' for?" Martin asked.

"Some guys I met at the park. They asked me to drop off a package for them, and I said I would."

"You dumb kid," Carlos said. "Los Reyes hangs out there. You've hooked up with Los Reyes, haven't ya?"

Again, Eduardo stood mute; his silence confirmed that Carlos had guessed the truth.

"They aren't just some 'guys.' These 'guys' could hurt all of us," Carlos said, drawing his fist back.

"Carlos, no," Angie yelled, trying to step between him and Eduardo.

"Get her outta here," Martin said to Ramon.

Once Angie was pulled out of the apartment, the three remaining cousins descended on Eduardo and beat him with fists and belts. Eduardo covered his face and took repeated lashes on his arms and legs. A few well-placed punches knocked the wind out of him. When he lay whimpering on the floor, his cousins dragged him into the bedroom.

"What are we gonna do?" Martin kept repeating. "What are we gonna do? We're either going to get in trouble with the cops or the creeps who have him delivering drugs."

Eduardo sat in the corner of the bedroom, rubbing the welts on his arms and considering what he himself must do. He was supposed to meet Miguel and the guys later. If he didn't' show, they would be waiting for him the next time he left the apartment. The front door opened, and he heard Angie crying. "What did you do to him?" There were sounds of a struggle and Ramon's voice telling Angie to stop.

"What are we supposed to do?" Martin asked. "Go to the police? Confront the guys he's workin' for?"

"None of those things, and you know it," said Angie. "The cops would send all of you back to Mexico, and I don't even want to think about what those drug dealers would do."

"Do ya think Alberto could help?" Ramon asked. Alberto, Angie's brother, was a school social worker.

"We could ask," Angie said. "He's got a lot of contacts, and he'd be careful not to create more trouble for you."

"Is he home right now?"

"He should be."

Pointing to the bedroom, Martin looked at Carlos and Julio. "Don't let the kid leave that room." He turned and walked out of the apartment with Ramon and Angie.

Eduardo heard his cousins leave and slowly moved to the bedroom door. He listened closely and cracked the door open to see what was going on. Julio was stretched out on the couch, his eyes closed. "Man, that felt good," he said. "I've always wanted an excuse to punch the little pest."

Carlos rose and slapped Julio on the shoulder as he walked into the bathroom.

"I'd like to kill the little creep," he said.

Eduardo waited until Julio's eyes were closed again and Carlos had shut the bathroom door. He crept noiselessly out of the bedroom. His money was scattered on the table along with yesterday's mail and a couple of glasses. Holding his breath, he slipped past Julio whose back was turned toward him. At the table, he began gathering up the bills when an empty glass tipped over and clattered to the floor. Eduardo ducked down just as Julio rose up off the couch. A breeze fluttered the curtains on the open window. "Crap," Julio said, lying back down.

Eduardo quietly exhaled. The front door was fifteen feet away. He knew he could make it to the door without rousing Julio again, but he doubted he could open it without bringing his cousin off the couch. As quietly as he could, he pulled the remaining bills off the table and crawled toward the door. He reached for the door handle and prepared to run. Just as he turned the knob, Carlos flushed the toilet, covering the sound of the opening door.

*   *   *

Not planning to ever return to his cousin's apartment, Eduardo had grabbed his jacket and stuffed his mother's cross into his pants pocket before leaving the bedroom. The living room clock read six. It was dark outside and starting to get cold. He didn't know where he would spend the night after leaving Miguel and the rest of the guys, but he hoped maybe Diego would take him in. He pulled the slip of paper from his pocket. In the glow of a street light, he could barely make out 406 Cordova Avenue, Apartment 102. It would only be a short bike ride, but he hated the thought of heading into that area after dark. He unlocked his bike from the back fence and started out. For the first few blocks, store lights lit his way; but then he entered an area of dilapidated shops, unkempt yards, and fenced-off junk heaps. Eduardo steered his bike into the middle of the road, trying to avoid shadows created by overgrown shrubs and trees, hoping not to be surprised by someone popping out to steal his bike or worse. Trash littered the undergrowth along the broken sidewalks spilling out into the street. He peddled as fast as he could. At this pace, he would reach the apartment way ahead of schedule, but he didn't' care. He'd just hang out and try to look like he belonged there.

The apartment building was easy to find. A small stretch of weeds and grass separated the building from the sidewalk. Half the numbers on the building were missing, but he found 102 at the far end on the ground floor. The door was open, and voices of several men could be heard laughing and talking inside. He walked his bike to a chain-link fence and padlocked it in place. Old candy and hamburger wrappers as well as drink cups and other debris lay where the wind had blown them against the fence. Eduardo jumped back with a sharp intake of air as something skittered past his feet. From behind him, a machete swung down and sliced the furry animal in two. Eduardo swung around to see Ernesto, one of Miguel's men. Ernesto had crept up so quietly, the boy hadn't heard him. Now the man stood there with a sarcastic grin on his face and the machete poised to strike.

"That's what we do to rats," Ernesto said, still smiling. "Human rats as well and this kind." And he pointed the tip of the machete at the dead rat. "Miguel wants you inside."

He nudged Eduardo with the tip of the knife and began walking in the direction of the open door.

Eduardo winced as he felt the tip of the machete against the skin of his back. The wince did not go unnoticed by Ernesto.

"Look at you," he said, "ya can't even take a little poke without makin' a baby face. You're such a wimp, and I told Miguel so. You're not gonna last through the night."

"Whatta gonna do?" Eduardo asked, his voice quivering.

"You'll find out soon enough," Ernesto said, pushing Eduardo through the door of the apartment.

Eduardo stumbled into a small crowded living room. Eleven solemn young faces, including Diego, stared at him from a soiled and worn couch and mismatched chairs that were roughly arranged in a circle. Eduardo heard the sound of men's laughter mixed with a woman's shrill protestations in a backroom and guessed there were at least two or three more men in the bedroom along with a girl. Lamps had not been turned on in the apartment, but the men and contents of the room were outlined by light that streamed in through the open door. Empty beer cans, overflowing ashtrays, and leftover food could be seen on a table next to the kitchen. The air was heavy with stale cigarette smoke and perspiration. Eduardo remembered the hotel in Tijuana, and his stomach knotted. Miguel pushed the boy into the center of the circle.

"Welcome, my little friend." He smiled. The female's sobs increased in the backroom.

Eduardo didn't know if he was more frightened for himself or the girl. "What's wrong with her?" he asked in a trembling voice.

"She's fine," Miguel said. Turning to the other men, he laughed. "She's mighty fine." Snickers erupted around the room.

The girl protested again. "Get off me." Eduardo stared at Diego, hoping to get some kind of reassurance from his friend, but Diego would not make eye contact. Eduardo's stomach churned, and acid rose in his throat. He thought he might vomit, and his heart pounded so hard he could hear it in his ears. *What am I doing here?* he asked himself, scanning the men sitting in a circle around him.

"Now," Miguel said, "ya think ya can withstand police interrogation. Well, we're not convinced, but if ya pass the test tonight, we'll rethink that. We test all new members to make sure they're strong enough to be part of Los Reyes. If you can take it, you're in. If not . . ." He laughed and looked at the others who smiled in return. "You've got to be tough to be one of us," he said, drawing his fist back and landing a punch on Eduardo's jaw. The boy dropped to the floor, stunned. The others rose and stepped toward Eduardo. He looked wildly about him, hoping for a way of escape, but a sharp blow from behind struck him in the back. Martin's belt was nothing compared with the bottles and baseball bats that began pummeling his body. He felt betrayed. *I'm dying*, he thought. *They're going to kill me.* Eduardo would have screamed, but repeated blows knocked the air from his lungs, and he thought he would pass out.

Over the laughter and jeers of the men, Eduardo heard the woman's voice now closer. "Stop it. You're gonna kill him," she yelled.

He curled into a ball and tried to shield his face from the blows, and then he lost consciousness.

"Hey, man, is he dead?" whispered Diego.

Miguel rolled the limp body onto its back with the toe of his boot. Eduardo moaned softly.

"He didn't even yelp," Miguel said. "I thought he was gonna cry like a baby." He turned to the woman. "Now that those apes are finished with you, sit down. The two of you are gonna get a nice little tattoo. Ernesto, get the needle." LRW inside a circle was drawn in blue ink on Eduardo's arm. He regained consciousness as Ernesto drew the needle of a used syringe through a flame. Then methodically, he popped in and out of the boy's left forearm, driving the ink into the dermis. In twenty minutes, the tattoo was complete, and Eduardo passed out a second time.

Hours passed.

Eduardo wakened to moaning and realized in the midst of the fog that resides between slumber and consciousness that it was his own voice rousing him. Miguel and some of the others lay snoring nearby. A stabbing pain in his right side brought another moan. Had they knifed him? Reflexively, he touched the right side of his chest to find the source of pain. Nothing protruded from his chest, although coagulated blood glued his shirt to his skin in patches. Gently, he probed the skin that overlay his ribs. He felt or perhaps heard a soft grinding noise. Eduardo breathed in sharply, and another moan escaped involuntarily as he pulled his hand away from the fractured ribs. He had never suffered such a beating in his life. Mentally, he began an inventory of his physical condition. Though his whole body ached, most probably bruises, he could feel no other broken bones. His right eye felt puffy, but his left eye was completely swollen shut. His teeth and nose were intact. Arms, hands, fingers, legs, and feet, although sore, still functioned. He wanted to run from the room, but he knew there was no real escape for him now. Cautiously, he pushed himself upright and leaned against the peeling paint of the living room wall. Was the torture over or would there be more? He tried to rise, but dehydration had reduced his total blood volume; and as he stood, darkness enveloped him. Leaning against the wall, he waited until his vision return. He would not rush, but he needed to find the bathroom. After relieving himself, he moved to the sink and cleaned as much coagulated blood from his arms and head as he could. He did not recognize the face that stared back at him from the mirror. He remembered Grandfather's mirror; and Grandfather's words echoed out of nowhere, taunting Eduardo, "Make me proud of you. Make your father and your beautiful mother proud of you." Tears welled in his eyes, but he could not let the others see his sorrow. Quickly, he wiped them and returned to the living room.

Miguel had awakened. He stared at Eduardo with as much empathy as he could muster. "Ya took it like a man," he said, putting an arm around Eduardo. "You didn't even squawk. You're one of us now, and we'll always be here for you.

Be here for me? Eduardo silently asked. A sense of betrayal rose from the pit of his gut as he stared at this man.

"We got a job for you," Miguel said. "We'll clean you up, get you somethin' for the pain, put some breakfast in you, and then, we're goin' for a little ride."

CHAPTER FOUR

Villa Perez

Palos Verdes Peninsula, California
October 21, 1984

Philip Perez drummed the end of a pencil on his desk, nearly driving his secretary nuts. She peered directly at him, but he was lost in thought. He was a good man, a kind man; but in the ten years she had been his assistant in the Los Angeles Unified School District, she had never learned to tolerate this nervous habit.

She looked outside. A light fog had come in from the ocean and collected into drops where it settled on trees and buildings. Thin rivulets ran noiselessly down the window of the office like so many tears adding to the gloomy pall the psychologist's mood cast over the room. The clock on the desk read two thirty. She was hoping to leave by three thirty, but if her boss didn't hurry up, she'd be leaving at four or five and that meant getting caught in traffic and missing the start of Othello. Perez had given her the ticket, though she wondered if he remembered.

The drumming continued.

"Dr. Perez," she said, breaking into his thoughts, "I have your latest reports to type."

"Should I do that and come back?"

"No, Martha. Sorry. I've got to get this letter out to the superintendent today, but I feel so distracted." He spoke as if the cause of his distraction was a mystery, but even Martha knew what preoccupied his mind. It was the anniversary of the death of his family. Martha had never asked him about the tragedy, and he had never offered any information. What little she knew of the deaths, she had learned from gossip and telephone conversations overheard throughout the years when the inner office door had been left ajar: a beautiful wife, an infant son, and his parents killed in an automobile accident. As the twenty-first of October approached each year, he became distracted and moody. With the passing of time, the effects had lessened, and he hadn't missed work for the last three years; but mentally, he was not in this office.

"OK, let's get this done," he said, suddenly pulling himself out of his own internal fog. He raised a palm and ran long fingers through his curly black hair. Martha knew a couple of young female teachers who would like to do that for him, but he showed no interest in new relationships. "Too busy with my work," he always said when his friends tried to set him up. Martha knew it wasn't his work. He had plenty of time for the theater and other arts. He held elegant gala parties at his villa to raise funds for a variety of charities. No, it wasn't a matter of time. Philip Perez was still in love with his wife after all these years. His hand moved from his hair to his face. He rubbed the five o'clock shadow, set his elbow on the desk, and rested a prominent jaw in his cupped hand.

"Use the usual heading, Martha, Jonathan Spalding, superintendent, Los Angeles Unified School District, yada, yada, yada. Dear Jonathan," he dictated as Martha recorded in shorthand. The letter summed up the last year of research and treatment that Philip had been responsible for related to gang activity and drug use among junior high and high school students in the inner city schools. The problem was growing, and in fact. Philip had spent considerable time in the schools close to his home in the last six months. Graffiti in the Wilmington and San Pedro areas indicated a branch of Los Reyes had moved outside of Los Angeles proper.

While Philip believed that peer groups were a great influence on young people, he found that the peer groups he had set up to combat drug and gang involvement were not resolving the problem or even keeping pace with its growth. "The family unit has the greatest hope of influencing young people against gangs and drugs," he dictated. "While school-initiated peer groups should not be disbanded, strategies that that focus on strengthening the family unit should be explored and developed. Research assistants provided to us from UCLA's psychology department were able to conduct interviews with over four hundred of Los Angeles's most successful students and their parents utilizing a tool that was tested for reliability and validity. When the data were organized and analyzed, it was found that these college-bound students had parents who—put this in bullet form, Martha—(1) talked with their children daily, (2) brought the family together for at least one meal daily, (3) had a strong faith that they passed on to their children, (4) supervised their children's homework, (5) attended extracurricular events in which their children performed, (6) discussed goals with their children on a regular basis." He continued reporting the pertinent facts and supporting research. "End it as usual, Martha."

As Martha went to her own desk and quickly typed his letter and the other reports, Philip sat pondering the gang situation. He was well acquainted with gang history in Southern California, and he knew that for some families, gang involvement went back multiple generations. Children were expected to join the clan-gang of their father. In the days of the ranchos, these gangs offered defense against thieves and outlaws and the encroachment of cowboys from other ranchos on one's property. But the new gangs had developed out of greed and despair, greed of the men at the top who preyed upon disenfranchised youth and coerced them into a slavery of sorts, drug dealing and gang membership with threat of harm if they failed to follow orders or showed disloyalty of any kind to the gang. Initiations were conducted with ruthless violence by many of the gangs; male initiates were beaten, and females were gang-raped and sometimes beaten as well.

Philip had pondered this practice many times and marveled that any young person would swear loyalty to a group that treated them so inhumanely. But then he always remembered the children who were victims of abuse by their parents. These children often defended the very persons who broke their bones and burned their bodies. Somehow they were convinced they deserved it. Philip had been brought to tears more than once by these small victims.

He had conferred with the police department in Lomita. He organized community meetings and brought his antigang curriculum into the local high schools and junior high schools. Being a man of means, he took out large ads in the local newspapers, outlining the cardinal signs of drug use or gang associated activity. He spoke in area churches and youth groups, he consulted with local hospitals. He organized the neighborhood associations into action groups to paint over graffiti. In concert with his antigang curriculum, he spent a few hours each Saturday counseling young people who had been detained by the police for suspected gang activity or drug possession. As a resident of the Palos Verdes Peninsula, Philip felt an obligation to his own community, and this work was done voluntarily and with great passion. He became a stone in the shoe of the Wilmington Los Reyes leader, Miguel Ochoa, and an opponent with the potential to impede, if not strangle, Miguel's growing business. Miguel hated the psychologist enough that the police had offered Philip protection.

"I will not be a prisoner in my own home," had been his oft repeated reply.

Martha typed the cover letter and attached it to the doctor's research papers. "I can mail it on my way out if everything's OK."

There was no need to reread the lengthy research documents and his analysis. Martha rarely made typos. He quickly scanned the cover letter, signed it, and handed it back to her as he left for the day. "Thanks, Martha," he said. "Accurate as usual. See you Monday morning."

"Have a good weekend," she replied, guessing it would be anything but good.

*   *   *

For generations, the Perez family had accumulated wealth by breeding horses, developing land, and investing in promising stocks and bonds. The estate had been passed down from father to son and now was at the disposal of Philip Perez. He was not a man given to ostentatious living, but he allowed himself the pleasure of building a new home in California. Villa Perez encompassed five acres of hillside overlooking the Pacific Ocean. Philip had spared no expense in its construction: imported tiles, copper plumbing, double-paned windows, and hand-carved doors salvaged from an old Mediterranean mansion. Although the villa was walled, the compound was no fortress. The perimeter wall, which enclosed the house and three acres of garden, was more esthetic than protective. It was in fact low enough to be scaled by anyone with supple joints and some muscle power. The wall's cream-colored stucco surrounded lush gardens behind the house and matched in color and texture the smooth exterior walls of the casa that sat beneath a red tile roof.

Philip had no guard dog on the grounds; and the only other residents were an older couple, friends of Perez's, who lived in a spacious apartment above the garage and helped him around the villa. Tomas had in fact encouraged Philip to consider a new start in California far from the loss he had suffered and all the memories of happiness he could never regain. A move of such proportions had seemed preposterous to Philip, and his grief had left him so paralyzed it had been difficult to even consider it. Ever so gently and persistently, Tomas began speaking to his friend of the possibilities such a move could bring. A fresh place and a meaningful new challenge might bring him peace if not happiness. Eventually, after months of consideration, Philip decided to take a sabbatical and head for California. He could always return to Pachua after all.

Philip's work among troubled children was known internationally, so when he approached school administrators in Los Angeles, he was welcomed with open arms. The work of evaluating the drug and gang problem in the Los Angeles area intrigued him; and as he started developing programs to deal with the issues, he felt a sense of energy returning. When after a year he decided to stay, he dove into building the villa and coaxed Maria and Tomas to join him, promising that there would be plenty of room for them. The couple had no family ties in Mexico City, and they found the climate very pleasant in California. Tomas was a quiet man, and it was years before even Philip's closest friends knew what type of work he had done in Mexico. He thrived out of doors among plants and quickly made the grounds of the villa his hobby. Tomas was a hard worker, and if he had not been so inclined to physical labor, Maria's cooking would have piled pounds on his lean frame. "Eat, Tomas," she often scolded him. "You are too thin for such a tall man." He laughed and piled his plate with more of her Tamales, beans, and rice; but he never gained weight. Though Maria cooked the finest Mexican food Philip had tasted since sitting at his mother's table, she did not limit herself to her native cuisine. She poured over cookbooks and magazines and mastered many ethnic dishes as well as basic American food. When Maria wasn't cooking, she fussed about the villa, supervising the housekeeper and wiping up the dust and cobwebs that had been missed. Tomas and Maria ate with Perez frequently, but they also enjoyed time alone and worked hard not to intrude on his privacy. It was a delicate balance that they achieved with seemingly little effort. Maria's jovial nature was a counterbalance to Tomas's quiet personality. She was quick to laugh, and she never seemed to tire in spite of her robust figure.

The acreage around the house reflected the thoughtfulness of Tomas's landscape planning. Palm and jacaranda trees and large bird of paradise planted in groupings against the rear wall formed a pleasing privacy hedge that extended well above the five-foot stucco boundary. Branches arched gracefully over beds of lilies, roses, and gardenias. Against the wall clung bougainvillea loaded with magenta blooms that hid sharp thorns. Here and there, jasmine grew among the bougainvillea, perfuming the garden with sweetness. Annuals claimed every inch of remaining space and were changed by Tomas and the gardener with the seasons to provide constant color and interest. A small gate in the back wall led to the orchard and extensive vegetable gardens. Over a dozen types of fruit trees grew behind the wall, and the fragrance of the lemon and lime blossoms made one feel they had entered a perfumery. Fresh vegetables grew eight months of the year; and winter kale, onions, and potatoes were available year-round.

A stretch of grass lay beyond the wide flower beds, sloping upward toward an area where a pool and tennis courts had been installed behind the main house. Here, ferns were interspersed amongst the palms and bird of paradise, creating a sense of tropical paradise around the free-form pool. Beyond the pool and to the left of the house sat a guest cottage, infrequently used, but immaculate and well-appointed. To the right of the pool lay the tennis courts, and beyond that, a four-car garage. The garage roof extended to the house, creating a breezeway between the two structures. Over the garage, Tomas and Maria made their home in a luxurious apartment. A service road leading past the cottage began a gentle descent to a set of wide wooden doors set below the grade of the main house. The doors opened into a large wine cellar and food warehouse, allowing provisions to be stocked without disturbing Perez or his guests. A dumb waiter enabled Maria and the housekeeper to deposit food and drink directly into the kitchen, saving many trips up and down the staircase.

The grounds in front of the compound were equally beautiful. Clumps of pygmy palms had been planted in groupings of three in front of the house. Colorful annuals grew thickly under the palms. A lane off the county road led to a large wrought iron gate in the center of the front wall. Past the gate, the lane became a circular drive that cuts through a broad expanse of dense grass and leads to the double front doors of the villa. The most notable feature on the front side of the villa, however, was the ocean view. Across the road from the villa, the chert-rich cliff dropped three hundred feet into the Pacific Ocean. Pounding surf crashed against its rocky foundation, providing sustained rhythmic percussion in a symphony of nature. Gentle breezes blowing off the water rustled clumps of native grasses, creating muted tones of haunting melodies that were punctuated by cooing doves and chirping robins.

Philip made his way to the solitude of his study after parking his car in the garage. Though the house was over six thousand square feet, this twelve-by-fourteen-foot room was his favorite and the place where he spent much of his time. It was sparsely furnished: an old desk, an even older couch in front of the fire place, bookcases, and a few odd tables. On the left side of the fireplace stood a sideboard where Philip kept brandy and cognac along with a few glasses. He was not given to indiscriminate drinking, but tonight he lifted a bottle of cognac from a tray on the credenza and poured a generous serving. Moving to the stereo, he selected Puccini's *Madame Butterfly* and settled onto the almost threadbare couch. On any other night, he might have listened to Vivaldi, Mozart, or Bach; but tonight the tragic strains of the ill-fated love story matched his melancholy.

Tomas and Maria had long ago stopped trying to coax Philip out of his October despondency. After so many years of living together, they knew his habits and were sensitive to them. His depression had lessened over the years, but Maria knew that some measure of it would always remain. She had given up the habit of trying to get him to join her and Tomas for meals at this time of year. Tonight she brought his dinner to the study and placed it on a TV tray in front of him. He attempted a smile, but it was halfhearted.

"Anything else, Philip?" she asked, and he nodded no. Whether or not he would eat, she couldn't say; but in her devotion to him, she had prepared a meal both nourishing and attractive to the eye and palate.

Once Maria closed the door, Philip closed his eyes. In his mind, he could see the face of the young woman who had stolen his heart so many years ago. Every nuance of her facial expressions remained alive in his memory. In spite of his grief, he smiled at the vision. *How appropriate for her to have a heart-shaped face,* he mused, a smooth broad brow narrowing to a tiny chin. Though the chin was delicate, it was not weak, and when Elena was incensed, the chin tilted up in defiance of the one who crossed her will. Her wide-set eyes were so dark they appeared black, and when the chin tilted, sparks flew from those obsidian eyes. His smile became a chuckle as he remembered Elena's occasional outrages. She had been a woman of passion, and that passion surfaced in anger as well as love. She was always ready to defend the defenseless whether man or beast, and when she found injustice, she was determined to correct it. Philip frequently told her she should have been a lawyer instead of a teacher. "You would wound the opposition with your beauty," he used to laugh. "And then you would kill them with your brains and passionate reasoning."

Perez finished his glass and, reaching for the bottle, found it empty. He mused how, like this bottle, his own life felt tonight, empty and lacking spirit. A wry smile softened the taught face. Empty and lacking in spirit, an analogy he would have enjoyed if it did not describe his own despair. The room seemed suddenly stifling, and he moved to open the window. He stood, savoring the fresh breeze. Bracing himself with hands resting on the lower window casing, he drew long breaths of salt-tinged air. It refreshed his body and soothed his soul. Moving to California had been a good thing. Remaining in Pachuca would have been torture, and yet selling the ranch had never even been a consideration. Would he ever return? It had been fourteen years since the accident and thirteen years since he left Pachua. He did not know; he just did not know if he could ever return in his lifetime. He would be buried there someday, next to the ashes of his family. Perhaps that was the only way he could return.

Philip turned and surveyed the room where he stood. It was a collage of quickly gathered utilitarian pieces with a few exceptions. In the dim light of a reading lamp, he could make out his books and Elena's Bible and guitar. The books and guitar brought him comfort as few things did. Friends brought him comfort, but friends left at the end of an evening. He had only shadowed memories to fill the void where love had once been, and love was the greatest treasure life had to offer. Oh, how his heart ached to hold Elena, to draw her to him, smell her scent, and caress her gently. Even after fourteen years, if he concentrated, he could still feel her softness, could still imagine her touch. Her dresses no longer hung in a closet next to his suits; and he no longer drew those dresses into his arms, burying his face in the fabric, and breathing her distinct smell. Such sweet torture that had been, and he had held onto the dresses long after her scent had faded.

This melancholy would pass. It always did, but in the midst of it, Philip felt the hopeless helplessness of one who has fallen into a deep pit. No one could rescue him but God alone, and God would bring him out of this despair once again.

Tomas and Maria took their dinner alone in the kitchen. "Nothing fancy tonight, Tomas," Maria said by way of apology for the soup and rolls she set before him.

"Looks good, my sweet," he replied. He was convinced that Maria could boil one of his old shoes and produce an epicurean delight. He took Maria's hand and said a blessing over the meal. "How is he?" he asked when they opened their eyes.

"It breaks my heart to see him like this," she said, wiping tears with her apron. "I used to think he might find someone else, but now I just don't think that will ever happen."

"Elena was the love of his life, and to lose not only her but their child and his parents . . ."

"He'll be OK. It seems each year he recovers a little faster," Tomas said.

"I know. He'll probably be fine tomorrow night. I just wish we could ease the pain somehow. He's such a good man." They talked of the day's happenings and the coming of cooler weather. "The house seems so empty, Tomas. Sometimes I wish we had children around or maybe a pet of some sort."

"There are little rabbits in the garden," he said, trying to coax a smile out of the woman he loved so dearly. For years they had tried to have children, but Maria never conceived. They finally conceded that they were fine as a family of two, and then Philip invited them to live with him. Still, he knew that Maria would never feel totally complete without a child.

They finished their meal and cleaned the kitchen together. "I think I'll see if Philip needs anything before we go upstairs," Maria said. "I can wash his dishes in the morning."

"I'll take the trash out and meet you upstairs, love."

Neither of them made it upstairs until well after midnight.

CHAPTER FIVE

Crime at the Villa

Villa Perez
October 21, 1984

It was midafternoon by the time Miguel and two of his men led Eduardo to a canvas-draped car parked behind the apartment. Ernesto and Luis carefully removed the cover, revealing a candy apple red Chevy lowrider with gleaming chrome bumpers and wire rims. Eduardo had seen Miguel cruising in this car down PCH on Friday and Saturday nights, but he had never been asked if he wanted a ride. The car was beautifully restored inside and out with custom leather seat covers that matched the paint job. Miguel tossed the keys to Ernesto and guided Eduardo to the door behind the driver.

"Get in, kid," he said. "You deserve a ride in the South Bay's coolest car."

"Thanks," Ernesto said, shocked that Miguel let anyone else drive this beauty.

"I'm trustin' you not to put a scratch on it," Miguel said to Ernesto. "I feel like bein' chauffeured this afternoon, plus I gotta show the kid some stuff back here while we're drivin'."

"What are we doin'?" Eduardo asked, feeling a little uneasy.

"In good time, my little man, in good time," was all Miguel would say.

They drove out of Wilmington, through San Pedro, and turned onto a canyon road that wound up a hill toward the ocean. From the summit, they had a one-hundred-and-eighty-degree view of the Pacific. A road skirted the bluff, and Ernesto turned the car to the right along this road. On the left, native grasses and cactus grew across a fifty foot shoulder that broke off sharply into the ocean three hundred feet below. It was drizzling outside, and the window wipers beat out a syncopated rhythm with Eduardo's pounding heart and the crashing of waves against the rocks below. The road was wet, and the car skidded as it followed the curve of the bluff. Eduardo gasped when Miguel's full weight was thrown against him.

"Slow down, idiot," Miguel said, thumping Ernesto on the back of the head. "Ya know how much money I got invested in this car?"

Forget the car, Eduardo thought. *You're gonna get us killed.*

"Sorry," Ernesto replied. "It's not my drivin'. The road's wet, but I'll be more careful."

"You better," Miguel said. "If you put one scratch on this car, I'm scratchin' your face. We got lotsa time. It won't get dark for another hour, so slow down."

Eduardo's brow crinkled, and he took a long look at Miguel. "What are we doin' up here anyway?"

"We're gonna teach somebody a lesson. Put a scare in him and everybody like him. You ever heard of Philip Perez?"

"Yeah, I think so," Eduardo replied. "Isn't he the guy who's tryin' to get rid of the gangs and street drugs?"

"Right on," Miguel smiled. "And we're gonna give him a little warning. Or should I say our newest member is gonna have that honor?"

Eduardo's pupils dilated. Were they sending him to kill this guy? Without thinking, he took a deep breath, sending his chest muscles into spasms and causing him to grab his side. This guy had never hurt him. Actually, when Eduardo saw him in a school assembly, he seemed like a nice guy. He didn't want to hurt the man, and in his condition, he couldn't exactly beat someone up. The boy's mind raced. What am I supposed to do? he asked.

"Set the house on fire," Miguel said, pulling a roughly drawn diagram of the villa and grounds from his pocket. "You're gonna scout the area and then wait until dark so you can get away without bein' seen. Pick one of these ground floor rooms." Miguel pointed to two rooms on the diagram. "They should have curtains. Cloth will ignite when you toss in the bomb. Light the bomb, toss it through the window, and run. We'll be waitin' in the car same place where we drop you off."

Eduardo looked at the diagram in the fading light.

"You're in the big time," Miguel said. "Diego hasn't done anything like this yet." He grabbed the back of Eduardo's neck and shook him playfully.

Eduardo winced. "Why me?" he asked." Why not Diego?"

"Rule number one," Miguel said in a suddenly serious tone. "Never question the guy in charge." This time, the shake of Eduardo's neck was not playful.

Eduardo fidgeted with the diagram for the next three minutes until Miguel directed his attention to a walled estate on the right. "That's the place," he said. Ernesto pulled the car into an ocean viewpoint on the left, just past the villa's front gate. The car came to a stop, and Ernesto turned the engine off. Miguel climbed out of the car and opened the trunk, removing a gasoline-filled soda bottle with rags sticking out of its neck. "Here you go," he said, handing it to Eduardo. He stuck a lighter in the boy's pocket. "Light the rags and throw the bottle through a window. Whatever you do, don't hold on to it after it's lit." He laughed, slapped the boy on the back, and climbed back into the car.

Eduardo half jogged, half limped down the road until he was across from the south corner of the wall. He crouched in the tall wet grass and shivered. His heart pounded as he studied the scene to mark his bearings before dark settled in. On the right, the service road led to a large gate on the south side of the wall that would accommodate delivery trucks. Groupings of palms grew on each side of the wrought iron entrance way. The palms were tight enough to allow Eduardo to gain a foothold at their convergence and boost himself to the top of the wall. This would be his entry point. Perspiration formed a band across the broad young forehead, and Eduardo's stomach churned in fear for what he was about to do. The school psychologist had done him no harm, and so he asked himself for the hundredth time, *Why should I hurt him?* And for the hundredth time, his answer was the same: because Miguel ordered it, because Miguel was the boss, and Eduardo had become Miguel's slave. *There is no escape, no escape for him or Perez*, he thought. Because Eduardo had been ordered to do this, his survival depended on it. He had no choice, and he knew that. Perhaps the psychologist's survival depended on this too. After all, it was a warning. Miguel's instructions were clear.

Suddenly, and without premonition, Grandfather's words rang in Eduardo's ears. "Make me proud of you. Make your father and your beautiful mother proud of you." *Would they be proud of this?* he asked himself, and the answer was obvious.

Eduardo shifted in the grass and lightly massaged the tender skin under his new tattoo. The letters LRW partially camouflaged an old burn scar that had been with him for as long as he could remember. He fondled the lighter in his pocket and set the bottle on the ground. The sun hovered near the horizon, and twilight was short in October. It would soon be time to scale the wall. A small sport car approached. Eduardo hunched down to avoid detection. The car stopped briefly in front of the main gate, allowing it to open and then passed into the compound. Eduardo's stomach knotted, and he yearned to take slow deep breaths to quiet his racing pulse, but the pain in his side prevented it. He crossed the road to the trees that would help him scale the garden wall. It was getting dark outside, and peeking through the wrought iron gate, he saw lights on in the house.

His sides ached, and he found some relief from the pain by bracing his back against the wall. He placed Miguel's fire bomb in the soft earth by his feet and stretched and tried to work out the knots in his calves to no avail. Unknowingly, his foot tipped the bottle, and gasoline began to leak. Were it not for the mist, Eduardo might have noticed the wet spot on his pants and sock.

Minutes passed slowly. Eduardo's breaths were shallow, an unconscious effort to minimize his discomfort. He could hear a grinding noise on his right side when he bent or stretched. The resulting pain was nearly unbearable. His will was strong however, and he never doubted his ability to scale the villa wall though hours of inactivity combined with the injury and pain rendered his muscles stiff and unwilling partners in his activity. His heart pounded, exacerbating his need for oxygen. The urge to breathe deeply battled with the desire to avoid pain. Eduardo slowly stood. Something deep inside told him he could wait no longer. He grabbed the bottle and placed one foot against a palm. Wedging his body into the space between the palm trunks, he was able to boost himself to the top of the wall where he sat for several seconds unobserved, willing his heart to slow its pace and struggling against the pain in his side. Setting the bottle down, he turned slowly, dug his fingers into the outer wall edge, and dropped his feet over the inside edge. He let out a shriek as his body slid down the wall, rubbing cracked ribs against stucco. Releasing his grip, he fell in a heap. He was no longer in control of his body as waves of sobs racked his chest. He buried his face in the earth to stifle any sound, fighting the urge to cry out. Eventually, the sobbing subsided. He did not know how much time had elapsed, but it did not matter. The whole night lay before him. He felt along the top of the wall until his fingers touched the bottle. It scraped sharply against stucco as he slid it from its perch. Turning toward the garden, he watched for any sign of his detection. Satisfied that he had not been heard, he took a minute to determine what lay about him. He was inside the compound, but how would he get out? He scanned the length of the wall for a tree that would provide a foot hold at the right height. A pepper tree sat ten feet from the wall and the upper branches spread over the top of it, but there were no branches low enough for him to reach. He slipped from bush to bush along the service road and came upon the guest cottage. Although he could not distinguish one bush from another in the dark, he could smell the soft fragrance of roses along the side of the cottage. He remembered the roses in the street markets back home. Their petals were all the colors of the sunset and so creamy and soft. Like a baby's skin, Grandfather had said. "Grandfather, oh, Grandfather, what am I doing?" he whispered.

"You can leave. You can still leave. This life is not for you." The words formed in his mind, and they were so clear he spun around startled, thinking he would see the speaker. No one was there, but the words had been so clear. "You can leave. You can still leave. This life is not for you." Eduardo sank down on the cottage porch and leaned against the front wall. Could he leave? Where would he go? His cousins had beaten him, and for that he had run away. He had endured the gang initiation, which was done to prove his loyalty, so that was different or was it? He didn't want to do their bidding right now, but how could refuse? He wasn't sure of his ability to escape this compound let alone the mess he had gotten himself into with Miguel. Los Reyes would not hesitate to kill him if he left them. He was sure of that. So if he hung with them, he was safe as long as he did exactly what they said. No, that wasn't true. He wasn't safe right now. If Perez found him on his property, he'd call the police. If he was turned into the police, he'd be sent in shame back to Grandfather in Mexico. He did not want to face the disgrace that would bring not only to Grandfather but to him. His mind raced. He argued with himself. There had to be a way. Slowly, a plan came to him. It just might work.

On the porch, Eduardo found a sturdy wooden chair. Setting the bottle down, he carted the chair back up to the wall. He would still have to hoist himself to the top of the wall, but the chair would give him enough added height that he was sure he could do it. He returned for the bottle, and using the corner of the cottage for cover, Eduardo surveyed the darkening scene. He judged that two hundred yards lay between him and the main house. He would approach by way of the road, which provided a direct and unobstructed route to the house. Cautiously, Eduardo slipped from the cover of the cottage and into the shadow of a large hibiscus that bordered the road. Could one man really own this whole place? The grounds were huge. Eduardo thought about how they must look in the daylight. He had never been so close to such magnificence.

Slipping from bush to bush, he reached the main house within a few minutes. He wondered again how much time had elapsed since leaving Miguel and hoped no one had been sent to see why this was taking so long. That would ruin everything. A window lay just ahead of him. He peered in, curious to see the interior of this mansion. It was backlit from lights in a hallway. He could see shadowed outlines of a huge dining table, chairs, and a china hutch. Grandfather's whole house could fit inside this one room. He wished he could linger at the window, or better yet he wished he could eat at the table. No matter what happened, he would always remember this room, and someday he would tell Grandfather about it. A light showed in a window several feet to the left of where he stood. *Maybe*, he thought, *I could just peek inside very quickly, but first I must get everything ready.* He moved a few feet away from the house to the dark shadows at the base of a small tree. Using his foot, Eduardo explored the dirt, searching for leaves that might have been blown to the ground. A soft crunch underfoot told him he had found what he was looking for. The leaves were soaked from the mist. He grabbed several handfuls and moved them into the grass bordering the flower bed. He had decided to tell Miguel that he lit the bomb and was just about to throw it through the window when Perez appeared, startling him. Eduardo would claim to have dropped the flaming bomb and run.

Now near the open window, he heard strains of sad, bitter music. It was very unlike the rap and rock he listened to or the mariachis his cousins favored. He crept to the edge of the window and was startled to see a man standing just inside, his back facing Eduardo. The boy backed away quickly, not seeing a large sprinkler with metal blades directly behind him. He tripped and lost his grasp of the bottle. His ankle twisted as he fell. The pain in his side was unbearable. He bit his lip to avoid screaming and prayed for the pain to stop. Rubbing the ankle with one hand, he searched for the bottle in an ever widening arc with the other. Instinctively and without thinking, he pulled the lighter from his pocket. In its faint glow, he saw the bottle lying intact in the soft dirt just out of his reach. He held the lighter closer to examine his ankle, and in that instant, his gasoline-soaked pant leg caught fire. All the sorrows of his life descended on him in that moment. He rolled and swatted at the burning cloth, screaming in agony. He was able to extinguish the flames but continued to writhe on the ground. He cried for the pain in his ankle, he cried for the pain in his leg, he cried for the stabbing pain in his ribs, but most of all, he cried for his beautiful mother and the comforting presence of a strong and protective father. He whimpered for his own wretched condition. He did not wish at that moment to belong to the gang. He did not want to return to the cousins or old Grandfather. He only wanted to bury himself in the softness of the earth and cease to exist.

*   *   *

Philip's reverie would have continued if a muted thud and anguished cry had not startled him into reality. The noise came through the open window from somewhere in the garden. Another cry and a low sustained moan assured him that his mind was not playing tricks on him. His first thought was for Tomas and Maria. Had one of them fallen while attending to some forgotten task outside? Philip rushed to the kitchen and found them both staring out the backdoor.

As Eduardo began to lose consciousness, he did not hear the voices or see the beam of flashlights as their rays sought him out. He never felt the gentle arms that lifted him out of the dirt and carried him to the warmth and comfort of the house.

*　　*　　*

Philip Perez was fully aware of the hatred the gang members felt for him, and he was ready to combat them with everything at his disposal. He could be an angry man, but he was no more inclined toward violence than the young man who lay unconscious on his couch. If they shared nothing else in common, they shared this one characteristic. He looked down with pity at the boy and stretched out his hand to smooth the hair away from a face streaked with tears and dirt while he waited for the ambulance to arrive.

Miguel and his men heard the ambulance. Suspecting it was the fire and police departments, they sped away in the opposite direction. Eduardo would have to fend for himself.

CHAPTER SIX

A Revelation

Villa Perez
October 12, 1990

Philip and Eduardo sat before the fire, warm from its glow and the effects of the cognac. "The years have passed swiftly, Eduardo," Philip mused. "We have just celebrated your twenty-first birthday and the end of my guardianship."

Eduardo stared into the flames flickering brightly, intent on consuming yet another chunk of almond wood. He was glad in many ways to have reached this milestone, but he was not ready to leave the security he had found with this man who he called Uncle Philip. "I don't want to leave this place," he said looking about him. "Or you," he added, searching the older man's eyes.

Philip swallowed hard. Focusing on Eduardo, he said, "I do not want you to leave. This place is now your home. You have become like my son, Eduardo, the son I . . ." His words trailed off, and he choked back a sob.

Eduardo stared into his drink, unable to speak. Philip Perez was responsible for the man Eduardo now was, a man confident of his abilities in business, a man who displayed comfort in formal social settings, a man who enjoyed books and music when left to himself. Eduardo could name and appreciate the works of important composers from Vivaldi to Bernstein. Although he preferred the bold color and geometry of a Cezanne, he could name the major pieces from the Renaissance and Baroque periods to the Modernists of the twentieth century. He could suggest a good wine or cigar, discuss ancient philosophers as well as yesterday's world happenings, dress with finesse, and conduct himself with the gentleness of another era. What Eduardo did not know was an appropriate response to Philip's emotion. He had no practice, having never witnessed Philip's tears in the six years he had lived with his mentor.

"A son is important to a man," was Eduardo's quiet reply.

"I had a son . . ." Control eluded Philip's voice.

"I did not know," Eduardo replied in truth. One comes to know many things about a person in six years, but the existence of a son was something Philip had never shared with his protégé. Questions raced through Eduardo's mind. He stole a glance at Philip, and the room grew silent as one man sat in pain, and the other sat helpless to relieve it. *It is a little like his dying*, thought Eduardo. His hand can be held and his wishes attended to, but he alone faces the end of his life. Would he, Eduardo, learn one final lesson from this man, the art of comforting one who faces death?

"Do you suppose you will marry someday?" Philip asked, his voice now in control.

The question startled Eduardo and roused him from his musings. "Am I a suitable candidate for marriage?" he returned.

"Ah, a question to answer my question. Are we playing chess, Eduardo?"

"You must admit, Uncle Philip, you have often been the one to discern what suits me best."

"You know yourself better than most twenty-one-year-old men, Eduardo. I would expect you have contemplated this question, especially where a certain young blue-eyed blonde is concerned."

Were the lights brighter, Philip would have seen the flush on Eduardo's face. "She's pretty sweet, Uncle Philip," he admitted.

A deep sigh escaped the older man. Leaning his head back, he smiled to Eduardo's relief. "To fall in love is a wonderful thing. I can think of nothing else that compares."

A whole new facet of Philip's life was presenting itself to Eduardo this evening.

Eduardo remembered with amusement a crush he'd had on his dance instructor. He had thought that was real love, and now the feelings he had for Emily. "Tell me about love," he said. "How do you know when it is the real thing?"

"I will tell you, Eduardo, and when I am finished, I have one last question to ask you."

"I owe you my life. There is nothing I would not do for you."

The smile left Philip's face, and his eyes focused on a different time.

"Our lives are like giant scales, Eduardo. There may be a little joy on one side, but there is always a little sorrow to balance on the other side. To experience great love, one risks great pain. There is no other way." Philip paused. The twinkle in the dark eyes brightened, and in the firelight,

Eduardo saw tears on the older man's cheeks. The room was quiet. Shear curtain panels hung still before the open window as if the evening wind itself waited for the story.

"The Perez Ranch sat in the hill country outside Pachuca, Mexico," Philip began. "It was near enough to the city that all conveniences could be accessed, but on the ranch, it was as if we were a million miles from the noise and chaos that a city produces. My father bred Andalusian horses." Philip paused again, appreciating in his mind's eye, the splendor of the animals as they pranced. "The horses descended from the finest stock in Spain," he continued, "and their beauty and grace were such that buyers came from all over the world to purchase them. Pedro was our foreman. He loved those horses, and if horses can love back, I am convinced they loved him." Here again, Perez paused as his mind transported him to another time and place.

CHAPTER SEVEN

Philip's Reverie

Pachua, Mexico
1948–1970

The early morning sun sent shafts of light through gaps in the wooden siding of the chicken coop. The hens cackled happily outside, pecking at the corn six-year-old Philip had scattered to distract them from their nests. A warm egg was plucked from each hen's resting place and carefully laid in the basket the boy carried. If he hurried, he had just enough time before breakfast to wash and candle the eggs. That would bring a smile to his mother Beatriz's face. She would be very busy this morning preparing food for the fiesta in town. Philip's excitement rose as he thought of the colorful celebration. He had hardly slept last night. His friends would be there, and they would eat many treats and play football and listen to the Mariachis. His parents would visit with neighbors and dance into the night. Philip turned to leave the coop just as Uncle Pedro stuck his head in the door.

"Philip, are you coming to the stable this morning?" he asked. "You had better hurry. There is a new colt, and he is the ugliest one yet." A broad smile broke across Pedro's weathered brown face, exposing a row of large white teeth.

"Really, Uncle Pedro, did the new pony come last night?" the boy asked, hardly able to control his excitement.

Pedro was not really Philip's uncle, but the boy addressed him as such out of affection and respect. Pedro and his wife Lupe were more like family than employees, and they were happily awaiting the birth of their first child. "I was up all night helping the mama. Now hurry, because if I don't get some sleep, I'm going to fall right here," the man said.

"Uncle Pedro, you call all the new foals ugly," Philip chided.

"But his legs are too long, and his knees are knobby," Pedro said.

"Newborn horses always look like that, Uncle Pedro." Philip laughed. "What about his eyes?" Pedro judged both man and beast by their eyes, and he was teaching Philip to do the same. Pedro smiled. It was evident that Philip had been listening to the lessons. He felt a sense of satisfaction knowing his wisdom was being passed to the boy.

As they neared the stable, Pedro turned to the lad. "You are six years old, Philip," he said. "Although six is very young, I think you can begin to judge for yourself. Look into his eyes and tell me what you see." With that, Pedro led the way to the stall where the mare and her newborn rested.

Were it not for chores and school, Philip would have spent the whole day in the stable. He loved the warm sweet smell of the horses and the earthy fragrance of straw. When his mother could not find him, the first place she looked was the stable. The new colt was in the brood stall with his dame. Philip entered the stall with a small gift of grain. It was not more than a handful, but it was gratefully accepted by the mare. The boy stroked her muzzle as she chewed the grain; and difficult though it was to avoid going directly to the colt, he stood patiently, as Pedro had taught him, allowing the new mother time to assess his intentions. The mare nuzzled and sniffed at the boy. When her head turned to her foal, Philip accepted the invitation, and he moved closer to the baby. He was beautiful. His coat was coal black except for a tiny white patch on his forehead. Though his legs were disproportionately long and his joints pronounced, he stood surveying his world with a regal air.

"You were very wrong, Uncle Pedro," the boy said. Pedro smiled with such delight one would have thought he had produced the foal himself.

"What about his eyes, Philip? What do you see in his eyes?"

The boy moved cautiously to the colt, using care not to alarm the new mother. He peered with all the seriousness a six-year-old can muster into the foal's eyes. The foal returned his steady gaze and did not stir. "He is not afraid of us, Uncle Pedro," the boy whispered. "He is very brave."

Pedro put his hand on the boy's shoulder. "Bravo," he said. "He is brave. He has much spirit I believe and is a prize to be treasured."

As they walked out of the barn together, Pedro teased, "I suppose you will be doing your schoolwork in the stable this afternoon," knowing the child had not had his fill of the foal.

"If that is all right, Uncle Pedro, I will not bother them," he said.

"I know," Pedro replied. "You are a good boy. The horses know this as well as I do." Philip turned and looked into the man's soft brown eyes. They were merry eyes, even with tiredness overtaking him. Pedro was a good man, honest, and loving.

"Thank you, Uncle Pedro, for taking me see the new foal."

"You are welcome, my little muchacho."

Philip spent many afternoons in the stable, reading or doing schoolwork near Majestic and her colt. He assumed the task of cleaning their stall and brushing their coats to a glistening sheen. His father allowed him to name the baby; and Philip chose El Viente, The Wind. Philip often played with El Viente in the meadow, and it was apparent to Pedro and Philip's father that one day, the colt would run like the wind. When the boy wasn't playing with El Viente, he was usually standing close by, watching the object of his delight cavort in the pasture with the other colts. The two became so attached, that when Philip whistled, El Viente stopped his antics with the other ponies and ran to the boy. Of course, Philip often had a small handful of grain in his pocket. One day Philip's father, Victor, leaned against the fence and watched his son and the colt walking side by side in the pasture. A look of concern furrowed his brow. When Philip saw his father, he ran to the fence, the colt trotting along behind.

"Papa, isn't he more handsome every day?" the child beamed, rubbing the colt's muzzle.

Victor's face softened a bit. "Let's take a walk," he said and helped the boy climb over the fence rail. "This is a horse ranch, Philip," Victor began, "and we breed the mares so we have more horses to sell." He stopped and turned, looking earnestly at his son. Understanding what his father was saying, the boy hung his head and allowed his tears to drop into the dust at his feet. The tears did not go unnoticed by the older Perez. Victor lifted his son and pressed the boy close. When Philip lifted his head, he saw there were tears in his father's eyes too. Silently, they walked back to the stable. Pedro was bringing Majestic and El Viente in for the evening. "Go on back to the house," Victor said. "Pedro will care for the horses." As the boy turned to leave, he saw Pedro give his father an odd look. Philip ducked into an empty stall to see what Uncle Pedro might say.

"You have told him we have a buyer?" Pedro inquired, the usual warmth lacking in his voice. Philip's heart sank. He knew his father was preparing him to say goodbye to El Viente, but he didn't think it would be so soon.

"No, I reminded him that the colt will not be staying here at the ranch, but I did not tell him we had an offer." Silence hung in the air like funerary bunting. "He is an extremely valuable horse, Pedro," Victor said with a defensive tone.

"Sons are valuable too," Pedro responded in a tone that was less accusing than the words.

A long loud sigh escaped from the father. "He is a spirited horse, Pedro, and he has great potential to race. There are many horses that would make a good pony for a boy."

"Sometimes it is good to look beyond the obvious," Pedro replied. There was silence except for the noise of horses munching hay.

"He will not be an easy horse to break," the father countered, "the unspoken question being can my son handle him."

"The presence of a strong bond will ease the task of breaking and training this beauty," Pedro said, stroking the colt's neck.

"And would you think it foolish if a man were to give a very prized young colt to a very young boy?" asked Victor.

"Yes, it would be a foolish thing to do," Pedro said, "if the boy was any other boy than Philip and the horse was any other horse than El Viente."

"Begin looking at possible replacements, Pedro," the father said with a smile on his face. "We are going to have one very disappointed and angry buyer."

Philip's heart rose from the pit of his stomach, and he thought it would burst through the roof. He ran from his hiding place and embraced his father and Pedro before burying his face in the neck of the pony.

*   *   *

A log broke, sending a stream of sparks onto the hearth. Eduardo rose and brushed the smoldering embers back into the firebox. "I am thinking you and that horse were inseparable for many years," he said, resuming his seat opposite Philip.

"Ah, yes, inseparable, indeed. Breaking him was not an easy task. It took many months of hard work, but he and I became like one as we flew across the countryside."

Philip sipped his cognac and stared into the fire.

Several minutes passed, and Eduardo stole a look in the older man's direction, fearing he might have fallen asleep. The eyes were open, and the glass held upright. The lines in his face had softened, and the corners of his mouth curved up ever so slightly. Eduardo remained quiet, unwilling to break the spell that had transfixed the older man.

Realizing his journey into the past had become a solitary one, Philip turned to Eduardo. "I'm sorry," he said. "I have not forgotten that you are here."

"I understand, Uncle Philip. The past has become very real for you tonight." *So real*, he thought, *I can almost see the horse in my own mind.*

Philip took another sip of the amber liquor, and the smile disappeared. Eduardo shifted in his chair, uncomfortably aware of the change in Philip's visage.

"Aunt Lupe was a beautiful woman," Philip continued. "And Uncle Pedro loved her above all else. Her skin was as fair as her hair was dark. But her eyes, her eyes were sparkling black with a frame of lashes that would make any movie star jealous." Philip smiled. "They were spirited eyes, kind but spirited. Lupe and my mother were the only women who lived on the ranch, and they shared gossip and experiences like best friends." He bowed his head in concentrated reverence as he continued the story. "One night not long after El Viente became my own pony, I was awakened by pounding and yelling on the front porch. I peered over the second floor railing as father opened the door. Pedro stood there shaking and begging for help. Lupe's baby was coming early and quickly. There was no time to drive to the hospital. Father and Mother went quickly to offer what help they could. I lay on the window seat in my room, staring toward the lights of Uncle Pedro's cottage. An ambulance arrived later, and I watched as two uniformed men wheeled a sheet-covered stretcher into the emergency vehicle. Uncle Pedro climbed into the ambulance, and Mother followed, a blanket wrapped bundle in her arms."

*   *   *

Young Philip had waited anxiously for his father to return home. It was a half hour before the lights in Pedro's house went out one by one, and Victor slowly made his way along a darkened path toward home. Philip met him in the hall, and his stooped shoulders and grim expression informed his son that something had gone very wrong. The light in Pedro's eyes went out that night as well. His Lupe was gone, and his life would never be the same.

During the day, Beatriz cared for the baby girl as if the child were her own. In the evening, Pedro sat in Lupe's rocking chair, holding the tiny girl close to his heart, knowing that in this child, a part of Lupe remained with him. Philip often sat with Pedro saying nothing, simply offering quiet companionship.

Pedro went about his normal work at the ranch. The horses were fed, groomed, and exercised; the stalls were mucked; and every other task required in maintaining the health of the animals was completed, but it was done robotically. It seemed as if when Lupe's spirit departed, Pedro's spirit left too.

In spite of his sorrow, Pedro showered great affection on his little girl, and the bond between the two was evident. When the baby was christened, Beatriz and Victor happily accepted the joy and responsibility of becoming Little Elena's godparents. The baby's large dark eyes and pale skin were constant reminders of her mother, but her smile was Pedro's. As she grew, she showed the spirited personality of her mother and the soft, sweet compassion of her father. Six years younger than Philip, she was like his little sister. When he was not teasing her, he tried to teach her all the things Pedro had taught him: feeding the chickens, collecting the eggs, and performing a dozen other chores around the ranch. Later he taught her the secret of searching the eyes and, under Pedro's supervision, the proper way to sit a horse. Beatriz spoke to the girl of her mother almost daily. She was determined that the little one would grow up with a sense of having known her mother.

"This is how your mama patted out the tortillas," Beatriz would say in the kitchen. Or "This is how your mama mended a tear," if they were fixing a shirt that had been caught on barbed wire. "See your beautiful eyes?" Beatriz would ask, holding the child in front of the hallway mirror. "They are so beautiful, just like your mama's." Elena would smile and touch her eyelids, saying, "Los ojos, los ojos." When she learned the word for mouth and said "Mama's mouth," Beatriz laughed and said, "No, that is not Mama's mouth. That is Papa's mouth-and-smile-for-sure."

Occasionally, Pedro's sister sent letters to him, insisting that he return to his hometown and bring Baby Elena with him. Pedro knew his sister resented the "Aristocratic Spanish" family, as she called the Perez's. The gentle foreman's people were of native Mexican descent, and though they were good and hardworking, they were poor and felt inferior to those whose life was more comfortable. Lupe had been fair-skinned and looked more Spanish than native Mexican. Pedro supposed that was why she never fit well into his family.

"You cannot trust the rich," Pedro's sister had advised him when he took the job in Pachua. To Lupe, she had said, "You will return to the village one day, begging to move in with us when those rich people tire of you."

One day, Philip wandered to Pedro's cottage and found Elena curled up in her father's lap as they rocked on the front porch. The child's little hands cupped Pedro's face. Intently, she stared into his eyes, studying whatever she might see there. She gently touched his eyes and said, "Papa's eyes." Moving her finger to her own face, she said, "Mama's eyes." Pedro groaned and pressed his daughter's head to his breast. Elena lay contentedly for a moment and then raised her little head. Tears coursed down her father's cheeks. "Don't cry," she said, kissing the tears away. "Don't cry."

Pedro wrapped his arms around his little girl and buried his face in her neck. The weeping continued while she patted his head and tried to sooth him. Philip crept quietly from the cottage, sensing even as a nine-year-old that he had intruded on a very intimate moment.

Some days Pedro's grief almost overwhelmed him. In town, he might see a dress that would be a wonderful birthday gift for Lupe only to be reminded in an instant that she was no longer with him. Elena might squint or put her hands on her hips in the same way her mother did. He never knew when a fresh wave of grief would overtake him, and so he was unprepared for the sudden tears and choking sobs that rose in his chest. Pedro was a man of faith, and he had no doubt that he would one day see his Lupe again. But that hope did not always soothe the pain during long lonely nights. In spite of his hope, the house was always dark and empty when he and Elena came home in the evening. The child filled much of the emptiness, but after dinner and play, after stories and bedtime routines, he was alone with his thoughts. He sat in Lupe's chair most evenings and read her Bible until his eyelids began to droop.

One night after dinner, Elena found her father's old guitar. Pedro sat the child in his lap and allowed her to strum the strings as he formed the chords. That became a favorite pastime for Elena until she was too big for Pedro's lap. By then, she had learned the chords herself. Pedro bought her a guitar; and in the evening, the two sat on the porch, contentedly singing and playing duets.

The day Philip left the ranch for university, Elena hid near the driveway. She could not bear the thought of bidding him goodbye. From her vantage point behind a camellia bush, she watched Victor pack the young man's bags into the trunk. The front door opened; and laughing, Philip and Beatriz walked to the waiting car. Pedro arrived from the stable, and as they said their goodbyes, Philip scanned the yard for Elena. "Where is my little sister? I can't leave without telling her goodbye."

"I think she could not bear your leaving," Pedro said, giving the young man one last hug.

"Elena!" Philip called out, sensing the girl was near enough to hear his voice. "Elena, come say goodbye or I will never speak to you again."

At that moment, Elena could restrain herself no longer. She flew to the car sobbing and clung to Philip. Holding her tight, he whispered in her ear, "Don't cry, little one. I will be back soon." He kissed her on the forehead, pinched her cheeks, and then was gone. He would return; of that, Elena was sure, but she sensed things would never be quite the same.

Victor drove his son to the University of Mexico that day to start what would become a six-year program resulting in a doctorate of psychology. There were trips home for the holidays, but Victor encouraged his son to spend the summers travelling. "It is important to develop an understanding of other cultures," he said, "especially, since you are studying human behavior." The whole third year of his studies was spent at the Complutense

University of Madrid where his parents visited him for a month. Together, they toured the Prado and viewed a special exhibit of works by Joan Miro. Philip had been especially anxious to view these paintings since Miro's work attempted to expose the subconscious mind. They returned several times to be able to fully appreciate this display as well as masterworks of Goya, Picasso, Velazquez, and others. They walked the Paseo de los Recoletos, the Gran Via, and through the Parq del Buen Retiro. They dined in fine restaurants as well as the haunts of the students in the Monloa area. Before the end of their stay, Victor and Beatriz travelled to Andalusia to see the best flamenco dancers and of course to visit the Pura Raza Espanola at the horse ranches.

Philip made use of long weekends to explore the rest of Spain. Barcelona was a favorite. He strolled up and down Los Rambles exploring small shops and the massive open air food market with its offerings of every imaginable staple and delicacy. He photographed the Gaudi buildings and spent an entire day at La Familia Sagrada. At a shop near the cathedral, his attention was drawn to a display in a store window. A small gold cross with tiny inset stones hanging from a delicate gold chain stood out from the others, and on impulse, he purchased it for Elena. Her fifteenth birthday was approaching, and this would be his quinceanera gift to her. He smiled remembering how she had cried when he left for university over three years ago. He had only seen her a few times since that day. He wondered then if he would see her again. His mother's letters indicated that Uncle Pedro would move back to his home village outside Guadalajara. Arthritis made exercising and caring for the horses increasingly difficult for him. His depression continued, and he longed to be back in the village where he and Lupe had started their life together. Philip knew his mother's heart would break when Elena left, so he was glad to learn that Elena would be spending summers at the ranch in Pachua.

Victor appreciated Pedro's dedicated service over the many years he worked at the ranch, and when his foreman left, Victor set up a trust fund that would help with future living expenses and Elena's schooling.

"If ever you have a need, you must contact me," he told his old friend in parting.

Philip's last three years were spent in Mexico City where the course-work became increasingly demanding. His parents attended his graduation with great pride. Following the celebrations, they prepared to return home to welcome their annual summer guest who would be arriving in another week.

"I am hoping this is not her last summer with us," Beatriz said. "She finishes school next week."

"She will travel to Guadalajara to attend university," Victor said before his son could frame the question.

Philip was relieved. Although he had never been to San Jenaro, he knew Elena would not be exposed to fine music, theater, or art where she was living. These things had become increasingly important to him during his studies and travel, and he wanted them for the young woman he thought of as his sister.

Two weeks later, Philip returned to his family home. He felt a surge of emotion as he drove his car down the long lane leading to the house. He sat for several minutes, drinking in the sight of the hacienda. Up the hill, behind the house, a lone rider galloped across the pasture. The lines of the horse were unmistakable. It was El Viente. His mane flew in the air as the rider urged him across the meadow. Philip could not distinguish the identity of the person who sat quite gracefully in the saddle. Descending the hillside, they disappeared behind the stable, and Philip turned his attention to the front door that had just swung open. His parents appeared on the porch, smiles on their faces, and he felt as if he had never left this peaceful place.

Beatriz had prepared coffee and pan dulce. Philip delved into the sweet bread greedily and conversed with his parents about the changes that had transpired over the past six years. His mother glowed, observing how handsome he had grown. Though he had been a man when he left for university, somehow his face was more chiseled and rugged. His eyes sparkled with self-confidence, not pride, but rather a certain self-assurance that he knew himself and where he was going. His father found pleasure in the fact that Philip showed knowledge of the world around him as well as an understanding of himself.

Eventually, as the conversation slowed, Philip felt the absence of his old mentor. "I wish Uncle Pedro was here," he commented.

"We all do," his father replied. "Elena says his depression continues, but his arthritis seems to have stabilized."

"Where is Elena?" Philip asked suddenly. "I thought she was coming here for the summer."

A look passed between Victor and Beatriz. "She is here," his father said. "In fact, she was out exercising El Viente when you came in. She is probably rubbing him down and feeding him. When she stays with us, she cares for that horse as if he were her own." Victor looked at Philip with a twinkle in his eye. "I think you will find she is much changed from the time you last saw her."

"In what way?" Philip asked, concerned that Pedro's depression might have worn off on her.

At that moment, the kitchen door opened; and in walked a willowy young woman, sweaty in her riding clothes. Her glossy black hair was pulled back in a bun at the nape of her slender neck. Philip gasped, "Elena?"

She giggled and ran to him. "Forgive me," she said. "I thought you would arrive this evening." The once stick straight figure now curved softly in all the right places. Her heart-shaped face had lost its baby fat and was more defined. The only thing that had not changed one bit was her eyes. Still framed in luxurious black lashes, they dominated her face and pulled the young man into their twinkling depths.

Philip reached to embrace her, and she leaned back. "No, silly, you're in a suit, and I'm all dusty and dirty." She leaned forward and pecked him on the cheek. Their eyes met, and Philip felt paralyzed, speechless.

Embarrassed, she broke the gaze and took a step back. "I'll get cleaned up, won't take me a minute." And with that, she sprinted up the back staircase to her room.

Elena's minute turned into thirty, and Victor observed Philip looking toward the staircase frequently. Smiling, he finally remarked, "Well, Philip, that's a woman for you. One minute turns into an hour. Let's go look at El Viente. Your mother will let Elena know where we are if she ever comes down." He looked toward his wife who was smiling.

After she had groomed him, Elena had released El Viente into the pasture. Philip and his father were not at the fence long before the horse came running to them. Philip climbed the rail and embraced his old friend. The horse whinnied and neighed in contentment. He nudged his owner toward the tack room, making Philip howl with laughter. "You were just out, old man," he said. "Give me a break." He offered a conciliatory handful of grain to the horse and rubbed his nose affectionately.

Beatriz called Victor to the telephone just as Elena appeared.

"You'll tear your suit," the young woman scolded, "climbing on the fence like that."

Philip flushed and jumped down, nearly losing his balance.

"Welcome home, Philip," she said softly, reaching out to steady him. Raising her hands to his broad shoulders, she placed a light kiss on each cheek.

Her hair was swept off her face by a velvet ribbon and hung in soft curls down her back. She wore just a touch of lipstick that matched the pale shade of pink on her cheeks. The cross Philip had sent her three years earlier lay on her chest. She touched the cross and smiled. "I love it," she said. "I have not taken it off since the day I received it." She had changed into peasant clothes, a scooped-neck billowy white blouse, full red print skirt, and sandals. The scent of roses lingered about her.

"I am glad you liked it," Philip managed, though his tongue was nearly tied.

* * *

Completely immersed in Phillip's story, Eduardo chuckled heartily. "I have never seen your tongue-tied in six years," he said. "Her impact upon you must have been incredible."

"Oh, it was," Phillip agreed. "In her presence, I felt like an awkward preadolescent. "Somehow those dark eyes made me feel exposed and vulnerable. It was as if when she looked at me, she saw my very soul. I had come home with such self-confidence, and in this young woman's presence, I was reduced to a weak-kneed, tongue-tied fool. I did not realize until later how obvious my discomfort was to others and the amusement this created for my parents."

* * *

Beatriz and Elena prepared a sumptuous dinner that evening. They talked of Pedro, of the old days, and of the future. "Uncle Pedro must miss you terribly when you are here," Philip said.

"Father will be OK," Elena replied. "He has his little house near his sister, and she visits daily. Although he loved this place, I don't think he could return for long. It reminds him of such a sad time in his life. You would think my mother had died only months ago. The pain is so fresh in his mind."

"I must go and see him sometime," Philip remarked.

"He would like that," she replied. "He asks about you often."

"Maybe at the end of the summer," Victor said. "You could drive with us to take Elena back home." He looked at his son for a reaction. "That is, if you are not busy with your work." Beatriz did not miss the smile as Victor raised his napkin to wipe his lips.

"Well, of course," Philip stuttered, "if my presence is not required at the university."

Elena did not hide her smile.

"When will you hear about the position at Universidad La Salle Pachua?" Victor asked.

"I meet with the dean tomorrow. It is a teaching and research position," Philip explained to Elena. "I am very excited about the prospect of doing the two things I love most."

"Don't let El Viente hear you say that." Elena giggled. Then in a more serious tone, she said, "I will say a prayer for you." Philip smiled and thanked her.

After dinner, Victor brought out his best Cuban cigars. He did not smoke often, but this was a celebration of Philip's return home. He clipped the ends and handed one to his son who placed it in his mouth.

"No, no," Victor said as if Philip had just violated a sacred code. Removing the cigar from the young man's mouth, he began rolling it between his hands. "You must pinch the cigar gently first," Victor said, demonstrating the technique he had learned from his own father. "That loosens the leaves and allows air to circulate between them." He handed the cigar back to Philip and watched as his son began gently pinching. Then Victor lit a wooden stick and held it to the cigar. "Never light a cigar with a match," he said, "or you will end up with the taste of sulfur. Now draw the smoke into your mouth, but do not inhale. Hold it for a moment, and let it escape."

That Philip was able to remember his father's instructions was remarkable and that he was able to appreciate the subtleties of the tobacco was even more remarkable, because as the two men strolled outside, Philip's thoughts were not on the cigar.

Elena had gone into the garden with her guitar; and even as father and son wandered away from the house, Elena's voice carried to them, sweet and clear on the evening breeze.

"Bella, no?" Vincent asked his son.

Startled out of his thoughts, Philip did not know if his father meant Elena or her voice. He decided to take the safer route. "Yes, her voice has matured into one of the loveliest I have heard," he offered.

Victor stopped and drew on his cigar. Releasing the tobacco, he looked directly at Philip and smiled. "I was not speaking of her voice, Philip, but that too is beautiful."

The younger man was grateful for the deep shadows in the orchard where they stood for he felt his face growing hot. "Oh, yes," he stammered in as offhand a manner as he could project. "Yes, she has grown into a very lovely young woman."

"Your mother and I love her as if she were our own daughter," Victor said.

"I have always loved her too," Philip replied. "She is like a sister to me." Even as he said it, the thought jarred him. At least I always thought of her as a sister, he reasoned to himself. But today, she had totally disarmed him; and in truth, he no longer knew exactly how he felt about Elena. The one thing he did know was that he wanted to spend more time with her, get to know the young woman she had become.

"I am not so sure she still thinks of you as a brother," Victor said, casting a sidelong glance in his son's direction.

A surge of emotion spread through Philip, sending a wave of warmth from his toes to his chest. He felt as if this wonderful man was reading his mind. It was disconcerting. He dropped all pretense of naiveté. "Father, I have never thought of her in any way except as a sister, but today, when I saw her again . . ."

"It is not surprising you have ambiguous feelings," Victor mused. "She reminds me very much of your mother. I remember the night I met Beatriz. Her beauty struck me like a force of nature. I was frightened because for the first time in my life, I did not feel in control of my emotions."

"What did you do?" Philip asked.

"I talked with my father. I had always gone to him for advice. He told me that this electric, instant attraction would not sustain itself forever. He said it is important to know a person deep inside. What were her convictions? What were her values?"

"Hmmm," Philip mused. For much of his life, he had known Elena very well. In fact, he had influenced her in many ways.

"You are not expected to solve questions like this quickly, Philip, not even with all your training. Time and patience will give you the answers you need, and Elena is still quite young."

Philip looked anew at his father with gratefulness for the example he had been and with admiration for his insight.

*   *   *

Philip received the appointment at Universidad La Salle Pachua and went to work the week after his arrival. His duties included preparing curriculum for the psychology department that was in line with the teachings of the Roman Catholic Church, under whose auspices the university operated. In addition to teaching, he would be allowed to conduct research in human behavior. With a developing drug problem on the streets, Philip was eager to look into the lives of the youth of the city and see if he could determine the reasons young people were turning to illicit drugs and how this problem could be reversed. His work was so demanding; he lived in Pachua except for weekends when he returned to the ranch.

His mother's cooking and his father's companionship provided welcome relief to the grueling schedule he kept in town. As he went about the days at home, he looked for opportunities to be near Elena. Each encounter left him feeling as though he was looking at her for the first time in his life. It was not that she had changed so much, but that she had deepened in character. As children, they had never discussed religion or politics. Now Philip found she was well informed on these and many other subjects. "Just as you see something new each time you view a great piece of art, there is something new and fresh each time I talk with her," he said to his father. To himself, he admitted that it was her beauty that caught his attention, but it was her gentle kindness that wrapped itself around his heart and would not let it go.

*   *   *

Philip looked at Eduardo with intensity. "I wish the same for you some day, a woman who is as beautiful as she is kind, but always remember, it is the kindness that will hold your heart."

The room in Philip's study grew still once more, and Eduardo sat contemplating what his mentor had said. "People speak of falling in love," he finally said, "as if it was something they could not avoid or control."

"That is a common misconception," Philip replied. "What people often mistake for love is physical attraction. Those feelings are very powerful." He looked at Eduardo and chuckled. "They can turn an articulate young man into a stuttering fool."

Eduardo smiled. "How do you know whether what you are feeling is real love or simply physical attraction?" he asked.

"That is one of the great questions of life," Philip said. Looking thoughtfully at Eduardo, he began quoting, "Love is patient and kind. Love is not jealous or boastful or proud or rude. Love does not demand its own way." He paused. "There is more. It is marked in Elena's Bible." He pointed to the shelf. Eduardo rose and placed the Bible in Philip's lap. As he thumbed to the thirteenth chapter of 1 Corinthians, the older man continued, "In Elena, I found all the qualities I so admired in my mother; virtue, modesty, compassion, a good work ethic, appreciation for the arts, and energy." He laughed at this last quality. "Boundless energy and laughter. Elena filled our days with joy."

"As fall approached, so did the time for Elena's departure. She would spend a week with Uncle Pedro and then go to Guadalajara where she would enroll in the university. She planned to be a teacher. Time did indeed give me the answers I sought," Philip said, smiling and twisting the simple gold band on his ring finger.

*   *   *

There were many horse paths on the hills above the ranch, and Philip enjoyed long rides astride El Viente each weekend. It was never hard to coax Elena to ride along, and today she brought a picnic for them to share in an old olive grove at the summit of one of the larger hills. A small shack had been erected in the stand of trees years ago. It housed an ancient olive press and a small fireplace where the workers could heat water for coffee. A lean-to on the side of the building sheltered a trough for watering the pack animals that were used to haul the harvest down to the ranch before the path was widened and graveled for trucks. There were never enough oil or olives for the market, but the orchard supplied the needs of the ranch.

Horses and riders slowly ascended, enjoying companionship and the view that spread out before them. Philip noticed the air becoming humid, and as he looked to the southwest, he saw dark clouds moving toward the valley. With a nod of his head, he indicated the sky to Elena. "Do you want to continue to the top or head back?" he asked.

She stood in the saddle and scanned the sky. "The clouds are moving in fast," she replied. "I think we'll get caught in a downpour if we turn around."

As she spoke, lightning flashed across the sky. "Let's go," Philip said, spurring El Viente toward the top.

They tethered the horses under the lean-to and filled the trough from a small brook that ran year around just as the deluge started. Laughing, they ran from the shelter into the shack.

"Remember the time this happened when we were kids?" she asked once she had caught her breath.

"I'll never forget," he replied. "Our parents were frantic, and I took the blame."

"Well, you were the oldest," she replied. "I never would have come up here on my own."

"You were pretty scared too," he teased. "Actually, if you want to know the truth, I was scared too, but I wasn't about to let you know."

"I never guessed," she smiled. "I thought you were so brave. Now you've ruined the image I had of you." She held her hand over her heart in mock disappointment.

Philip grimaced and began loading the fireplace with kindling. It wouldn't give off much heat, but they were both shivering and anything would help. The kindling caught, and as it snapped and popped, Philip added larger pieces of wood. The shack was drafty; but in a tiny space, directly in front of the fire, there was warmth. Elena spread a thin blanket and extracted fruit, sandwiches. and a jar of agua fresca from her backpack. "Poor horses," she said as they huddled in front of the fire and ate.

"El Viente will be fine," Philip said, "but I'm a little worried about the mare. She was skittish when we tied her up." The rain continued outside. Elena rose to look out the window just as a bolt of lightning struck and split a tree in the grove. She screamed loud enough to be heard across the valley below. Stepping back, quickly, she bumped into Philip who had risen right behind her. Trembling, she turned and sank into his chest. "Shhh," he cooed to her. "It's all right."

The fire had warmed them both, but his strong arms around her brought warmth that had nothing to do with the fire. Tentatively, she wrapped her arms around his waist and rested her head against his shoulder, no longer afraid of the storm, but feeling she was on the verge of something else that could be both wonderful and frightening. Philip raised a hand to her chin and tilted her face until their eyes met. Moments passed as they caressed one another with their eyes, each searching deep within the other. He lowered his face, kissing her neck, taking in deep breaths of her essence. His lips moved up her neck, to her chin, and finally to the lips that waited impatiently. Elena did not know if lightning flashed again outside or within her brain, but shivers coursed through her and aroused a longing she had never experienced.

They sat caressing and kissing in front of the fire, wishing the rain would never cease. It was late afternoon when the torrents stopped and the sun streamed through chinks in the walls. Twilight was brief in Pachua, and Philip knew his parents would be concerned if they did not return before dark. "I'll be in trouble again if we don't hurry," he laughed as they stuffed their backpacks.

El Viente stamped restlessly as they rounded the corner of the shack. He whinnied and tugged at his tether as Philip approached. "Easy, boy," Philip said. "The storm has passed." And then he noticed the mare was gone.

"She must have bolted when the lightning struck," Philip said. He walked out into a clearing and scanned the hillside. "Hopefully, she headed back down the path." He shook his head, trying to decide whether to stay and look for the mare or start back home, hoping she had retraced their steps. It would be dark in a half hour, making the descent on a rocky path dangerous for El Viente. He decided to take Elena to the ranch. If they did not find the horse on the way, he would come back up with some of the ranch hands armed with rifles and torches. He knew the horse would not survive a wildcat or coyote attack. Philip swung up in the saddle and pulled Elena onto his lap as he had done many times before she learned to ride on her own.

"It's a bit more crowded now," she said.

"But I'm enjoying it more," he replied with a smile and hugged her to him.

It was almost dark when they reached the ranch. The mare had not returned home. Victor assembled his men, and they rode off in the twilight armed with torches and rifles. He had never lost a horse to wild animals, and he didn't want this mare to be the first.

"I'm so sorry, Father," Philip said as he rode alongside Victor.

"Don't blame yourself, Philip," his father replied. "That storm came up fast. I'm just glad you and Elena made it home safely." Then he turned to his son with a smile that could only be discerned in his voice. "At least you won't get a spanking this time."

It took almost an hour to reach the olive grove. They listened for noise as they ascended the hill, but there was no sign of the little mare on the trail. At the summit, the men split up into groups of two and spread out using flashlights to illuminate the brushy hillside. Philip and his father took the steeper backside of the hill. Victor wore an old miner's helmet, which left his hands free to grab the rifle in his saddle holster. He hoped he wouldn't need it. Philip carried a flashlight that he moved back and forth, scanning the brush. Their descent was slow. The ground was rocky, and the rain had muddy it. There were snake and ground squirrel holes that could trap and break a horse's leg.

After thirty minutes of searching, Victor dismounted. "Pedro and I scouted this area years ago. There's a rock overhang above on the right. It's about thirty meters ahead of us. Everything beneath it broke loose and slid down the hill centuries ago. The horses can't walk through the scree, and it would be dangerous for us to try. We'll have to turn back."

Philip dismounted and handed his reins to his father. "Let me go as far as the overhang and take a look," he said. Unbeknownst to the men, the little mare stood just yards from them. She had traversed a narrow path beneath the overhang and now stood on its far side, her wandering interrupted when she came up against a large group of boulders. She sensed the presence of the men, and a nervous whinny broke the silence of the night. Victor grabbed his son's shoulder. "I'll follow behind as far as I can go with the horses." He pulled his rifle from the saddle holster and tied El Viente's reins to the harness of his own mount. "Hopefully, she's not hurt." Victor hated putting one of his animals down, but if her leg was broken, he knew they would never get her off the mountain.

Philip edged ahead cautiously, casting the beam of the flashlight back and forth. The overhang was in view, and he moved toward it. A rocky, uneven piece of ground running eight feet beneath the overhang appeared intact enough to support his weight. Below it, the scree fanned out for three hundred feet, ending in a mass of boulders. He swung his torch in slow, wide arcs, but there was no sign of the horse below. Philip backed into the hillside and maneuvered himself toward the ledge. If the mare was on the other side, there was just enough room to bring her back, but it would be a risk in daylight let alone in the dark. The horse whinnied again. Philip aimed his light ahead and spotted her past the far side of the ledge. "I see her," he called back to Victor. "She's standing, and I think I can get to her." He inched forward until he was under the overhang. She could not move away from him without falling, and he hoped she would not panic and try to charge past him. The path was muddy, and Philip moved cautiously toward the horse. He was sure he could reach her, but he was not confident he could bring this skittish mare back to where his father waited.

"Easy, girl," he soothed. She whinnied and backed away. "Easy, girl," he continued. "It's me. I've come to bring you back to a nice warm stall and pan of oats." The horse knew him, and her behavior puzzled him. He continued his reassurances as he moved forward. Philip reached the far side of the ledge just as an inhuman scream pierced the night air. He shuddered as all three horses began to whinny in response to the wildcat's cry. Instinctively, he took a step back.

"I think it's on the outcropping above you," his father yelled. "Stay under the shelf, and I'll see if I can get off a shot." He knew the cat would bolt at the sound. The problem was that the mare might bolt too. He aimed his rifle in the air and sent off a round. Another scream followed from farther up the hill. Was there a second cat or had the first one made a run for it uphill? Philip called softly to the mare. She lowered her head and neighed. "Come, girl," he said. The little horse took a tentative step forward. Philip edged out from the overhang and grabbed the reins. He patted the horse and soothed her with his voice. "Dad," he called, "I've got her."

Philip moved slowly, coaxing the mare as he went. He aimed the light off the path just long enough to judge the distance to his father when his boot struck a rock. He lost his balance and tripped, sliding and tumbling three hundred feet, smashing sideways into a boulder. He had released the reins as well as the flashlight when he fell. The horse stood as she had been left beneath the outcropping. Victor watched as Philip slid, unable to help his son. "Philip," he called. "Philip, can you hear me?" He quickly tied the horses to a nearby bush and edged to the spot where his son had slipped.

Grabbing the flashlight, he searched the scree until he saw Philip, crumpled against a boulder. "Son," he screamed.

Philip lay unmoving, trying to regain the breath that had been knocked out of him. His right arm was wedged against the boulder, but he was able to raise his left arm. He took a deep breath, and pain seared his right shoulder.

"Philip, can you hear me?" his father yelled. "Please, son, can you hear me?"

"Yeah, Dad," Philip replied in a weak voice. "I can hear you, but something's wrong with my arm and shoulder."

Victor fought to push back panic that was rising by the second. He forced himself to think. He needed help, but he couldn't leave his injured son alone. "Can you move?"

Philip raised his left arm and with great difficulty pushed himself to his knees. "It's my right arm, Dad," he said. "It's broken, but I think I'm OK otherwise."

Victor worked as he spoke to his son, removing the coiled ropes from the saddles of his and Philip's mounts. He tucked a first aid kit inside his jacket and tied one end of each rope to the horn of a saddle. He wrapped the other ends of the ropes around his gloved hand and moved to the top of the scree. Locating his son in the beam of a flashlight, he began his descent. A shower of rocks slew out from under his feet, but anticipating this he had positioned himself so the cascade would miss Philip.

When he reached the base, Victor moved sideways until he was at Philip's side. He ran his hands up and down his son's legs and found nothing broken. He moved to Philip's left arm, which was also intact. The right forearm had an obvious midshaft brake, but the upper arm and shoulder seemed fine. Vincent found a reasonably straight stick close by and bound it to his son's arm with tape from the first aid kit. Philip was conscious and oriented to his surroundings, and Vincent prayed he would stay that way. Tenderness in his son's upper right quadrant troubled Victor, and though there was no obvious injury to the shoulder, Philip grabbed it periodically with his left hand and moaned. Victor worked quickly, creating a harness around his son's pelvis.

"I'm going to move to the right," Victor said, "and I'll pull myself up with this second rope. When I get to the top, I'll use the harness to pull you up." He rolled his son on his back to prevent bumping his abdomen. "Hang on with your good hand," he instructed, placing Philip's hand on the rope and the miner's hat on Philip's head. Victor's ascent was slow, but when he reached the top, he was glad to see two of his men rushing toward him.

"We heard the rifle," the first one said. "And we figured you had either found a wildcat or an injured horse."

"Here, give me a hand," Victor said, climbing up onto the path. "Roberto, Luis, help me pull my son up."

They pulled as smoothly as possible until Philip was off the scree. His back was bloodied from being pulled against sharp rocks. The three men lifted him as gently as possible onto his horse. In the light of the torch, his skin took on an ashen hue. Victor reached for his son's arm and was alarmed to feel a thready, racing pulse.

"Go on ahead, Luis," he instructed. "Get to the house as quickly as you can and call an ambulance. Then come back to the shack with a truck."

Luis moved his mount as quickly as possible, and when he reached the road, he spurred the animal on like a race horse. It was nearly ten o'clock when he reached the ranch house. An ambulance was called; and the women waited in agony and fear, while Luis returned to the olive grove in the truck.

*   *   *

"The blood loss was significant," Dr. Ortega informed Philip's family when he came out of surgery. "He had a laceration of the liver. Thank God it was small or he would have bled to death. Dr. Arroyo reduced the fracture of his right arm. Other than that, there is a lot of bruising, and his back looks as if wild animals had gotten to him. Expect him to be sore for a while, but he should recover just fine."

Victor shook the surgeon's hand. "What about his right shoulder? It caused him a lot of pain."

"That was referred pain from blood pooling under the diaphragm. The shoulder itself is fine."

Victor continued to pump the surgeon's hand. "Thank you, doctor," he said with tears in his eyes. Beatriz and Elena refused to leave the hospital that night. Victor offered to arrange a hotel room in town, but they would not leave.

"Go home and get some sleep," Beatriz begged her husband. "We'll call you if there is any change."

When Philip had recovered enough to return home, his father jokingly decreed that the olive grove was off limits to him and Elena. "We'll have no more adventures up on that hill if I have anything to say about it," Victor teased.

Surrounded by the love of his family, Philip's physical wounds healed quickly. But his sleep was troubled for weeks as he lay in bed each night, reliving the accident and considering how differently things could have turned out. Victor had been prepared for any eventuality, and Philip was grateful for his father's good judgment and quick action.

The night before Elena returned home could not have been more perfect. Beatriz and the girl prepared a delicious meal made even better by lively conversation and laughter.

Victor watched his son wander into the garden as the table was being cleared. He resisted the desire to join him, suspecting the two young people might want some time alone in the moonlight. Although Victor and Beatriz did not pry, it was evident that something besides the bolting of a skittish mare had happened up in the hills: the adoring looks that passed between Philip and Elena, the way they touched as they brushed past each other, every free moment spent together. "They are in love," Beatriz announced to her husband as if he could not draw this conclusion for himself. Victor raised a window in his study, allowing a cool evening breeze to refresh the air in the room. Rosemary, heated by the afternoon sun, had released its oil and scented the air with a pleasant fragrance. He breathed deeply and left the window when he caught a glimpse of Philip through the leafy redbud trees lighting luminaries that Beatriz had placed on the garden wall.

The moon was full, casting its light into the garden and creating shadows under the trees that sheltered the old brick terrace from the house and surrounding gardens. Beatriz's luminaries created a soft glow. Philip took a seat near a jasmine bush and waited; then he rose and paced and sat again. Surely the kitchen was clean by now. He withdrew a small box from his pocket and lifted the lid. The ring was simple, a gold band with inlayed stones that matched those set in the cross he purchased in Barcelona. His and Elena's initials were inscribed inside the band. Was it too simple? He had friends who spent a fortune on wedding rings with huge stones, but Elena was not impressed with material things. No, this was perfect, but would she say yes? She was young and had her whole life before her. Maybe she wasn't ready for this step. He rose and paced some more, rehearsing the words he would say. "Elena, I love you. I don't ever want to be apart from you. Will you marry me?" *No, there wasn't enough feeling in that.* "Elena, you've been in my life since the day of your birth, and I can't think of living without you. You are the most beautiful woman I have ever known and the only one I have ever loved. Elena, will you marry me?" *No, too shallow.* It was more than beauty that drew him to her. Maybe if he said the words out loud, they would come out better. He cleared his throat and, in a soft voice spoken to the tree before him, said from his heart, "Elena, we grew up like a brother and sister. I tried to teach you all the things our parents taught me. We laughed and played together. Sometimes we teased and pulled tricks on each other, but I always tried to protect you. I loved you like a brother loves a dear sister, but that has changed. I see your patience, your kindness, your humility, and the love in your heart. You put others before yourself. You go about the day with a smile on your face that lights my heart afire. Elena, I no longer love you as a brother because I have grown to love you as a man loves a woman. I am hoping that you love me too and will accept this ring as a pledge to marry me."

He had not heard the soft footsteps approaching, but when a small gasp escaped Elena's lips, he spun around and found her with tears streaming down her cheeks. Philip reached for her and drew her to him. Holding her close, he soothed, "Don't cry. Please don't cry. If you do not love me this way, I . . . I . . ." He tried to think of what he would do if she did not love him. The words were out there. He had uttered them. If she did not love him, there was nothing he could do. He felt like a fool. The idiocy of this hasty proposal astounded him. How could he have been so stupid? Elena was going off to university. The whole world awaited her. He had embarrassed her and now himself. He took a deep breath, and just as he released her, she spoke.

"I have had a crush on you since I was a little girl. Did you not know? Your mama saw it. She told me that crushes pass away, but real love endures. I have found that to be true, Philip, because I no longer have a crush on you . . ."

He hung his head. So it was over. It was just a summer romance. They had kissed and embraced, and for Elena, the feelings had burned out. "I'm so sorry," he interrupted.

Placing her hand over his mouth, she continued, "Because I love you, Philip. I truly love you with my whole heart, and I trust you with mine."

Philip took two steps backward, and then her words replayed in his head. "I love you, Philip. I truly love you . . ."

Reaching for her, he stammered, "You love me?"

She smiled. "How could I not?"

Philip wanted to shout, he wanted to cry, but all he could do was stare into her eyes and pull her into his arms.

*   *   *

"We all agreed that Elena should attend university that fall," Philip told Eduardo. "I got my feet on the ground, and when the next summer came, we were married in Pachua."

"So did you see Uncle Pedro again," Eduardo asked.

"Oh, yes," Philip said, raising his eyebrows, "and the whole family."

*   *   *

Pedro descended the steps of the bus and shielded his eyes from the sun. It had been years since he had seen Philip, but he knew he would recognize his young friend. His joy at the upcoming nuptials was hard to contain. Many of his family would be arriving in the next few days; but Pedro wanted time alone with his old friends, and especially his future son-in-law, so he made the trip alone. Elena had been in Pachua for two weeks, completing wedding preparations with Beatriz. Pedro worried about the arrival of his relatives. He knew how they felt about the Perez family. His sister was especially troubled by the reality that if Pedro spent any money on his daughter or grandchildren, there would be less to share with her. Pedro's return to the village with the trust Victor had set up had made his sister's life a little easier. There was always some money to help her buy things she had never been able to afford for herself ore her children. *Well*, Pedro thought, *I have had enough sadness in my life. I am not going to let my sister's jealousy spoil this happy moment.*

Outside the terminal, Philip shifted from one foot to the other, watching travelers exit the building. "Why are you so nervous?" Elena laughed.

"Because"—he grinned down at her—"I have to ask your father for your hand tonight, and what if he says no?"

Just then, he spotted his old mentor. "Uncle Pedro," he, called rushing toward the man.

*   *   *

That evening, the three men wandered out into the garden to reminisce. It was so good to be together again. "Please, Pedro," Victor begged, "come back to the ranch. You can have your old house back and be near your daughter and any grandchildren we are blessed with."

"Your offer is tempting," Pedro said thoughtfully, "But I can't live here anymore. Everything reminds me of Lupe." Looking at Philip, he smiled. "You will not deprive me of seeing my grandchildren, will you?"

"No, Uncle Pedro," the young man replied. "We will come as often as possible to see you, but if you lived here, you would influence your grandchildren just as you have influenced Elena and me."

The old man frowned and shook his head slowly. "I fear I would fall into that depression again, and I would influence no one for the good," he replied.

"If you ever change your mind, there will be a room in the main house waiting just for you," Victor said.

*   *   *

Philip sighed and looked at Eduardo. "If only he had agreed to stay. Things would have been so different."

"So you were married," Eduardo said.

"Yes. It was a beautiful wedding. Elena wore my mother's white lace mantilla. We were so happy. Uncle Pedro stayed with my parents until Elena and I returned from our honeymoon in Spain. I showed Elena all the places I knew . . ."

The room grew quiet once again. Eduardo stole a look at the older man whose face had been transfixed by a peaceful glow. *Were it not for the sunken cheeks*, Eduardo thought, *Philip Perez would appear to be a healthy man once again.*

"What is it Eduardo?" Philip asked, noticing the young man's stare. "Have I suddenly sprouted a second nose?"

Startled, Eduardo stuttered, "No, you just . . . you just look so happy. You must have been incredibly happy."

"We were indeed," Philip replied. "Two years later, our son was born. He was perfect in every way and brought even more joy into our family." Philip looked at the young man. "We had three and a half years of absolute bliss, and then it was all gone." He shook his head slowly back and forth and repeated, "Gone, all gone."

Eduardo shifted in his seat, uncomfortable but not knowing what to do to ease the mental pain that had taken possession of Perez and erased the look of health from his face.

A log broke on the grate, sending a shower of sparks onto the hearth. Eduardo rose and brushed them back into the firebox, stirring the remaining coals to a bright glow.

"Put that big log on top," Perez instructed.

Eduardo looked at the man. It would take two hours for the large log to burn down. He was sure Perez needed to rest, but he did as he was bid.

Perez sighed heavily. "When Uncle Pedro learned of Elena's pregnancy, he regressed into a deep depression. I think he feared that Elena would die as her mother had. We visited him when we heard he had been hospitalized, but he was almost catatonic. When the baby was six months old, Elena decided we must introduce him to his grandfather. Uncle Pedro had improved enough to leave the hospital, and Elena hoped that seeing her and his new grandson would brighten his spirit. My work at the university kept me from making the trip, but my parents happily bundled Elena and Alejandro into the car and headed off to see Uncle Pedro. That was the last time I ever saw any of them."

The door of the study opened, following a soft knock. Maria poked her head in "It's getting late. Would you like Tomas to help you to bed, Philip?"

"Thank you, Maria," he replied. "You and Tomas go on to bed. Eduardo is here if I need any help."

The older woman smiled at Eduardo and mouthed the words, "We'll be upstairs."

Eduardo studied Philip's face in the firelight. His eyes lacked luster, and his voice had become hollow. "I am told that my parents and Elena never even made it to Uncle Pedro's house. On the way, there was a collision with a fuel truck. The car was incinerated with everyone in it." Perez broke down, sobbing uncontrollably. Eduardo moved to Philip's chair and wrapped his arms around the man's shoulders, wishing he could bear at least a part of this man's burden.

When the sobbing eased, Philip began again, "In one brief instant, I lost my family." He shook his head as if in disbelief and covered his eyes with one hand. "The following weeks are a blur to me," he continued. "Maria and Tomas, friends from the university, convinced me to leave Pachua for a while. So after a year, I move to California. Here, I found work among troubled children, which gave some purpose to my life. Eventually, I convinced Tomas and Maria to join me, and even though I would never sell the ranch, I built this villa as a place to live out my life. Tomas and Maria have been a comfort, but you, Eduardo, have given new meaning and purpose to my life."

Again, there was an uncomfortable moment of silence.

"Do you need a refill?" Eduardo asked, brushing aside his earlier concerns about the alcohol.

"That would be good."

The young man poured the cognac in silence. Philip savored a sip and smiled wanly. "It is a gift to be comfortable with silence, Eduardo. This quality will serve you well in life."

Eduardo did not feel comfortable, but he was relieved to know he appeared so. "This is painful. Are you sure you would not like to continue tomorrow?" he asked.

"I am fine, Eduardo. The pain of my story will be there tonight, tomorrow, or whenever I tell it." Philip sighed and continued. "I could not have known that I would never see my family again."

Eduardo unconsciously rubbed the burn scar on his left arm. He did not remember his own brush with death, nor could he remember his parents, but he had some understanding of Phillip's grief. "I have no words that can express my sympathy adequately," Eduardo murmured.

"We share the grief of having lost those most precious to us, Eduardo. You understand my grief, and perhaps that is the source of the bond we have with each other."

"I do not have the memories you have," Eduardo replied. "I think the pain is more intense for those who remember the voices and the touch of lost loved ones."

"There are reminders every day," said Philip. "Elena's Bible, her old guitar in the corner, sometimes I think I hear her voice on the evening breeze. That is why I finally left the ranch. I could not bear the reminders everywhere I looked. Alejandro would be a young man like you, Eduardo, a fine young man like you." Their eyes met, and Eduardo felt a deep longing for the father he had never known.

CHAPTER EIGHT

Hunting and Healing

Palos Verdes Peninsula
October 1984

The young would-be arsonist awakened to soft moaning that was his own voice. Hushed male voices indicated that he was not alone.

"Give him a little more morphine, Maggie," Dr. John Montoya directed. Eduardo slipped into a calm sleep. Turning to his companions, the doctor began again, "The burn is deep but small. It may need a graft, but I think not. Aside from multiple contusions and abrasions, he has a badly sprained ankle and three fractured ribs. Fortunately, he doesn't have a flail chest or internal injuries." The doctor shook his head as if in unbelief. "Whoever beat this kid did a good job."

"I'm making it my business to find them. So far, no one has reported him missing," Police Chief Mike Lolich said. "We can always contact local schools, but that may be hard on the weekend. If his family did this, they'll be punished."

The doctor held up the boy's limp left arm. "Here's your answer, Mike. Los Reyes. The tattoo looks new, so I'm guessing the injuries are from his initiation. I just don't understand how these kids can pledge loyalty to a group that would beat them like this."

"It is a strange but not uncommon phenomenon," Philip Perez said. "Kids who have been chronically abused at home will usually defend their parents. Often enough, they feel they deserved the abuse. This may be a similar phenomenon, but I am thinking it is probably more of a demonstration of machismo and loyalty." Turning to face Mike, he asked, "What will become of him?"

"A lot depends on his family. Not much will happen until John says he's ready for release from the hospital. You can go ahead and file charges tonight, but it's late. Why don't we take care of that in the morning?"

"And if I file charges, then what?" Perez asked.

"What do you mean *if?*" the chief asked.

"My question first," Perez said.

"If he's as young as he looks, he'll probably go to the juvenile detention facility in LA"

"And if I don't press charges?"

The chief looked at Perez in disbelief. "Philip, for heaven's sake, the kid was going to burn your house down. Look at his arm. He belongs to Los Reyes Wilmington. That's not a social club for exemplary youth."

Perez looked long and hard at his friend. "I'm well aware of who Los Reyes Wilmington are, Mike."

"This kid could be a victim of circumstances or he could be real trouble," John Montoya offered. "I can evaluate his physical condition, but I have no idea regarding his psychological health."

"Well, I guess that is my area of expertise," Philip said grimly. "We'll locate his family first, and I'll offer my assistance. We'll go from there.

*   *   *

At Eduardo's cousin's apartment, Martin's anger at finding the boy missing flared in Julio's and Carlos's direction. "How could you be so stupid?"

"We're better off without 'im," Carlos said, when Martin's lecture subsided. "He was a nuisance we never wanted to deal with in the first place. Who cares what happens to him?"

Martin put his head in his hands. "Ya know we're gonna have to tell his grandfather sometime. The old man will blame us for not keepin' a closer eye on the kid."

"Who cares?" Julio asked. "The old man spends half his time in the hospital. He'll probably die before we have to say anything about all this."

"Julio's right," Ramon said. "Even if we have to tell the old man the kid ran away, so what? We already got what we wanted . . . the money to come to California."

Martin stared at his brothers. They were right. The old man had given them what they wanted. There was no need to worry. "OK," he said. "If the kid shows up, fine. If not, who cares?" He shrugged his shoulders.

*   *   *

By Saturday afternoon, Eduardo had not been reported missing. He refused to tell the police his name or address. "Somebody's got to be looking for him," Lolich said. "We've positioned a couple extra officers and two plainclothes guys in the hospital. If someone comes looking for this kid, we'll try to intercept them."

*   *   *

Each time Eduardo awakened, he became acutely aware of pain, pain in his ribs, pain in his leg. The first time he fully regained consciousness, he thought he was back in his cousin's apartment, lying beaten on the floor. He could open his right eye just a slit. From first glance, it was obviously not the apartment. He was alone in a room he did not recognize. Cautiously, he lifted himself on his left elbow. Contracting intercostal muscles pulled at the broken ribs, and Eduardo fell back against the mattress. His swollen left eye was patched with something moist and soothing. His right eye was fine, and although the room was in shadow, he could see from the glow of a dim light on the wall over the head of the bed. A bandage was taped to his left forearm just above the tattoo. Unconsciously, he rubbed the tattoo and discovered a small tube running from the bandage to a fluid filled bag hanging on a pole alongside the bed. *A hospital*, he thought. Although he had never been in a hospital, he had seen them on TV. People went into hospitals to die. His heart began racing. Was he dying right this minute? He lay still, concentrating on what he could feel. Any effort to raise his head and look around caused excruciating pain in his chest. His right leg burned. Feeling the leg with his left foot, he discovered a bulky bandage. Carefully, with his right hand, he began exploring his body. Other than the bandage over his left eye, his face felt unremarkable. He slipped his hand beneath the sheet that covered his body and began to gently feel his chest. His right side was taped over the area that caused the most pain. Moving his hand up his chest, he found a small pad stuck to his skin with a wire leading from it. He tugged gently on the wire, and it popped off the pad. He dug at the pad and pulled the tenaciously sticky foam rubber from his chest. His hand had just moved to the left side when a woman ran into his room.

"Well, you're not dead," she quipped, as she pulled the sheets back to reveal his upper torso.

So I'm dying, Eduardo thought. *She expected me to be dead when she came to check.*

The nurse busied herself examining Eduardo's chest. "Aha!" she exclaimed. "Here is the culprit." She placed the disconnected wire on the bed, reached into the bedside drawer and produced another sticky pad. "Now I don't think this came off by itself," she said. "So I want you to leave these pads alone."

Eduardo's eyes followed the nurse as she moved quickly and effortlessly to smooth his sheets and adjust his pillow.

"My name is Keri, and I am the nurse who will be taking care of you for a few more hours. You've had quite an accident it seems. Your right leg is burned, and you have some broken ribs and a sprained ankle, not to mention that beauty of a black eye. In spite of how you must feel, you're going to be fine, but," she said and shook her finger at him, "you have got to leave those wires alone. Dr. Montoya wants us to watch your heart rate for the rest of the night. When you pull the pads off, it sounds an alarm at the nurse's station. If you take them off, I'll be right back and replace them. Understood?"

Eduardo shook his head in the affirmative.

"We don't know your name," she said. "I need to write it in your chart."

Eduardo turned his face to the wall.

"OK," she said, "I guess you'll remain John Doe for now, but I really need to know if you have any allergies."

"What's that?"

"Allergies," she repeated. "You know, foods or medicines that make you sick if you eat them."

Eduardo shook his head no.

"Are you having pain?" she asked.

Once again, he shook his head in the affirmative.

"I'll get something to take care of that," she said, leaving the room.

The medication helped Eduardo sleep, and when he awakened the next time, he knew where he was.

*   *   *

When Eduardo did not show up at Miguel's apartment the night of the attack on Villa Perez, the Los Reyes Wilmington leader knew the boy was either dead, injured, or in police custody. Eduardo had endured a severe beating at the hands of the gang without a whimper, but Miguel was not sure how his resistance would fare if he was being interrogated by the police. Miguel needed to know where the boy was and whether he had placed Los Reyes in any danger. Nervously, he paced the apartment, hoping that

Eduardo would show up or that one of his guys would bring word of the boy. Around ten o'clock, he got in his car and drove to the park where he knew Diego would be waiting.

Diego was on his skateboard, perfecting his turns at the crest of the ramp, but as soon as he saw Miguel, he hopped off and sauntered over to the picnic tables. "What happened last night?" he asked.

"Whada ya know?" Miguel replied, looking angry. He kept punching his left fist into his right palm. Diego took a step back. "I asked ya a question," Miguel said in a menacing voice. "What did ya hear about last night?"

"Not much," the boy responded. "When you guys left for the Perez place, we all kinda wondered what was comin' down. Alberto said you was goin' to burn down Perez's house. A bunch of us hung around for a while and then went to get some burritos. I been looking for Eduardo this morning. Know where he is?"

"No. I was hopin' you'd heard somethin'." Miguel related the events of the previous evening. "Eduardo had been gone about forty minutes when we heard sirens screamin' up the hill. The kid must have screwed up. Maybe he set off an alarm. Maybe Perez shot 'im. I don't know. We took off, and he never showed up all night."

"You mean you just left 'im?" Diego's face mirrored the contempt he felt for Miguel.

"Whadda ya think we shouldda done?" Miguel growled menacingly. "Stay there and wait for the cops?"

"Couldn't Ernesto or Luis sneak in and see what was goin' on?"

"You're not as smart as I thought," Miguel said, thumping the boy on the head.

Diego studied his leader. How had he expected Eduardo to get back to the apartment on foot? He knew Miguel had flipped a coin to decide which boy would take this job. He could be in Eduardo's shoes right now, and the thought scared him.

"You're gonna find out where the kid is," Miguel informed him. Diego stared at the man. "You got friends at school. Find out if any of them have seen him. Go to his cousin's place and see if he went back there. If that doesn't work, I want you to go over to the county hospital and see if he's in there. No, go to the hospital first," he said, having a change of mind. "There was an ambulance."

"Drive me to the hospital?" Diego asked.

"I'll drop you," Miguel said. "You can take a bus back. Be at my apartment no later than five."

Diego groaned. The bus would require a couple of transfers. "Can I leave my skateboard in the car?"

*   *   *

A strong antiseptic smell assaulted his nostrils as soon as Diego entered the main door of the county hospital. If Eduardo was injured, this was probably where he had been taken. It was a level I Trauma Center for the South Bay area, but he felt like he was entering a prison. Guards were posted at the entrance, and he had to place his backpack on a conveyor belt that went through an X-ray machine. "No guns," he joked at the guard as he passed through the arch of a metal detector. The guard did not smile. Diego waited at the other end of the conveyor belt for his bag. The guy watching the screen looked at Diego, backed the belt up, and ran the backpack through one more time. As soon as the bag was within his reach, Diego grabbed it and slung it across his shoulder. He didn't see the look that passed between the guard at the X-ray and a plain clothes sheriff's deputy wearing a hospital badge about twenty feet away. Diego looked across the huge entry space, hoping to see a reception desk, but there was none. The deputy wandered over. "You look lost," he said. "Need help finding someone?"

Diego eyed the badge. "Uhhh, just looking for my friend. Heard he got hurt, and might be here."

"Name and age?" the man asked.

"Diego. I'm fifteen."

"Your friend," the man said.

"Oh, yeah," Diego laughed nervously. "He's my age. His name is Eduardo."

"Last name?"

"Rodriguez."

"Check at the reception desk. Just follow the blue line around the corner. You'll come to a desk. Give them your friend's name, and they can help you." Diego looked down at the floor. Wide strips of tape had been stuck to the worn linoleum. Blue tape led around a corner to the right, and yellow tape led to a hall on the left side of the entry.

"Thanks," Diego said to the man as he made his way to the corner.

The deputy walked to the guard at the X-ray machine who was not looking very happy. "Looked like about five bags of weed," the guard said. "Better not let him get it to his friend." The guard did not like this break in protocol. He rarely found anything of note in visitor's bags and purses, but when he did, it was confiscated and the owner held until the police arrived. This morning, the guards had been instructed not to detain anyone or confiscate their property. If there was anyone or anything suspicious, the guards were to notify deputies placed strategically throughout the building. The plainclothes deputy simultaneously looked around the room for anyone that might have entered with the boy and pressed the button of his walkie-talkie. "Got a hot one here, Matt, a kid. He's about five foot five, a hundred thirty pounds, Latino male, blue jeans, black tee, blue plaid flannel shirt. He's got a black backpack with probably five bags of weed, and he's looking for a friend. Friend's name is Eduardo Rodriguez. Tell Gabe to call it in and see if there are any police or school records under that name. We may have just ID'd our perp."

"Got it. The kid won't get past reception. They've got their instructions. I'll have Joe make sure he doesn't sneak past, and then I'll wait outside."

Diego found a line of five people at the reception desk. A tall skinny guy with long blond hair and well-worn clothes was giving the receptionist a hard time. "I know he's here," the guy kept saying. "Don't give me that bull about not having his name listed. I saw them bring him in."

"Look, mister," a man at the head of the quay said. "There's a line here, and you just crowded in."

"Is that it?" he asked the receptionist. "Do I need to get in the line and then you'll help me?"

"You can wait in line all day," she said. "If I don't have the name down, he's not here. It's very possible he was seen in ER, treated and released. It happens all the time."

The man slammed his fist down on the counter, sighed, and walked past the line of people who had grown to seven. As he passed Diego, he nodded and took note of the boy's clothes, backpack, and face. He sauntered to the front hall as the receptionist shook her head and then turned to the next visitor.

When Diego's turn arrived, she smiled sweetly and asked his age. "Why do you need to know my age? I'm not sick," he replied.

"We have an age limit for visitors, dear."

"I'm fifteen and a half."

"I'm very sorry. You can't visit the wards unless you are sixteen."

"I'm almost sixteen."

"I'm sorry," she repeated and looked past him to the next person in line.

"Well, can I at least leave a note for my friend?" Diego pulled the backpack off his shoulder.

"Of course. Why don't you step to the side and when you're finished writing your note, I'll have one of the candy stripers take it to . . . what was the name?'

"Eduardo. Eduardo Rodriguez."

"Rodriguez, Rodriguez, did you say Eddie?"

"Eduardo."

"We don't have an Eduardo. How old is your friend?"

"Fifteen like me."

"No, no, Eddie is sixty-seven. No, we don't have an Eduardo. Sorry I couldn't help you," she said, raising her eyes from the roster and smiling again."

Diego made his way to the door, considering where he would look next. He stepped outside into the October sunshine.

"Looks like you didn't have any luck either."

Diego spun his head around and saw the tall skinny guy leaning against the building and lighting a cigarette. "Want one?" he offered.

"Don't smoke," Diego said, shaking his head.

"Not my preferred tobacco if you get my drift," the guy said. "So your friend wasn't there either?"

"No," Diego said and slumped down on a step. "I gotta find him."

"Car accident?"

Diego gave him a funny look. "I don't know. He just disappeared, and I heard he might have gotten hurt."

"Rough neighborhood?"

"Yeah,"

"My friend OD'd last night. I'm just hoping he's not in the morgue."

Diego's head shot up. "How ya gonna find out?"

"I've got a friend works there as a guard. He's picking me up in"—the guy looked at a cheap watch on his wrist—"five minutes."

Diego considered this. He was sure Eduardo had not returned to his cousin's apartment. He wasn't at the hospital, and he wasn't at Miguel's. The only other options seemed to be police headquarters and the morgue. Miguel said the fire department and an ambulance had gone to Perez's house last night.

"You think he'd let me come along?" Diego asked.

"Don't know why not," the man said, stomping his cigarette on the step. "He's here right now. My name's Matt by the way."

"Diego," the boy said, extending his hand.

"Hey, Gabe," Matt said, stepping up to the driver's window of a 1950 Ford and leaning in, "this kid wants to come along."

"No problem," the driver replied. His dark hair was shorter than Matt's but just as unkempt. He sported a few days' beard growth and had a tattoo of a dragon running up his left arm.

"Hop in," Matt said, opening the back door of the car. He surprised Diego by sliding in alongside him. The boy scooted to the far side of the backseat and then noticed there was no handle on the inside of the door nearest him. On further inspection, the window handle was missing too.

Diego turned to Matt with the look of a trapped animal. "Nobody's gonna hurt you, kid," the undercover narcotics officer said.

"Who are you?" Diego asked, his voice betraying fear.

"Like I said, nobody's going to hurt you. Now let's make this as easy as possible. Who sent you to the hospital?"

Diego stared mutely at the man who called himself Matt and backed as far as he could into the corner.

"Who sent you, Diego?"

"Let me out," Diego yelled, banging on the door.

"Ain't gonna happen," Gabe said from the front. "Door's welded shut."

"Let's see what we got here," Matt said, grabbing the backpack that had slid off Diego's shoulder.

"Give that to me," Diego yelled, pulling at the bag.

Matt had a firm grip on the backpack and pulled the top zipper down. He dumped the contents on the floor. "Looks like we got a drug bust here," he told Gabe, holding up a bag of marijuana. "Why don't we just head on over to the station?"

"No," yelled Diego. He pushed and banged on the door and beat at the window.

Gabe made eye contact with his partner through the rearview mirror. Matt reached for the boy's hands. "You're gonna rip your hands apart, you little tiger," he said. He slipped a handcuff on Diego's right wrist, pushed the other through a leather strap hanging from the roof, and had the second cuff on before Diego could respond. "We're not going to hurt you," Matt said in measured tones.

"I'm not afraid of you," the boy screamed. "I'm not afraid of you." He began kicking with his feet. He kicked the front seat; he kicked at Matt. He raised his left leg up and brought his foot down on Matt's thigh. "OK, I'm outta here," Matt said, and Gabe pulled to the curb. Matt got out. Diego pulled the cuffs back and forth, sawing away at the leather strap.

"Hey, stop," Gabe said, turning and grabbing the boy's wrists. The sound of the trunk opening startled Diego. He craned his neck to see what Matt was doing, but the trunk lid obscured his view. In a second, Matt returned to the driver's back door with a roll of duct tape. Gabe got out and held the boy's legs together, while Matt ran the tape spiral fashion from ankles to just above the knees. Diego gathered a mouth full of saliva and spit at the men.

Matt held the roll in front of Diego's face. "See this?" he said. "I have a whole lot left, and if you do that again, I'll wrap it around your face."

"You're gonna get me killed," Diego screamed.

"We're not killin' anybody," Matt said. "If you get killed, it's because you're runnin' with the wrong guys, guys who would send you out to do a job and then leave you when you got hurt doing it, some kind of friends."

"You know what happened to Eduardo," Diego said. "You have him."

"Maybe we do, and maybe we don't," Matt replied. "Now who sent you to find him?"

Diego pressed his mouth in a firm thin line. He had no intention of squealing on Miguel.

"Isn't it funny, Gabe," Matt remarked, "these guys are so loyal to their leader, but when they get in trouble, the leader hides like a chicken."

"Buc, buc, buc," Gabe crowed from the front seat. "They send their guys out to do the dirty work, while they stay safely out of harm's way."

Diego glanced out the window. He no longer recognized any of the streets or buildings they were passing. "Where are we?" he asked. "Where are you taking me?"

"Just driving around," Gabe said. "No place in particular."

"I gotta be back home by five," Diego said. "If I'm not home by five, my mom will call the police."

"Gabe, why don't you call in and have someone stop by Diego's apartment and let his mom know he may not be home by five."

"No," the boy yelled. "You gotta let me out." He began the sawing motion with his wrists again.

"Don't gotta do nothin'," Gabe said, "until you're ready to help us out a little."

"I told you they'll kill me," the boy cried.

"Could be true," Gabe said, looking back at Matt.

"Yeah, I wouldn't doubt it one bit," Matt replied. "Remember what they did to that kid up in LA?"

"What kid? What are you talking about?" Diego asked.

"Hated to tell the mother about that one, ugliest body I ever saw," Gabe continued.

"How long do you think it took that kid to die, eight, ten hours?"

"At least. The kid must have really been screaming, one toe at a time, then the feet. They just kept chopping their way up the body until they got to the head. Never saw anybody with their eyes poked out like that." Diego began retching. "You're not gonna throw up in my car, are you?" Gabe said. "Matt, he's not gonna throw up in this car. Do something."

Matt grabbed the empty backpack and held it in front of Diego's mouth. The boy retched until vomit spewed in to the bag. Gabe threw a box of tissues back to Matt who wiped the boy's face. "I need a drink," Diego breathed when he had finally stopped vomiting.

"I need a drink," Matt said. "Hey, you doin' anything tonight, Gabe?"

"We might be driving this kid around."

"Crap, you think we're gonna pull another all-nighter?"

"Looks that way. Tell you what, let's drive around for a few more hours, and if he doesn't cooperate, we'll put him in a cruiser and have the uniforms take him over to, oh, let's say we drop him off someplace near Cordova."

"Yeah, and we'll have the cops thank him real loud for all the information."

"You're not gonna do that," Diego said. "You're just trying to scare me. You guys are nuts."

Matt looked at the boy and raised his eyebrows. "Hmm. Maybe we are. Maybe you're locked in this car with a couple of psychos. Hey, what time is it, Gabe?"

"Twelve thirty," Gabe said. "Want a burger?" Looking in the rearview, he made eye contact with Diego. "Want a burger, kid?"

"I just threw up," Diego replied.

"You sick? Think you got the flu?" Matt asked. "Hey, Gabe, did you get your flu shot? I didn't get a flu shot yet. You think this kid's gonna make us sick?"

Gabe shook his head and pulled into an *In N Out* drive through. "Best burger around," he said. "Sure you don't want one?"

"How am I gonna eat it? You've got me all tied up."

"He's got a point, Gabe. If we go down to the station, we can put him in a room and let him eat."

A young female voice sounded from a speaker, "May I take your order?"

"Three double doubles, fries, and"—turning to the kid—"what do you want to drink?"

"Help," Diego yelled.

"A coke and two ice teas," Gabe said.

"Help me," Diego screamed again.

Matt slapped a piece of tape across the kid's mouth and covered him with a blanket.

"You guys," the female voice laughed. "Behave yourselves and drive forward."

Gabe paid for the meals and set them in the front seat. The aroma was driving Diego crazy. He hadn't eaten since eight o'clock, and that was now sloshing around in his backpack. He struggled to shift the blanket off his face.

"To the house or the station?" Gabe asked. "What do you think?"

"The house, I guess," Matt replied, "at least to start with. If we don't get anywhere, we can always move to the station." He grabbed a black hood from the front seat and pulled it over Diego's exposed head.

"I can't breathe," the boy mumbled through lips held tight by the tape. "I can't breathe."

"Sounds like he's breathing just fine," Gabe said from the front seat and sped off. They drove for ten minutes before the car stopped, and Diego heard a metal gate open. The car moved forward slowly and dipped down an incline. The gate closed behind, and the car turned to the left before coming to a stop.

"I'll guide you, and as soon as we get inside, I'll take the hood and tape off," Matt said.

Matt removed the handcuffs from the leather strap and then locked them on again, while Gabe cut through the tape so Diego could walk. They went up a set of stairs, through a door, and into an elevator. Diego counted three dings of the elevator before they came to a stop. Matt guided the boy down a hall and through a second and then third door. "OK," he finally said. "Mask off, tape off, and lunchtime."

Diego looked around. The windows were boarded up so he had no idea where they were. It felt like they had been driving for ten or fifteen minutes, but he hadn't known where they were when they stopped at the burger place. He held his hands out to have the cuffs removed. "Eat with them on," Matt said. The boy sat in a chair, and Matt placed his food on a desk. He looked around. There was a cot, a couple more chairs, and a small bathroom through an open door.

"This is kidnappin'," Diego said.

"Kidnapping?" We better haul him down to the police station so he can file a complaint."

"No!" the boy stammered. "If Miguel sees me comin' out of there, he'll think I snitched." The name was out before he realized he'd said it, and a look of horror came over his face.

"Look, Diego," Matt said sitting on the edge of the desk. "This is how it's gonna come down. We're taking that gang out. If you want to remain loyal to Miguel, you'll go out with him. You keep dealing and you'll end up in a stinking rotten prison where a nice kid like you will become some thug's lackey. He'll dominate you and use you like a girl until another good-looking young guy comes in. Then he'll drop you and leave you for one of his boys to take over where he left off. I'm not kidding. You're likely to pick up that new HIV virus or hepatitis. When you get out of the joint, you'll die a slow miserable death all alone because no girl is gonna want to be with you then." He stared long and hard at the boy.

Diego put his cuffed hands to his face and began crying. "He's gonna kill me. I'm a dead man." The burger and fries grew cold, and the ice melted in the Coke while Diego cried.

When the crying subsided, Matt said in a much gentler tone, "We can help you, but you gotta help us."

"Nobody can help me," Diego said. "I've seen those cop shows where they promise to protect somebody, but the bad guys get them anyway."

"Those are shows, made for Hollywood. If there wasn't some drama, they wouldn't sell at the box office. We'll keep you and your mother safe."

For the first time, Diego made eye contact with Matt. "How do you know about my mom?"

"We've been watching you for months," Matt said. "We know where you live, we know where you go to school, and we know where you make your deliveries. We could have hauled you in a long time ago, but that wouldn't stop Miguel or the people above him."

The boy's face registered shock and then resignation. "What do you want me to do?"

"We want you to help us find Miguel's supplier. We've been watching Miguel ever since he came into the area, and as much as I want to put him behind bars, we'd prefer to get the guys above him first. I don't want you to do anything out of the ordinary. Don't start asking a lot of questions. Just be normal. If you see anything or anyone suspicious, let me know."

"So I'm just supposed to walk down to the police station and hand them a note for you?" Diego asked sarcastically.

"Not exactly," Matt said. "I'll meet you tomorrow morning in the park. I'll ask where I can get some weed. I know the drill. I've been doing this for a long time. When Miguel gives you the go-ahead, he'll tell you to give me a number where I can call for more drugs, right?"

Diego shook his head.

"I'll call once a week and ask to have the stuff delivered to an address over on Cordova."

Diego considered this. It would work. "But what about right now?" he asked. "Miguel is expectin' me at his apartment at five. I don't even know what time it is."

Gabe looked at this watch. "It's two o'clock straight up."

"What were Miguel's exact instructions?" Matt asked.

"He said to check at the hospital, check if anyone from school had heard anything, and to check with Eduardo's cousins."

Gabe and Matt looked at each other. "OK, let's figure out a timeline." Gabe pulled a piece of paper from a desk drawer and began writing as Matt dictated, "He dropped Diego at the hospital around eleven. It takes the kid fifteen minutes to find his way to the reception desk and find out Eduardo's not there. He walks to the bus stop, another five minutes. The bus comes in ten and drops him . . ."

When a plausible timeline had been developed, Gabe and Matt once again hooded the boy and took him to the car. After ten minutes of driving, they dropped him at a bus stop near Wilmington. "You know where Eduardo's cousins live, right?"

Diego nodded. "Just two blocks from where me and my mom live."

"OK, go to their apartment. If no one's home, that's it. If someone answers, tell them you're a friend from school and you haven't seen Eduardo for a few days. When they say they haven't seen him either, walk to the park and ask around there."

Diego looked at Matt and wrinkled his brow. "You know he's not at his cousin's," he said. "You have Eduardo, don't you? Is he OK?"

Matt looked at the boy intently. He wished he could tell him that Eduardo would recover from his injuries. Whether the boy would be OK or not depended on a lot of things, but right now the plan was to keep Eduardo's whereabouts confidential. "Just tell Miguel you hit a dead end. Eduardo's not at the hospital, he's not at his cousin's, and nobody at the park has seen or heard from him. For all you know, he died in the ER or caught a ride back down to Mexico. You got bus money?"

"Yeah," the boy said, getting out of the car. These guys knew something, and he was beginning to think that his friend was dead.

"Damn," Miguel said when Diego reported back to him. He got in the boy's face. "You sure Eduardo wasn't at the hospital? I got a friend works over at Four Star Ambulance, and he said an ambulance was dispatched to Perez's house and took a patient to the county hospital last night."

"Maybe he died in the emergency room," Diego said, genuine anguish on his face.

"It's possible. "I'm gonna see if Raul's girlfriend can look up some records. She works over there."

"The lady at the desk said he wasn't there," Diego reminded Miguel.

"Yeah, sure, kid. If he's in police custody, they'll do things like that."

"You mean . . ."

"Yeah, I mean he could be over there under a different name. They may not even know his name if he was hurt bad enough and if he didn't have any ID. He just better not rat us out," Miguel said, "or I'll cut him into little pieces."

Diego shoved his hands into his pockets to keep Miguel from seeing the tremor he'd just developed. Maybe Matt hadn't been lying about the kid up in LA, and maybe Eduardo was alive.

*   *   *

"So, Eduardo Rodriguez, you don't want to go back home," Mike Lolich said when he visited the boy Sunday morning.

Eduardo shook his head no, wondering how they had learned his name and what else they knew about him. Miguel and the guys may have beaten him, but so had his cousins. He didn't want to return to any of them. "We know you came into the country illegally," Mike continued. "Do you want to go back to Mexico?"

They knew everything he realized. They probably knew about Miguel and Los Reyes too. Absentmindedly, he rubbed the tattoo on his left forearm.

The action was not missed by the astute chief of police. "Yeah," he said, nodding toward the tattoo, "We know about them too. Did you think they were your friends? Real friends don't get you into trouble or run when you need help."

A look of fear came over Eduardo's face. He could not say a thing about Los Reyes or they would kill him.

Mike could see the boy was afraid and knew he was in danger. "You don't have a lot of options here," Mike said. "Looks like your cousins haven't been treating you very well, and we can see what Los Reyes did to you. They'll come after you. You know that, don't you?"

For the first time, Eduardo shook his head in the affirmative.

"You could end up in a juvenile detention facility or do you want to go back to Mexico? That is an option."

Eduardo wanted to be with his grandfather more than anything, to be with Grandfather and feel safe and loved once more. But how could he return? What would he tell the old man? I've failed you? I joined a gang and ran drugs. His grandfather would end up with another heart attack. He also knew that even in Mexico he wouldn't be safe from the gang. Eduardo shrugged his shoulders as tears filled his eyes.

Emotion was what Mike Lolich was looking for, any emotion that would help him see inside this boy. The pain he saw in Eduardo's eyes informed him that the boy was a victim of his circumstances. He was not a hardened streetwise kid who would endanger Perez . . . if he was properly supervised. "OK, we have one more option, young man. Philip Perez, the man whose house you were trying to vandalize, has offered to take you home."

Eduardo's mouth opened, just a little. His eyes dilated, and he stared mutely at the police chief. Why would Señor Perez take him into his home . . . unless he planned some great punishment?

"No," he stammered. He shook his head violently. "No, he'll kill me."

Mike threw back his head and laughed.

They're going to torture me together, Eduardo thought. He slipped his feet off the bed, preparing to run.

"Hold on there, son," Mike told him, pressing gently on Eduardo's shoulder to keep him in the bed. "Punishment is the farthest thing from Philip Perez's mind. He won't hurt a hair on your head, but he's going to expect a lot of you. You will probably end up working harder than you have ever worked in your life."

Eduardo relaxed. So that was it. He would be Perez's slave. As an undocumented alien, Perez would work him from dawn to dusk, and he wouldn't have to pay Eduardo a cent. Eduardo's mind raced. He had gotten into Villa Perez, and he could get out. Once his injuries healed, he could easily scale the wall and run. The boy looked at Mike Lolich and shook his head in the affirmative for the second time. "OK," he said.

CHAPTER NINE

The Cousins and Angie

Wilmington
October 1984

A meeting with Philip Perez and Chief Lolich had answered Martin's questions about where his cousin was. "We could charge you with child abuse," Mike told him. "That kid was pretty beaten up when we found him, and we understand that some of the bruises resulted from a beating you and your brothers gave him."

"Look," Martin said defensively, "we never asked to take care of the brat. Our uncle made us promise to look after him, and it's tough trying to work and take care of a child too. We didn't even know he was in that gang."

"Señor Perez is willing to take the boy into his home and assume responsibility for him," Lolich offered. "If you are willing to agree to that arrangement, he'll take care of the legalities."

Martin looked at Perez as if he had a contagious disease. "Why would you want to do that?" he asked suspiciously.

"Because I think I can help him."

"Dr. Perez works with the schools to try and prevent gang involvement," Lolich interrupted.

"Doesn't look like it's working very well," Martin sneered. "I don't know what I'm going to tell his grandfather, but as long as you're taking good care of him, yeah, it's OK. I'll sign whatever you need me to sign."

Perez and Lolich raised their eyebrows in unison when Martin expressed his concern that Eduardo received good care. "Are you here with migrant status?" Lolich asked.

"Yeah," Martin lied. "We'll be going back now that the crops are in."

"I'll have my attorney draw up the papers this afternoon in that case," Perez said. "Can we meet here tomorrow afternoon?"

"Yeah, I guess."

"Take my card," Lolich said, sliding his business card across the desk. "If your uncle wants to get in contact with Eduardo, he can do it through my office."

* * *

"Have you seen that place?" Ramon asked his brothers after Miguel told them about the meeting with Perez. "Angie and I drove by once, and you can't even see the house from the road, and there's a gate to keep people out."

"I hope they work the hell out of him and beat him every night," Julio said, throwing a magazine down on the table.

"Why are you so mean?" Angie asked. "He's a really nice kid, and I've never understood why you hate him so much."

"He's a pain," Carlos said. "I wish Abuela had sent him back to his father."

"What are you talking about? His father's dead. Eduardo told me both his parents died in a car accident."

The four brothers looked at each other and smirked. "Let's just say when Eduardo's folks brought him to San Jenaro to show him off. Abuela took advantage of an opportunity to keep the little guy at Uncle's house. Uncle was sick in the head, and she thought having his grandson might clear things up for him. When he's happy, he throws a little more money her way." The men all laughed at this. "It kind of backfired on Abuela, but by then, she was stuck with what she'd done. If she'd told Uncle the truth, he'd have been so angry he'd have never talked to her again," Martin finished.

"I don't get it," Angie said.

"Don't try," Ramon advised her. "It's all in the past; better forgotten." He turned to Martin said, "Shut up."

"But if his dad . . ."

"Let it go, Angie. We're never going to talk about this again."

She gave him a look that said we'll see about that, but she changed the subject. "I'm graduating in two months. Mom and Dad said when I get a job and save a little money, I can get my own place. When I do, you guys can come over to my place to eat."

"Hey," Ramon said, "why don't we get a place together?" The other brothers cast knowing looks at one another and grinned. They knew Ramon could work fast, but this was warp speed.

"Forget it, Ramon," she replied. "I may be your girlfriend, but I'm not that kind of girl."

Ramon noticed his brother's smirks and flushed in embarrassment. "Who do you think you are? There are hundreds of girls out there who'd jump at the chance to move in with a handsome guy like me."

"You are so full of yourself," she said. "Looks aren't everything."

"Well, good luck finding a new boyfriend," he said, "'cause guys think looks count for a lot."

"Just what are you implying?"

"Figure it out for yourself. You think you're so smart." He walked into the bedroom and slammed the door.

"What just happened here?" Angie asked no one in particular. She went to the bedroom and banged on the door. "Ramon, come out here and talk to me or I'm leaving." Tears welled up in her eyes as she added, "Please."

When there was no answer, Angie walked to the front door. She turned to look at the three men standing there and saw amusement in their eyes. Without another word, she walked out, got in her car, and drove home.

"Good riddance!" Ramon yelled, hearing the door open and close. His brothers erupted into uncontrolled laughter.

Angie cried all the way home. She really liked spending time with Ramon, but in her heart, she knew he had a dark side. She wondered why she was so attracted to him. When she arrived home, she found her mother in the kitchen. "Angie, what has happened?" the woman asked.

The girl sat down, put her head on the table, and sobbed. "Mom, it's really nothing. Ramon hurt my feelings, we had a few words, and I walked out. I'm never going over there again."

"You know, your father and I were never very happy that you spent so much time with him," Christina Dominguez replied. "You're father said more than once that he could not understand what you saw in Ramon. Of course, he is quite handsome, but what could he offer you, my daughter? We suspect he did not come into this country legally, and if he did not—"

"Oh, Mama," Angie interrupted, "he is the first man who ever showed me any attention. I have never had a boyfriend, and at first, he treated me so nice."

"Angie, Angie," her mother soothed, hugging the girl. "When you were little, you always ran to help the child who had fallen down. You shared your toys and treats with others. Sometimes you even gave you toys away. As you got older, you helped slower children with their schoolwork. There were children who received attention from no one else but you. I think you have been kind to this man because he needed you. Perhaps he knew the things to say that would make you feel special, right?" She looked into her daughter's eyes. "There will be another, I promise. There will be someone who treats you as nice as your father treats me. It is good to be kind to people who are needy, my love, but that is not how you choose a boyfriend or a husband."

Angie raised her head to face her mother. "I did like helping him," she said. "I liked cooking and straightening up his place. I felt like I was doing something good. I especially liked cooking for Eduardo, the youngest one."

"It is good to help other people, but that is not how you choose a husband," her mother said again.

"Ramon said something about me not being pretty," Angie said. "I'm not, Mama. I know that."

"You are beautiful, Angie. You are one of God's precious children, and you are beautiful inside and out."

That night, Angie studied her face in the mirror. She had always been chubby. She liked to eat, and her mother was an excellent cook. She ran her fingers through her hair. She hadn't cut it in a very long time, and she never took the trouble to wear cosmetics. Maybe there were a few things she could do for herself. She smiled, turned the light out, and crawled into bed. She needed some good rest because finals were coming up.

CHAPTER TEN

A New Beginning

Palos Verdes Peninsula
October 1984

Philip met with John Montoya on Wednesday after the doctor made rounds at the hospital. "He's progressing nicely, Philip. John looked at his friend sideways while shuffling the court documents Philip had placed on his desk. "You are taking a big risk here," he cautioned. "They already tried to hurt you once, and those gang members aren't just going to just stand by while this kid comes to live with you."

Philip shifted in his chair as he considered his response. "Many important things begin with risk, John. This is a risk I am going to take."

"You may be putting Tomas and Maria at risk also."

"They will tell me if they feel unsafe," Philip answered. "They are intuitive and very wise. We have discussed it, and they agree with me. This child is young enough to respond to a positive environment, and I am well qualified to provide that. Detention facilities are overcrowded, John, and he would probably be out on the streets and in trouble again in a few months."

The doctor shook his head. "I don't know whether to admire you or tell you you're nuts, Philip. And I must be nuts too for sitting here, listening to this." He rose and shook his friend's hand.

"It's settled then," Philip said. "Maria will need instruction and maybe some assistance in caring for the boy's injuries when he is ready to be released."

"Eduardo will need to stay here for a couple more days. Bring her over when it is convenient, and I will tell the nurses to teach her."

The doctor gave his friend one last long look before exiting the room. "Don't get your hopes too high, Philip. This young man has already made a choice regarding his loyalties." He tapped his arm in the same place where Eduardo's tattoo had been applied."

"Perhaps he had less of a choice than we imagine in the matter."

Philip made a quick stop at the hospital before going home. He stood watching the boy sleep and finally could not resist the impulse to stroke the teenager's head. His black hair was thick and slightly wavy. Phillip ruffled it ever so gently. "We have a lot of work ahead of us, young man," he murmured. "I believe that with enough care and positive influence, we can give your life purpose beyond what you found with your gang friends. I hope we can learn to overcome our lack of understanding of each other." With that, he stepped out of the room.

Eduardo strained to open his right eye ever so slightly. He watched as Philip Perez exited his room. Eduardo did not understand what had just happened and the warmth that had surged through his body when Perez touched him. The boy reached to touch his own hair in disbelief and confusion.

Dr. Montoya arrived early Thursday morning to inspect Eduardo's injuries. "You're lucky, young man," the doctor informed Eduardo as he gently removed the dressing on the burned leg. "The burn is small. It will heal without surgery."

Eduardo winced as the nurse cleansed the white ointment off his leg.

"Philip Perez is sending his friend, Maria, by today to learn how to care for the boy," the doctor informed a nurse who had introduced herself to Eduardo as Michelle.

"Hold off on the next dressing change until she arrives."

Michelle frowned in puzzlement over the doctor's remark.

"Perez wants to take him home," Montoya smiled, answering Michelle's unasked question.

The nurse shook her head and wrapped a gauze roll over a generous slathering of fresh white ointment on the leg.

"You're a lucky kid," the doctor said again as he ruffled Eduardo's hair. He left a puzzled boy who could not understand how being a slave could be the result of luck.

To the boy's relief, the pain in the injured leg subsided quickly after the wound was covered, but his anxiety remained. The day passed slowly as Eduardo, lonely and uncomfortable, tried to comprehend what lay in his future.

Around four in the afternoon, Michelle entered Eduardo's room with an older Latina.

"Hey, Eduardo, how's it going?" Michelle asked, and without waiting for an answer, she introduced Maria. "This is Maria. She lives at Dr. Perez's villa. Maria is going to watch me do the dressing this afternoon."

"Por que?" Eduardo asked the woman.

"It seems you are going to live with us for a while," Maria answered in English. "Your injuries will need attention if you are to get well quickly. You are an unbelievably lucky boy."

"I don't understand," Eduardo said.

"You don't understand English?" the woman asked.

"No, I mean yes, I understand English. But why does everyone tell me I'm lucky to be going to Señor Perez's house? He must be very angry, and the police said he will make me work very hard."

"Well, I cannot deny that," the Maria answered. "I just hope you appreciate the chance Señor Perez is offering you."

This did nothing to answer Eduardo's question, but he sensed he would not find the answer with these two women as they busied themselves with the dressing. Michelle was quick, and Maria assisted. The pain, though intense, was over quickly.

"You are brave, Eduardo," Maria said. He did not feel brave, but he treasured the words and even more the kindness in the woman's voice.

"I can do this," Maria told Michelle as if she changed burn dressings every day.

"I'll let Dr. Montoya know. He needs to rest the sprained ankle for a few days. Fortunately, it's not too bad. The rest of it is a piece of cake. He'll also need to protect that side from bumps. We don't want him puncturing his lung with a broken rib." The last was said as much for Eduardo's benefit as Maria's.

Instinctively, Eduardo placed a hand over the injured ribs.

*   *   *

The boy was discharged to Phillip Perez's care three days later. "I am sure you wonder what is going on, Eduardo," Perez said as he helped the boy into the passenger seat of his sports car. "I will explain everything in due time. Today, you will rest, but tomorrow, after breakfast, we will discuss my house rules.

Were it not for music coming from the stereo, the ride to the villa would have been accomplished in silence. The music was painfully slow and lacking the beat Eduardo favored. He eyed the tape player with disdain.

Had he possessed more courage, he would have pushed the buttons to switch to a radio station.

Philip glanced at the boy from the corner of his eye. "You don't like the music," he said in a matter-of-fact manner.

Eduardo shrugged his shoulders as if the music were of no importance.

"I know it is probably not what you are used to, Eduardo, but give it a chance. It grows on you."

Eduardo wrinkled his nose. He could not imagine this music growing on him.

"This piece was written over three hundred years ago by a man named Johann Pachelbel. It is one of his most loved works. Perez pressed a button to roll the windows down. They were on a road high above the ocean. A light breeze blew through the car, filling it with the smell of the sea.

Eduardo squirmed in his seat. The slow pace of the music was agonizing. "I like rock music," he said, "or the mariachis."

"Hmm," Perez mused. "I don't think we have any rock music at the villa, and I know we don't have any in the car. I like the mariachis too, but for now I think we'll make do with the Canon in F major."

*   *   *

Eduardo was escorted to a room on the second floor at the front of the house. "This is where you will sleep and keep your personal things," Perez explained.

Eduardo gazed about the room. The largest bed he had ever seen dominated the room. *It would hold three or four people*, he thought. "Who else stays in this room?" he asked innocently.

Perez resisted an urge to laugh. "No one, Eduardo. This room is just for you."

When the boy still seemed not to comprehend, Perez said, "This is one person's bedroom, and for now that person is you."

Eduardo looked about the room, trying to absorb Perez's words. This was a mansion, and this room was the room of a rich man, not a slave. The boy turned slowly, studying the furnishings. In addition to a table on each side of the bed, there was a tall chest on the wall to his right, a long dresser opposite the bed, and a desk to his left, under the window. All of the furniture was of matching dark wood with intricately carved legs. A chair, lamp, and small round table sat in the corner near the desk. Eduardo moved toward the bed and felt the softness of the coverlet. The room smelled sweet like the air after a morning rain before the tequila trucks stirred up dust at home. For reasons unknown to him, the boy thought of his mother. Perez moved to a door beyond the chest. "This is your closet," he said, and then walking through a doorway that was open, he beckoned Eduardo. "This is your bathroom. I think Maria has stocked it with everything you need, but if something is missing, let her know."

My bathroom, Eduardo thought. *My bathroom?* Thick white towels hung on racks near the sink and shower. A white cotton rug lay on the floor. On the counter were a comb, brush, toothpaste, and toothbrush. "Whose things are these?" Eduardo asked, moving toward the counter.

"Those are toiletry items Maria purchased for you. As I said, if there is anything you need and can't find, let Maria know. Now I must go downstairs. Maria will bring you some supper, and later she will help you get into bed. If you are strong enough in the morning, we will have a tour of the house." And with that, Perez left Eduardo alone in the room. The boy sat in a chair by the window, staring into the front yard and beyond to the sea until Maria arrived with a bowl of vegetable beef soup. When he had finished, she helped him into pajamas, instructed him to brush his teeth, pulled the curtains, and left the room. Too tired for anything else, Eduardo crawled into the bed and imagined he was floating on a cloud.

When Eduardo awakened, the curtains had been drawn, and the room was filled with sunlight. A tray at his bedside smelled of goodness from the kitchen. "How are you doing, Eduardo?" Maria's cheerful voice greeted him. "I am glad to see that you are finally awake. I have duties to tend to, and I cannot sit at the bedside of a sleeping boy all day. Señor Perez will talk with you now that you are awake. Go ahead and eat while I get him." The woman continued to prattle as she plumped his pillows and then left the room, her voice fading into unintelligible noise.

Eduardo lifted the cover from the tray and to his delight found eggs, two of them, and fresh warm tortillas. His body ached as he rearranged himself, and he wished he did not feel so queasy. It had been a very long time since he had last tasted eggs. Perhaps if he ate slowly, his stomach would not reject them. He was so engrossed in the meal that the approaching footsteps were unnoticed.

"Good morning, young man. I'm glad to see you looking improved."

So startled was Eduardo that he dropped a forkful of egg on the bedding. Hastily reaching for a napkin, he tipped a glass of orange juice off the tray and onto the carpet."

"Maria, we have a spill," Perez hollered toward the door and then headed into the bathroom to get towels. Returning to the mess, Perez's eyes locked with the boy's. There was embarrassment in the child's gaze or was it fear for having just made this mess?

"Don't worry about the spill, Eduardo. It can be cleaned up, and Maria will bring you more juice. You and I have much to discuss, and I will talk while you finish eating."

Maria appeared, clucked her tongue, and cleared away the juice-soaked towels.

"Please bring another glass, Maria," Perez asked as she left the room. "Actually, bring two. I think I'll have a glass myself."

"How are you feeling, Eduardo?" Perez queried.

"Fine," Eduardo replied.

"Fine you are not," Perez corrected. "Dr. Montoya says you have three broken ribs, a sprained ankle, and multiple bruises. Your left eye, though no longer swollen shut, is still quite discolored. You were badly beaten before you came into my garden and started the fire that burned your leg. Chief Lolich believes it was your cousins or Los Reyes who hurt you. Is this correct, Eduardo?"

Eduardo turned his face from Perez and kept silent. He would not indict his cousins or his gang brothers in spite of the beatings. One did not betray family or Los Reyes no matter what the circumstances.

Perez waited a few moments before trying a different tack. "Do you want your cousins to visit you here, Eduardo, or your friends?"

"No!" Eduardo shouted. The word escaped before he could stop it, and he searched Perez's eyes to assess the man's reaction.

"OK," Philip responded. "Did you have a plan when you broke into my garden last night?"

Again, Eduardo turned from Perez.

"The police believe your plan was to burn my house down. Is this true?" Perez's tone was not accusing but factual. Validation of the police suspicions was not forthcoming from Eduardo, but neither was denial. "I am not a harsh man, Eduardo, but I do insist on the truth from someone living under my roof."

Eduardo turned toward Perez and stared.

"You have a few choices to make this morning," Perez stated in a calm but firm voice. "One of the choices you must make is whether or not to be truthful with me. If you are willing to be truthful and work hard, you may stay here in the villa as my charge. I will arrange legal residency for you. If you chose not to stay, I am afraid you will be placed in a juvenile detention facility or be deported back to Mexico."

"I can take care of myself," Eduardo said with a hint of stubbornness in his voice.

"How, Eduardo? How will you take care of yourself?" Perez asked as he moved the desk chair next to the boy's bed and sat. This was not a rhetorical question, and he waited for Eduardo's answer.

"I'll get a job," Eduardo said. "And I'll buy a car."

"Well," Perez mused, "I think you had a job, working for Miguel." He stared into Eduardo's eyes and saw them dilate in surprise. He was on the right track. "Is he a boss you want to go back to?"

The shake of the boy's head was barely perceptible.

"Then we must look for a job for you, because it will take a good job if you plan to support yourself and buy a car. Maria," he called down the hall. "Maria, will you bring me the morning paper, please?"

Maria appeared a few moments later with two glasses of orange juice and a folded newspaper on a tray.

"Wonderful," Perez murmured as he picked up the paper. "Now let's see," he said, turning to the classified advertisements. "What kind of car do you want, Eduardo?"

Eduardo shrugged his shoulders. "A Chevy," he said, remembering a conversation Martin and Carlos had one evening about lowriders.

"Any particular year," Perez asked, peering above the paper.

Eduardo shrugged his shoulders again. He really didn't want to play this game.

"OK," Perez said. "Let's look at used Chevy's." He reached into the desk drawer to extract paper, pencil, and a small calculator.

After checking the price of several cars, computing the monthly payment, tagging on the price of gas, insurance, groceries, rent, and utilities, Perez gave a low whistle. "You will need at least $25.00 an hour to make this work." He rechecked his figures and set the calculator on the bed. "Now let's see what is available in the help wanted section." Turning the pages of the paper, he asked Eduardo what kind of work he thought he might like.

"I could work at the grocery store," Eduardo said, "or maybe a gas station or a carwash. Or maybe I could work at McDonald's."

Perez scanned the paper and wrote down a few numbers. "Eduardo, you will be making less than $4.00 an hour doing those things. You could work very hard at two or three jobs, and maybe, if you are very careful, you could save enough money in a year or two to buy a used car. But if you are working that hard, when will you have time to do anything that is fun?"

Again, the question was not rhetorical. Perez locked eyes with the boy and waited for an answer. Eduardo lowered his gaze, thinking of his cousins. They worked five or six days a week, but there rarely seemed to be enough money for even a new pair of shoes.

Eduardo became acutely aware of Perez's eyes on him. With head bowed, he raised his eyes to meet those of the man.

"I don't want to talk about this," he said.

Philip looked deep into Eduardo's expressive brown eyes and noted they did not yet reflect a hardened or callous attitude. "Well, I'm sorry," he said softly, "but these are the facts of life. They aren't going to change just because you do not want to face them." Perez cleared his throat. "Life is full of many challenges and many difficulties, Eduardo. You have already experienced some very hard things." The man broke the gaze this time. He paused, cleared his throat again, and looked out the window as if his thoughts had taken him elsewhere. Looking back at the boy, he found the child giving him full attention. "You can change your circumstances, Eduardo, but it will take work. It will take a lot of work."

The boy's expression revealed confusion and a little hostility. "I am not afraid of hard work," he said. "Do you mean you will pay me for the hard work?"

This time, it was Perez who wore the confused look. "Well, no. I won't be paying you." The light dawned suddenly. "Eduardo, do you think you have been brought here to work for me, to pay off some debt?"

The boy's steely gaze almost bore through Perez.

"Oh no," he said. "No, no, no. We have a misunderstanding here. You will be working for yourself, not me. Let me start over. I am a psychologist. I work with the schools to try and help kids stay out of gangs. I do research and intervention." He paused and began again thoughtfully as if remembering it was a child, not an adult, he was addressing. "I believe that friendship and love and knowledge about the world around you are important in order to be successful in life. People who have these things are lucky indeed. I also believe that determination, discipline, and persistence are important. Not everyone has these characteristics, but they can be developed." He looked at the boy to see what effect his words were having. The boy was clearly confused. Perez sighed deeply. "Eduardo," he began again, "if you continue on your present path, you will end up in jail. You need an education to make a good life for yourself. You need to work hard at your studies even when it is difficult and you feel like giving up." *You need care and love even more*, he thought. "I am willing to help you by providing education and training, but I need to know if I can expect some things from you in return."

The child picked nervously at the bedcovers. He knew nothing in life came for free; and what this man, who seemed to have everything, might ask in return roused discomfort somewhere in his young gut. He was afraid to ask what that something might be.

Phillip sensed the boy's uneasiness. "What I am asking in return is that you are truthful and willing to work hard at your lessons," Perez said. "If you are honest with me and persist at your lessons even when they become difficult, you may stay here in this house instead of going to a detention facility or another foster home. Our justice system will not release you to live on the streets trying to care for yourself. Neither will they return you to your cousins. Do you understand?"

Eduardo was not entirely sure that he did understand. Friendship he understood, although he felt betrayed by the only friends he had here in California. Love, he understood. Grandfather had shown him love. In his dreams, Mother cradled him or Father held a protective arm around him. That is love, the boy reasoned. But lessons meant school. Eduardo did not like school. He did not read well, and his English was basically the language of the streets. Since he didn't fit in with the studious kids, he hung out with Diego and Los Reyes.

"Do you understand?" Perez asked again.

For reasons unknown to him, Eduardo did not want to hear the sound of his own voice. He did not want to be a part of this conversation. Perhaps he was afraid to voice disagreement or maybe he did not want to feign agreement. Perhaps he was frightened by the honest answer, so instead of answering the question, he lowered his head and stared at his hands.

"Perhaps you do not agree. That is all right, but I would be interested in knowing why." Perez paused and waited for Eduardo's answer.

Uncomfortable with the long silence, the boy ventured feebly, "I don't like school."

"I see," replied Perez. "But may I assume that you agree that friendship and love are important things?"

Eduardo nodded yes.

"So you do not like school," Perez sighed. "There is much to learn in this world, Eduardo. Some learning requires study, but much learning takes place outside the classroom. Both ways are important."

Eduardo's wrinkled brow, and his tightly pressed lips bespoke his confusion.

Taking a different approach, Perez pressed on. "Why did you come here Friday evening, Eduardo?" Again, he paused.

Eduardo squirmed, even more uncomfortable with the course of the conversation.

Unable to think of an acceptable response, he said, "I wanted to see your house."

Perez frowned at the lie. "That is an unacceptable answer, Eduardo. I will accept nothing but the truth."

Eduardo felt cornered. He hated Miguel for putting him in this spot. "They made me do it," he said.

The revelation of who "they" were was not important to this conversation, so Perez asked, "Do they have power over you?"

Eduardo cocked his head to the side and frowned. "No."

"They must have power over you if they made you do something."

Eduardo wanted to escape this conversation and this room. His anger was building, and he looked longingly toward the door beyond Perez as he unconsciously rubbed the tattoo on his arm.

"And that must have hurt," Perez said, nodding toward the tattoo. "Did you use a clean needle?"

Eduardo winced. "They cleaned it in a flame," he said, fear gripping his stomach. He knew AIDS and hepatitis could come from a dirty needle. That was one thing he had learned in school. Perez closed his eyes and took a deep breath. "Well, Eduardo," he said at last, "your friends—"

"They're not my friends," Eduardo interjected quickly.

"Well, not many people would risk AIDS, hepatitis, or arrest for mere acquaintances,"

"If you don't have friends in Los Reyes, just exactly why did you let them put that on your arm?"

Eduardo swung his legs out of bed. "I don't want to talk about it," he yelled. "I don't want to talk about it, and I want out of here." He slid to the floor and faced Perez.

"Where's my clothes?"

"Tomas and Maria went out and purchased new clothes for you," Perez said, motioning toward the closet with his head. "What you were wearing was burned."

Eduardo hobbled to the closet. Opening the door, he found a pale blue dress shirt, Khaki slacks, and a blue blazer. "What's this?" he asked, pulling the slacks off the hanger.

"Your replacement pants," Perez said pleasantly.

"I can't wear these," Eduardo whined. "Everyone will make fun of me."

"What do you care?" Perez reasoned with him. "They're not your friends. You said so yourself."

Perez's logic was tripping Eduardo, and his anger increased. "I don't want your stupid pants. Bring me my own pants." Then suddenly remembering something precious left in the pocket, he pled, "Please, where are my pants? Just let me see them."

The intensity of his pleading roused Perez's curiosity.

"Maria," Perez shouted out the door, "has the garbage man been here yet? Eduardo wants his old pants back."

"I'll be back up with the pants if they're still around," Perez said, leaving the room and closing the door behind him.

The pants were still in the garbage can. Perez opened the plastic bag they had been placed in at the hospital and gasped from the odor. He dumped the contents on the patio. Damp and charred when paramedics cut the pants off the boy, they were now mildewed. Maria might be able to wash them, but he doubted they could ever be repaired; each leg was cut from hem to waist. He marveled that the nurses had not discarded the bag. Perhaps as personal property, they had to be returned to the patient regardless of their condition. Gingerly, he grasped each item and dropped it back in the plastic bag, tying off the top.

"He has no gratitude," Maria grumbled when Perez walked back inside, bag in hand.

Perez returned to Eduardo's room and knocked on the door.

"Yeah?" Eduardo responded.

"I've got your pants," Perez replied.

The door opened, and Eduardo grabbed the bag.

Chapter Eleven

The Contract

Perez Estate
October 1984

The smell from the bag almost knocked Eduardo over. He pulled the wet clothes out and tossed them into the bathtub. Kneeling, he grabbed the denim and found the left front pocket that contained a sizable lump deep inside. Ignoring the odor, he put his hand into the pocket and extracted a knotted old handkerchief full of mildew.

With some difficulty, he untied the wet knots and lifted a tiny gold cross and chain from the soiled linen. Carefully and lovingly, he wiped the moisture from the cross. Moving back into the bedroom, he chose the drawer in the bedside table as the place where he would store it. In the bathroom, he opened the window before reexamining his pants. He had learned to launder clothes, but even if he could get rid of the smell, the pants were not wearable. No seamstress could repair the hem to waistband cuts that had been made to quickly remove his clothes. Cursing loudly, he stuffed them back in the bag and tied it off. He stepped outside the room and threw the bag down the staircase.

Eduardo sat for close to an hour, contemplating his situation when the low rumble of an engine alerted him that a car was coming up the driveway. His pout having been interrupted, he stood to the side of the large bedroom window, seeing without being seen. He recognized Lolich as the man exited his car. "Damn!" the boy said under his breath. Obviously, Perez had sent for the police to take him away. Angry as he was with Perez, he reasoned that this house was probably a better situation than juvenile detention or any other foster home. Eduardo moved toward the closet and hoped he wasn't too late.

"How's it going?" Mike greeted Perez.

"Could be better, could be worse."

"Changed your mind?"

"No, but ask me again in a few more days." Perez laughed. "Or maybe a few more hours. We just had our first run-in."

"Well, at least it looks like you came out on top," Lolich observed.

"Time will tell. You know, they cut his clothes off at the hospital, so Tomas and Maria went to the mall and bought him some new things. I just showed them to him, and he's not exactly happy about the cut."

"Knowing you, it's probably a suit."

"Almost," said Perez sheepishly. "Khakis, button-down shirts, and a navy sport coat."

"Give me a break," Lolich howled. "I suppose you gave him a tie too?"

The deepening color of Perez's face was answer enough for the cop. "You've got to be kidding," Lolich said. "That kid has never had a suit jacket on in his life, let alone a tie. He probably doesn't know whether it goes around his waist or his neck."

"So what brings you up here this morning?" Perez asked, eyeing a bag in Lolich's hand and deftly changing the subject.

"I went by Eduardo's cousin's apartment and spoke with Martin again. That man could care less about the boy. He's admitted they beat the kid when they learned he was dealing for Miguel, but he claims they didn't injure him. I'm inclined to believe it. I'm sure Miguel and his hoodlums were responsible for the cracked ribs and black eye. Anyway, it'll be up to you and Eduardo whether you want to press charges against them or not." He handed the small bag to Perez. "They gave me the kid's stuff. It's not much, but it might be important to the boy, especially with the new wardrobe." He grinned.

"What's inside?"

"Just clothes," Lolich said; "shirt, pants, underwear."

"I don't know whether to thank you or not," Perez said, "I'm sure Eduardo will be grateful, but I think I'll have Maria launder the clothes and hang onto them for a while."

Perez led the police chief into the study to enjoy a cup of coffee before returning to the station.

"What's the plan, Philip?" Mike asked when they had settled onto an old couch before the fireplace.

"His safety is my first priority. Los Reyes is not going to just let him go, and I'm concerned about my ability to keep him safe."

"I think your plan to educate him at home is a good start. We already know they can scale the wall and break in, but he would be even more vulnerable at school. I've brought a list of items for you to consider:

motion-sensitive outdoor floodlights, an alarm system, and a security guard."

Philip took the list and scanned it. "Hmmm, I think most of these things could be easily installed, but a guard, Mike? I don't think I want an armed guard patrolling the grounds."

"I was afraid you'd balk at that. I'll tell you what, I'll send a patrol car up here twice a day, and you have Tomas call in twice a day to let us know things are OK. Can you live with that?"

"I can live with that," Perez said, smiling.

"And get a guard dog."

"A guard dog?"

"Yeah," Mike said, smiling. "You've got a boy. Now you need a dog."

Perez considered this for a minute. He loved animals, but his busy schedule had not left him time to care for a dog. Getting a dog for Eduardo, something for him to take responsibility for, might be a very good thing. "You know, I like that idea," he said.

Upstairs, Eduardo was struggling with the tie. By the time Lolich and Perez had entered the study, Eduardo had the shirt and pants on, but he couldn't figure out how to secure the tie.

A quiet knock on the door startled the boy. *This is it*, he thought. *They're going to haul me out of here.* He went to the door ready to plead repentance and was startled to find Tomas standing there.

The older man smiled. "Good," he said simply. "You have decided to stay."

"I don't know what to do with this stupid thing," Eduardo said, pulling the tie from his neck.

"I will show you," Tomas said, and with that, he led Eduardo to a mirror and taught him the four-in-hand. Repeatedly, the old man knotted and unknotted the tie until he was satisfied that the boy could complete the task. "Here," he said, handing the length of fabric to Eduardo. "Now you tie it."

Eduardo grasped the tie, looking as though he had been asked to prepare the noose for his own hanging. Awkwardly, he repeated the steps Tomas had shown him, achieving a presentable knot. If his living situation had not depended on it, Eduardo would have ripped the tie from his throat. He felt as if he would choke.

"Am I going to have to wear this all the time?" he asked Tomas, poking a finger between shirt and neck, trying to loosen the noose.

"You will get used to it," was the answer, and as quietly as he had come, the older man left the room.

Eduardo paced his bedroom floor, anticipating he would be called down and sent away with Lolich, so he was surprised to hear the car start up and drive away. A few minutes later, there was a knock on his door. Eduardo answered the knock and once again found Tomas in the hall.

"Señor Perez wishes to see you in his study," Tomas said. "I will show you the way."

The furnishings of the study were impersonal. "I have never gotten around to buying decent furniture for this room," Perez said as the boy came in and looked around. "And strangely, it is the room where I spend most of my time."

The fact that Eduardo sported his new suit did not escape Perez's glance, but he wisely chose not to comment. "Have a seat," he said, motioning the boy to the couch. "We need to talk about what happened upstairs."

Eduardo shrugged his shoulders. "I didn't want to put these clothes on," he said.

"But you did." The boy looked at the dirty sneakers on his feet. Perez's glance followed the boy's. "Shoes have to be properly fit," he said, explaining the fact that there were no new shoes to go with the clothes.

Eduardo shrugged as if it didn't matter. "Do I have to wear this stuff all the time?" he asked.

"Much of the time," Perez commented coolly.

"I can't breathe," Eduardo complained, prying at the shirt and tie with his hand.

"You will get used to it," he heard for the second time in the last half hour. "It appears that you have decided to stay here."

"It beats juvenile detention or deportation," Eduardo said.

"That's not good enough. If that is your attitude, I'll call Chief Antonovic back, and you can leave."

"What do you want from me?" Eduardo asked, the anger rising once again.

"I want a commitment," Perez said. "It will be just as if you are in school here, and I want a commitment that you will work your heart out. I want a commitment that you will persist even when you don't feel like it. I want a commitment that you will be truthful with me. If you are willing to sign a contract of commitment, you can stay."

"Why do you care what happens to me?" Eduardo asked.

The question drew Perez up short. He thought about his motivation and admitted to himself that there was a self-serving motive to what he was doing. It wasn't just about the boy. It wasn't just about the community, although he cared deeply about the community. The boy presented an opportunity to prove a theory he had been working on for the last several years. It was an opportunity that might not come this way again. He felt sudden shame. Was he using this child for his own ends? No, not exclusively, and there was something that eluded him, something about the boy. "I think I can help you change your life," Perez said tentatively.

"Why do you care about my life?"

"If I can help you, I can help others."

"So you don't really care about me in particular," Eduardo said. He didn't understand why that was important to him. He had never been very important to anyone except Grandfather and of course his parents. Somehow it was important, though.

Come on, Perez told himself. *What's going on here? I'm a psychologist. I'm not supposed to be stumped by a fifteen-year-old.* He rose and paced the room, rubbing his chin between thumb and forefinger as he thought this out. Walking about the room, the light came on. Eduardo did not want to be used. He wanted to be valued.

"There are many levels of caring," Perez started. "I don't know you well, Eduardo, and you barely know me," he continued. "I would be lying if I said I care about you as I would care for a child of my own or even a good friend. I do care about you as a human being, and I value you as a person. I believe that you have something to offer this community, and I would like to be a part of helping you discover what that something is."

"Why me? Why not some other kid?"

"You're the one who tried to break into my house."

The boy stood, considering this for a few moments. "So I'm going to go to school here?" he asked.

"That's right."

"All by myself?"

"Right again," Perez said. "You will have the full attention of me, Tomas, and any tutors I decide you need."

"What about sports? I love sports."

"There are sports that don't need a team," Perez said.

The room grew quiet as both the man and the boy were lost in their own thoughts.

"Do you need more time to think about what I have said?"

"I will stay," Eduardo answered as though he were doing Perez a favor.

Perez moved to the desk. "I have a contract that I am going to ask you to sign, Eduardo. It is not a legal contract. You are too young to sign a legal contract. This is an agreement between the two of us. It says I will provide you with a home, clothing, food, and an education. It also says that you agree to work diligently at your lessons and that you promise to be truthful with me. Are you willing to sign this?"

Eduardo rose and moved to the desk. The agreement was short, and the language simple.

"There will be times that you will feel discouraged. You will probably feel angry with me. When those times come, I want you to know those feelings are OK. But no matter how you are feeling, you cannot give up." Perez looked deep into the boy's eyes. *Yes*, he told himself, *there is enough determination there.*

Eduardo nodded his head in agreement, this time holding Perez's stare. "Do you have any questions?"

Eduardo's mind was racing. More questions were swirling in his head than had ever been there before, but he did not know how to put them into words. Instead, he picked up the pen and signed his name, Eduardo Rodriguez.

"Now," said Perez, "how would you feel about getting a dog?"

* * *

"First a boy, now a dog," Maria said, picking up a stack of newspapers from the study.

Tomas turned and smiled to himself. She might have sounded like she was complaining, but he knew his wife. She was happy beyond belief to have the boy and now the thought of a dog in residence. Eduardo had already infused new life into the house, and he knew a well-trained dog would be fun for everyone.

"I hope Philip gets plenty of chew toys. Puppies will chew everything in sight if you don't give them something to gnaw on."

"Well, my dear," he said, "at least the puppy won't be chewing your things. Our stuff is safely off limits."

I guess it's a good thing Philip has never purchased nice things for the study," she said. "But that pup better stay out of the dining room. The table and chairs in there are antiques."

* * *

Eduardo was surprised when Perez suggested a dog. He had never owned a pet, but he loved dogs. A serious talk followed the suggestion, outlining the work involved in caring for and training a dog. "It is a big responsibility, Eduardo. You have many new things to contend with here. Are you willing to take care of a dog?"

"Yes." Eduardo's answer was emphatic. A dog would be a friend and companion.

"We will help you care for him, but you will have the main responsibility for feeding, walking, and cleaning up after him."

They set out that afternoon for the shelter. The choice had been difficult. There were so many dogs waiting for a good home, but Perez wisely considered what his household needed, a dog that would be able to help guard Eduardo and the house and had a reliable temperament. Several young dogs were brought from their kennels, but one stood out from the rest, a six-month-old German shepherd.

"He's bright and already housebroken," the attendant said. "His owner moved into an apartment that doesn't allow pets. He's had his shots, and he's neutered."

The dog's name was Lobo. "He looks like a wolf," Eduardo said, kneeling down and stroking the animal. The dog licked Eduardo's face and tried to climb into his lap.

Philip smiled. "I think this is the one, Eduardo. What do you say? Shall we take Lobo home?"

The boy smiled at Perez for the first time and hugged the dog. "Yes."

CHAPTER TWELVE

Lessons

Palos Verdes Peninsula
November 1984

"Children are resilient," Dr. Montoya said in a mater-of-fact voice after concluding an examination of Eduardo. He nodded his head toward the exam room where the boy was dressing. "It has only been two weeks since his injury, but look at him."

"The emotional wounds are still as fresh as two weeks ago," Philip commented. "They will leave scars much larger than the small one on his ankle."

The door opened, and Eduardo joined the two men in Montoya's office. "I don't think you need to see me anymore, Eduardo," the doctor said. "Your burn is almost healed, and the X-ray shows your ribs are healing also. I see you have gained a couple of pounds." He turned to Perez and chuckled. "Must be Maria's good cooking."

Perez returned the laugh. "Yes, I think we are going to need to start some physical education."

"No contact sports for a month," the doctor cautioned. "Maybe we should X-ray in six weeks if you are contemplating anything like that."

"He can swim," Perez said. "That big heated pool is going to waste in the backyard."

"I d-d-don't swim," the boy stuttered. Perez noted the fear on the boy's face and let the subject drop.

"Well, we'll find some reason to get him outside," Philip said, "even if it's just to walk the dog."

"Dog?" the doctor asked, eyeing Philip with amusement. Things were really changing at the Perez household.

"Yeah," Eduardo said. "We got a dog. His name is Lobo, and I'm taking care of him."

"And doing a very good job of it too," Perez added.

"Well, that's fantastic," the doctor replied. "Just don't let my kids see the dog or they'll be begging for one too. Now let's see, running would be good for the boy. Stress on the bones encourages deposition of calcium. His sprain is healed, so as long as he's careful not to twist it—"

"I'm a fast runner," Eduardo interrupted.

"Well, I think it's time to get some running shoes," Perez said, "especially after the last two weeks of music appreciation."

Eduardo's brows raised, and his mouth opened in anticipation of more good news.

Perhaps the music lessons were over.

The look did not escape Perez. "Sorry, Eduardo, music appreciation will continue." He shook the boy's shoulder playfully. "You're going to love Mozart in a few more weeks."

The boy wrinkled his nose. He couldn't envision himself loving the music Señor Perez played. The only rock music he had heard in the last two weeks came from a car stopped beside them at a light on the way to the doctor's office. "Even the dog hates the music," Eduardo informed the doctor. "He sits outside the study and howls."

"He's singing along." Perez laughed.

"I think I may start singing with him," Eduardo said.

*   *   *

The professor's music appreciation classes had begun on Eduardo's second morning at the villa. Freshly bathed and dressed in his "uniform," he reported to Perez's study after breakfast.

"The Perez prep school uniform," Perez had announced with obvious pleasure in his voice. "We really need to do something about the shoes, though."

The clothes were soon forgotten as Perez presented his own music appreciation course to the boy. "Music is soothing, and I think it will be a good place to start while your body is healing," Perez explained. "Music is part of a classical education, and it is my intention to see to it that your course of study is well rounded."

Sitting side by side at a table in the study, Perez began reading about the basics of music from a large book. He drew notes and symbols on a lined pad of paper, and Eduardo copied the drawings on an identical pad. At intervals, Perez turned on his tape player to demonstrate a sound, an instrument, or a rhythm. For two weeks, the study of music was the focus of Eduardo's day. They moved from the basics of reading music to a study of the great periods and composers of those periods. Eduardo could barely tolerate the lessons much less appreciate the music they were about. He fidgeted from the time he sat down until Maria interrupted them for their morning break with a plate of freshly baked pan dulce, coffee, and milk. The scent of the warm bread was intoxicating, and Eduardo inhaled appreciatively each time she placed the tray on a low table between the fireplace and couch. Store purchased baked goods rarely tasted as good as those made at home, and Maria's bread was some of the finest he had ever tasted. He always ate greedily, the crumbs falling on his lap, the couch, and the carpet.

"Hungry?" Perez asked one morning.

"Yeah," Eduardo replied, his mouth full.

Perez pressed his lips into a thin line and studied the boy. The boy was painfully aware of his teacher's gaze. He laid the bread next to him on the couch and scrubbed his new slacks free of crumbs using a crumpled napkin.

"Try not to step in the crumbs when you get up," Perez cautioned. "The housekeeper can vacuum them up more easily if they aren't trod into the carpet." Perez knew that Eduardo's presence had increased his housekeeper's workload. Maria was trying to help out, but though she never complained, she looked more tired in the evenings.

Eduardo lifted his feet to look at the mess he had created. There were crumbs everywhere. "I'm sorry, "he said, squatting to try and scoop the crumbs into what was left of his napkin. He wished he was outside where the crumbs would likely be cleaned up by hungry little birds.

Perez watched the boy appreciatively. A willing spirit could make up for many deficiencies. "It's OK, Eduardo," Perez said. "Consuelo will bring the vacuum cleaner in and take care of it. Let's get back to work."

"I think I would rather run the vacuum cleaner for Consuelo," Eduardo said. Perez laughed. "You said I must always tell the truth," Eduardo added, a grin on his own face.

*   *   *

"Why do I have to study this crap?" Eduardo asked one morning as they concluded a particularly noxious lesson on Renaissance composers. He had asked the same question so many times Perez's patience was reaching its limit.

"First of all, you will not refer to the music or anything else in this house as crap. And I have told you more times than I can count that music appreciation is an important part of a well-rounded education. I do not want to hear this question again. If I do, I will have to think up some appropriate punishment," Perez warned in a state of total frustration.

"This *is* punishment."

"Perhaps we need to take a different approach. I was going to wait a couple of weeks, but . . ." Perez moved to a cupboard and retrieved a box. Opening it, he turned and presented the contents to Eduardo.

"What is it?" the boy asked. It was a straight wooden tube with holes down the front. There was a tapered piece at the top, and the bottom was flared a bit.

"A recorder," Perez replied. "It is a very primitive instrument, and you are going to learn to play it."

"I'd rather play the drums or guitar."

"All in good time, but we'll start with something simple." Perez pulled a second well-used recorder from the cupboard. "This one is mine. I've had it since I was a child."

Eduardo had already memorized the notes and signature of a simple scale. Perez set some sheets of music on a music stand and beckoned Eduardo to stand next to him. The tune was simple, and after Perez showed the boy the key holes that corresponded to the notes on the page, they played the song together. When Perez saw the grin on Eduardo's face, he knew he had steered the lessons in the right direction.

"It sounds a little like the pipes some of the South American people play, but it doesn't look like their pipes," Eduardo quipped.

"You're right. Both are very ancient instruments. The flute you are referring to is sometimes called the pan flute. The pipes are closed at one end, and you blow across the top to make music. The recorder was a very popular instrument in Europe from Medieval to the Baroque period."

"We were listening to Baroque music this morning."

Perez smiled. Did he have a breakthrough here? "Would you like me to bring out some Baroque sheet music?"

"Yeah, maybe it would be more fun to play it than listen to it."

"I'll show you what it looks like, but I think we should keep this beginners book out because some of the Baroque pieces are fairly difficult."

After that session, Perez could not keep the boy away from the instrument. He played in the house, and he played in the garden. He could be heard playing after he went to his bedroom in the evening. Much to everyone's delight, Eduardo became proficient on the instrument within a short period of time.

*   *   *

After the visit with Dr. Montoya, Perez made good on his promise to purchase new running shoes for Eduardo. "We have both worked hard for the last two weeks," he said. "You may not appreciate these lessons, but at least you are paying attention, most of the time," he qualified the statement. As Perez ushered Eduardo into his car, he asked, "How about a trip to the mall for those new running shoes?"

"Cool," Eduardo exclaimed.

*   *   *

"Good shoes are imperative if you intend to run," the sports shop clerk said. He pointed out several styles with "a good midsole" that would cushion Eduardo's feet.

Eduardo tried on a pair, and they felt like nothing he had ever worn. He bounced repeatedly, appreciating the unaccustomed spring they gave his step.

"We'll take those and a couple pair of running shorts and some shirts," Perez told the clerk who pointed Eduardo to the rack where he could choose from several colors. After the purchases were made, Eduardo moved anxiously toward the door of the shop, hoping Perez would not linger too long talking with the salesman. He couldn't wait to get home and put on the shoes.

It was all Perez could do to keep his stride paced with the boy's once outside the shop. Eduardo headed toward the parking garage, but Perez turned the opposite direction, drawing him into yet another shop. "You need more than running gear," Perez reminded him. "As long as we are here at the mall, we might as well get a few more things."

After stopping at a large department store, Perez and Eduardo emerged with several more bags containing three pair of slacks, several shirts, one pair of everyday sneakers, brown leather loafers and black dress shoes, more pajamas, and underwear. In the car, Eduardo's confusion was apparent. He had never owned more than one pair of shoes at a time. Little had he known that when they returned home, he would be carrying four new pairs of shoes along with new clothes.

Except for the tape player, the car was quiet as Eduardo pondered how he would ever manage to wear so many shoes. Perez cut into Eduardo's thoughts. "Whose music are we enjoying?" he asked the boy.

Eduardo thoughtfully listened to string instruments sending their energetic pulsed staccato through the car's speaker system. The music was bright with a repetitive rhythm. He searched his mind a few seconds before remembering the Baroque composers. The four he studied over the last week were Vivaldi, Telemann, Bach, and Handel. He did not enjoy the music, but this particular melody was becoming familiar. The shopping spree had put Eduardo in a playful mood, so he said, "*You* are enjoying Vivaldi." There was smug grin on the boy's face.

"Bravo," Perez replied in admiration. "And do I take your tone to mean that you are not also enjoying this?"

"Not this movement," Eduardo replied. Then glancing sideways at the professor, he continued, "I prefer summer."

The piece had just moved from presto of summer into the third movement, autumn.

The boy had identified the piece as Vivaldi's "Four Seasons." Perez could hardly speak.

"Tell me why you prefer summer over autumn," Perez said in astonishment.

"No school during summer," Eduardo said and doubled over with laughter. The child was having fun at the expense of the concerto and Perez; but he had identified the composer, placed him in the correct period, and distinguished between the movements of the concerto, which he had also correctly identified. Perez could have shouted to the skies, but he resisted the urge and quietly basked in the wonderful knowledge that this child who he had decided to help was very clever and very quick to learn.

When they reached home, Eduardo raced to his room, packages in hand. He opened each shoebox, placed the shoes side by side on the closet floor, and sat staring at them for several seconds before picking up the running shoes. Donning the running gear and lacing up his shoes, he jogged in place, pretending to lead the pack. When his fantasy had run its course, he placed the shoe polish bottles and waterproof solution on his shelf in one neat row. The slacks were neatly hung, the shirts and pajamas placed in drawers. He carried the packages of underwear down to the laundry room and started a wash cycle much to Maria's surprise.

*   *   *

Perez found Consuelo in the dining room, vacuum-cleaning a mess from under Eduardo's chair that had been made at breakfast.

"He is going to have to eat outside if he keeps making such a mess on the floor," Consuela grumbled as she unplugged the cord from the wall socket. "You cannot even have guests. His manners are so bad."

"I know, I know, Consuelo," Perez said, feeling as though he had betrayed this woman who had worked so hard for him over the years. "Your workload has increased, and it is my fault. Manners are one of the first things I should have addressed. I thought he was nervous and that was why he kept spilling things, but he eats like a little hamster, scattering crumbs all over. It's as if he doesn't grab what he wants, it will all disappear."

"Perhaps there was not enough on the table when he lived with his cousins," Maria said, entering the room.

"You have a good point," Perez answered. "However, I promise he will begin to learn good manners tonight at dinner."

The nod from Consuelo and the satisfied look on Maria's face were all the thanks Perez needed. He cared deeply for these people, and he would do nothing intentionally to make their lives hard. Maria and Tomas were the closest thing to family that he had, and they had been friends for over twenty years. He would not allow Maria's or Consuelo's frustration to continue if he could remedy it.

CHAPTER THIRTEEN

The Sting

Wilmington, California
November 1984

Diego met twice with Matt at an apartment on Cordova, and Matt was starting to like the kid. "He's good at the core," the undercover cop told his partner, Gabe, one afternoon. "He's just misguided. His dad was killed in a drive-by when Diego was only three. His mom works three jobs to try and support him, so he's unsupervised most of the time."

"Too bad we can't take him out for some hoops once in a while," Gabe said.

Matt swung his legs over the side of the cot where he'd been resting and hung his head in despair. He saw too much of this, kids who might have turned out differently if they had someone to listen to them, someone to talk with and to emulate. "I set up a delivery for this afternoon. I think I'll head on over there."

"Still early," Gabe said, checking his watch. "I'm going for a burger. Wanna eat first?"

"No," Matt replied, patting his stomach. "If I get any fatter, I won't be able to pull this charade off anymore."

"You think you'll get anything out of this kid?"

"We never know, do we?" Matt said, rising and taking his keys from the desk.

Matt was about an hour early when he arrived at the apartment, so he was surprised to find Diego waiting for him. "What are you doing here so early, man?" he asked, unlocking a shabby door and ushering the boy ahead of him. Diego was anxious or scared; Matt couldn't decide which. "OK," he said, sitting the boy down on a worn couch. "What's going on?"

"There were some guys in Miguel's office this morning. He has a kind of office over on—"

"Yeah, I know, I know," Matt interrupted.

"Well, two guys came in this morning while I was there picking up my cut. I'd never seen them before, but they walked right in like they owned the place and went to the backroom. Miguel told Ernesto to finish paying the guys, and he went into the back and shut the door."

Matt cocked his head to the side and looked at Diego. "I bet a lot of guys come in to that place. Were they buying from Miguel?"

"No, they have a big delivery for him," Diego said. "I heard them talking about it." His voice betrayed urgency.

"OK, buddy, calm down. What exactly did you hear and how did you manage to hear it with the door closed?"

"There were two other guys getting their money from Ernesto, so I said I was going to take a dump while I waited for my turn. I went into the bathroom, which is right next to the room Miguel and those guys were in. I put my ear to the wall, and I could hear everything. They said they had a load of cocaine just off shore on a fishing boat. They're gonna bring it in tonight, and they told Miguel he could buy it for half a million."

"What did he say?"

"He said he didn't have a half a million. If they were willing to give him the stuff, he could unload it in two days, and he'd give them the money plus a bonus for fronting him. They said they'd do it if he'd join forces with them. You know, let them be his new supplier."

This was probably the biggest single deal Miguel had ever been involved in. The potential was mind-boggling, and it had to be stopped. "Did you hear anything else?" Matt asked.

"Miguel said he couldn't break with his current supplier under penalty of death. The men got kind of mad and told him they could deal with the other guys. They sounded really angry and said they were taking over. Miguel could join forces with them or face the consequences. I was getting scared just listening, so I flushed the toilet like I'd been doing my business and walked out to get my money. Some of the guys were hanging around, so I joined them. After a while, everybody came out of the backroom, and the men left. Miguel walked over to where we were and said that there was going to be a war." The boy looked scared.

Matt put is head in his hands. Boatloads of coke off the coast, a gang war, this was big stuff; and he wondered how safe Diego would be. "What happened next?"

"The guys all started talking about a war. Miguel went to the phone and called somebody, and I left to come here."

"If war breaks out, there's going to be a lot of shooting," Matt said. "A lot of people are going to get killed. You're not safe."

Diego hung his head. "I don't want to die, Matt. I was just looking at making a few bucks, plus the guys treated me like family, at least they did at first."

Matt put his hands on the boy's shoulders and looked into his eyes. "What you've told me is extremely important. We can intercept the cocaine without much problem, but stopping a war between Los Reyes and this cartel may be another story. I want you to go home and stay there until you hear from me. If Miguel or anybody asks where you are, tell them you're sick. Tell them you've been spewing your guts out in the toilet."

They boy slipped out, and Matt reached for the phone.

"I hope that kid did just what I told him," Matt whispered to Gabe as they sat outside Miguel's office that night.

"I hope they weren't setting him up," Gabe said. "It doesn't look like much is going on here. Do you think we should drive to Miguel's apartment and see if there's any action over there?"

"Let's check inside this place, and if there's nothing of interest, we'll head over there." There were no lights on inside the building, but a lone flood light at the corner of the roof lit a triangular area in front of the man door and the roll-up door alongside it. The two undercover cops climbed out of the old Ford, scanning for movement as they made their way to the back of the building. A chain-link fence surrounded the property, and the back gate was locked. Matt pulled a tool from his pocket and had the lock off in less than a minute. They closed the gate behind them and left the lock on a link of the fence. There was a small side yard to the left with overgrown weeds, empty oil cans, and old tires. The right side of the building was piled halfway to the roof with used construction materials. Gabe shined a small arc of light on the back door, while Matt jimmied the lock. The backroom was about nine by ten feet. A folding table and four chairs sat in the right corner next to a littered counter. Dirty glasses and mugs filled a small sink. Half a pot of coffee remained in a coffee maker next to the sink. Gabe felt the carafe. "Still warm," he whispered. He moved the arc of his flashlight into the other corners of the room. Three long boxes were stacked against the far wall. *Should have brought some tools inside*, he thought. He motioned to Matt that he was returning to the car and slipped out the back. Matt opened the inner door and looked around. Another desk shoved against the back wall; a couple more chairs, and what appeared to be a working garage. A second door close to the one he had just come through was ajar, and a light was on in the room. His crepe soles made no sound as he moved toward the door. He peered through the crack between the door and the sill to assure himself no one was hiding behind it, and then he pushed the door open. It was the little bathroom Diego had eavesdropped in. He heard Gabe return with the tools and walked to the backroom. "Hey, man, need a little light?" he asked, turning his flashlight on his friend.

"What are you doing here?" Miguel demanded. He held a Glock in his right hand.

Matt slipped into his dope addict personae, hoping he could make it work. "Hey, man, put that thing down. Somebody could get hurt." "What are you doing here?" Miguel demanded a second time.

"Just looking for a place to sleep," Matt lied. "It's cold out there, and I got kicked out by my old lady tonight. Hey, you're the guy I get my fix from. Got anything in here?"

Miguel eyed him suspiciously. "You're undercover. You're a narc!" He raised the gun and pulled the trigger just as Gabe came bursting back inside.

The bullet hit about three inches to the left of its intended mark and grazed Matt's neck. Gabe pummeled Miguel to the floor and had the cuffs on him in one sweeping action. "Are you OK?" he asked his partner.

"I'm fine except for my pride. My cover's blown." He blotted his neck with the tail of his shirt.

"You've been hit!"

"Grazed is more like it. I'd be dead if you hadn't come through that door. Let's get this guy down to the station. We can send another team out her to see what's in these boxes."

Miguel was processed and placed in a cell. "What are the charges?" the captain asked.

"We've sent Maxwell and Kent back down to Miguel's place to open some boxes we found. We think they probably hold automatic weapons. More than likely, they'll find drugs too. We're waiting till the guys get back with the evidence to charge him."

"You better get over to St. Mary's and have that wound looked at," the captain ordered. "Max and Kent can finish the paperwork for you."

When Matt and Gabe returned to the station four hours later, they found Miguel's cell empty. "Hey," Matt said to the sergeant at the desk, "where's my bust?"

"Had to release him."

"What the—" Matt stormed through the office with Gabe at his heels. Maxwell and Kent were just finishing up some paperwork. Matt slammed his palm down on Maxwell's desk. "What the hell just happened here?"

Maxwell looked at his partner. "You wanna tell them?"

Officer Kent cleared his throat. "We got down there probably twenty minutes after you called."

Maxwell interrupted. "We were just wrapping up a domestic or we'd have been there five, ten minutes sooner."

"Like I said," Kent continued, "we got there, and the back gate was locked. We jimmied it and went inside. There was nothing. We tore the place apart, no boxes, no weapons, no drugs."

"We didn't lock the back gate," Gabe said dumbfounded.

"Somebody must have come in and took the goods after you left."

"I've been shot," Matt yelled. "I've been shot, and you let the guy go."

"Self-defense," Kent said. Matt and Gabe shot him a look of disbelief. "He claimed it was self-defense. He came into his shop, found a burglar, and said you pulled a gun on him, self-defense. There will be a hearing, but that's what he'll plead. We had to let him go. Good news is"—Kent yelled behind the two as they strode toward the door—"the feds made a big bust tonight, coke coming into the harbor via fishing boat, street value of about a million."

The front door banged open and slammed shut.

* * *

"I'm glad you weren't far behind," Miguel said to Ernesto. "Getting the guns and drugs out saved my neck."

"The boxes were a piece of cake, but I had to send Luis up in the attic for the drugs, and you know how scared he is of rats."

"Luis and me both," Miguel said. "I don't know where that little rat is right now, but we're going to find him one way or the other. He just about got me sent up the river."

CHAPTER FOURTEEN

Etiquette

Palos Verdes Peninsula
November 1984

Philip took his usual place at the head of the table the evening after his discussion with Consuelo and Maria. Tomas sat at the opposite end, and Eduardo took his seat on Perez's left.

"Hungry?" Perez asked as Eduardo slipped into his seat.

"Very hungry," the boy replied, grabbing a tortilla.

Perez's hand came down on top of the boy's, and the flat bread remained in its basket. "Well, as usual, Maria has prepared a wonderful meal for us, and such a lot of food. We always seem to have enough to satisfy our needs."

Eduardo looked from Perez's face to his hand. He was unsure of what had just happened.

Maria set the last of the hot dishes on the table. "You let me know if you are still hungry after dinner," she said. "I will go right back into that kitchen and cook until you are full. Philip Perez always has enough around here to feed an army." She took her seat and winked at Perez.

So all right, thought Eduardo, *let's start eating*.

"I will say a blessing upon the food," Perez said, removing his hand from the boy's.

"And then we will eat."

Eduardo colored. He had not prayed and had not been to church since leaving Mexico. Perez always said a short prayer of blessing and thanksgiving before eating. Eduardo had been too long out of the habit his grandfather had established at home, and he kept forgetting.

After the prayer, Perez addressed Eduardo. "To begin, Eduardo," he said, picking up his napkin, "this goes on your lap."

The boy picked up the napkin, opened it to a single fold, and placed it in his lap, copying Perez's actions. His stomach rumbled in reaction to the smell of the fresh warm tortillas and a savory meat stew, but something new was transpiring; and Eduardo was learning to wait and watch.

"Now we will eat this meal very purposefully without attacking it," Perez continued.

Eduardo's brow furrowed.

"You know," Perez explained, "that is how you generally approach your food. You attack it. And nothing behaves well when it is being attacked . . . like the piece of steak that slipped off you plate last night."

The boy was embarrassed. It was true. He had jabbed his knife and fork at his food as if it would escape his plate at any moment.

Reading the boy's expression, Perez said kindly, "You are a typical hungry boy, Eduardo. You come to the table appreciative for what has been placed in front of you. I just want you to slow down a bit. There will always be enough food to satisfy your appetite, I promise." Smiling, Perez lifted the basket of tortillas, offering the contents to Eduardo, who gratefully accepted one.

Perez demonstrated the proper way of holding knife, fork, and spoon. Eduardo, used to grasping the implement handles as a baby grasps a rattle, struggled with the seeming awkwardness of the grip.

"It will get easier," Perez said, encouraging the boy. "Take small bites and chew well. Your stomach will appreciate that."

My mouth appreciates big bites, Eduardo thought, but he dutifully cut the meat he had speared into smaller pieces.

The meal proceeded slowly with strained conversation; the boy could only concentrate on one thing at a time. But for the first time in over two weeks, there were no spills for Maria to clean after dinner.

Etiquette lessons continued nightly. When it appeared that Eduardo was comfortable with the basics, Perez moved on to more formal issues.

Maria and Consuelo were asked to prepare a five-course meal. At 7:00 p.m., the household assembled in the study. An array of hors d'oeuvres had been set out on the coffee table. A sideboard held Perez's usual assortment of stemmed glasses; liquors; and, this evening, a bottle of sparkling cider nestled in a silver ice bucket.

"What's going on?" Eduardo asked.

"Party practice," Perez said.

This was unlike any party Eduardo had ever attended, but then many things that occurred at Villa Perez were strangely new to him. While the boy scrutinized the tidbits intended to stimulate his already ravenous appetite, Tomas opened a bottle of wine, tasted a sample, pronounced it spectacular, and filled all but Eduardo's glass. To Eduardo, he offered a glass of sparkling cider.

"Can I have soda instead?"

"You know, Eduardo, I don't like you drinking soda pop. It's not good for your bones and teeth," Perez said. "Once in a while on special occasions, you may have it."

"This looks pretty special to me."

Perez stared at the boy and then shook his head. "OK, go to the pantry and get a soda, but be quick. These hors d'oeuvres look wonderful, and I can hardly wait to try them."

Eduardo was back in less than three minutes with his soda. *Perez was right*, the boy thought, *the little snacks look good*. He took a small plate and moved toward the food.

Perez cleared his throat, a sign that Eduardo had come to learn. He looked at the man who nodded toward Maria. Eduardo offered her his plate and stepped aside. As Maria made some selections, Tomas moved in behind her. Eduardo looked at Perez, and the man once again nodded his head, affirming that Eduardo could now help himself. He grabbed a plate and quickly took one of everything except the oysters. The small meat-filled pastries were the best, and he quickly went back for more.

"Careful," Perez said. "These little offerings are a prelude to the meal. I know you are hungry, but if you eat too many, you won't have room for the rest of the meal."

Eduardo finished what was on his plate and eyed the table enviously. Eventually, Consuelo, who had stayed late, rang the bell; and the group moved into the dining room. Steaming plates of thin soup and tiny dumplings were set before them. The soup didn't look very interesting, but when Eduardo took his first sip, his mouth exploded with savory flavor. "What is this?" he asked appreciatively.

"Chicken consume with dumplings," Maria said proudly. "I found the recipe in a magazine and thought it might be good for one of Señor Perez's parties. What do you think?"

"I could eat three bowls full," Eduardo said as he greedily slurped. "I hope we will have it again."

Maria smiled. "I will make it for you often, Eduardo. It is always nice to cook for appreciative diners, but you must not show your appreciation by slurping." She lifted a spoonful of soup to her mouth and quietly drank it.

Eduardo raised an overfull spoon to his own mouth and dripped on his napkin. Looking up, he saw all eyes on him. He tried a smaller portion, slipped the soup from the spoon to his mouth noiselessly and received a smiling approval from his dinner companions.

Soup was followed by a wedge salad. A section of iceberg lettuce seemed so plain, but with Maria's homemade blue cheese dressing and bacon crumbles on top, it was another winner. Prime rib of beef was served next. It was salty and succulent. Eduardo shunned the horseradish sauce; he had never eaten it before. Perez encouraged him to try a small amount, telling him he might grow to like it. The first taste made him grimace, but once it was down, he decided to try a little more. He loaded his baked potato with sour cream, butter, and chives. The plate was garnished with a few small baby carrots, which he ignored as he dove into the meat. About halfway through his cut of meat, he slowed down.

"Full?' Perez asked.

"Getting there," the boy replied and rubbed his stomach.

"Don't overdo it," Maria warned him. "We can put the leftovers in the refrigerator for tomorrow's lunch. Save some room for dessert."

The conversation continued. Since his eating had slowed marginally, Eduardo started to join in the discussion of current events, bringing a smile to Perez's face. The young man stuffed the last piece of meat in his mouth and looked at the half-finished potato and carrots. There was no room for them in his stomach if he was going to have some of Maria's dessert. Her desserts were always the best part of the meal, but tonight Eduardo did not know how she was going to surpass what they had already eaten. As she rose to help Consuelo clear away the dishes, Eduardo stood with her and took several plates into the kitchen.

"You're making great progress," Tomas said when the boy left the room.

"It's been a real team effort, Tomas," Philip replied, "and I could never have done it without my two best friends."

*   *   *

Science, mathematics, and other scholastic pursuits continued daily in the professor's study. Eduardo enjoyed composing stories and reporting on events around the community, and it was soon evident to Philip that the child had a natural gift for writing. It was not long before Perez decided it would be to the boy's benefit to bring in tutors. He was not willing to place Eduardo in a classroom setting because of potential distractions. There was also the concern about the boy's safety. He called the local high school to locate teachers who would be willing to come to the villa two or three times a week. Though more subjects were added to Eduardo's schedule, the music lessons continued, much to the boy's dismay. One afternoon, Perez placed a tape in the player and left the room. Eduardo covered his ears with both hands and shook his head. "I hate this, I hate this, I hate this," he mumbled.

"Persistence, Eduardo," encouraged Perez from the next room. "Even Lobo is learning to like the music." It was as if Philip Perez could read Eduardo's mind, a characteristic the boy was beginning to believe the man truly possessed. Why was Perez making him listen to this music?

"Culture," Perez said. "Any cultured young man must know the music of Bach, Beethoven, Mozart, and the other masters, Eduardo. You do not have to like it, but you must recognize it." More than once, Eduardo wondered if juvenile detention would be a better fate than this musical interment.

"This is the art of the fugue," Perez instructed one afternoon when the lesson concentrated on Bach. "Before the time of Bach, the fugue was used, but Bach perfected it." He smiled in obvious contentment at hearing the repeating strains of melody overlaying each other in the violin Concerto in D Minor. Eduardo checked the clock on the desk. Thirty minutes and the lesson would end. This afternoon, he was to meet with Perez's tailor; and as violins and woodwinds wove the melody of the Baroque fugue into a rich tonal tapestry, Eduardo's mind wandered to thoughts of the new suit that would be sewn just for him, though what use he had for a suit he did not know.

*   *   *

Measuring for the suit took place in Eduardo's bedroom with the professor sitting by.

The process was boring, but when they sat to review Mr. Chang's fabric, Eduardo's interest was piqued.

"It will need to be light winter weight, I assume," Mr. Chang suggested.

"I suppose. Winter is never too cold here," Perez replied.

Eduardo flipped through the dark swatches feeling the texture of the fabrics as he looked for something colorful. He stopped when he reached a particularly smooth cut of navy blue fabric and rubbed it gently between his thumb and forefinger. It was soft like a kitten. *What a wonderful feeling,* he thought.

"That is an exceptional wool/cashmere blend," Mr. Chang said. "It is 120s," he commented to Perez, referring to the twist of the fabric, "but it would not be suitable for a tuxedo."

"Perhaps another time. I will be hosting a formal party during the Christmas holidays," Perez said, turning to the boy. "We will both wear tuxedos, which are special black suits."

Eduardo wrinkled his nose. "Black is for old grandmothers."

"Well then, I guess we will have to liven it up with a cummerbund and pocket kerchief. Mr. Chang, what colors do you have available?"

The tailor opened a book of colorful swatches that drew Eduardo's interest.

"Anything?" the tailor asked Perez.

"Anything." Perez smiled, knowing he might regret his words.

"I am going to a Christmas party?"

"Yes," replied Perez who was now examining the navy fabric that first caught Eduardo's eye.

"I will choose this," the boy said, pointing to a bright red brocade fabric.

"Very, well," said Mr. Chang. "That will be quite festive, indeed."

Perez cast a glance at Chang and nodded his approval. "Do you really like this?" Perez asked Eduardo, holding up the wool/cashmere swatch.

"It is very soft," Eduardo replied. "It would not itch like some clothes." This was an indictment of his new slacks, which Eduardo said felt "prickly."

"The high twist makes it lighter weight than the standard 60 to 80 twist. It would wear well through all the seasons here in Southern California," Chang offered, hoping to make another sale and a very profitable one at that.

Perez fingered the fabric. "I might like a jacket of this myself," he mused. "You wouldn't mind, would you, Eduardo?"

*   *   *

Two weeks later, Eduardo had the final fitting for his tuxedo. "I can't move," he complained, once the studs had been affixed to the heavily starched shirt and the tie and cummerbund were in place.

"Perhaps you should wear it around the house for a few days to get used to it," Perez said. He had been joking, but then announced, "Actually, that's not a bad idea." He ignored the look of horror on Eduardo's face. "Mr. Chang, we'll take an extra shirt, just in case, and we'll need the suit cleaned and pressed just before the party."

It took Eduardo forty-five minutes to dress the next morning. He moved about the house sullen and quiet, mimicking a robot whenever he thought someone was watching.

Perez instructed Tomas and Maria to ignore the boy's behavior, but it was difficult at times to keep a straight face. "You would think that suit was made of tin," Maria said with amusement one evening when she and Tomas were in their apartment over the garage.

"Try one sometime," Tomas said with a wry smile, "and you won't find it quite so amusing."

"It could not be any worse than a tight evening dress and high-heeled shoes," she replied with mock indignation.

Tomas patted her backside playfully. "It has been a long time since I saw you in a beautiful gown. Too long," he said. "You are a beautiful woman, Maria, and you deserve a little glamour."

"It will be fun, Tomas. Philip is so good to make up part of his life." She gave him a tender kiss.

"Are you truly happy, my love?" he asked.

"Truly," she managed before his answering kiss led to other things.

*   *   *

By the end of the week, Eduardo had the studs and cummerbund under control, and he managed get to the breakfast table on time. The shirts had each been washed more than once, but Eduardo was developing a comfort with the clothes that he had not anticipated. He seemed to stand taller when wearing the tuxedo. Whether that was from the stiffness of the clothing or his pride in seeing himself in every mirror he passed was anyone's guess.

CHAPTER FIFTEEN

Revenge

Palos Verdes Peninsula
Thanksgiving Day, November 24, 1984

"He's going to need another pair of running shoes before Christmas," Maria said as Eduardo dashed out the door Thanksgiving morning. The boy had been running since Perez bought appropriate shoes for him. He enjoyed the feeling of freedom being out of doors provided as well as the comfort of loose-fitting clothing. At least twice a week, Tomas drove the car out to the road and paced Eduardo. Running was a sport at which the boy excelled, and as he saw his times improving, it boosted his self-esteem and that showed in his overall attitude. The dog, Lobo, usually ran with Eduardo; but this morning, the boy was afraid of losing sight of his best friend in the fog. "Wait for me here, boy," he said as he prepared to leave the house. The dog whined and scratched at the back door.

The air was cold. Fog moved in quickly off the ocean in moist masses, and Eduardo marveled at how rapidly familiar shapes were obliterated by the advancing vapor. Taking his usual route, he turned to the right and onto the road at the end of the driveway. Surf beating against the base of the cliffs and a foghorn with its bass monotone created the only sounds in an eerily quiet world. The smell of the sea filled his nostrils as his hungry lungs drew in large draughts of air. The fog thickened quickly, and by the time he was one thousand feet down the road, all visual markers had disappeared.

Eduardo shivered as a sense of loneliness and disorientation almost overwhelmed him. The fog horn bellowed its woeful note every few seconds, warning passing ships off the rocks like a gigantic sea lion warning other males away from his territory. As much as Eduardo loved to run, he was anxious to finish and return to the warmth of the house this morning. He salivated as he thought of the feast Maria was preparing. By the time he opened the kitchen door, the whole house would be filled with the aroma of baking fruit pies. In a few hours, a succulent turkey filled with Maria's savory dressing would be pulled out of the oven.

The sound of an approaching engine intruded on Eduardo's thoughts, and he slowed his pace. He found the edge of the pavement with his foot and moved into the grass; the car was behind him, and no driver would see him in this fog until the car was on top of him. He moved further from the asphalt; and his jog became a walk, waiting for the car to pass. The car did not pass, and the engine noise died. He wondered if he had imagined the car, and then there was a quiet, almost imperceptible closing of a car door. On the far side of the road was a turnout where motorists sometimes stopped to admire the scenic view, but no one would be enjoying the view today.

Logic led him to believe the driver was lost in the fog and had judiciously pulled over to wait for it to lift. The fog had come in quickly and could move out just as fast, though most probably, it would linger all day. The occupants of the car might have a long wait ahead of them. Eduardo shivered again. He was damp with perspiration, and his body had cooled with the slower pace. He moved to the road and began running to warm up. A low gust of wind whipped the mist at his feet, swirling it in visible currents. One moment he was on the road, and the next moment, his right foot slipped off the asphalt, twisting his ankle. He bent and massaged the joint, relieved that it was only minimally uncomfortable. *Lucky that was just a change in terrain and not a squirrel burrow*, he thought. Squirrels holes on the ocean side of the road had turned the hill into an obstacle course. Stepping in one of those holes, especially while running, could snap an ankle. The cliff was eroded in two or three places where the tiny engineers had placed their tunnels too close together. Treading in those areas guaranteed a quick trip to the rocks three hundred feet below.

As Eduardo rose and turned toward home, he thought he heard footsteps ahead. He stopped and listened, but the mechanical sea lion barked the single note in its repertoire obliterating all other noise. A slight breeze stirred from the ocean driving the icy dampness through Eduardo's shirt. He hugged himself, slapping his arms against his chest repeatedly as he tested his ankle, springing lightly in place to gauge its ability to support his weight. He began a light jog, touching the toe of his right foot to the ground. It was OK, but he was glad he had not run his usual distance this morning. He focused on the ground not wanting to slip off the pavement and twist his left ankle. He could see just enough to assure that his leading foot came down on asphalt. Maintaining his position on the edge of the road took all of his concentration, so he did not see the two figures waiting in his path until he slammed into them.

"Whoa," he said, grabbing the larger of the two to maintain his balance. He immediately recognized the man he held as Ernesto, Miguel's second in command.

"Well, well, well, what have we here?" Ernesto asked.

"Looks like we got us a rat," the other man replied.

Ernesto grabbed Eduardo's left arm. "Luis, tell Miguel we got 'im."

"What do you want with me?" Eduardo demanded, though he wasn't as confident as his voice sounded. He tried to pull himself free, but Ernesto grabbed both his arms from behind. Eduardo could not break the man's grip.

"Nobody squeals on Miguel and lives," Ernesto said.

"I didn't squeal on anybody," Eduardo protested.

"Why don't you tell that to Miguel," Ernesto hissed, pushing the boy forward. "He got busted last week, and now it's payback time. You're gonna run yourself right over the cliff, but not until after Miguel and us guys beat the crap outta you. Your own mother won't recognize you when we're through." Eduardo thought he could see the outline of a car several feet away. A door opened and closed, and Miguel stepped through the fog. He walked to where Ernesto held the boy and grabbed Eduardo's lower jaw. Miguel squeezed until the boy's face was contorted grotesquely. Eduardo struggled harder against the assailants and shook his head to release it from Miguel's grip. He knew these hoodlums weren't lying about killing him. "I didn't give the police any names," Eduardo insisted. His mind raced. If he could not free himself, he knew he would die. Miguel took Eduardo's left arm and twisted it unmercifully, bringing the tattoo within inches of Eduardo's face.

"See this," he said, shaking Eduardo's arm. "This is the mark of Los Reyes. You became our property the moment the needle drove the ink into your skin, but you don't deserve to have it now. Before we kill you, we're gonna break your arm off and throw it over the cliff first."

"I got caught," Eduardo yelled. "I got burned with your fire bomb, and I was caught. You guys ran and left me."

"Looks like you ain't complainin' much about being caught, now are you?" Miguel said. "Is that what it took to break you, a cozy life in the biggest mansion on the hill?"

"I didn't turn you in, I swear," Eduardo said, trying again to wrench his arms free.

The fog was lifting, almost imperceptibly, and Eduardo could see the curb of the turn-out at his feet. A plan was beginning to form in his mind. He leaned against Ernesto on his right. "You're crowdin' me," he whined.

"I'm gonna do a lot more than that," Ernesto laughed, but he moved ever so slightly away from Eduardo, unaware that the boy had begun to guide their steps.

Back in the kitchen, Maria fretted as she prepared the traditional Thanksgiving turkey. Lobo was fretting too as he continued to scratch at the door and whine. *That's not like him*, she thought to herself. When Tomas appeared to refill his coffee cup, she put a voice to her concerns. "It is too foggy for that boy to be running this morning. Even Lobo thinks so."

Tomas raised his eyebrows and moved to the window. He couldn't see three feet into the yard. "It came in fast," Tomas observed. He was used to Maria's fussing, but silently, he agreed that she was right. He was sure the boy was fine, but if Eduardo got lost, he could slip over the bluff. A man of quiet determination and few words, Thomas moved into the back hall and donned his heavy coat. It wouldn't hurt to wander outside and see if he could find the boy on the road, though he would suffer tonight with his arthritis for having gone out in this cold. He grabbed a sturdy walking stick kept by the back door and headed for the door. Lobo was ready to go. "No, boy, you wait here," Tomas said as he slipped out of the house.

"Go turn the car on," Miguel said to Luis, beating his arms against himself to ward off the cold. "Nobody's gonna hear us. We got the snitch, and I doubt anyone else is stupid enough to leave the comfort of that house on a morning like this. I want this car nice and warm for the ride home."

Luis walked to the car, climbed in, and started the engine. He flicked the heater to high. The sound of the engine alerted Tomas to the presence of a car before he could see it. *Strange*, he thought as he neared the end of the driveway. *Why would a car be stopped out here unless* . . . Terror gripped him as he realized that Eduardo, unseen in the fog, must have been hit by a motorist. Ignoring the pain in his knees, Tomas raced toward the sound of the car. At the end of the driveway, he instinctively turned right. Having paced Eduardo many times, Tomas knew the boy never altered his route; but before he could turn, he realized the sound of the engine came from his left. The car had stopped before reaching the driveway. Tomas turned toward the car, but a loud scream from across the road stopped him in his tracks.

Miguel's pager went off as he clenched his fist for the first blow. Without thinking, he reached into his pocket to check the number. Eduardo took advantage of the loosened grip and wrenched his left arm free. The move was unanticipated, and Miguel dropped the pager. Eduardo swept the ground with his foot, quickly finding the device. A well-placed kick arched it into the air and to the right of the trio, landing on the grassy bluff just as he had hoped. Cursing, Miguel grabbed Eduardo's arm and moved the other two in the direction of the buzzing pager. They left the turn-out in ten quick steps. Eduardo kept his eyes on the ground. The pager went silent.

"I'm gonna kill you," Miguel yelled, drawing his fist back. Ernesto shifted his grip, holding Eduardo from behind with both hands. Instead of struggling, Eduardo bent slightly forward and then rammed his weight against Ernesto. The man staggered, trying to maintain his balance. Instinctively, he moved his left foot back to widen his base of support. As the foot came down, it sank into the opening of a squirrel hole. Ernesto fell back, pulling Eduardo with him. The force of the boy's weight against him caused Ernesto's left leg to snap midshaft. His scream split the air. Miguel, unsure of what had just transpired, lurched toward the sound of the pager, which had begun buzzing once again. Eduardo rolled off the moaning Ernesto and into the cover of the fog.

Tomas's first instinct was to walk in the direction of the scream, but he turned instead and hurried as fast as possible to the gate phone. It took only seconds for Maria to answer, and she moved quickly to alert Philip and call the police.

Once he had retrieved his pager, Miguel turned toward Ernesto. The man writhed on the ground, his foot trapped in the squirrel burrow. "Where's the kid?" he yelled.

"How should I know?" Ernesto gasped. "He got away."

"What do you mean he got away?" Miguel screamed. He grabbed Ernesto's leg and pulled until the foot was free.

"What are you doin' to me, man?" Ernesto howled. "My leg's broke."

"Shut up," Miguel said as he strained to see through the fog.

Moving away from the sound of the ocean, Eduardo avoided Ernesto's fate by staying on his hands and knees. When he felt asphalt under his hands, he stood and cautiously moved across the road. Miguel's car, still running, was ahead and to his right. He would swing clear of the car and, hopefully, Miguel too.

Tomas left the phone and walked cautiously toward the road. His heart compelled him to walk in the direction of the screams, overriding his head, which told him to wait for Perez. Crossing himself, Tomas prayed that Eduardo was all right. His pace was slowed by aching knees and hips, and he leaned on the stick as he made his way toward the road. The wind swirled fog up off the ground in clouds of varying translucence, revealing the ground in some places and obscuring it in others. Shadows began to appear in the fog. Tomas saw movement twenty feet ahead on the road. "Eduardo?" he yelled. "Is that you, Eduardo?" The figure turned. It was not Eduardo.

Seeing the slightly stooped figure, Miguel yelled a word of warning. "Stay out of this, old man. Go back to the safety of the house or you will follow Eduardo over the cliff."

"If you have hurt the boy, I will kill you," Tomas yelled.

Miguel spun to face Tomas once more. "You'll what?" He laughed.

"I will kill you," Tomas yelled, advancing toward Miguel, his stick drawn back like a lance.

"Old fool," Miguel spat, no longer amused by the old man's threats. In one smooth move, he wrenched the stick from Tomas's hand, whirled it in the air, and brought it against the old man's side, dropping him to his knees. Tomas grabbed his side and wheezed, trying to refill his empty lungs. With no effort, Miguel kicked Tomas onto his face. Placing his boot on the old man's neck, he leaned close and hissed, "It could be over just this quick." He brought the stick down over his knee, breaking it cleanly and dropped the pieces on the road.

Walking toward Ernesto's cries, which had resumed, Miguel yelled to Luis. "Move the car back a bit." He didn't bother adding, "And run over the old man lying there."

Eduardo had just reached the driveway when he heard the exchange between Tomas and Miguel. Stomach churning and heart pounding, he ran toward Tomas. "Can you move?" he whispered, leaning close to the old man's ear.

Still struggling to fill his lungs, with air, Tomas nodded. Eduardo slipped his arms under Tomas's shoulders and tugged him to his knees as the car backed up. *We're going to be run over*, the boy thought. Not knowing what else to do, he pulled Tomas back down and rolled to the left of the car. The old man moaned involuntarily. The car crept past, missing them by inches. They lay stunned, but only for seconds before Eduardo once again pulled at Tomas. "We've got to get out of here," he whispered. He pointed toward the driveway and motioned for Tomas to follow him, but the old man resisted, indicating that Eduardo should go without him. Sweeping the road with his hands, he lifted the pieces of his walking stick from the pavement. *OK, you've got your stick. Now let's get out of here*, Eduardo said to himself and motioned once again to Tomas. He thought he saw a trace of a smile on the old man's lips as Tomas pointed toward Eduardo and then jabbed his finger repeatedly toward the house. Turning, Tomas crawled toward the idling car. At that moment, Perez approached the end of the driveway in his Mercedes. Recognizing the sound of the engine, Eduardo sprinted to it and pressed his face to the glass of the passenger's window. Perez released the lock, allowing Eduardo slip inside.

"Where is Tomas?" he asked. The fact that Tomas had come out of doors in this chilly weather was unusual. That he had called the house for help was concerning. But now where was he?

Before Eduardo could explain, the old man rapped on the driver's back door.

"Hurry, hurry, lock the doors," Tomas warned, crawling in back and pulling the door shut. The fog had dispersed enough for the three to see Miguel and Luis, dragging Ernesto into their waiting car. Miguel and his henchmen had also heard the Mercedes.

"Get in," Miguel yelled as he slipped behind the wheel. "The cops are probably on their way." Miguel slammed his foot on the accelerator and made a wide U-turn. Three tires squealed, but smoke rose from the driver's rear tire, which began dragging rather than rolling. Miguel realized he did not have full control of the car as it spun in a wide arc. Not knowing what else to do, he slammed on the brakes, spinning the car in ever widening circles until it left the road and cascaded over the embankment.

Perez and Eduardo reached for their door handles simultaneously and rushed across the road just as the car exploded into flames on the rocks below. Tomas remained in the warm comfort of the car. "Must have picked up a nail," he quipped, running his thumb and forefinger along the sharp metal point at the end of his broken walking stick.

CHAPTER SIXTEEN

Thanksgiving

Palos Verdes Peninsula
Thanksgiving Day, 1984

The fog disappeared as quickly as it had come, leaving a cloudless blue sky. The winter sun, now unobstructed, warmed the peninsula and dispelled the gloom of the morning; but its rays were powerless to dispel the gloom in Eduardo's heart. Miguel's car, crushed and burning on the rocks below the cliff, had seared its image into his mind.

"The occupants were undoubtedly dead on impact," the police assured the residents of Villa Perez. A team would be sent to "retrieve the remains," and the police chaplain would notify the deceased's families.

"I don't think there will be any more trouble," Mike Lolich told Perez before leaving. "The gang was fairly small as gangs go, and I think it will fizzle out, but we'll keep an eye on the known remaining members. We had recently arrested the leader, Miguel for suspicion of narcotics trafficking, but there was not enough solid evidence to hold him. It may be that he thought Eduardo had divulged some information to us."

"It was our worst fear," Perez said. "It's reassuring to think that this problem might be resolved in spite of the horrible outcome."

"Remember, they were going to kill Eduardo," Lolich reminded him. "So don't waste too much time feeling sorry for them."

"Keep me updated, Mike, and if there is anything I can do, let me know. For our part, Eduardo will not go out alone until we feel sure that there will be no further threats to his life. He has confided in me that he had one friend in the gang, a kid named Diego. The rest, he knew only marginally."

"We'll be sure to keep an eye on them," Lolich reassured Perez. "We will have to release information to the press, of course, but there is no need to mention that Miguel and his group had any contact with Eduardo or Tomas.

We will simply say that a group of young men from Wilmington drove off the cliff in the fog this morning."

"Thank you, Mike," Perez said and breathed a sigh of relief. Perhaps everything really would be OK. "Happy Thanksgiving."

"Same to you," the chief said. "I guess you really have something to be thankful for today."

Maria's much-anticipated Thanksgiving dinner would have been a subdued feast were it not for the arrival of Philip's closest friend, John Montoya, and his family. The three Montoya children bounced into the house, laughing and chattering. It was a special treat to be taken to "Uncle Philip's" house. They were especially anxious this day to meet Eduardo. Their father had revealed very little of Eduardo's background, and their natural curiosity demanded more information. They were disappointed to find a rather morose and uncommunicative young man. And then Lobo came bouncing into the room. The children squealed with delight, and Lobo was happy to find three more children ready to scratch his belly and throw his ball.

In his study, Philip poured drinks for John and Tomas as they waited for the women to call them to dinner. "There seems to be a little tension in the air," John remarked. "Is something going on with Eduardo?"

"You will have to excuse us if we seem a bit off balance today," Perez said to his guest, and he began recounting the events of the morning. "I didn't want to say anything in front of the children. It's important for Eduardo's continued safety that he is not be connected to the accident."

"Of course," John replied. "I won't say a thing, but if they tried to harm Eduardo once, they'll surely try again."

"Mike knows who most, if not all, of the remaining gang members are. It's a small group, and he doesn't think any of them have the ability to lead the others. At any rate, he promised to keep an eye on things."

*   *   *

When they sat down to dinner, it was a feast that made Maria proud. All of the traditional American dishes plus a few Mexican specialties were set before the gathered group of friends. When Philip offered a prayer of thanksgiving, he mentioned special thanks for Eduardo and for the safety and health of everyone at the table.

Thirteen-year-old Emily Montoya sat on Eduardo's right side. She glanced sideways at him and blushed. He was cute, and his quiet demeanor made him appear very mature in her young eyes. His table manners were better than most boys she knew. She chattered constantly in spite of her mother's admonitions not to talk with food in her mouth. To Eduardo, it was annoying. When she wasn't trying to engage him in conversation, she talked to her younger siblings, Maria, her parents, or anyone who looked her way.

"You're not eating very much," she said to Eduardo.

Eduardo eyed her morosely. "Don't need you to tell me how much to eat," he replied. Philip sent him a scorching look, and the boy got the message. He turned by to Emily. Her deep blue eyes, half hidden behind glasses, held him with a steady gaze; and in spite of her chunky braces and plump form, he pasted a smiled on his face and said, "I'm sorry, Emily. My stomach's kind of upset."

Glad to pick up any thread of conversation with her handsome table partner, she replied proudly, "If you're sick, tell my dad. He's a doctor." She began a monologue informing Eduardo that she might be a doctor some day or maybe a nurse like her mother. Eduardo thought about his music lessons. As much as he disliked them, he wished he could put a tape of Vivaldi in the player right now and crank the volume to the max.

*   *   *

Mike Lolich was correct in predicting the gang's behavior following Miguel's death. Perez checked in with the school, and though he was guarded and quiet, Diego was now attending classes regularly.

As Christmas approached, Eduardo resumed his routine of running every morning. He never ran in the fog, he always took Lobo with him, and he heeded Chief Lolich's advice to be alert and aware of his surroundings. His vigilance was commendable; but it was not flawless, for every morning, as Eduardo ran, unbeknownst to him, an older man wielding a walking stick and a pair of binoculars stood warmly bundled and unobserved at the edge of the driveway, watching.

*   *   *

"A dance instructor is coming this afternoon," Perez told Eduardo two weeks before the Christmas party.

Eduardo laid his toast and butter knife down and looked at Perez. "What kind of dance are you going to learn?"

Perez's eyebrows raised, and he peered at his young charge over the top of his glasses. "I learned to dance when I was a boy," he replied. "The instructor is for you."

Eduardo frowned. "Break dancing?" he asked, knowing that Perez would not hire a break-dancing instructor.

"It is not break dancing you will be learning this afternoon," Perez informed the boy, preparing himself mentally for another battle of wills. "We'll save that for another day."

"Today, you will learn the waltz. Some of the guests will bring children to our Christmas party, and you will be expected to entertain the children and dance with the girls."

Eduardo sighed deeply. Emily would be in that group, he was sure. He had begun to realize the futility of arguing with Perez; and like it or not, in two weeks, he would be guiding Ms. Emily Montoya around the dance floor to something by the king of waltz, Johann Strauss, no doubt.

Eduardo spent the rest of the morning trying to work out algebraic equations.

"Math is a precise science," Perez told Eduardo as the boy struggled with a particularly vexing problem.

"If it is so precise, why do I get a different answer every time I work out this equation?" Eduardo scrubbed the paper with the stub of a well-used eraser.

Math had not been Perez' favorite subject either, but with patience, he guided the boy to the correct solution. "I think we both need a break," Perez said just as the sound of an approaching car signaled the arrival of Eduardo's dancing instructor.

"Kristen is Dr. Carter's daughter," Perez informed Eduardo as he introduced the young woman to her pupil. "She helps to teach dance at the community college when she herself is not in class or helping father out at his office."

Eduardo had not seen Kristen in the dentist's office, and he suddenly regretted that his return visit was not for several weeks.

Kristen smiled and reached for Eduardo's hand. "I am so happy to meet you," she said. Eduardo stared dumbly at the most beautiful girl he had ever seen. She held his hand as if waiting for a response from him.

"Uh, hello," he stammered.

Perez glanced at the boy, inwardly coaxing him to say more.

As if he heard the unspoken urgings, Eduardo added, "I'm happy to meet you too. Thank you very much for coming. I don't know anything about dancing."

"Well, that's about to change," Kristen giggled. "Now I think we had better get started. We only have a short time before the party."

Perez led teacher and pupil into the living room. The carpet had been rolled back to expose the hardwood floor. An appropriate tape was put in the tape player, and the instruction began.

"Since you are the man, you must lead," Kristen said. "Hold my right hand like this and put your right hand on my back."

"How can I lead you if I don't know how to dance?" Eduardo asked.

Kristen giggled her soft tinklelike laugh. "That's why I'm here. I'll tell you and show you what to do. Now listen to the beat of the music." Standing in place, she bobbed up and down until Eduardo was mimicking her movements in time with the music. "Watch my feet now," she said as she began moving them rhythmically. Eduardo did his best to copy in reverse what Kristen was doing. "Glide, Eduardo, glide," Kristen coaxed as they danced around the room.

Eduardo made his best effort to glide, but his legs felt like stiff boards, and his heart pounded with such force he could hear the whoosh in his head. He was uncomfortably conscious of perspiration beading up in his hands; and, becoming aware of it, it worsened with each passing second. He wanted to run from the room, and yet he wanted never to move from Kristen's light embrace. What a strange sensation. He was excited and confused, and he never wanted these feelings to leave him.

"Pay attention, Eduardo," Kristen said, looking directly at him. Her eyes were blue like the sky. She was taller than Eduardo, with long slender legs capable of sweeping strides that he was able to match in a much less graceful fashion. "You're doing well," she encouraged, giving him a smile.

Eduardo blushed, and sensing the warmth on his cheeks, the color deepened. He glanced down, hoping to hide his embarrassment, but Kristen removed her left hand from his shoulder and lifted his chin gently. "You've got to keep your head up," Kristen warned, laughing, "or you'll run me right into the table."

Eduardo glanced at the table inches from Kristen's back and managed to move her far enough from its presence to avoid any accidents. He struggled to get his mind off the closeness of her body and attend to his footwork, but it was not easy. His eventual success was more likely because of some innate ability rather than his purposeful attention to the instruction she gave.

"It is wonderful, the things a beautiful young woman can accomplish," Perez said to Tomas who had just come into the hall with boxes of Christmas decorations.

Tomas raised his eyebrows, and a smile spread across his weathered face. "Perhaps she knows algebra," he suggested.

Perez cast an appreciative glance at the old man and laughed.

By the end of two hours, Eduardo had relaxed enough to produce a smile and a passable glide without looking down at his feet. Kristen praised him and declared the lesson to be over for the day. The discrete change in Eduardo's expression went unnoticed by Kristen, but Perez saw a shadow pass across the boy's face.

"Do you teach the tango, Kristen?" Perez asked as he helped her into her jacket.

"I teach all the Latin dances," she smiled. "But they take more than one lesson, even with a disciplined student like Eduardo."

"I think we would like to engage you for a series of lessons then," Perez said.

Eduardo bit his lip to keep from shouting his enthusiastic approval, and with a quick hug of her handsome young pupil, Kristen was out the door.

*　　*　　*

Eduardo had three additional lessons before the party, and he became more comfortable with the closeness of Kristen as they worked on the tango.

"This is a dance of passion and tragic love," she said. "It was developed in the late nineteenth century in Buenos Aires. At first it was not accepted in high society because of the close body contact, but over the years, it was adapted to people's tastes and became quite popular. It tells a story of love and rejection. The dancers come together in a passionate embrace and then push each other away."

"Why would they do that?" Eduardo asked.

"Love can be a complicated thing," She replied. "Perhaps a man loves a woman, but she does not love him back in the same way. Maybe she likes him, but she doesn't really love him."

"If someone loves you, why wouldn't you love them back?" Eduardo demanded.

"Well, maybe she loves someone else," Kristen giggled.

Eduardo didn't think it was funny. "Then she shouldn't be dancing with him. He thinks she loves him because she's dancing with him."

Kristen saw the confusion on his face. "Maybe he hopes that if he dances with her, he can make her fall in love with him. So he pulls her to him, and she pushes away. Oh, maybe you'll understand it when you get a little older," she said.

"I'll never understand that no matter how old I get," he replied.

They worked on Eduardo's steps and posture for an hour. He was sweating when they finished. "You're a natural," Kristen said when they finished a particularly strenuous passage. "Your footwork is exceptional for a beginning student." She hugged Eduardo and gave him a light kiss on the cheek. "I may have to bring you to class to help me out," she laughed.

Eduardo's hand went to his cheek, and he felt the spot where the kiss had been placed. Suddenly, he felt a little taller, a little older.

That night, Eduardo dreamed of Kristen; and as they danced the tango, each time she moved away, he pulled her back. Looking deeply into her eyes, he was convinced that she did not really want to draw away from him. When the dream-dance was finished, she allowed him to pull her back into his arms and hold her tight. "I love you," he said, and after echoing his words, she drew his face to hers and kissed him deeply. "The tango is not for us," he whispered. "We must always dance the waltz." Kristen drew back slightly, smiled, and nodded her agreement.

CHAPTER SEVENTEEN

The Christmas Party

Villa Perez
December 17, 1984

The day of the party arrived. Eduardo walked from room to room in the villa, entranced by glass ornaments, garlands, poinsettias, and candles that had been carefully arranged in anticipation of the evening ahead. A ten-foot Grand Fir adorned with colorful glass balls and twinkling white lights stood in the front hall, its aroma scenting the air around it and wafting gently through the adjoining rooms. Even the guest bathrooms had special towels, candles, and floral arrangements. In the alcove off the front hall, a barman arranged glasses on a linen-covered table in preparation for thirsty guests.

Eduardo lingered to study the various bottles behind the bar. On the floor, he saw cases of cola and determined that at least one of those cans would be his this evening. He'd only had one soda since coming to the villa because Philip Perez said soda was bad for a growing boy's bones. The dining room doors were shut, but Eduardo slid them apart just enough to view the sumptuous fare being laid out under silver candelabra and miniature topiary trees. Round linen-covered tables and linen-draped chairs had been placed in the family room. French doors on the back side of the room were open, and the seating spilled out onto the used brick surface of the terrace. A Mariachi band assembled on the terrace under heaters on tall stands that had been set up for the comfort of ladies likely to arrive in bare-shouldered gowns. A string ensemble was scheduled to replace the Mariachi's after dinner to provide music for waltzing, an event he anticipated with mixed feelings. He would be obliged to dance with Emily Montoya at least once; but if he was lucky, for the remaining dances, he would have his arms around Kristen. Luminaries lined the garden's walkways, lighting the paths just enough for a romantic stroll in the moonlight. Eduardo walked to the front of the house as cars began arriving.

Uniformed young parking attendants efficiently escorted guests from their cars and whisked the vehicles to a small parking area removed from the house. Eduardo checked his tuxedoed image in a gilded mirror and felt very grown up. He adjusted his tie and dutifully took his place at Philip Perez's side ready to greet their guests.

Emily Montoya arrived a few minutes past seven with her parents. Eduardo greeted her formally and hoped she would find something or someone besides himself to occupy her time. She wandered to the bar with her parents and ordered a soda. Eduardo licked his dry lips and shifted his weight from foot to foot, worrying that the sodas would be gone before he got to the bar. In his head he knew that the supplies were ample, but the little child inside agonized over each soft drink he watched being poured. He remembered the sugary taste of his favorite drink, but remembering was not the same as having.

As Eduardo watched the disappearing figure of Emily, cola in hand, a familiar voice rang from the doorway. He spun around to see Kristen Carter approaching. In less than one second, the party had turned from drudgery to delight. Eduardo turned quickly to peer in the mirror one more time. He pushed down a stray lock of hair, straightened his tie, and displayed his brightest smile.

Phillip Perez held the girl at arm's length in total admiration. "That is an exquisite dress, my dear," he said. "You look lovely."

"You like it, Uncle Philip?" she asked with obvious pleasure. "It's a Pepa Pombo that Andrew brought me from Mexico City."

"Andrew," Perez said to the young man standing behind Kristen. "You have excellent taste, and not just in haute couture."

Giggling, Kristen turned to Eduardo, kissing him on each cheek and informing him she expected a dance. Eduardo thanked her and studied the dress. Made from long strips of knit golden ribbon sewn together and clinging ever so slightly to the slender form it encased, it was elegant and unique.

"Hello," said Andrew, taking Eduardo's hand. "I am Kristen's friend, Andrew."

"We're happy you can be here," Eduardo said, not sure he meant that. In fact, he knew he did not mean it as Andrew slipped his arm around Kristen and the two moved to the bar. Eduardo had fantasized about this woman every day since he met her, and now another man stood beside her as he had envisioned himself doing. Eduardo's no longer bright smile suddenly looked pasted in place. He remained at his post, but his attention was elsewhere;

and every few minutes he strained to see if Kristen was nearby. Briefly, from time to time, he caught a glimpse of her head bobbing in the crowd, the shiny blonde hair pulled into a sleek, sophisticated knot. She was laughing when he chanced to see her face, and always, Andrew stood at her side.

Emily reappeared as the last guests arrived. "Do you want to hear the Mariachi's?" she asked.

Eduardo craned his neck, looking in vain for Kristen. Realizing she too might be on the terrace, he said, "Sure, let's go." He walked past the bar, forgetting the coveted soda.

The band was good, and guests moved appreciatively to the rhythm of the music. On any other day, Eduardo would have sat enthralled, enjoying this music he thought worth listening to, but his mind was far removed from music tonight. He saw a golden head directly in front of the band and strained to see if it belonged to Kristen just as Perez appeared at his elbow.

"Are you enjoying this?" Perez asked, putting an affectionate arm around the boy.

Eduardo swung around startled by the intrusion on his thoughts. "What?" he managed.

"The music, you must be enjoying it. You were concentrating quite intently."

"Yes, the music," Eduardo said. "It's nice."

Perez gave the boy a strange look before his attention was drawn away by a group of flirtatious bejeweled middle-aged women who felt they "really must have Philip's opinion" on their latest fundraising project. Would he allow them to host a tea at the villa? they wondered, batting heavily mascaraed eyelashes.

Eduardo quickly returned his attention to the blonde head in front of the band, but it was gone. He scanned the crowd, anxious to find Kristen, but she was nowhere to be seen on the terrace. He had forgotten Emily who stood tenaciously at his side.

"There are rabbits in the garden," Emily said to Eduardo.

"Huh," Eduardo replied, only half listening.

"Rabbits, there are little rabbits in the garden. They come out at night. Have you seen them?"

"How do you know there are rabbits out there?" Eduardo asked, somewhat skeptically.

"Tomas feeds them. He showed me one evening. Hasn't he showed them to you?"

Eduardo looked at Emily and said nothing. Tomas had not shown him the rabbits, but he wasn't going to reveal that to Emily Montoya.

"Come on," she said. "If we're quiet, we might see them."

Eduardo was getting irritated. "Why don't you go find them?" he said. "I see them all the time."

Emily dropped her head and said nothing. Eduardo glanced at her out of the corner of his eye. He wanted Emily to get lost, and he might just as well have told her so. Shame flooded his heart for the coldness of his remark. How many times had he felt rejected? How many times had he repeated to himself, "I'll never do that to anyone," and yet he had just done it to this girl?

"I'm sorry, Emily," he said. "I was looking for someone, but I can look after we see the rabbits." She smiled, her braces catching the glint of the twinkle lights overhead. "Come on," he called as he headed toward the lighted path. His stride was long and quick. Emily had to skip to keep up with him.

"I bet the music has scared them," Emily said after ten minutes of hunting.

"They probably went back by the wall. Let's take a look there before we give up."

Emily hesitated. "It's too dark back there. It scares me."

"Don't be afraid, Emily," Eduardo said, feeling rather brave in the face of her apprehension. "I won't let anything happen to you."

Emily grasped the tail of his jacket and smiled. She was unnerved at the thought of moving into the darkened garden, but she felt an element of excitement at the thought of being there with Eduardo. Had Eduardo been more attentive, he would have noticed her body leaning lightly against his own, but even Emily was unaware that her heart was beating slightly faster. Stealthily, they crept across the lawn toward the back wall, Emily's hand securely grasping Eduardo's jacket.

"That's a good place for them to hide," Eduardo whispered, pointing toward a berm planted with a large magnolia and clusters of lilies. As the rabbit hunters made their way slowly toward the mound of earth, a small rabbit hopped from behind a lily, lifted its front feet off the ground, and sniffed. "Look," Eduardo whispered, pointing toward the bunny. The children approached cautiously; but the rabbit, sensing them, scampered back into the bushes.

"Oh," Emily breathed, "it's so small I could hold it in one hand."

Eduardo parted the lilies, hoping to find the little creature. There were no rabbits to be seen, but soft rustlings in the undergrowth signaled their presence. "They're here somewhere," he whispered, planting a black leather dress shoe in the soft soil of the flower bed. Quietly, he bent over and began poking beneath the plants, methodically searching out the elusive little squatters in Perez's garden.

Eduardo was completely absorbed in the pursuit of the rabbits when a woman's squeal on the other side of the berm alerted him and his companion that they were not alone.

In the dim moonlight, Eduardo could see Emily's hand go to her mouth. Her eyes were wide with fear. Eduardo grabbed her free hand and pulled her down into the cover of the bushes. They listened intently for further sounds, and hearing none, they crept quietly to the end of the berm. Peering around the shrubbery, they saw two forms locked in a passionate embrace. A shaft of moonlight rested upon the couple, a tall young man in black tuxedo and a slender young woman in a gown of gold.

Eduardo wanted to yell at them to stop. He wanted to punch the young man. He wanted to cry. But instead, he turned, still holding Emily's hand, and pulled her toward the house. "Let's get out of here," he told the grinning girl.

The rest of the evening passed in a blur for Eduardo. He was poor company for Emily who thought the episode in the garden was "soooo romantic." She was sufficiently enraptured by the scene that she did not immediately recognize Eduardo's change of demeanor. When she did notice, she thought maybe she was a fault. She began asking herself what she had done to put her companion in such a gloomy mood. Her need to know led to a series of questions that she posed to Eduardo.

Eduardo answered without engaging in conversation. "Nothing," he replied to her repeated "What's wrong?" They sat quietly at their assigned table through dinner, and Emily watched from the corner of her eye as Eduardo pushed the food around his plate.

The woman on Eduardo's left made a feeble attempt to coax a few words from him but soon gave up, dismissing his gloom as a typical teenage response to being invited to an adult party.

Tomas had noticed too and was keeping a watchful eye on Eduardo. The boy had never previously failed to empty his plate, but each course from melon and prosciutto to crusted rack of lamb was being returned uneaten. Tomas studied the boy's face. There was no anger or petulance. *No,* Tomas mused, *the boy looked hurt.* Emily was a nice little girl. He was sure she had not caused Eduardo any pain. There were a few wealthy couples at the party who did not understand why Perez had brought Eduardo in to his home. It was possible the boy had overheard an unkind comment. Tomas studied the plump matron next to Eduardo. He did not know her well; but she looked offensive, her silver blue hair pinned and lacquered firmly in place, her back rigid and turned toward Eduardo. Tomorrow, he would talk to Philip. Tonight, he would talk with Maria. *If that woman has hurt the boy, I hope Philip does not invite her back into this house,* he thought.

As Tomas continued to watch the boy, he noticed Eduardo glancing in Kristen Carter's direction frequently. She was especially radiant this evening. Young Andrew Morgan, sitting on her left, leaned close and whispered in her ear. She blushed, dipped her head, and smiled. She was obviously happy, and her smile seemed to hold some lovely secret.

Tomas remembered Eduardo's reaction to his attractive dance instructor at their first meeting. He turned his attention once again to the boy whose woebegone look was now fixated on Kristen. *Ah, one of the hard lessons of life,* Tomas said to himself. *This is a wound of the heart.* He felt suddenly guilty for having suspected the elderly matron.

As dessert and champagne were set before the diners, Dr. Carter rose from his chair and asked for everyone's attention. "Philip has graciously allowed my family to share the spotlight with him and Eduardo this evening." Carter paused and lifted his glass in the direction of Perez and Eduardo in turn. "My wife and I have a very happy announcement to make. As you all know, Andrew has returned from his post at the embassy in Mexico for some additional training. He tells me"—and here Dr. Carter turned and smiled at Kristen and Andrew—"that he would like to take Kristen with him when he returns in the spring." Oohs and ahhs arose from the table. "And so Eileen and I are very pleased this evening to announce the engagement of our daughter Kristen to Mr. Andrew Morgan."

Applause erupted from the tables followed by excited chatter. There were only two people who were not smiling, Eduardo and Tomas. Tomas shared in the good wishes and congratulations of everyone at the party, but his immediate concern was for the young man who was now rising from the table.

"Excuse me," Eduardo said to Emily, his voice cracking. "I am very sorry to leave, but I have a terrible"—and here he paused—"a terrible toothache." He put his hand to his jaw and rushed from the room.

Emily rose and went directly to Dr. Carter. As soon as dessert was finished and guests had been directed to the living room and terrace for cordials, cigars, and more music, the dentist, with Philip in tow, went to Eduardo's room.

"He had one small cavity when I checked him a couple of months ago," Carter said as they ascended the stairs. "I planned to take care of it after the holidays."

Tomas saw the two men leave, concern on their faces. He handed his glass to a server and followed. When he reached Eduardo's room, the dentist, with a flashlight in hand, was searching in vain for the source of Eduardo's distress.

"The gum and tooth he's pointing to look fine," he reported to Philip, shining the light on the tooth Eduardo indicated. Noting Eduardo's tear-stained face and wet pillow, he added, "But it is obviously causing him a great deal of pain,"

Tomas caught Philip's eye from the doorway and cupped his hands over his heart.

Perez stared at Tomas in confusion. Tomas pointed to his own ring finger, then to Dr. Carter, and finally clutched is heart again. It took Philip only seconds to understand his insightful old friend's message. He shook his head in acknowledgment, and Tomas slipped away as quietly as he had come.

"Perhaps we should give him an anti-inflammatory and let him sleep," Philip suggested.

"Well, frankly, I don't know what else to do," Carter replied.

"Go ahead and rejoin your family," Philip told the dentist. "I'll have Tomas bring the medicine and help Eduardo out of his tuxedo."

"If it persists tomorrow, call me," Dr. Carter instructed. "We'll open the office and get an X-ray."

Philip sat on the edge of Eduardo's bed and stroked the boy's head. "It is not your tooth that hurts, is it?" he asked.

Eduardo did not respond immediately, but new tears escaped his tightly shut eyes.

Philip's hand moved to Eduardo's back. "You know, she did not hurt you on purpose."

Eduardo rolled over and opened his eyes. "How did you know?" he asked. He had never said a word about his feelings for Kristen.

"What young man would not fall in love with her? There are probably a few more men downstairs tonight who wish they could have left the room as you did."

Eduardo quietly considered what Perez said.

Philip placed his hands on the boy's shoulders and looked directly into the pain-filled eyes. "It will get better, Eduardo," he said. "Trust me on this."

Eduardo raised his arms and embraced his mentor, and suddenly, he was not the only one with tear-filled eyes.

CHAPTER EIGHTEEN

A Friend Poses a Puzzle

Palos Verdes Peninsula
January 1985

"Hello, Angie," Dr. Carter said when the dental office opened after New Year's Day. "We're glad to have you here for your internship. This is my daughter, Kristen. Kristen helps me out when she is not in class or spending my money on wedding preparations." He turned to give his daughter a smile. "My regular hygienist is ill today, so Kristen will give you a tour of the office and help you get the feel of things." He turned to his daughter. "When you're through, Kristen, bring Angie back to my office. I'll discuss what my expectations are and what she can expect of us during her internship."

The day was heavily booked. Since the regular hygienist was ill, her appointments had been rescheduled. The hours whizzed by as Angie helped Dr. Carter at the patient's chair. "You've done quite well today," he told her as they closed up the office. "You managed to keep up with me. Marla called and said she's better, so you'll spend the day with her tomorrow. She'll take the first two patients and then observe as you take the next ones. Are you up for that?"

"That's exactly what I've been preparing for, sir," Angie replied.

"Good girl. The school gave you a very high recommendation. I'm expecting great things."

"She seems like a really nice girl," Carter told his daughter that night at dinner.

"I really liked her," Kristen replied. "Maybe I'll ask her out to lunch some afternoon when we're having a slow day.

"When does that ever happen?" He laughed.

Angie was pleasantly surprised a few days later when she found Eduardo sitting in her chair at the end of a long day. "Angie," he shouted when the girl walked into the exam room. He jumped from the chair to give her a hug. "I've missed you. What are you doing here?"

She ruffled his hair and planted a kiss on his cheek. "I've missed you too, Eduardo. I finished my studies, and I'm doing an internship here in Dr. Carter's office. How are you doing?" She looked him up and down and decided she really didn't even need to ask. He looked like he'd grown a bit; he was nicely dressed, but even more important, he seemed happy.

"I'm great, Angie. I got away from that gang, and I've been studying really hard. I learned to dance." He laughed as Kristen poked her head in and waved. "How are you, Angie?" he asked suddenly serious. "Are you OK? Is Ramon being nice to you?"

"Ramon and I are finished," she said. "I haven't been over there for weeks."

"I'm glad, Angie. He isn't good enough for you."

She smiled a kind of sad wistful smile and placed a drape over his chest. "I've got a schedule to keep up with." She winked. "What do you say we make a date to go out for an ice cream sometime?"

"What's this?" a voice said from the door. Philip Perez stood smiling at the pair. "Is this young man getting fresh with the hygienist?"

"This is Angie," Eduardo said. "She used to date my cousin Ramon."

Philip raised his eyebrows, thinking this might not be a good encounter. "We're not seeing each other anymore," Angie said, "not since I found out what kind of guy he is."

"Angie was the only person who was nice to me until I met you," Eduardo said.

Philip tilted his head and smiled. "Eduardo and I are going out for pizza when he's finished here, Angie. Kristen's parents have an engagement this evening, so I've invited her to come along. Would you like to join us?"

Angie grinned and gave Eduardo a squeeze. "I'd love to," she responded.

They ate at a little pizza parlor near the mall. "Kristen taught me to dance," Eduardo beamed. "She's promised to save a dance for me at her wedding, and we're going to do a tango." He held one hand above his head and the other at his waist and snapped his fingers.

"Take a picture," Angie said, "because I'd love to see this."

"I'm even going to be wearing a tuxedo," Eduardo informed her.

"Well, then I really want to see," she laughed.

"Dr. Carter says you're doing a very good job at the office," Perez commented.

"I love the work," Angie replied. "Everyone has been so helpful. Dr. Carter is a great dentist." Turning to Kristen, she continued, "The staff are the best."

Philip and Kristen's eyes met, and they smiled a knowing smile. "Well, I've got dance class tonight," Kristen said, rising. "Thanks for the pizza, Uncle Philip."

"Sounds like fun," Angie said, clearing up their table.

Kristen cocked her head to the side and looked at Angie. "Why don't you come along?"

"Do you think I could?"

"Yeah. It'll be fun, but prepare for a workout. Good thing you're wearing comfortable clothes." The girls continued talking as they walked to the parking lot.

"I've missed Angie," Eduardo said wistfully as the girls walked away.

"Then we will have her over sometime," Philip said.

"Really?"

"Really." Perez smiled.

It was two weeks before Philip had a clear schedule. Remembering his promise to invite Angie for dinner, he consulted with Maria and then suggested that Eduardo invite her over the following evening. "I hope she doesn't have any trouble finding way in this fog," Eduardo said as he stood at the window and watched it roll in off the ocean.

"It's not too heavy yet," Philip said, glancing up from his newspaper. "Didn't you say Kristen drew a map for her?"

"Yes, I guess she won't have any trouble."

"Tell me a little bit about her while we wait," Philip suggested, noting the boy's anxiousness. "How did she meet your cousins?"

"My cousins do farm work and dig ditches, things like that," Eduardo started.

"Day labor," Philip interjected.

"Yeah, I mean yes. They were talking about work one night and trying to figure out how they could get better paying jobs. Ramon said he was going to find a girl and get married. Then he could get American citizenship. He said with citizenship, he could get a job on the docks, you know, something that would pay him more money. The girls like Ramon because he's good-looking and knows how to talk to them."

"I see," said Philip

"He started hanging around the college because he said that's where the chicks were. I guess Angie fell for him. I'm just glad she's not seeing him anymore."

"What happened?"

"I don't know. They broke up after I came here." The buzzer rang for the front gate, and Eduardo ran to release the lock. He watched from the windows flanking the door as Angie pulled up in front of the house. "Angie," he said, flinging the door wide.

"Hey, buddy," she said, hugging him and kissing his cheek. She had a large round tin in her hand, which she gave to Philip, who had joined Eduardo at the door. "My mom sent some cookies."

Philip peeked under the cover. "Mexican wedding cakes," he exclaimed. "They're one of my favorites."

"I would have made them myself," she apologized," but I've been so busy with the internship."

"I'm glad you're enjoying it so much." Philip led her into the living room, which contained two sitting areas, one in the rear comprised of chairs and small tables gathered near a grand piano and one closer to the windows where Philip directed the girl.

She glanced about the room. A fire had been lit in the stone fireplace on the far wall, and its warmth radiated to the couch she settled into. "Dr. Carter is so nice to the staff. When Kristen leaves, I'll really miss her."

Maria and Tomas appeared from the kitchen with a platter of hors oeuvres and a tray of drinks. "Angie, I would like to introduce you to Tomas and Maria," Eduardo said, rising to relieve Maria off her load. "They are Señor Perez's good friends, and they live here too. Tomas and Maria, this is Angie Dominguez."

"Dominguez," Tomas observed. "That was one of the original families to settle in this area."

"You know California history," Angie said. "Yes, my father descended from that family. I wish we owned all the land they once held." She laughed as she took a glass of white wine. The conversation soon turned to Eduardo. "Are you going to school? Are you in any danger from the gang?"

Eduardo recounted the events of the past Thanksgiving morning and then gave her a brief synopsis of his scholastic pursuits.

"Wow," she said, "I'm really impressed."

"I'm glad you're not seeing Ramon anymore," he said.

"We had an argument shortly after you left." She looked at Philip as if she might say more, but she dropped her eyes and shifted in her chair.

"You're too good for him, Angie," Eduardo replied.

Sensing some discomfort in the recent turn of conversation, Maria suggested that Eduardo help her with a few last things in the kitchen while Philip gave Angie a tour of the house.

"I'm learning to cook too," Eduardo crowed as he followed Maria out of the room.

"Well, you've seen the living room," Philip said. "It's probably one of the best rooms in the house for a view." He led her from the gold and maroon striped sofas to the drapery framed front window where they looked out over a fog-blanketed ocean. Catalina is right over there," he said, pointing. "When the fog dissipates, we can see it." Philip followed her glance to a telescope situated near the window. "It's not only fun looking at passing ships," he said, "we can see a lot of stars on clear nights too." He moved to the door. "My office is right here across the hall. Not much to look at, but one of these days, I'll get around to decorating it properly." Behind the office was the dining room, which was set with fine china for dinner. Further back, Maria and Eduardo were plating salad in the kitchen.

"You'd better finish the tour, Philip. We're about to set things on the table," Maria warned.

"Just give me another second, Maria, and we'll be done with the first floor." Philip led the girl to a large room behind the living room. "We call this our family room," he said. Here there were also two seating areas. The closest faced a stone fireplace identical to the one in the living room and a projection screen television that sat in the corner. Shelves lined the walls, providing storage space for books, videos, recordings, and games. The second seating area consisted of game tables and chairs and was near a set of glass French doors that led to a terrace. "There's a guest bathroom over there," Philip said, pointing to a door at the rear of the room, "and another off the front hall." He smiled. "Well, I suppose Eduardo will want to show you his room after dinner, and then we can take a stroll outside. The gardens are nice even in February." He turned to lead her back to the dining room when she placed a hand on his arm.

"Dr. Perez, may I have a private word with you after dinner?"

"Of course," he said, somewhat puzzled. She smiled and walked ahead of him to join the others.

"Angie," Eduardo said, helping himself to a third tamale, "I used to think you were the best cook in the world. Then I came here and tasted Maria's food."

"Eduardo," Maria chided, "you will make her feel bad."

"That's OK." Angie laughed. "I know world-class tamales when I taste them, and yours just might beat my mother's in a cook off."

Philip liked the girl. She was honest and unassuming, but he wondered what she needed to discuss with him. *Well*, he thought, *I guess I'll find out later.*

"Would you like dessert now," Maria asked, rising to clear the plates, "or would you like to have it later?"

"It's still light enough for Angie to see a bit of the back garden," Philip said. "Why don't I show it to her and then we can settle in the family room for coffee and dessert?"

Eduardo really wanted to join them, but a stern look from Perez informed him that he needed to help clear the table. "I'll see you outside," he told Angie, grabbing a stack of plates and hurrying into the kitchen.

Philip grabbed Angie's jacket from the front hall and led her through the French doors to the terrace. Garden lights shined up into the trees at the perimeter of the yard. To the left lay the swimming pool, its underwater lights illuminating blue tiles that lined its walls. The fog lay in patches overhead, and Angie shivered in spite of her jacket.

"Eduardo's helping with the dishes," Philip said. "But if I know him, he won't be long. Did you have something you wanted to discuss with me?"

"Yes," she said. "Shortly after Eduardo ran away, I was at the apartment. Ramon and the others were discussing the whole situation. They were glad to be rid of Eduardo, but they were jealous that he had ended up here. Julio said he hoped you would beat Eduardo and work him very hard. I asked them why they were so mean to him, and then Carlos said something very strange."

"Go on."

Angie closed her eyes and tilted her head back as if trying to remember the exact words that had been spoken. "He said, 'I wish Abuela had sent him back to his father.'"

"Sent him back?" Philip said, astonished. "How could she send him back? His parents died. Do you think he meant he wished that Eduardo had died too?"

"When I questioned them, they laughed. Martin said something about his grandmother taking advantage of a certain situation that allowed her to keep Eduardo at his grandfather's house. When I said I didn't understand, Ramon told me not to try, and he pretty much shut the conversation off. He told me we would never talk about it again."

"So what you are telling me is that you think Eduardo's father may be alive."

"I think that is a possibility."

"Have you said anything to Eduardo about this?"

"No! I really didn't have the chance, and even if I did, I wouldn't want to give him false hope. Who knows, maybe his father didn't want him."

Philip mulled this over in his mind. "I know Eduardo and his grandfather were very close. I would think if the father was alive, the grandfather would have told Eduardo unless the man was not fit to care for the boy."

"I just thought I should—"

"Angie, want to see my room?" Eduardo came bouncing out onto the terrace.

"Sure," she said, glancing one last time at Philip.

"Thanks," he mouthed before she turned to go inside with the boy.

"Do you think we should investigate to find out if the father is alive?" Tomas asked when Philip related the conversation to him that night.

"Perhaps," Philip said. "But even if he is alive, he has been away from the boy so long. His sudden reappearance might create more issues than the boy could handle right now."

"You make a good point," Tomas replied. "We do not even know what kind of man he might be. If he was cruel like Eduardo's cousins, the boy would be better off without him."

"If he is alive, why wouldn't he make himself known to Eduardo unless he did not want him?" Philip searched his own soul and wondered how that could possibly be. "I will contact Marco down in Mexico City and see if he can snoop around a little."

"I think that is a good idea," Tomas replied. "If there has been a missing person's report for a boy Eduardo's age, Marco will locate it. We can go from there."

"Do you know the parent's names?" Marco asked from his desk at the office of Marco Ramirez, Investigador.

"No, we only know the boy's name."

"Well, you know, he could be living under a name other than the one registered at his birth," the investigator told his old friend.

"I hadn't thought about that. Well, just snoop around and see if anyone has put in a missing persons report for Eduardo Rodriguez. It could go back fourteen or fifteen years."

"I'll let you know if anything turns up, my friend."

"Thanks, Marco. I'll wait to hear from you."

The call from Marco came a month later. There had been no missing persons report filed for a child by the name of Eduardo Rodriguez. Marco had gone back sixteen years just to be sure. "Do you want me to pay his grandfather a visit?"

"No," Philip replied, although he had a decidedly unsettled feeling about it. "Perhaps at some point in the future, but I don't think it is really in the boy's best interest at this time."

"Am I being selfish?" Philip asked Tomas that evening. "I know what I would do if I was in Eduardo's father's shoes. I would stop at nothing to find him."

"First of all, we do not know for certain that the father is alive. If he is alive, why isn't he looking for his son? You said yourself that no missing person's reports have been filed."

"I just keep thinking what I would want if I was his father."

"But you are not his father," Tomas said.

CHAPTER NINETEEN

Kristen and Andrew's Wedding

Palos Verdes Peninsula
May 18, 1985

Although Eduardo did not at first believe Perez's reassurances, his feelings of loss regarding Kristen faded rather quickly. And such is the resilience of youth that his heart was fully mended in time to enjoy a tango with Kristen at her wedding reception the following spring. It was a beautiful day in every way. The sun shone brightly, and the roses and jacaranda trees were in bloom. Eduardo sang as he showered following his morning run. The wedding was at four in the afternoon, hours away; but he wanted to take his time dressing and look his best for that special dance he was anticipating.

Philip, Tomas, Maria, and Eduardo arrived at the church thirty minutes prior to the start of the ceremony; and a large number of guests were already present. "The bride's family and friends are seated on the left," Perez whispered to Eduardo when they entered the foyer, "and the groom's family and friends are seated on the right. An usher will offer Maria his arm and lead her down the outside aisle. Tomas, you and I will follow them."

The church was resplendent with roses, lilies, orchids, and hydrangeas. Eduardo breathed their fragrance as he took his sear between Tomas and Philip. The Montoya family had already been seated in the pew ahead of Eduardo, and Emily turned to give him a big grin. "I'll see you at the reception," she said in a loud stage whisper. Her mother brought the girl to attention with a yank of the arm, and Emily reluctantly turned to face a string quartet playing musical selections that were now familiar to Eduardo.

At precisely 4:00 p.m., Andrew entered the sanctuary with the minister and groomsmen. They took their places near the altar, and the strings began playing Pachelbel's Canon. Four young women in gowns of creamy yellow walked slowly down the center aisle. As the last bridesmaid reached the altar, the music increased in volume and Kristen's mother stood. The congregation followed Mrs. Carter's lead as two large doors in the back of the sanctuary opened, revealing Kristen and her proud father. Eduardo gasped. The bride was dressed in a white silk strapless gown with beaded bodice. She had been transformed from beautiful to angelic. As Kristen passed Eduardo's pew, he noted her smile, barely perceptible through the thin veil covering her face. A three-foot train trailed behind her, and Eduardo thought she looked like a princess. Slowly, on the arm of her father, Kristen made her way to the altar where she met a beaming Andrew and exchanged marriage vows with him.

The reception was held in the church hall. The new Mr. and Mrs. Morgan and their parents received their guests in the courtyard patio just outside the hall. Eduardo followed Philip to the reception line, anxious to offer congratulations to the new couple and remind Kristen of the promised dance.

Inside the reception hall, Eduardo found his name card next to Emily's at a table reserved for the Montoya and Perez families. "I hope your tooth is OK today," Emily said when Eduardo took his seat, "because you still own me a dance." Eduardo noticed she had slimmed down a lot, but the attitude did nothing for her feminine appeal.

If I give you a dance, will you never pester me again? Eduardo wanted to say. He felt a kick under the table coming from the direction of Perez, so he smiled and said, "I'm fine, and thank you for your concern." Apparently, Emily had been kicked also, because she let out a yelp and shot a surprised look at her sweetly smiling mother.

Emily got her dance and an extra one too. She was actually a good dancer, and together they looked "so cute" that Emily's mother took several pictures of the young couple.

Kristen had invited her father's new dental hygienist to the wedding and placed her at the Perez-Montoya table, rounding it out to an even eight people. It was evident from the easy banter passing between Angie and Eduardo that they were friends. Emily was not very pleased, and when the young usher led Angie to the dance floor, the pouting fourteen-year-old turned to her mother hissing, "Who is she?"

"That's Dr. Carter's new hygienist."

"Well, she looks too old for Eduardo."

The band began a waltz. Eduardo took Angie's right hand in his left and placed his own right hand on her waist. "You've lost weight," he said before he had even thought out his comment.

Angie laughed to his relief. "Thanks for noticing. Kristen got me involved in dance classes, and I've never worked out so hard in my life."

"You look nice," Eduardo commented. *She really did look pretty,* he thought. *Something about her smile, and the light touch of makeup didn't hurt one bit.*

"You look pretty handsome yourself," she replied.

Kristen eventually freed herself from the other guests long enough for the promised tango with Eduardo. They performed it so well that everyone else left the floor and watched. When the music ended, the bride and her usher stood laughing, and nearly out of breath, alone in the middle of the dance floor. Applause went up around the room.

"You are a very special young man," Kristen told him as she gave him a hug, "and if I had not known Andrew first, I am quite sure I would have fallen in love with you."

Eduardo, now feeling a little more mature, laughed and replied, "And I am quite sure you would have become impatient waiting for me to grow up."

"The woman who captures your heart will be lucky indeed," she replied.

And I hope she is as beautiful as you, he thought to himself with just the slightest twinge of regret for what would never be.

*　　*　　*

With the coming of summer, Philip considered how he might coax Eduardo into the swimming pool. Unwilling to fuel the boy's fear of the water, Perez put his psychological wizardry to work. It began with a backyard barbeque to celebrate the Fourth of July. Family friends were in attendance with their children. Perez hired a local band that had gained popularity with the community's younger generation. Croquet and badminton were set up on the lawn. The children had been invited to bring swimsuits for a late-afternoon splash in the pool, and in spite of the other games and amusements, the pool became the focus of the fun.

Eduardo donned his own swimsuit when he perceived he was drawing unwanted attention in his slacks and shirt. He stood, towel around his shoulders, watching the others splash and dive before eventually moving to the edge of the pool and dangling his feet in the water. Emily Montoya, gliding beneath the surface, dolphinlike, headed straight for Eduardo and tugged playfully at his feet.

"Stop," he yelped, kicking water in her face before pulling his feet onto the deck.

"You can't hurt me," she giggled. "I'm already soaked." And with that, she sliced her hand across the surface of the water, shooting a wave into the air that descended on Eduardo's head. As quickly as she had soaked her host, Emily dove underwater and swam to the opposite end of the pool.

Emily's eleven-year-old brother, Matthew, plopped down beside Eduardo. "Aren't you gonna get her?" he asked.

"I will if she comes back over here."

"Go get her," Matthew urged. "Come on," he said, jumping into the pool. "I'll help you." Without waiting for Eduardo, Matthew swam to his sister's side and began jumping at her, trying to push her head under water. Emily dodged her brother, and a wrestling match ensued. It wasn't long before Matthew banged his knee on the side of the pool. After the knee had been dried and a Band-Aid applied, Matthew rejoined Eduardo. "You should have helped me," the boy said. "Why didn't you?"

Eduardo was ashamed to admit he couldn't swim. "Just didn't feel like getting into a fight."

"I was fighting for you."

His pride pricked, Eduardo leaned to the boy's ear and said in quiet tones, "I don't know how to swim, but I don't want anyone to know."

Matthew pulled back from Eduardo and scrutinized him carefully. "Really? So that's why you're not playing with everybody else?"

"Yeah, really, and like I said, I'd appreciate it if you don't tell anybody."

"It's our secret." He gave Eduardo a high five. "I could teach you," he said a few minutes later, excitement rising in his voice.

Eduardo looked at him with skepticism. "What if I don't want to learn?"

"Why wouldn't you want to learn?"

"I don't like getting water up my nose."

"So? Nobody likes getting water in their nose. Just breathe out real slow, and the water can't come in." Matthew jumped back in the pool and put his face in the water. He exhaled through his nostrils, and a slow stream of bubbles rose to the surface.

"See, it's easy."

"But that's not swimming. Anyone can stand in shallow water and blow bubbles out their nose."

Matthew flopped onto his back, pulled his arms through the water, and came alongside the edge. Looking up at Eduardo, he said, "You can do this. It's easy."

"What keeps you from sinking?" Eduardo asked the boy, not realizing a crowd was gathering around the two.

"Nobody sinks," Emily's tall friend, Lindy, replied. "You think you will at first, and that makes you lift your head up. When you lift your head, you really do sink. What you've got to do is stretch out and tip your forehead back like this." She lifted her feet from the bottom of the pool and fell backward, tipping her head slightly. "See," she said, "Now you try it."

The last thing Eduardo wanted to do was lay on his back in the water. As he considered what excuse he might use, a chorus of shouts went up from his assembled guests."

"Come on."

"You can do it."

"Watch me."

Eduardo jumped into the pool. The water came to his chest. *Well, even if I sink to the bottom, I can stand up*, he told himself.

"It feels weird at first," Lindy said. "So I'll put my hand under your head. Hold onto the gutter with one hand and stretch out."

Eduardo grabbed the edge of the trough as if his life depended on it. He lifted his feet off the floor of the pool and raised them to his chest.

"Good," said Lindy. "Now straighten your legs and tilt your head back." She slid her hand beneath Eduardo's head and pressed gently so he felt her support. "Tip your head back more. That's right. Now arch your back a little."

Eduardo felt as though a hundred eyes were on him. *I can't blow it now*, he thought.

"Let go of the side," Lindy said, "but keep your head tilted back, and whatever you do, don't bend at the waist." Eduardo released his grip, and Lindy continued to support him with one hand beneath his head. "See, now you're floating. I'm going to move you away from the wall just a little bit, and I want you to move your arms in the water."

Eduardo began moving his arms. "Perfect. Now you're doing it." Slowly, she slipped her hand from under Eduardo's head.

As soon as he felt her hand move, he did exactly what he was cautioned not to do. He bent at the waist, and his bottom sank into the water. Kicking and flailing, his feet found the bottom of the pool, and he stood but not before he had gotten a nose full of water. Coughing and sputtering, he reached for the edge of the pool.

"It's OK. Its OK," Emily said. "That happens to everybody the first time."

"Come on, Eduardo," Matthew said, "you can do it."

Eduardo shook the water out of his hair and stared at his cheerleaders.

"One more time," Lindy said. "You just about had it."

Eduardo lay in the water, concentrating on keeping his back arched. Slowly, he pushed his arms though the water in practice strokes. This time, as Lindy removed her hand, Eduardo did not sink. She peered into his upturned face and smiled. Eduardo grinned back and began gently kicking his feet.

From a chair on the patio, Perez smiled and lit a celebration cigar.

The next week, Perez engaged a swimming coach who came to the house three times a week. Eduardo ran in the morning before breakfast and swam every afternoon. "He's developing muscles," Philip observed as he and Tomas watched the boy dive into the pool one hot afternoon.

"Why can't I have summer break like the rest of the kids?" Eduardo asked Perez one day after his math tutor left.

"You've had a little catching up to do. You're doing very well though, and I think it's time for a vacation."

"Really? It's just two more weeks until the others go back to school. Can I take the next two weeks off?"

"Well, I was wondering, now that you swim so well, how would you like to fly to Hawaii for ten days and do some snorkeling?"

"You're kidding," Eduardo said. "No way!"

Perez smiled. "Yeah, I was kind of thinking I could use a vacation too, so I booked our airfare and hotel. Maybe you could learn to surf too," he said, ruffling the boy's curly hair. "You're beginning to look like a surfer with that long hair."

CHAPTER TWENTY

The Vacation

Hawaii
August 1985

The flight took almost six hours. They exited the Honolulu airport into what felt like a steam bath. "I feel like I can't breathe," Eduardo said, placing a hand over his chest.

"It's the humidity. Remember your study of weather?"

"Yeah, the temperature stays pretty constantly warm near the equator. That causes evaporation of water and increases the moisture content of the air. I just didn't know it would feel so awful. I don't think this is going to be a very fun trip."

"We're staying on the beach, and the breeze off the ocean will improve our comfort. Don't give up yet." They caught a taxi to the Royal Hawaiian Hotel, and as Perez had promised, it sat right on the beach, its own private beach.

The hotel looked like a pink mansion to Eduardo. When a bellman greeted them at the door and took their bags, Eduardo looked at his companion with concern. "Where's he going with our stuff?"

"He'll deliver everything to our room. Don't worry. Your dress clothes will probably be in the room before we get there." He threw his arm playfully around the boy's shoulders.

"They can have my dress clothes," Eduardo said. "Just don't let them take my swimsuit."

"You wouldn't have said that a year ago, would you," Perez quipped, squeezing the boy's shoulders a little tighter.

After checking in, they walked through the lobby and out onto the terrace to get a view of the ocean. A cool breeze blew through the trees and picked up the scent of plumeria, jasmine, and ginger from the gardens.

Waves crashed slowly on the sandy beach, inviting observers to pick up their gentle rhythm. A few puffy clouds drifted slowly toward the island from the line of the horizon, and high above, the sun shone bright.

"See that rocky mountain going down to the ocean?" Perez said, pointing to the left. "That's an extinct volcano."

"Diamond Head, Tomas gave me a book about Hawaii before we left, and I read that the islands were created by volcanoes. I'm glad that one isn't active any more. It's too close for comfort."

Perez smiled. "We have a lot of things to do here on Oahu, but next week, we'll fly to the big island of Hawaii. While we're there, we'll take a helicopter tour to see a volcano that has been erupting since last year."

"No kidding?"

"No kidding, but now let's go unpack and get ready to swim." Just as Perez had promised, their luggage was waiting when they entered their suite. "Unpack and hang your shirts and slacks so they don't wrinkle too much," Perez called out from his bedroom. "There are robes in the bathrooms that we can wear down to the beach." Eduardo had never unpacked so fast. They trekked through the lobby, past the terrace, and onto the beach where they claimed lounge chairs and dropped towels and sandals.

"I'll race you to the water," Eduardo yelled, sprinting toward the breakers. Perez was not far behind, feeling more like a child himself than he had in years. "It's a lot warmer than the ocean at home," Eduardo remarked and splashed Perez in the face, provoking a water fight.

They played and swam in the ocean until they were exhausted. "We'll eat in the hotel tonight and go to a seafood restaurant tomorrow," Philip told the boy, "but day after tomorrow, I have a special surprise for you."

After a steak dinner, they sat on their balcony and watched boat lights out on the water. "I love the sound of the surf," Perez said in sleepy voice. "It makes me feel so calm." The night breeze ruffled palm fronds, and somewhere below their balcony, an ensemble of frogs croaked a primal melody.

"Lobo would be down there sniffing in the bushes, catching those frogs, if he was here. I miss him and Tomas and Maria."

"I do too, but I'm kind of glad we're here."

"Oh, I wouldn't trade this for anything," Eduardo said apologetically. "It's just that, well, do you ever get a funny lonesome feeling at night, especially when you're in a new place?"

"Hmmm, yes, I know what you are talking about. Some people call it homesickness." Perez looked at the boy in the dim moonlight. "Do you ever get homesick for your cousins, Eduardo?"

"No, never. I think about my grandfather, though. He used to sit in his rocking chair after dinner and read to me from the Bible. I never listened very well, but I'd give anything to sit next to him and hear him read again."

"Do you ever think you would like to move back there?"

After a long pause, Eduardo replied, "I wish I could finish school and bring him to California. That's what he really wanted. He's a good man, and I love him so much. He's not like my aunt Juanita or my cousins, not at all."

Perez breathed a sigh of relief. He had developed a fondness for this boy that startled him, and he was glad the boy did not want to run back to Mexico. *I'll have to see what we can do about that,* he thought, but he vowed not to make any promises to Eduardo that he could not keep. "They were pretty mean to you, weren't they?"

Eduardo hung his head and was quiet. Perez did not push it but allowed him space to direct where this conversation was going. "I just don't know why they never liked me," he finally said. "In my family, only Grandfather showed me love. Grandfather said my parents loved me very much, but they died when I was a baby. I don't remember them at all, but sometimes after I go to bed at night, I imagine what they must have been like and the things we would have done together."

"Hmmm," Perez mused. "What kinds of things would you have done together?"

Eduardo paused again as if considering whether he wanted to share the most intimate part of his soul with this man. Finally, he said, "I think we would have talked and hugged a lot. Father would have played soccer with me, and Mother would have read me stories." Looking up at Perez, he continued. "Grandfather said my father was a good man, and Mother was very beautiful. She played the guitar and sang." Then grinning, he added, "Maybe she would have given me guitar lessons." They sat in silence for several minutes, Eduardo thinking of his lost parents and Philip thinking of his lost family. "I think I would have done some of the same things I am doing now," Eduardo finally said, "except I would not have shamed them by getting involved with a gang. Maybe grandfather no longer loves me, and if my parents can see me from heaven, they probably don't love me anymore either." At this, he lowered his head and covered his eyes with his right hand. Quiet sobs racked his body.

Moved with emotion, Philip rose from his chair and crouched beside the boy, wrapping an arm around him. "We all make some poor choices. That's part of growing up. The important thing is to realize that the decision was poor. The hard part is to change direction, and you have done that. You are very bright, and you are doing well in your studies. It is not about being perfect, Eduardo. It is about being forgiven, and God is willing to forgive you. Your parents and grandfather don't hate you. They are very proud of you, of that I am sure."

"You don't know that," the boy said in a voice choked with grief.

"Yes, I do," Perez responded with emphasis.

"How?"

"Because if you were my son, I would love you very much."

Eduardo threw his arms around Perez's neck and sobbed openly. "I wish you were my father," he said.

A sob rose from the depths of Philip's being and shook his own body. He raised a hand and ran his long fingers though the boy's tousled hair. "I do too," he said. When the sobs ceased and the tears had dried, they sat in peaceful silence for a long period.

Turning to Perez, Eduardo said, "Even though I don't remember him, I love my father. I just think he would have been a lot like you."

Understanding the boy's remorse at saying something that could be misconstrued as disloyalty to his father, Perez replied, "I am honored you think that I might be like your father. I am sure if we had met, we would be great friends, and you would have called me Uncle Philip."

Eduardo looked up at the man and smiled. "I think he would have liked you very much."

"Then it is settled. I am Uncle Philip."

Eduardo's smile grew as he repeated "Uncle Philip" over and over in his head.

During the night, clouds rolled in from the ocean, and Philip and Eduardo woke to a torrential downpour. Eduardo stood amazed at the window, listening and watching.

"We've got things to do today, Eduardo," Philip said, poking his head into the boy's room. "Get dressed. We can watch this little squall from the terrace while we're eating breakfast."

"You mean we're going out there in this rain, Uncle Philip? We'll get soaked."

"We're going to get wet anyway. We have surfing lessons at ten."

"Won't it be cold?" Eduardo asked, shivering at the thought.

"It's only cold because your air-conditioning unit set too low," Philip said, adjusting the temperature. "This rain shower won't last long, and then it will be warm and humid outside. A dip in the ocean will feel good."

After breakfasting on eggs, bacon, and fresh pineapple, they strolled the gardens of the hotel, allowing their meal to settle. The rain had stopped, and the air smelled of tropical flowers. A parrot perched noisily on a stand near the terrace. When Eduardo approached, the bird hopped onto his shoulder. "We need to come back later with the camera and get your picture with this guy," Philip said, "but right now, let's get ready for our surf lessons." The clouds were gone, and the sun shone down on the sparking blue water.

A surfing instructor gave a group lesson on the hotel's private beach. He stressed safety and gave pointers on breaking through the surf to get to the point where they would wait to catch a wave. Eduardo and Philip carried their boards into the water with the other surfing students. When they had waded out to hip level, they threw their boards down and lay atop them. It was hard work paddling through the waves, but they finally made it to calm water. Each tried to crouch on their board and then stand. Philip fell off immediately and climbed back on the board to try again. Eduardo stood on the first try. It felt a little like being on a skate board. Once they had mastered standing, the instructor told them to lie back down and paddle to a swell. As the wave started to break, they were told to stand quickly. This time, Eduardo fell, and if it wasn't for the strap that held his board to his ankle, he would have lost it. He tried again, and finally on the fourth try, he made it upright. It was an exhilarating feeling, even though the wave had been rather small. By the end of the morning, Philip had conquered his first wave, and he was exhausted. They carried their boards back to the surf shack and stretched out on lounge chairs.

"Did you see the muscles on the instructors?" Eduardo asked.

"I can understand why," Philip replied. "I feel like I've done a day's worth of hard labor. You can go back out this afternoon if you want, but I'm staying right there on the beach."

Eduardo did go back out after lunch, and Philip got a few nice pictures that he knew Tomas and Maria would enjoy seeing. That night, after a dinner of fresh fish, the boy slept very well.

The following morning, Philip announced that they would attend a luau in the evening. "It is a Hawaiian feast," he explained to Eduardo. "The hotel staff will dig pits in the sand where they will roast whole pigs the way native islanders used to prepare them. They will serve other native dishes like poi, which is the cooked root of the taro plant. Dinner will be served on the beach, and there will be bonfires, singing, and hula dancing."

"Sounds like a real party, Uncle Philip."

"I know we will have fun, but right now, we have the whole day ahead of us. What would you like to do? We could take a tour of the island, go snorkeling, or surf again."

"All of those things sound fun. My muscles are a little sore from surfing yesterday, so could we snorkel today and surf again another day? I don't want to forget the things the instructor told us."

It wasn't long before they were floating on the surface of the water in Hanauma Bay. The water was clear, and Eduardo found the fish were as curious to see him as he was to see them. Schools of Manini and other varieties of tang fish, reef trigger fish, and trumpet fish swam near. A foot-long creature came into view and began slithering toward Eduardo. Thinking it to be a poisonous snake, he panicked and, in his effort to get away from the creature, began flailing and sucked water into his snorkel tube. This caused further panic. He managed to kick his flippers and thrust himself above the surface of the water where Philip spotted the boy's distress. The newly self-appointed uncle swam with sure swift strokes and pulled the boy up to the surface where he could cough out the seawater and get a gulping breath of air. "There's a snake," Eduardo yelled when he could talk.

"I think it's probably an eel. It's not likely to bother you." Philip stayed close to the boy the rest of the morning. They left the water in the early afternoon to enjoy a picnic lunch of sandwiches, fruit salad, and cookies. After a rest on the beach, they dived back in the water for some more snorkeling. The eel returned, but Philip was at Eduardo's side and was able to reassure the boy that he was in no danger.

It was late afternoon by the time the snorkelers returned to the hotel, and a short rest was in order prior to the luau. "We wouldn't be resting in the afternoon if we were home," Eduardo said. "Here we are on vacation, and we're so tired we're taking a nap."

"We may be on vacation, but we put in a hard day of work." Philip laughed.

The sun hovered over the water like a giant red ball when Philip and Eduardo walked out onto the beach for the luau. Tiki torches had been driven into the sand around the perimeter of the party area. Four men worked a few yards away, lifting the roast pork from the pits. The aroma was intoxicating, and Eduardo's mouth began watering. "Traditionally," the master of ceremonies told the gathered guests, "participants in a luau would sit on the sand to eat, but we have provided tables and chairs for your comfort. Please take a seat, and the party will begin." The meal was bountiful, and Eduardo enjoyed everything but the poi.

"Do I have to eat it all?"

"Certainly not," he was told. "But I am happy you tried it. I do not care for it either. I am sure it is an acquired taste, kind of like horseradish," he said, smiling.

"I like horseradish now, but I don't think I would ever like this poi."

"I am sure you will find many things in life that are not to your liking," Philip replied. "Some will be worth trying, and some will be best left alone. The trick is to figure out which is which."

"Like the difference between trying poi or marijuana?" Eduardo asked.

"Yes," said Philip, "that would be an example. There will be things that tempt you, and there will be people who tempt you to try things. It is important to develop the judgment to know what is good and what is not good."

"Grandfather used to read to me from the book of Proverbs in the Bible," Eduardo said. "He talked about wisdom and good judgment and not letting other boys talk me into things I know I shouldn't do."

"He is a wise man," Philip said.

"But I didn't follow his instructions when I met Diego and Miguel."

"I hope you can eventually forgive yourself," Philip said. "God is willing to forgive you if you just ask Him to, and I know your grandfather will forgive you too."

The boy thought about these things. Perhaps there was forgiveness for him. He wanted to ask Uncle Philip more questions about God's forgiveness, but just then, a group of men and women in traditional Hawaiian dress began playing their ukuleles and singing songs of the islands. After dinner, a dance troupe joined the musicians and performed the hula. Guests were encouraged to join in. They learned that the hand motions were a type of sign language telling stories of many things including the sea, the islands, and love. At one point, the pretty girl dancers pulled male guests onto the stage to participate in the dance. Many of the men were embarrassed, but Philip joined in happily, much to Eduardo's delight. He fumbled the steps and exaggerated the hand motions, and Eduardo doubled over laughing. They returned to their room in a joyful mood, and Eduardo had fun at Philip's expense, mimicking his performance. Unknown to Philip, the boy had taken a few shots of him with the camera so Tomas and Maria could also have a good laugh.

The next day, the travelers boarded a bus to tour the island. They were taken inland to the Nuuanu Pali Lookout where a famous battle was waged in 1795 between the warriors of Nuuanu and King Kamehameha I. The king was victorious, and many of his opponent's soldiers were driven over the cliff to their death. Eduardo could not help but think of Miguel, Ernesto, and Luis. As they stood there, a howling wind rose up the side of the cliff and pressed against the tourists with unexpected force. From the lookout, they travelled to the windward side of the island. The driver stopped at a fenced area and explained, "A movie set is being built on the other side of this fence. How many of you have seen the *Karate Kid*?" A few hands went up among the small group. "Well," the guide said, "they are already planning the sequel, and an Okinawan Village is being built here for that movie." Ohhs and awws went up as people stepped up to the fence to see the activity on the other side.

"Do you think we could see that movie some time?" Eduardo asked.

"We have no special plans this evening," Philip said, so let's get some burgers tonight and go to the movies.

The last stop on the tour was the Arizona Memorial, a beautiful structure designed to honor men and women who lost their lives when Pearl Harbor was attacked on December 7, 1941. There was such an air of reverence Eduardo almost felt like he was in church.

The movie, *Karate Kid*, was a hit with Eduardo and Philip as well. The psychologist was surprised by the emotion the film stirred in him. He naively expected the movie to be a shallow martial arts demonstration, but at the heart of the story was the relationship between a fatherless teenage boy and an older Japanese man. He left the theater with a warm feeling in his heart.

After a couple more days of surfing and sunbathing and a shopping trip to the open-air International Market place, they boarded a small plane for the big island of Hawaii. A shuttle bus took them to a hotel on the north end of the island where there were beaches for swimming. They rode in an outrigger canoe and went kayaking in the ocean. Eduardo loved riding the waves to shore in the kayak. He body-surfed and board-surfed but decided his favorite activity was kayaking. They took a helicopter ride in a large circle over the southeast end of the island, seeing Kilauea, which had erupted the previous year. It continued to spew molten rock through lava tubes into the ocean where its heat boiled the water and turned it into clouds of steam. Lush green jungle and cascading waterfalls lay below them as they coursed their way above the island.

On the last day of their vacation, they took ukulele lessons. By the end of two hours, they had a repertoire of three songs. "If I can play this, I bet I could play the guitar," Eduardo said playfully.

"I give up," said Philip, holding his hands up in surrender. "When we get home, we'll see about guitar lessons."

That evening as they sat on their terrace enjoying the sunset and the tranquility of the sea and gentle breeze, Eduardo began recounting the activities of the past ten days. "This is the best vacation I have ever had. In Mexico, I just stayed home and played soccer with my friends and helped Grandfather around the house."

"I'm glad you enjoyed it, Eduardo. It has been one of my best vacations too."

"Uncle Philip, when we were at the luau, I was going to ask you a question, but the dancing started and I didn't have a chance."

"You can ask me anything you want," Philip replied.

"You said you are sure my grandfather and my parents forgive me, because you would forgive me if you were my father."

"That's right."

"You also said God would forgive me, but how do you know?"

"The Bible says, *If we confess our sins, He is faithful and just and will forgive us our sins and purify us from all unrighteousness.* Do you understand the meaning of that?"

"I think it means if I ask God to forgive me, He will."

"That is right, Eduardo. The Bible says we are all sinners, and God is so righteous He cannot tolerate sin. We all sin, so that separates us from God. No matter how hard we try to be good, we can never be good enough for God."

"Then how can He forgive me if I can never be good enough to please Him?"

"Let me tell you a story. There was a group of prisoners who were going to be put to death. They had all done horrible things like murder and burglary except for one man who was innocent. Someone had falsely accused him of committing a horrible crime, and the judge believed the accuser. When it was time for the execution, the jailer lined the men up. He put the innocent man first in line because he was accused of the worst crime. He handed the man a cup of poison and told him to take a drink and pass it down the line. If by any chance the cup was empty when it reached the last of the prisoners, they would go free. The first man, the innocent one, took the cup and drank the whole thing. He died, and everyone else went free."

"That's not fair. The guy who died was innocent. Why would anyone do that, especially if they weren't guilty?"

"Love. He felt great compassion and love for the people who stood in line behind him." Philip looked deeply into Eduardo's eyes. "That is what Jesus did for us. He was innocent, a perfect man, and He died in our place to pay the penalty for our sins."

Eduardo drew a deep breath. Many of these things he remembered from church and from Grandfather's teaching, but he had never heard it so clearly before. Tears came to his eyes as he considered the thought of someone being willing to die in his place. He looked up at Philip. "I am so sorry for some of the things I have done."

"The Bible says if we repent or turn from our sins and ask God to forgive us, He will. Would you like to pray right now, Eduardo?" Philip knelt on the terrace with the boy as Eduardo poured his heart out to God and accepted the forgiveness he had been longing for.

Eduardo found it hard to say goodbye to the island. He missed Lobo, but this had been so much fun. He thanked Philip profusely for the adventure, but somehow words seemed to fall short of expressing the gratitude he felt. He wondered what he could give this man as a token of his appreciation, but he was at a loss. Browsing through a shop in the airport, he found a card with a picture of a man, a woman, and a child gathered on the beach at sunset. He bought the card and opened it to the blank page inside. "*Thank you for being my family,*" he wrote. "*I love you very much.*" He placed the card in its envelope, sealed it, and slid it into Philip's briefcase.

CHAPTER TWENTY-ONE

The Lessons Continue

Palos Verdes Peninsula
1985–1986

Eduardo's lessons resumed as soon as the travelers returned from their vacation. Ms. MacDonald, who had been Eduardo's math teacher in public school, agreed to come to the villa two evenings a week to oversee lessons in algebra. "I can't believe this is the same kid," she told Philip after the first evening. "He was unengaged in the classroom, possibly because his English was a little limited, but there was more to it than that I believe. I always felt he had given up."

"I think your assessment was fairly accurate," Perez said. "He lost his parents when he was so young he doesn't remember them. His only bond seems to be with his grandfather who apparently is not well. The grandfather sent Eduardo to California to live with his cousins and get an education beyond grade school. When Eduardo arrived here, the cousins were anything but welcoming, and then Diego, the one friend he had found, introduced Eduardo to Los Reyes."

"It doesn't sound like he had much of a chance."

"He certainly saw it that way. Could I offer you a drink, Ms. MacDonald?" Philip said rising to go to the bar.

"Please, it's Maggie," she said. "And if you have white wine, I would love a glass while we discuss Eduardo's education plan."

"White wine it is, and you must call me Philip," he returned.

"What are Eduardo's plans, exactly?" she asked when they were settled on the couch. Eduardo's latest math test lay on the cocktail table before them.

Philip cleared his throat and furrowed his brow. He felt suddenly uncomfortable because he realized that in his eagerness to educate the boy, he himself had set all the goals: music, math, English, history, current events, swimming. Only running had been Eduardo's idea. Not once had he asked Eduardo what course of study he wanted to pursue. Philip threw his head back, closed his eyes, and took a deep breath.

Maggie MacDonald pursed her lips and looked down at her wine glass, realizing that the school psychologist was about to admit he made the same misstep he had railed at parents and teachers for or he would present her with a bald-faced lie. She hoped it was the former.

Philip took another deep breath and looked sheepishly at the red-haired teacher sitting next to him. Sensing his gaze, she turned and met him with the bluest eyes he had ever seen. His expression was so guilty she couldn't restrain a giggle. "Stop laughing," he said. "It's not funny." This made her laugh even harder. A rosy glow blended into the freckles that fanned out from the bridge of her nose. She covered her mouth with a small hand and regained composure with no little difficulty. When she looked at him again, he was smiling too. "I can't believe what I've done," he said. "After years of lecturing and writing, the psychologist is guilty of not taking his own advice."

She cocked her head to one side and studied Philip as if she was seeing him for the first time. Her first response had been to offer a quick sorry-this-is-none-of-my-business, but it was her business. She was the teacher, and she was doing what he had helped train her to do: make sure the child was invested in the goals set forth in the individualized education plan. "You weren't behaving as a psychologist," she said. "You were behaving as a parent, a parent who wants what is best for his child." Her words stunned him.

Philip rose and went to the door.

"Look," she stammered, thinking she was about to be ushered out of the house.

"Eduardo," Philip called out. "Eduardo, can you come in here?" Lobo bounded into the room, carrying a large chew toy. "Where's Eduardo, boy?" Philip asked, giving the dog a pat.

Eduardo was not far behind the boy. "I'm sorry," he said. "I thought I was through, so I was playing tug-of-war with Lobo." Noticing Philip's face, he asked, "Is everything OK? I did the best I could on the test."

"The test was fine, Eduardo, but Ms. MacDonald reminded me of something I have neglected to do. Come pull a chair up. We would like to talk with you for a few minutes." When the boy had seated himself, Philip began. "Eduardo, when you came to live here, I was sure I could help you move ahead in life with purpose. I wanted to see you develop an interest in books, music, and culture. I hoped you would excel scholastically and go to college one day." Eduardo nodded his head, agreeing with everything Philip said. "What I did not do, and what Ms. MacDonald has reminded me, is to consult you about your goals. I know many of the things I have forced you to study were things in which you had no interest. I still believe those studies have enriched your life, but we have come to a place where you really need to participate in setting goals."

Eduardo looked from one face to the other. Ms. MacDonald smiled at him. "What do you want to do when you finish school?" she asked.

"Grandfather asked me that same question before he sent me away," Eduardo replied.

"What did you tell him?" Philip asked.

Eduardo thought about this for a moment. He had been worried that Grandfather would laugh at him, but he hadn't. *Would these two laugh?* "I want to be a soccer player," he said, looking straight a Perez. The man's expression changed almost imperceptibly. Ms. MacDonald looked down at her papers and shuffled them neatly into a pile.

"Well," Perez said, exhaling deeply. "Well, a soccer player." Turning to Eduardo, he asked, "Are you good? What position do you play?"

"I haven't played since Mexico," the boy replied.

"They're having tryouts this weekend," Ms. MacDonald said quietly.

Eduardo shot her a glance. She was looking at Uncle Philip with raised eyebrows as if expecting one of her students to give her a correct answer.

"I guess we better find out where," he said. Secretly, he hoped the boy would develop other interests in a couple of years, but he was committed to support him in this pursuit, provided Eduardo kept up with his studies, that is.

The next day, Philip interrupted Eduardo's history lesson and took him out on the lawn for a little soccer practice, explaining that he used to play in college.

"I was the goalie," Tomas said from the sidelines. "I couldn't do it now with this arthritis, but I can sure give you some pointers." He rolled the ball, lifting it up with his right foot, and shot it to Eduardo.

On Saturday, Philip drove Eduardo down to the high school playing field for league tryouts. They signed the appropriate paperwork and took a seat, waiting for Eduardo to be called to the field. Tomas was almost as excited as Eduardo and had asked to go along. Sitting on one side of the boy, he patted his young friend's leg and said, "I will be cheering for you, muchacho." Eduardo's excitement was evident; he grinned from ear to ear and talked nonstop, seeing nothing but the players already on the field.

A tall thin man with shaggy blond hair took a seat in front of Philip. He threw his arm across the shoulders of a Mexican boy who looked close to

Eduardo's age. "I wish my mom could be here today, but thanks for coming with me, Matt," the boy said.

"Wouldn't have missed it for the world, Diego," the man replied.

Though the boys' voice was lower in register than Eduardo remembered, it struck a chord of familiarity. He rose from his seat with a startled look on his face and began climbing over Tomas's long legs. "Whoaa, where are you going, Eduardo?" Philip asked, reaching out to restrain Eduardo. "You haven't been called yet." Philip saw the look of panic on Eduardo's face and turned in the direction the boy was staring. The young Latino sitting in front of him sported a familiar tattoo on his left arm.

The words were not completely out of his mouth when Diego turned. "Eduardo," he yelled. The smile on the boy's face indicated his joy at seeing his friend again. Eduardo was hesitant but stopped pulling against Philip.

Matt turned and rose, extending his hand to Philip. Philip glanced quickly at Eduardo before releasing him. "Matt Connors," the man said.

"Philip Perez," Philip said, shaking the extended hand. "Looks like our boys know each other." Philip's eyes travelled once more to the tattoo.

"Eduardo," Matt said. "So you're Eduardo." He extended his hand to the boy.

"Look," Philip said again, "we don't want any trouble."

Matt grinned and flashed his badge. "You won't get any from us," he said. "I kind of developed a fondness for this kid when I was working undercover." He grabbed the back of Diego's neck and gave it a friendly shake. "He was out looking for Eduardo when we met at the hospital."

"I'm not in the gang anymore," Diego said emphatically. "Matt kept pestering me, and then when Miguel and some of the guys died, well—"

"It was a little easier for him to leave once the head of the snake had been cut off," Matt said. "It was pretty scary going there for a while."

Eduardo sucked in a breath. "You gave the gang up?" he asked.

Diego shook his head in the affirmative. "I'm really ashamed I ever got you involved. When Matt finally talked with my mother, she just about killed me. We were going to move away, and then the accident happened, so we didn't have to. The gang just dissolved."

The boys were called down to the field, and Matt moved up alongside Philip. "We didn't know Eduardo's name until Diego showed up at the hospital looking for him. That kid was in over his head. It didn't take a lot of talking to convince him he was in for a life of misery."

Philip shared what had been going on with Eduardo but held back any invitation for Diego to visit the villa. His feelings regarding this friendship would take some time to sort out, but in the meantime, he praised Matt for the help and support he was giving Diego.

The boys were placed on separate teams, which eased Philip's mind. They had found their way into trouble once before, and he was not completely convinced they would not do it again.

Eduardo was made his team's goalie, which brought a certain measure of joy to Tomas. "He's just like me," the old man bragged to Maria. "He's turning out just like his old Uncle Tomas."

Philip may have missed a game or two because of work, but Tomas did not miss any. He often dragged Maria along to help cheer for their favorite goalie. Eduardo was skilled in his position and could drop to fend off low balls or stretch to catch the high ones. He thrived with the exercise, and Philip wondered if his young charge really did have a career in the sport. "Would you be disappointed if he chose professional sports over college?" Maggie asked him one evening after a lesson.

Philip smiled and looked at her. "I'm going to be honest," he said. "Yes, I would be disappointed, but I am committed to support whatever he chooses to do."

"The nice thing is he's good at the game. If he seriously wants to play professionally, some team is going to pick him up."

Philip looked at her curiously. "I didn't know I'd spoken that much about his ability," he said.

"Oh, you haven't," she replied. "But I've attended most of his games, and I know talent when I see it."

"Does he know you're there watching?"

"Yes, and I think that is part of the reason his studies have improved. I showed interest in what he is doing outside my discipline, and he's reciprocating very nicely."

"You amaze me, Maggie," Philip said appreciatively.

"You're pretty amazing yourself," she said, coloring.

"What would you like to do for your birthday?" Philip asked Eduardo as the day approached.

"I've never been to Disneyland," the boy said.

"Well, as amazing as it sounds, neither have I."

"If we go, could I take a friend?" the boy asked.

Philip looked at him with curiosity. "Who do you want to take, Emily?"

"Yuck," Eduardo replied. "Would you let me take Diego?"

Philip considered for a moment. "Let's call Matt and invite them both."

"Great," Eduardo whooped. "You old guys can hang out, while Diego and I ride the scary rides."

Philip called the number Matt had given him. "I have an uneasy feeling about fostering a friendship between these two," he told Matt honestly when they met for coffee. "They've been in serious trouble before, and I worry about the negative influence they might have on each other."

"I hear you," Matt responded. "I'm not the expert, you are, but I've gotten so close to this guy. I'd hate to push the button that would send him back into the abyss. I have an idea though. What if they wash away the past, so to speak, by going together to get those awful tattoos removed?"

"Is that possible?"

"Yeah; it's painful, but possible. We have a few guys on the force that had stupid stuff put on their arms in the military, and there's this doctor in Long Beach who's removing them. It's not perfect, but it's not too bad either."

"I like the idea," Philip said. "I've worried that the tattoo might be a hindrance to Eduardo in the future."

"It's not like he's going to get a job as a bank president with a gang insignia on his arm," Matt laughed.

"There are a lot of companies who won't welcome that. Have you spoken to Diego about this?

"A million times. He's afraid it will hurt."

"I wonder if they would make a pact to do it together," Philip mused. "They certainly endured enough to get into the gang."

October 12 dawned clear and mildly warm. *Aa perfect day for standing in lines at an amusement park*, thought Philip. He drove Eduardo to Diego's apartment where they picked the boy up along with Matt. The boys chatted excitedly in the backseat about which rides they wanted to try first. "Space Mountain is my favorite," Diego said. "Then the Matterhorn, Big Thunder Mountain Railroad, and the Pirates ride."

"I think the important thing is to choose a place where you want to start and see everything in that area before moving on to the next section," Matt said. He turned to Philip, "I took my nieces last year, and they ran my legs off going from one end of the park to the other."

Eduardo was so excited he was practically jumping in his seat by the time they left their car in the parking lot. A tram took them to the front gate where Philip insisted on paying for all the tickets. "You're our guests," he told Matt. The line was already forming to get into the park, which hadn't opened yet. They choose the shortest line and only had to wait a few minutes before they were at the entrance gate.

The boys were both dressed in short-sleeved shirts, and when they reached the ticket booth, the man glanced at the exposed tattoos and then at Philip and Matt. "There won't be any trouble," Matt said quietly, flashing his badge. The ticket taker nodded and ushered them through. Eduardo's eyes darted everywhere as Diego tugged him toward Tomorrowland. "Space Mountain first," he called back to the lagging men. By noon, they had seen all of Tomorrowland and all a sixteen-year-old boy cared to see of Fantasyland.

"Time for lunch, I think," Philip said. "That is, if you think you can keep food on your stomach and ride roller coasters too."

"You mean there's another roller coaster?" Eduardo asked.

"One more," said Diego. "Big Thunder Mountain Railroad."

"Let's try the Golden Horseshoe for lunch," Matt suggested. "My treat this time."

After lunch, Philip insisted the boys wait at least a half hour before going on another roller coaster. "There are plenty of other things to do while our lunch settles," he said, so they boarded the rafts for Tom Sawyer's Island. The boys explored while Matt and Philip sat and enjoyed each other's company. "I think the boys had a moment of panic when the ticket taker saw their tattoos," Matt said.

"It might be good to start a discussion at dinner tonight," Philip suggested.

"Just what I was thinking," Matt agreed.

"That was so much fun." Eduardo laughed as the foursome disembarked from the Pirates of the Caribbean ride.

"Matt and I thought we could eat dinner at the Blue Bayou, that restaurant where we got on the boat if you guys are hungry," Philip said.

"You mean the place that looks like you're eating in a swamp?" Diego asked. "I've always wanted to eat there."

"Looked pretty cool," Eduardo agreed.

They were given a table near the water and were halfway through their dessert when Matt asked how they had felt when the ticket taker had looked at their tattoos.

"I was afraid they weren't going to let us in," Eduardo said.

"I was pretty sure they would let us in. I just thought they'd probably keep an eye on us to make sure we weren't trying to sell drugs or something."

"It kind of marks you as something you no longer are, doesn't it?" Philip commented.

"Yeah," Eduardo said. "I wish I'd never gotten it."

Diego looked at his friend. "Matt's been trying to get me to take mine off."

"You can't just take this off, Matt," Eduardo said. "You can't even scrub it off with steel wool."

"Don't tell me you tried," Philip said.

"Yeah, I rubbed some of the skin off. I quit when it started bleeding."

"You have to go to the doctor to get it off, stupid," Diego said.

Eduardo looked at Philip in surprise. "You mean Dr. Montoya could take this off?"

"No, but another type of doctor could, a skin doctor."

"It hurts, man," Diego said.

"You think that steel wool didn't hurt? If I can stand having it put on, I can stand having it taken off."

"What we were wondering," Matt said, "is if you guys would like to go in together and have them removed, kind of a new start together."

The boys looked at each other. "Let's do it," said Eduardo.

"It won't be perfect," Matt warned them. "You'll still have a bit of a scar, but at least it won't advertise to the whole world that you used to belong to Los Reyes."

"He'll be ready for calculus in the fall," Maggie told Philip at their conference the following spring.

"I'm not sure he's going to be happy with that."

"Are we still on course to play professional soccer?"

"He certainly excels at the game."

"Maybe it's time to revisit goals," she suggested, looking at Philip out of the corner of her eye. "You've developed a wonderful rapport with him."

"Tonight," Philip told her. "We'll talk tonight."

"He's a very gifted writer," she said.

That evening after dinner, Philip joined Eduardo as he walked Lobo. "You've been keeping yourself pretty busy," Philip observed; "what with running, soccer, swimming, and your studies."

"Yeah, I guess you're right," the young man responded. "But I'm really enjoying everything, even though some days I feel like I don't even have time to think."

"Maybe it's time to lighten the load," Philip advised. "Have you thought about giving anything up?"

"School work," Eduardo said, grinning. Philip ruffled the boy's hair and smiled himself. "Seriously though," Eduardo continued, "I like everything I'm doing, but soccer is taking up too much of my time."

Philip studied the young man's face. "You're very good out there on the field," he said.

"I love the game," Eduardo said, "and I will always want to play, but"— and here he looked at Philip again—"maybe not professionally."

Amazing, Philip thought to himself. *He has come to this decision on his own.* "Diego will be disappointed. He planned on the two of you going professional together."

"He'll get over it," Eduardo replied. "He really isn't that good of a student, but he's a great soccer player."

Philip smiled. "I have a question for you then. If you don't want to play professional soccer, what do you want to do?"

"Be an actor," the boy said. Philip almost choked. "And I think I'd be a pretty good one too," Eduardo continued, "because it looks like I had you fooled, Uncle Philip." He started laughing.

Philip stared at the boy and couldn't restrain his own laughter. "You nearly gave me a heart attack, you know. Maybe you should be a stand-up comedian. But can we get serious for a minute?"

The boy looked at Philip and shook his head. "I don't really know what I want to be anymore. My favorite subject is writing. When I wrote that recycling article and they put it in the community newsletter, I felt pretty good.

"That was a good article. It raised awareness in the neighborhood. The waste management company said recycling is up 20 percent." He smiled at Eduardo again. "You know, you really don't have to decide right now. You may not even know when you start college. Some young people have an undeclared major, and some change their major after a year or two. How about we just play it by ear?"

"Sounds good to me," Eduardo replied. Just then, Lobo spotted a rabbit and took off on a run. Eduardo was after the dog in a split second, while Philip stood and laughed. It seemed Eduardo would be as busy as ever.

The summer came and went in a flash, or so it seemed to Eduardo. There were the usual activities: running every morning, swimming in the afternoon, and Philip had provided tennis lessons three days a week. "He's good," Barton Levy told Philip, "but he should have started years ago if you want him to go pro."

"This is strictly recreation," Philip assured the instructor. "I want him to just enjoy the game."

"Well, he's pretty good. He could have been—"

"That's OK, Barton. I'm happy with the way things are."

Early in the summer, Philip had asked Eduardo if there was any place he would like to visit before school resumed. "We sure had fun in Hawaii last year," Eduardo said.

"I was thinking of something different for this year," Philip mused. "I have a colleague who has asked me to speak at a conference he is sponsoring in January in Oregon. He's invited us to go up for a couple of weeks this summer so he and I can talk and plan. If we go, you will be spending time with his sons. They have a cabin on a little lake just east of Portland. What do you think? You could learn to waterski."

"No kidding?"

"No kidding. He tells me the weather is really nice in August, so we'll plan to go the last two weeks before school resumes."

Without summer studies to take up his time, Eduardo found himself spending time in the garden working with Tomas. "He's gonna have me out of a job," Tomas said to Maria one night. "He is learning the Latin names of all the plants, and he knows when and how to feed them. He's a good student."

"You are a good teacher, my dear," she countered. "He loves spending time with you almost as much as he loves being with Philip."

He smiled. "Anyone who didn't know their story would think they were father and son."

Philip decided to book their flight to Portland a couple of days before they were to join the Garrett family on the lake. "We can see the city for a day or two before heading out to the Garrett's," he told Eduardo. The flight lasted an hour and forty-five minutes, and when they landed, they caught a cab for a hotel in the city center. While Philip checked in, Eduardo grabbed a handful of sightseeing brochures from a rack in the lobby. In their room, Eduardo spread the pamphlets out on his bed. "Do you want to plan our two days here?" Philip asked, knowing this would be a good experience for the boy.

Eduardo looked up with surprise. "Sure."

"We've got an hour before dinner, so why don't you grab a pen and paper off the desk and make a list. The concierge can help make reservations when you've finished."

There were brochures for the beach and brochures for Mt. Hood. "Hey look, Uncle Philip," Eduardo yelled over the sound of the shower in the next room.

"I've got shampoo in my hair," Philip called back.

"Is it OK if we take a hot air balloon ride? It's a forty-minute ride south of the city, and we have to be there at seven in the morning."

"We'll have to be up by five thirty," Philip warned him.

"I can do that," Eduardo said. "And then if the afternoon, we can go to the rose gardens and, if we have time, the zoo or Japanese Gardens."

Rose Gardens, Philip thought to himself. *Since when is that boy interested in roses?* Then he remembered Eduardo's work outside with Tomas. "Sounds like a winner. What about the next day?"

"We could take a walking tour of the downtown area or we could take a boat ride up the Columbia River to the Bonneville Dam."

"Why don't you call the concierge and book the balloon tour for tomorrow and the boat excursion for Friday?"

Eduardo felt very grown-up making the reservations. "All done, Uncle Philip," he reported. "I wrote down the conformation numbers. A town car will pick us up at six o'clock tomorrow morning, and the concierge said they'll have a thermos of coffee waiting downstairs for you. We get a champagne breakfast after the ride is over."

"I get champagne," Philip said, poking his head in the room. "You'll have sparkling cider. Are you ready for dinner?"

They went to the hotel's steak restaurant on the ground floor where they shared chateaubriand accompanied by potatoes Lyonnaise and asparagus. Dessert was molten chocolate cake; and when they were finished, the waiter brought a cheese, fruit, and nut plate.

"I think we should take a little walk and then go to bed," Philip said. "We have an early start tomorrow." They exited onto Broadway and walked past the lighted shops and restaurants. When they reached Alder, they turned left and circled Pioneer Square before heading back to the hotel.

The alarm rang before Eduardo was ready to wake up. "Come on, buddy," Philip said, hitting the boy with a pillow. "Rise and shine."

Glad he had showered before going to bed, Eduardo crawled out and slipped into his jeans and T-shirt. "It's still dark out there," he reported after drawing the drapes. "And it looks cold."

"Take a light jacket," Philip warned.

The town car took them south on Interstate five until they reached the Tualatin Sherwood exit. Passing through farming communities, they turned onto Ninety-Nine West and headed to the Newburg air field where the balloons were being laid out on the ground. Walking up to one of the pilots, Eduardo began asking questions.

"Would you like to help?" the pilot asked. He showed Eduardo the bottom rim of the balloon. "I'm going to turn the flame on in a minute. What I'd like you to do is hold this rim so the flame heats the air inside the balloon. As the air warms up, the balloon will start to lift. When that happens"—and here he turned to Philip—"if the two of you will take opposite sides of the basket and turn it upright, we'll be ready to go."

It took a while for the balloon to fill, and Philip clicked several pictures of Eduardo holding the rim. When the balloon was finally full and the basket was upright, they climbed aboard. "You almost need a ladder." Philip laughed. When everyone was onboard, the pilot and ground crew released ropes, and the balloon slowly lifted. They sailed with four other balloons in the early daylight over the small college town and toward fields ripe with wheat and hops, and orchards of nut trees. When they hovered over the Willamette River, the pilot dropped the balloon until the bottom of the basket dragged the water. Then he fired the burner to raise them again.

After an hour, they landed in a harvested field. The chase truck was waiting, and they all helped roll the balloon and put it in the truck bed along with the basket. Vans took them back to the air field where a hearty breakfast had been set out.

Eduardo and Philip arrived back at their hotel in the early afternoon, and after a brief rest, they caught a cab for the International Rose Test Garden in the hills high above the city. They walked through rows and rows of rose beds. Eduardo took pictures of blooms he thought Tomas would admire and shot some views of the city with Mt. Hood in the background.

"Look over there," Philip said, pointing to the left. "That must be Mt. St. Helens. It used to have a perfectly rounded top until it erupted a few years ago." Eduardo turned the lens of the camera toward the flattened top of the mountain. A small wisp of smoke trailed upward from the cone.

They wandered into the Shakespearean Garden and admired the cozy little spot bordered by hedges and filled with colorful perennials. Moving back out to the rows of roses, Eduardo stopped to read the name tags posted by a particularly fragrant section. "I didn't know there were so many varieties," he continued. "Climbing roses, floribunda, hybrid tea, miniature roses. There are millions, but I like this one the best," he said stooping to inhale a whiff of a coral-colored tea rose named fragrant cloud. In the gift shop, they found a bottle of rose water and glycerin for Maria and a 1986 rose pictorial calendar for Tomas.

They wandered over to the Japanese Gardens, which lay on the hillside just above the rose garden. It was a quiet place with pools and bridges, a traditional tea house, and a pebble garden. "It's such a serene place," Philip commented.

That night, they sat at a table overlooking the Columbia River and ordered fresh grilled salmon. The fish was served with rice pilaf and spinach soufflé. They lingered over dinner, watching running lights mark the path of sailboats as they slid into their moorings for the night. "The reflection of lights on the water is so pretty," Eduardo observed. "Sometimes I see the lights of ships out on the ocean when we are home. I always wonder where the ships are going and where they have been. I think it would be fun to travel and see many different places."

"Travel is educational," Philip said. "It gives you the opportunity to learn about other cultures both past and present."

"Like the Mayans and the Incas?"

"Yes, and like many other ancient cultures in Asia, the Middle East, Europe, and Africa. Did you know that the Icelandic tongue has been kept so pure over the centuries that Icelandic people understand the Viking sagas? The bloodline of their horses has been kept pure since Viking times also. If a horse is taken off the island, it can never return."

"Wow," said Eduardo. "They must be very isolated."

"Not really. Many Europeans visit Iceland every year, and many European young people go to Iceland for a year of college."

"Is it all ice covered?"

"No," Philip laughed. "Although there is snow in the winter and on the higher elevations year-round. There are glaciers and volcanoes, hot geysers, and pools. Iceland has one of the world's most beautiful sites, Gullfoss Waterfall. During the summer, Iceland never gets really dark at night, and during the winter, its dark almost all day."

"I know," said Eduardo. "That's because of the tilt of the earth. Iceland is close to the top of the world. Norway, Sweden, Finland, and parts of Russia are like that too. I think I really want to see all of those places."

"Hmm," said Philip smiling. "I wonder how a man could get paid for travelling to all of those beautiful places."

Eduardo wrinkled his brow and thought about this long into the night.

The next afternoon, a motorboat took Philip and Eduardo along with several other tourists from the heart of Portland to the place where the Willamette merged with the mighty Columbia. They entered the larger river and travelled upstream until they came to the Columbia River Gorge. "Here, the river flows through a narrow pass between cliffs of columnar basalt," their guide informed them. "The gorge becomes a wind tunnel when the east wind blows, and for that reason, this area has become the wind surfing capital of the world." They passed Rooster Rock, Multnomah Falls, Crown Point, and finally came to the Bonneville Dam. "The dam was begun in 1934 during the depression and provided employment for thousands of people," the guide said. The boat entered a lock and thirty minutes later exited into Lake Bonneville. Travelling a little further, they came to the town of Cascade Locks. "The bridge you see is called the Bridge of the Gods," their guide told them while waiting for the boat to tie up at a dock. "There was a natural bridge across the river centuries ago that was created when the Cascadia landslide sent about five and a half square miles of debris into the river, effectively blocking it for a period of time. The river eventually breached the dam and washed it away. The Native Klickitat people have a legend about the natural bridge. They say that their chief god, Tyhee Saghalie, gave land to each of his two sons. Pahto took the land north of the river, and Wy'east took the land to the south. Their father created the earthen dam so they could visit each other. When the two brothers fell in love with the same maiden, they fought so furiously that the earth shook and the dam collapsed."

Lunch was on the patio of a restaurant overlooking the river. A few wind surfers skimmed through the water, catching a light breeze that blew west from the Cascades. The sun reflected off the mast of a sailboat whose spinnaker was unfurled in a show of red, blue, and yellow. Bees buzzed around a field of blue lupine and yellow balsamroot, and a woodpecker hammered away an old elm tree with rhythmic staccato. Eduardo stretched in his chair, letting the sun hit his face. "I could stay here for a long time," he said lazily.

The next morning, Philip's friend Robert met the two travelers in front of their hotel and drove them to his family's lake house east of the city. "My father built the house when I was a little boy," Robert said. "Mom would pack the four of us kids up and take us out to Blue Lake for the whole summer. There are a lot of good memories associated with this place." He turned the car on to Interlaken Lane and drove two-thirds of the way down the road before pulling onto a gravel driveway. The house was two stories with three visible dormer windows on the backside. Varying shades of weathered brown shingles covered the exterior sides as well as the roof. Robert popped the trunk and lifted their suitcases onto the grass, eyeing them with amusement. "You're going to need one pair of jeans, a pair of shorts, a couple of shirts, and a swimsuit while you're here," he said. "I think you may have overpacked."

"We did that in Hawaii too." Eduardo grinned at an embarrassed Philip who had insisted the boy pack dress clothes.

"We're all about casual here," Robert said. "My boys pretty much live in their swimwear. Do you waterski, Eduardo?" he asked, leading them up a gravel path to the side door.

"No, but I learned to surf last year."

Robert opened the door and ushered them inside. "It's a little different than surfing. The boys are out on the water right now. When they come in for lunch, you can meet them and then give it a try."

The house smelled of wood smoke and cedar. A large living room with exposed beam ceiling lay to the right of the door. A stone fireplace stood in the middle of the front wall between two large windows that faced the lake below. A door on the far side led to a deck complete with hot tub. On the left was a set of stairs and a hall. The hall led to a bathroom and two bedrooms, and the stairs led to a loft over the back half of the house. Straight through was a large dining table and to the left of that the kitchen. An oversized couch and two chairs in faded floral print stood in front of the fireplace. A sturdy maple coffee table sat on top a large rug that had been braided from scrapes of colorful fabric. Robert's wife, Dee, poked her head out of the kitchen for introductions. "We're so glad you could come," she said with genuine warmth in her voice. "Ken, Rob, and Tim will be here shortly, Eduardo. They've been looking forward to meeting you. Robert, show Philip his bedroom, and have Eduardo put is things up in the loft. I'll have lunch on the table in less than ten minutes."

Eduardo set his suitcase down and followed Philip and Robert to the guest bedroom in the back of the house. It was nothing fancy, just a bed, dresser, chair, and bedside table. There were two small windows and scenic photographs of Oregon on the cedar walls. "The photography is remarkable," Philip said, stepping up to take a closer look at a framed shot of turbulent surf as seen from the opening of a coastal cave.

"Thanks," Robert said. "This is all Ken's work. He's received several awards, and he's been pretty successful selling his work at street fairs the last three summers. He'll be going back down to Otis in a couple of weeks where he hopes to get his BA with a focus on photography.

"Wow," said Philip appreciatively, "the Harvard of art schools."

"Yes," Robert said. "It is prestigious. I'm very glad he got a scholarship, because it's also expensive."

"What will he do when he finishes?" Eduardo asked.

"Right now, he thinks he wants to be a photojournalist. We'll see what happens between now and the three years it will take him to graduate, but I think he's got the talent to do it." A door opened in the front of the house, and the banter of young male voices drifted to the bedroom. "We better get your stuff upstairs or we'll miss lunch," Robert said, smiling.

"Ken, Rob, Tim, come meet our guests," Robert called when they reached the living room. The boys were carrying a platter of sandwiches and armloads of tableware and condiments to the deck. The set their loads down and came back in. "Hi, Dr. Perez. Hi, Eduardo," they said, offering their hands.

"Dad," sixteen-year-old Rob said laughing, "you're not going to make Eduardo stay upstairs, are you? Ken snores so loud Eduardo won't get any sleep." The tallest of the three boys playfully slugged Rob in the shoulder.

"At least I don't sleepwalk," he said.

"Yeah," the youngest chimed in. "Last week, Rob got all the way down to the dock before he woke up." They were stair step images of each other: sun-bleached blonde hair falling below the jawline and tanned, muscular bodies.

"Lunch," Dee called, and the boys jostled each other as they followed their guests out to the deck.

"Mom says we have to wait for an hour after we eat before we can go in the water," Tim said as he loaded his sandwich with pickles.

"I think it's a conspiracy," said Ken, winking at his mother.

"Yeah," agreed Rob. "In an hour's time, we can get the dishes done and help fold laundry and sweep the floors."

"Hey," she said, "it's my vacation too, you brutes." They laughed and chatted, teased each other, and finally sat back stuffed full of tuna fish and macaroni salad.

"OK, I wash," Ken said, stacking Eduardo's and Philip's plates on his own.

"I'll dry, and Timmy can put things away," Rob said.

"Quit calling me Timmy. I'm a teenager now. I want to be called Tim."

"Yes, sir," his brothers said with mock salutes.

"You can have the bottom two drawers of the dresser on the left upstairs," Ken said, turning to Eduardo. "Why don't you unpack while we help mom, and then we'll go out on the lake. Tim was just exaggerating about waiting an hour. Mom only makes us wait a half hour."

Eduardo unpacked, donned his swimsuit, and came downstairs to keep the boys company while they finished their chores. "I don't know how to waterski," he told them. "I can surf, though."

"Oh, this is nothing like surfing," Ken said. "I do some surfing when I'm down in LA. With waterskiing, you have to lean back as you take off on the skis. If you ever lean forward, plop, you're in the drink."

"And don't hang on to the rope when you go down," Tim cautioned. "I did that and got dragged through the water for a mile until Kenny stopped the boat and came round to get me."

Eduardo's eyes widened.

"It wasn't a mile, stupid," Rob said, bopping his brother on the head. Looking at Eduardo, he warned, "You always have to have a spotter, someone in the back of the boat who watches the skier to make sure nothing happens and to let the driver know when he wants to go in."

"Is it hard to get up?" Eduardo asked.

"Most people fall at least once or twice before they're up on the skis," Ken said, "But once you're up, it's kind of like riding a bike. You get the hang of it, and it just gets easier and easier."

"OK," Ken announced, "time's up." Pointing to a narrow door under the stairs, he said, "Grab a towel from the closet, Eduardo, and let's go." He waited for Eduardo, and then they charged out of the house after the younger two boys. The path from the deck led down a bush-covered hillside to the boat dock forty feet below. Halfway down the hill, a sizable spot had been leveled for a fire pit. "We have bonfires here in the evening," Ken said. "The guys and I take turns hauling the lawnmower down once a week to mow the grass, and that's a pain in the neck."

They reached a short set of stairs leading to the dock. "Careful here," Ken said. "We have a few treads that need replacing. They don't last very many years around all this water." Moss grew on the sides of many of the stair treads as well as parts of the dock. There was a wet algae smell that permeated the area. Eduardo sat on the edge of the dock and lowered himself into the water. His left foot slid on a mossy rock nearly sending him to the bottom. Holding the side of the dock, he walked toward the end of the structure, judging the depth of the water. Something slimy wrapped around his right leg, and he hoisted himself up on the dock in a panic.

"What's this?" he asked, holding up a long string of slimy green weed.

"Lake grass or seaweed, whatever you want to call it," Rob said. "Every year when we open the cabin up, we spend the whole first day pulling that stuff out of the lake so the boat motor doesn't get fouled by it."

"Plus, it's not very fun to swim in it," Tim added.

The afternoon turned into evening before the boys finally brought the boar in and tied it to the dock. It had taken Eduardo three tries before he had gotten up on the skis. Once successfully upright, he had taken several turns around the perimeter of the lake, and his arms and legs ached from the strain. In spite of his discomfort, he trudged quickly up the hill with the Garrett boys, lured by the smell of grilling burgers on the deck. "I'm starved," a grinning Eduardo announced to the three adults who were surveying the loaded picnic table.

"Go take a quick shower with the boys and get dressed," Dee said. "We get a little breeze as the sun goes down, and you'll be chilly in that wet suit." The boys were taking turns rinsing off under an outdoor shower. Eduardo soaped himself up and rinsed as quickly as he could in the cold water. He wrapped his towel around his dripping suit and ran inside to change. Two burgers later, he sat contentedly listening as his three new friends regaled Philip with stories of their waterskiing prowess. Philip finally turned to him. "You're awfully quiet this evening," he remarked.

"I'm too tired to even talk," Eduardo replied to the amusement of everyone at the table.

"I hope you get your second wind," Robert said, "because we're going to take a twilight ride on the lake and then roast marshmallows over a bonfire. Run inside and get a jacket. It'll be cool on the water."

Eduardo was glad for the jacket because as Dee had promised, a breeze came up and cooled the air considerably. Robert drove the boat slowly around the lake with the running lights on. "We have to limit our speed after dusk," he said, "and no power boats after ten o'clock." They cruised past large modern houses and small cabins. On the far side of the lake, families were driving out of a public park that had a roped-off swimming area and a large slide. The boaters returned to the dock and walked to the campfire where kindling had been neatly stacked in the fire pit. Tim ran to the house to get marshmallows and roasting sticks. Ken brought his guitar down, and they sang and ate s'mores and watched the embers of the fire ascend into a midnight blue sky.

The next two weeks were filled during the days with swimming, skiing, hiking, and boats rides. The neighbors took the boys out on their sail boat and taught Eduardo the basics of handling the sails and tiller. In the evening, the family gathered around the fire and talked. The last evening, the conversation turned to Ken's pursuits. "You know we expect you to spend some time with us when you're in LA," Philip told the nineteen-year-old.

"I'd love that," Ken replied. "Thank you for the invitation."

"What made you decide you want to be a photojournalist?" Eduardo asked the young man who sat next to him.

"Since Mom and Dad bought me my first camera, I've loved taking photos. I found it was a challenge to capture something worth hanging on a wall. I mean, we travel places and we take pictures, but how many of them belong on a wall someplace? I took a photography class and leaned a few tips, and the next thing I knew, I was selling my stuff at markets and fairs."

"Do you make any videos?" Eduardo asked.

"No, I decided to stick with photography, you know, kind of freeze a moment in time. You can tell a story with photos, and I like that idea."

"Will you keep selling your pictures at street markets and fairs?"

"Oh, I hope I go beyond that." Ken laughed. "I will probably have to fund my own trips at first, but I'm hoping to sell my work to magazines. I especially like the idea of doing work worthy of the *National Geographic*."

"Wow," the younger boy said. "That sounds exciting, travelling all over the world, taking pictures, and telling stories."

"I don't think it will always be easy or glamorous, but exciting, well, yes, I think it will be exciting."

Goodbyes were said the next morning, and Robert drove Philip and Eduardo to the airport. "I can't thank you enough," Philip said, shaking his friend's hand. "This has been one of the most relaxing periods of time I have had in years."

"Then we should make it an annual event," Robert said. "You're willingness to participate in the conference up here this winter has sent registrations soaring."

"My pleasure," Philip said. "I'll see you in January."

On the short flight home, Eduardo could not get the conversation with Ken off his mind. Travel and storytelling, to be paid for doing these things was a compelling idea that would engage his thoughts and imagination for a very long time.

CHAPTER TWENTY-TWO

College

Los Angeles
1987–1988

Eduardo's seventeenth birthday was celebrated at a steak house in Santa Monica with Philip, Tomas, Maria, and the Garrett's oldest son, Ken.

"Happy birthday," Ken said after a hostess led him to the group "Here, I hope you like this." He handed Eduardo a long flat package.

"Can I open it now?"

"Please," the young man said with an air of expectancy.

Before the wrappings were off, Eduardo knew Ken had given him a framed photo. In fact, it was a series of three photos. The first photo showed Eduardo, Rob, and Tim in a water fight. The second photo was shot from the boat, a beaming Eduardo on one waterski. The third photo was taken at the campfire; Eduardo was sitting on the ground in front of Philip with his head leaning into the man's chest. Philip's arms were draped around Eduardo's shoulders, and his chin rested on the boy's head. Embers rose from the fire like thin streaks of light. Eduardo examined each photo in speechless wonder.

"Do you like it?" Ken asked.

"It's beautiful," Eduardo answered. "It's the story of my vacation. Thank you."

"How did you get the night shot?" Philip asked, slightly unsettled by the emotion the photo roused in him. "I didn't even know you were taking it."

"That's the point," Ken said. "I don't like posed photography. I think the magic of the moment flees when people realize they are being photographed. To answer your question though, I used a very slow shutter speed, the light from the fire to illuminate your faces, and a block of wood to stabilize the camera. I think I caught that magical moment I was looking for."

Lessons had grown more intense as Eduardo labored through what would be his final year of study at home. "You will need to start applying to colleges," Maggie informed him. "Have you thought about where you would like to go?"

"I think I want to stay close," Eduardo said. "I actually like the idea of going to UCLA."

"They have a great liberal arts program there," she said. "For one of your assignments, I'm going to have you make an appointment with an admissions counselor to discuss the application process and a possible course of study." It all seemed slightly overwhelming to Eduardo, but Maggie helped him break it down into manageable steps.

Christmases were never a parade of materialism at the Perez household, although there were parties and beautiful decorations. The whole family went to church on Christmas Eve, and Philip read the story of Jesus's birth before they opened small gifts Christmas morning. The gifts were sometimes homemade; and when purchased, they were never expensive, perhaps a book, a painting, or a tape of music. One year, after learning to play the recorder fairly well, Eduardo made a tape of his instrumentals and presented it to the others.

Maria always prepared a sumptuous meal at noon, and one or two other families often joined them. During the Christmas break following Eduardo's seventeenth birthday, Tomas and Maria accompanied him and Philip on a trip to Mammoth. While Eduardo took ski lessons and Philip tackled some challenging slopes, Maria was content to crochet a new afghan, and Tomas read by the fire. "You don't need that blanket around your knees, Tomas," she said one afternoon. "It's seventy five degrees in here."

"I see the snow outside, and it doesn't matter how warm it is in here. I shiver. I'm keeping the blanket."

With spring came an acceptance letter from UCLA, including the notification that he had been granted a four-year soccer scholarship. There was a celebration in the house that night. "I'm not declaring a major just yet," Eduardo told Philip that evening. "Do you think I'm foolish?"

"Absolutely not," Philip replied. "I want you to remember, though, there will be many temptations that will present themselves to you in college. While I hope you enjoy an occasional party, if you get involved in alcohol or drugs, you will lose your scholarship and may ruin your life."

"Uncle Philip," Eduardo said, "I have seen the side of life that accompanies drug abuse. Even when I was running drugs for Miguel, I was never tempted to try them. I promised myself I would never do that, and I am promising you the same. I have watched my cousins drink until they passed out. I do not want that to ever be part of my life. If I drink any alcohol, it won't be until I am twenty-one, and it will be in moderation like you and your friends."

After spending two weeks at Blue Lake, Eduardo began studies at UCLA. The university was a one-hour drive from the villa, which would have cut into valuable study time, but staying near the university was an expense Eduardo could not afford. He kept distractions to a minimum by studying at the library between classes.

"You must be making a lot of new friends," Maria remarked one Friday when he arrived home late. "Have you seen any cute girls?"

"I don't have time for that," he laughed. "I go to class, study, eat, and sleep. I don't even know if girls attend UCLA," he joked. That was not exactly the truth as Maria suspected. He had not only noticed a pretty brunette by the name of Tiffany Sebring in his history class, he was also thinking of inviting her to see a movie at the local theater some evening if he could raise the courage to do so.

The opportunity to invite Tiffany out presented itself one afternoon when she dropped a pile of books on the long study table opposite Eduardo and dropped into a chair. The commotion drew his attention away from the text he was reading, and when he made eye contact with the girl, she smiled.

"You're in my history class, aren't you?" she asked.

"I think so," he lied, deciding he shouldn't be too obvious about having observed her. They talked for almost an hour, and by the time Tiffany rose to leave, they had a date for coffee the following afternoon. Eduardo arrived at the coffee shop fifteen minutes early and dropped his books and jacket at a small table in the corner. His heart was pounding, and his face felt flushed. He had grown used to being in all types of social situations, but this strange reaction to spending time with Tiffany was both exciting and disconcerting. He sat back in his chair and took a few deep breaths.

Tiffany arrived a few minutes late, breathless but laughing. "Sorry I'm a little late," she apologized. "Some of the fraternity guys were pulling off a practical joke, and I just had to watch."

They both lost track of time, and when the young man hit rush-hour traffic on his way home, he knew Maria would be probing into the reason for his late arrival. He smiled to himself and decided he would tell Maria the truth, even though he knew Uncle Philip would probably worry about the distraction.

Tiffany's name came up often enough in conversation that Philip decided it was time to meet this girl who was the object of Eduardo's interest. "Bring her over next Saturday," Philip suggested, "and let the rest of us meet her." When she arrived two days later, Philip was pleased to find the young lady was gracious and seemed to enjoy conversing with the older inhabitants of the house. She had thoughtfully brought small gifts for him as well as for Tomas and Maria.

"You are well informed regarding geopolitics," Philip commented at dinner. "Many young people are not interested in what transpires outside their circle of friends."

Tiffany had already told Philip of her desire to become a news commentator. "I know that the commentator's presentations on air are canned. I told Eduardo I want him to write my stories." She looked at the smiling young man and giggled. "That way, maybe the news can be presented without a political or big business slant."

Philip raised his eyebrows. This young lady really was informed.

Tiffany was not only bright, but she was pretty. Maria took note of the girl's long glossy brown hair, which she had swept away from her face with a headband. Her features were delicate with warm hazel eyes and a slightly upturned nose. She wore little makeup, just a touch of mascara on her lashes and gloss on lips that were prone to smile. Philip was happy that she came from a family that put high value on education. Tiffany's father was an anesthesiologist, and her mother was a teacher. Philip suspected that Eduardo would be meeting them soon. Things seemed to be off to a good start, but he hoped the budding romance would progress slowly.

*   *   *

"Where do you see yourself in three years?" Philip asked Eduardo during the summer between his freshman and sophomore years of college. Eduardo was quiet for a long time. "Perhaps as an overseas correspondent or working on documentary films," the young man replied. "Ken really made me start thinking about things like that."

Philip hoped it was the latter. Correspondents for news networks were often assigned to places of danger, earthquakes, floods, war zones. Of course, depending on the type of documentary film Eduardo produced, there could be danger in that too. There were many human rights violations in the world, and for every violation, there were people who did not want the violation exposed. Philip sighed. "You seem to be headed for a life of adventure and peril. Are you ready for that?" he asked, the concern evident in his voice.

Eduardo considered this for a moment. He saw glamour in the work of a foreign correspondent, but he had not given a lot of thought to the dangers he might incur. He had faced danger and uncertainty more than once in his young life. In his dealings with Miguel and Ernesto, he had shown considerable resourcefulness. "I would like to try it," he said quite honestly.

"I have a friend at CNN," Philip said. "Would you like me to inquire about an internship there?" Eduardo's face said it all. Philip placed the call as promised. It was too late for an internship that summer; but his friend, Hal Brightwood, suggested Eduardo apply for the following summer.

"It's pretty competitive, Philip, and it's not as glamorous as most of the kids think it will be."

"I understand," Philip assured his friend. "I want him to get a taste of the real world of journalism though, and this would be a wonderful opportunity."

"In that case, have him write a piece on some subject of his choosing, preferably a current event. It should be written as if it would be read on broadcast news. He can send it to the network and mark it to my attention. If it passes muster, we'll bring him in for a summer stint. Let's see what your kid has to offer."

*   *   *

"CNN," Tiffany squealed when Eduardo told her. "That's unbelievable, Eduardo."

"It's not a done deal," he said, "and it would mean a whole summer apart for us." He reached for her hand as he led her through the garden behind Perez's house.

"But it's an opportunity you couldn't refuse." She smiled at him. "The summer will go by fast, you'll see."

They had reached the end of the lighted path; and a giant moon, sitting atop the hills to the southeast, cast shadows into which Eduardo led the girl. Though she wore a sweater, she shivered with the coolness of the evening. He drew her next to him and wrapped his arms around her. "I think I'm getting addicted to you," he whispered in a hoarse voice. "I don't' know if I can make it three months without seeing your sweet face." He moved his left hand to her cheek and looked deeply into her eyes. Tiffany raised her own hands to his chest. Ever so gently, Eduardo brought his face to hers, drawing her even closer as their lips met.

"You'll make it," she said when the kiss ended, "because I'll be waiting right here for you when you return home."

"Promise?"

"I promise."

*   *   *

With the return of summer, Tiffany travelled to Minnesota with her family, and Philip and Eduardo returned to Blue Lake. Robert Garrett helped Philip find a small cabin to rent on Blue Lake. "This makes more sense than buying a place," Robert said, "unless you're going to spend several months here each year." The place was perfect: two bedrooms, a loft, and a great room. It was about a half mile from the Garrett's, a nice walk or bike ride.

"No boat, and not Tiffany," Eduardo said with disappointment.

"You can't ski by yourself, dummy," Rob reminded him.

"Who's Tiffany?" Ken wanted to know.

"Come down here as often as you like," Dee offered. And so they spent a whole month swimming and sunning and waterskiing. Tomas, Maria, and Lobo joined them until Tomas said the dampness got to his arthritic joints.

*   *   *

At the beginning of Eduardo's sophomore year, he declared his major, journalism, and a minor in film making. He became a writer for the school's newspaper, the *Daily Bruin,* and worked on several student films.

"Have you talked with Ken recently?" Philip asked one evening. "He'll be interested to know about your major."

"I haven't talked with him since we returned to LA."

"Why don't we invite him over for dinner?" Philip suggested. "You could invite Tiffany and a few other friends too if you like."

The evening with a couple of friends quickly became a party for twelve when Ken brought a few friends to join Eduardo's group from college. After diving into a lavish buffet Maria had spread on the dining table, the young people drifted into the family room and split into two groups for a lively game of charades. "Hey, we've lost a couple of people," one of Ken's friends announced. Eduardo noted that the two missing people were Ken and Tiffany.

"They'll probably be here in a minute," someone suggested. "Ken can be on our team, and Tiffany will be on Eduardo's team." Twenty minutes after the game commenced, Ken and Tiffany were still missing. Philip poked his head into the room and chuckled at the antics of the kids as they acted out movie and song titles.

Everyone seemed to be having a good time except for Eduardo. It was then that Perez noted the missing members of the group. He left the kids with a puzzled look on his face and checked the downstairs rooms for the missing guests. His search led him to the backyard where he spotted Ken and Tiffany so deep in conversation that they seemed to have shut out the rest of the world. Philip's presence went unnoticed until he coughed. Ken looked up and rose from the bench he'd been sharing with Tiffany.

"Dr. Perez," Ken said in a startled tome, "I didn't see you standing there."

"I think the other kids are beginning to miss the two of you," Perez said.

Tiffany arose, her face noticeably red in the pale light. "We started talking about Ken's goals and then mine, and we sort of lost track of time."

"I think you can probably join in the second round of charades if you hurry," Philip advised.

Without further comment, Ken and Tiffany made their way into the family room, hoping they wouldn't be required to explain their absence.

The rest of the evening went rather awkwardly. Eduardo could not help noticing the frequent looks Tiffany gave Ken. Ken did not seem to be having a very good time and spent most of the rest of the evening with his head down, avoiding eye contact with Eduardo and everyone else. "You don't look so good," Ken's roommate, Gavin, remarked. "Want to head back to the apartment?"

"Yeah," Ken replied. "I think I'm coming down with something." He rose and thanked his hosts for their hospitality.

"Since you're headed back into Los Angeles, can I hitch a ride?" Tiffany asked. "It'll save Eduardo a long drive."

Ken looked at the UCLA group. "Our car's loaded," the other driver said.

"It'll be a bit of a squeeze, but yeah, we can take you," Gavin said.

Tiffany thanked Philip and gave Eduardo a weak smile. A deafening silence followed their departure, and rest of the kids nervously grabbed coats and bid Eduardo and Philip a hasty but grateful farewell. Eduardo went straight to his room, although Philip feared the boy would probably not sleep easily. It was not clear what had transpired on the back patio, but whatever it was, Philip hoped either Ken or Tiffany would call Eduardo in the morning and explain.

Sleep may have eluded Eduardo, but it also eluded Ken. An uncomfortable silence had hung in the air all the way back to Los Angeles. Ken said little to Tiffany other than "Good night," when he walked her to her door. Even at that, their eyes had met for the briefest of moments during which he felt almost paralyzed.

"Call me?" Tiffany asked.

"Eduardo's my friend," Ken said, agony written across his face.

"Do you believe in love at first sight?" she asked, moving closer.

Ken held up his palms as if to fend her off. Tears welled up in his eyes, and he turned and raced to the car.

Eduardo failed to come downstairs for breakfast. Philip was about to check on him when the doorbell rang. A disheveled Ken stood in the doorway. The young man tried to find his voice, but he choked on the words that failed him. He lowered his head and put a hand to his eyes. "I've ruined our friendship," he managed to say.

Philip slipped an arm around Ken and guided him into the study. When the boy regained control of his voice, he looked at Philip. "I don't know what happened," he said. "We were standing around eating, and Tiffany started asking me about my studies. Somehow we ended up in the garden, and it was like . . . I don't know . . . like sparks were flying between us. She told me about her goals, and we laughed about how she might report the news I would be photographing . . . you know, how our careers might intersect. She was just so fun to talk with I completely forgot about everyone else, including Eduardo." He broke eye contact and held his head in his hands, for all appearances a broken man.

"Are you going to see her again?"

"No! She asked me to call, but there's no way. I never meant to step between Eduardo and his girlfriend."

"It sounds like her relationship with Eduardo is over . . ."

"That's beside the point," Ken said. "I will always associate her with the pain I've caused my good friend."

"Would you like to talk with Eduardo?"

Ken shook his head in the affirmative.

Philip left the young men alone to sort things out. Their meeting was strained and painful, but Ken would not leave until he sensed the friendship could be restored. When he finally departed, he wrapped his arms around Eduardo at the front door and buried his face in his friend's shoulder while his body shook with emotion.

Tears filled Eduardo's eyes. He didn't know whose broken trust had caused him the most pain, but he suspected it was Ken's.

"You will get past this," Philip reassured Eduardo when Ken had left.

"I believe that, Uncle Philip. It's just going to hurt for a while."

Chapter Twenty-Three

The Internship

Florida
1989

The internship materialized the next summer in Florida, and that was as close as Eduardo got to an assignment abroad. The young apprentice spent most of his days running errands for a producer and learning the workings of a television studio from the ground up. While the experience afforded him no glamour, it gave him an education in programming that he would not have received in a classroom. He worked hard and often spent extra hours in the sound or editing rooms after the other interns had left for the evening. His efforts did not go unnoticed, and Perez received regular updates from Hal Brightwood, the producer Eduardo worked under.

"This kid is great," Hal told Perez one evening on the phone.

"I'm so grateful for your updates because we hardly hear from him."

"That's probably because we practically have to drag him out of the studio at the end of the day. In fact, when I left this evening, he was still there. I'll ask him tomorrow if he's talked with you lately. He's doing great, Philip, and if he keeps this up, we'll be glad to offer him a job when he graduates."

Philip smiled at the thought of how far Eduardo had come in such a few years.

As promised, Hal asked Eduardo how everyone was at home, and Eduardo was on the phone by the end of the day. "I'm sorry I don't call more often," he said when Philip answered the phone.

"I hear they're keeping you pretty busy."

A ten-minute dialogue followed as Eduardo described his apartment, his duties, and the people with whom he worked. He lived in a two-bedroom apartment with another intern, Dylan Cox, a nineteen-year-old from Oregon who was studying for a career in film and television. Over the course of the two-and-a-half-month internship, the two young men developed a friendship that would last for the rest of their lives. When they said goodbye at the end of the summer, they vowed to try and find work together when they had their degrees.

As Eduardo packed to return to the West Coast, he could not get his grandfather off his mind. It had been five years since he last saw the old man, and Eduardo had changed greatly since then. He did not know if his grandfather would recognize him. In fact, he did not know if his grandfather still lived. Eduardo put his final paycheck in the bank, checked his balance, and then called the airline. He had enough money to cover a change of itinerary. He placed a call to Philip and explained his wish to visit his grandfather on his way home.

Perez had often wondered when this time would come. It was to be expected that Eduardo would one day want to see his grandfather again. There had been no contact with him or the cousins since Eduardo had come to live at the villa. Perez too wondered if the grandfather was still alive. For Eduardo's sake, he prayed the old man lived. Eduardo was exceptionally mature for his age, and Phillip had no doubt that he could manage the details of the trip. What he feared was Eduardo's reception in his grandfather's village.

"Are you sure you want to do this?" he asked Eduardo over the phone. "Your cousins may have returned home by now."

Eduardo had not considered that prospect. They were sure to give him a hard time, and they might try to prevent him from seeing his grandfather. His excitement of the past hour began to wane. "I hadn't thought about that," he said. "Still, I would like to go." But this time, the words were more tentative.

"Would you mind calling me daily?" Philip asked. Concern was evident in his voice.

"I promise," Eduardo said and hung up the phone.

The trip was long and tiring. Arranged on short notice, it had been pieced together, a flight into Mexico City with a one-day layover followed by a flight to Guadalajara and a bus ride to San Jenaro. After landing in Mexico City, Eduardo checked into the Camino Real Mexico, a short ride from the airport. His flight did not leave until the next afternoon, and he soon grew restless. Before an hour had passed, he was in a cab that carried him into the neighborhood of Polanco, where some of Mexico City's finest shopping is located. The district was crowded. It appeared that people from all over the world had converged on the area. Eduardo strolled slowly down a street lined with designer shops. He had never seen so many beautiful women.

Dressed in the latest styles of South American designers as well as those of the great houses of fashion in Europe, many of them could have set for the covers of *Vogue* or *Cosmopolitan*. Turning to admire a colorful grouping of dresses in a window, something tugged at Eduardo's memory. He studied the dresses that seductively clung to thin mannequins, and his thoughts turned to Kristen. The dresses were similar to the design she had worn the night of her engagement. It suddenly occurred to him that Kristen was here in Mexico City. He found a phone and called the American Embassy.

"Excuse me," Eduardo said to the receptionist answering the telephone, "I am a friend of Kristen, Kristen and Andrew Morgan. I am in Mexico City for just a day, and I was wondering if it would be possible to contact them."

"Your name?" the pleasant young voice asked.

"Eduardo Rodriguez. I'm a friend from Los Angeles."

"Eduardo Rodriguez," she repeated. "One moment please, Señor Rodriguez. I'll see if Señor Morgan is available."

Was there amusement in her voice, he wondered, but he did not puzzle over the receptionist's tone long. A cheerful male voice came on the other end of the line.

"Hello, Eduardo. What brings you to Mexico City?"

"Andrew?"

"Yes, how are you? Kristen and I think of you and Philip often."

"I'm well. And how are you and Kristen?"

"Couldn't be better."

After a few minutes of catching up, Andrew offered to send Kristen to spend the afternoon escorting their American visitor as Andrew put it. "Stay right where you are, and she'll be there in twenty minutes. That is, if you don't have other plans."

"I can't think of anything I would like better," Eduardo replied.

Twenty minutes later, a cab pulled up; and Kristen bounced out, laughing and looking just as he had remembered her.

The next hours flew by. Kristen had become as good a tour guide as she was a dance instructor.

"Have you a gift for your grandfather?" she asked as the afternoon wore on.

"No, I need to purchase something." He could not believe his thoughtlessness. He was grateful Kristen had remembered this simple but important courtesy.

"Let's go down to the old market," Kristen said. "I think he would appreciate something hand-crafted much more than an Armani shirt we would find in this store."

A cab drove them to a district of small shops where local crafts were hand-made.

Wandering into an old leather shop, Eduardo scanned rows of ornately carved boots.

"Beautiful, aren't they?" Kristen commented at his side.

"I would love to buy him a pair," Eduardo said, "but as Uncle Philip says, shoes must be fitted properly."

"We have belts," the proprietor suggested.

Kristen wandered to the back where rows and rows of belts hung from long nails pounded in the wall. The selection was good. "How big is he?" she asked before realizing that Eduardo was not at her side. She turned and scanned the shop, not seeing him. A moment of panic gripped her heart. This was one of the most colorful parts of the city, but not the safest area. In an instant, Eduardo's head popped up from behind a table piled with hides.

"What are you doing?" Kristen asked, relieved to find him.

"Look at this," he said, motioning her to join him.

"Needs some work, and I think it would be much easier to carry a belt to your grandfather than a desk."

Eduardo laughed. "Look at this." With some difficulty, he pulled a drawer loose and turned it for her inspection.

"The workmanship is beautiful," she agreed. "But would you really buy a desk for your grandfather?"

"No, this is not for grandfather. It's for Uncle Philip. This desk belongs in his study. Stripped of the paint and oiled to a shine, it will look beautiful in his study."

"Oh," Kristen said. "I thought you were going to drag it down to San Jenaro. You simply want to cart it to LA." She looked at Eduardo as if he was crazy.

"It's beautiful, isn't it, Kristen?" he coaxed.

Kristen pulled hides from the top of the desk. "Well, it's not damaged. And other than having too many layers of paint, it is in good shape. Yes, it's a beautiful piece. I'll tell you what, because you are such a good friend, if they'll sell it to you, I'll make sure it gets crated up and shipped to Villa Perez."

Eduardo smiled and slipped an arm around his friend.

"Now," she said, tugging him toward the wall, "let's find that belt."

Before they left the market area, Eduardo purchased a lacy black shawl for Aunt Juanita. "Maybe it will soften the shock of my return," he said.

*   *   *

Kristen and Andrew asked Eduardo to be their guest at dinner that evening. "I'll send a car around at seven thirty," she said when she dropped him off at his hotel. "Jacket and tie be fine. We might have another guest, "she added, laughing. And with that, she was off.

Eduardo checked his watch. It was five o'clock. With luck, he could catch a quick nap before showering and changing for dinner. He sent his slacks to be pressed and his shoes to be shined before lying down. He always strived for a neat appearance, but for some reason unknown to him, he took extra care this afternoon.

The car arrived sharply at 7:30 p.m. Eduardo was grateful the driver had the air-conditioning on. The humidity was high, and the heat of the day had not dissipated.

He smoothed his tie. It was a gift Kristen insisted on purchasing that afternoon during their shopping trip. A similar tie was packed in his suitcase for Philip. "The color and fabric are good," she had said, ignoring the price tags. The silky softness was smooth and cool beneath Eduardo's hand. Orange red in color with small yellow dots, it contrasted beautifully with his navy jacket and crisp white shirt.

"Could you stop just a moment?" Eduardo asked the driver. On the corner, a flower vendor was gathering up his wares. Eduardo stepped outside the car and purchased the man's last two dozen long-stemmed roses. They were a beautiful shade of coral. The driver smiled. Mrs. Morgan loved roses, and she always kept vases of them about the house.

The trip was reasonably short, and soon they arrived at a villa with a large iron gate in the front wall. The driver pulled to the entrance and pressed the combination on the key pad that opened the gate. A short driveway led to an old Spanish-style hacienda. Pulling up to the front door, the car stopped, and Eduardo exited, his arms laden with roses. He pulled a chain that rang the doorbell, and Andrew appeared.

"Eduardo, what pleasure to see you."

"Thank you for inviting me, Andrew. It is good to see you too."

"Please, come in. It's so hot this time of year. Can I get you something to drink?"

"I'd like to set these flowers down first," Eduardo said, "and then if you don't mind, a tonic water on ice.

"Come into the kitchen then. I think we'll find Kristen and Em there along with a vase, some tonic, and ice." He clapped Eduardo on the shoulder and led him through the front hall to the back of the house where Kristen labored over pots while chatting with another guest.

"Honey, Eduardo is here bearing flowers," Andrew announced.

Kristen spun around. "Oh my gosh," she said. "They're gorgeous. How did you know I love that color?"

"Lucky guess." Eduardo smiled.

"Em, could you get a vase in the pantry . . . if there's one large enough?" Kristen laughed.

A slender blonde, dressed in a simple black jersey dress, went into the pantry and returned with a large crystal vase. "This should do," she said. "Would you like to do the honors, Eduardo, or should I?"

Eduardo frowned at the sound of her voice. "You answered the phone today at the embassy," he said.

The young woman giggled. "You don't know me, do you?"

Eduardo's brow became more furrowed. "Should I?"

"Would you like to go rabbit hunting in the garden after dinner?" she teased.

"Emily," he exclaimed, his eyes wide. This was no chubby, bespectacled thirteen-year-old with braces on her teeth. He looked into her eyes, and it was unmistakable in spite of all the other changes. Her eyes were the same clear blue eyes of his young dancing partner.

"Emily," he said again, laughing, and gave her a gentle hug.

"Emily is helping us at the embassy during the summer—" Andrew began.

"And getting some fantastic experience," she interrupted, while filling the vase with water. She smiled up at Eduardo, displaying the arrangement for his approval.

"Now how is it," Eduardo asked, "that some people can shove the flowers in the vase and make it look like a piece of art? I always get them clumped onto one side or the other."

Emily's cheeks glowed bright pink.

"Put those roses on the hall table, Em," Kristen said. "Then we'll sit down to dinner."

*   *   *

Dinner was wonderful, and Eduardo was not surprised. He suspected there was nothing Kristen did not do well. The surprise had been Emily. Having not seen her for a few years, he knew he would never have recognized her on the street, and for the first time ever, he did not feel like running from her. He stole a glance in her direction and found her looking at him. He smiled, and she beamed back.

Dinner was enjoyed leisurely, and as the women cleared the table, Andrew and Eduardo wandered into the garden. "Lovely night," Andrew commented.

"Beautiful," Eduardo replied.

"So you're going to see your grandfather tomorrow?"

"Yes." Glancing toward the house, Eduardo added, "But I kind of wish I had a couple more days in Mexico City."

"Change your ticket."

"I really can't," he said regretfully. "I've got to be back in LA when school starts next week."

"Let me know if you need anything while you're in San Jenaro. Philip told us your grandfather hasn't been well."

"Thanks, Andrew. I really appreciate that."

"So I think you were a bit surprised seeing Em tonight."

"I can't believe how much she has changed," Eduardo said. "I would never have recognized her. Did you know we were in the garden chasing rabbit's the night you and Kristen announced your engagement. We thought we were alone near the wall until we heard a certain young lady's delighted squeal.

"We thought we were alone too," Andrew laughed. "I had just slipped the ring on Kristen's finger." He paused, folded his arms, and looked at Eduardo. "I heard you had a toothache that night."

"Well, actually, the pain was a little lower than that," Eduardo confessed, patting his chest at the level of his heart.

"Hope it's better now," Andrew said.

"Getting better all the time." Eduardo smiled, looking in the direction of the kitchen.

*   *   *

Eduardo arrived back at the hotel well after midnight and was glad his flight didn't leave until one in the afternoon. He packed his bag and crawled into bed, but sleep eluded him. The vision of Emily Montoya would not leave his head, and he smiled to himself as he thought of her. His smile deepened as he remembered how desperately he had tried to avoid her just a few years ago and how those feeling had changed tonight.

*   *   *

San Jenaro was just as he had left it. He exited the bus a few blocks from Grandfather's neighborhood and walked slowly in the direction of the old man's house. It was late afternoon, and the smell of fresh tortillas and savory stew wafting from kitchens reminded him that he hadn't eaten since morning. He felt suddenly weak and sat down on an old wooden crate in the shadow of a large tree across the street from his grandfather's house. Children played soccer in the road, raising a cloud of dust that settled like brown powder on their bodies. The obvious signs of poverty were present: patched clothing, bare feet, and a ball that had lost its bounce. But the children played with gusto, and Eduardo smiled as he watched their animated game.

His attention was suddenly drawn from the children to an old man who slowly moved onto the porch across the street and seated himself in a rickety rocking chair. The man was a little thinner and more fragile-looking than Eduardo remembered. The young man stared for several minutes, nervously contemplating how he would approach his beloved grandfather and what he would say. Had he been sure of Grandfather's reaction, he would have run into the old man's arms, but he feared his sudden appearance might give the man a heart attack. The old man seemed well. Eduardo had harbored fears that Grandfather might not be alive; and yet there he sat, rocking in his favorite chair. Juanita came out the front door and said something to Grandfather before walking down the street.

Eduardo reached inside his pocket and felt his mother's cross. He remembered the day Grandfather gave it to him, wrapped up in a soft cloth. He remembered losing it after his wet clothing had been stripped off him at the hospital. Holding the cross now between thumb and index fingers, he summoned his courage, rose, and walked across the street.

The old man paid no attention as Eduardo approached him. There were no noises coming from the house, and Eduardo hoped his grandfather was alone. He knelt in front of the old man and put his hand on his grandfather's knee.

"Grandfather," he said softly, "it is Eduardo, your grandson." The old man's eyes rested on Eduardo's face. The two men were transfixed for a moment, holding each other's gaze until Grandfather slowly stood, bringing the young man up with him, wrapping his arms around Eduardo, and sobbing.

"Where have you been, my son?" Grandfather asked. "Your cousins told us you got into terrible trouble." Here, the old man's voice cracked again. Eduardo guided his grandfather back into the chair, took a seat at the old man's feet, and relayed his story. The old man looked deep into Eduardo's eyes and was satisfied that what he heard was the truth. "I always knew you were a good boy, Eduardo. I knew you would not disappoint me in the end."

"Are you OK, Grandfather?" Eduardo finally asked.

"I am fine," the old man smiled. "I am better than I ever thought I would be. Come," he said. "Come inside. We must celebrate your return."

The old man placed food before the boy and insisted he eat. Hours passed as evening wore into night. Eduardo told his grandfather of his good fortune in being taken into the household of the man he referred to as Uncle Philip. "I will have my citizenship as well as my college degree in a couple of years, Grandfather. Then I will be able to get a good job and bring you to live with me."

"If God wills," the old man said, smiling.

"You will like it there," Eduardo said. "You will meet Tomas and Maria, and I will take care of you."

The old man patted his grandson's arm. "There is something I wish to give you." Rising and moving to an old dresser, he took a tattered picture from a drawer. "You and your parents," he said, handing the picture to Eduardo.

Eduardo carefully took the picture and studied the faded images of a serious young man whose arm was protectively drawn around a beautiful young woman with long black hair and laughing eyes. In her arms was a baby. He had never seen the photograph before, but it was as if the images had been in his head forever. "They are exactly as I always imagined them," he said in wonder. "You never showed this to me when I was a child, Grandfather. Why?"

The old man's eyes filled with tears. "I thought it was lost. I only found it recently where I had placed it with some old papers. See how happy they were."

"Tell me about them, Grandfather," Eduardo begged. "You have never told me much about them."

The old man pulled a handkerchief from his pocket, blew his nose, and looked into Eduardo's eyes. "You have only to look in the mirror. You are like both of them," he said. They talked long into the night until the old man could no longer hold his eyes open.

The following morning, Eduardo was awakened by the noise of trucks rumbling down the road to the factory. He rose and found his grandfather on the porch with Lupe's worn Bible. Eduardo sat at the old man's feet. "Grandfather, I used to hear your voice in my head, reciting verses when I went to live in California. I knew you would not be happy about my involvement with the gang. In fact, I was afraid you would hate me if you found out what I was doing."

"Hate you?" the old man said. "No, I would never hate you. I was very disappointed, and I always feared I had made the wrong decision in sending you to live with Martin and the others. Do you remember the story of the Prodigal Son, Eduardo? His father received him back into the family because he showed true remorse over his waywardness. If we repent, God is willing to forgive us. How could I do any less?" The two men sat in thoughtful silence until Grandfather took Eduardo's hand and prayed. They rose, embraced each other, and went into the house to prepare breakfast.

Just as they as they sat to eat, steps sounded on the front porch, and Juanita entered. Eduardo greeted her and placed his gift in her hands. She tossed the shawl on the table, landing its fringe in a bowl of polenta.

"What are you doing here? You are not welcome. Martin and the others told us what trouble you were in, how you disgraced the family and brought shame upon your grandfather's name. You gave him another heart attack. Now get out of here before you cause his death."

"Grandfather," Eduardo whispered, turning to the old man. He had never wanted to cause Grandfather any harm. He took the old man's hand. "You did not tell me you were sick again."

"I am fine, Eduardo." Turning to his sister, the old man said, "You are the one who will leave this house. Leave now."

"He has only come for your money," Juanita yelled. Turning to Eduardo, she spat venom. "But you will not get it. I am not stupid, Eduardo, though you may think I am."

Eduardo stared at Juanita in confusion. What was she talking about? Grandfather was not rich. Why would she say such a thing? Then he remembered the day he left for California. Grandfather had handed the truck driver a large amount of money. Eduardo never knew how Grandfather had come to have such a lot of money. Old questions were being supplanted by new ones.

"Don't play stupid," Juanita hissed.

"What?" Eduardo said, only partly paying attention to the woman. His mind was spinning, trying to put the pieces of information together, but there was too much missing to form a solid picture.

"I know you've come for his money, but you're not getting a dime," she repeated.

"Silence, woman," Grandfather demanded. "You will leave this house at once."

"I don't want any money," Eduardo said. "I came to see my grandfather."

Grandfather rose and walked to the door. "Out," he commanded to the woman.

Without saying another word, Juanita walked out of the house.

Eduardo was stunned. "Grandfather," he said, "I don't understand what Tia Juanita is talking about. I want nothing from you, but the love you have always shown me."

The old man shushed the boy. "I know," he said. "I know."

*   *   *

The following day, Eduardo slipped the photograph in his shirt pocket and bid his grandfather a tearful goodbye. "I will return for you, Grandfather. I do not know if it will be in a few months or a few years, but I will return. Please take care of yourself and remember that I love you." The young man walked out of his grandfather's house and to the bus stop. In Guadalajara, he spent a sleepless night in his hotel room, mentally sorting out what had transpired in San Jenaro. Of the money, Grandfather would say nothing. Eduardo did not press for more information, afraid his curiosity would be misinterpreted as interest in gaining some of the money for himself. He learned that Carlos and Julio had returned to Mexico and were working in the tequila factory. Miguel and Ramon were still in California. Ramon was married and had a child.

Grandfather seemed well in spite of the heart attack he had suffered. The old man had assured Eduardo that the care he received in Guadalajara was good. The doctors said his heart had not suffered permanent damage. This positive report did not assuage Eduardo's guilt after learning that the heart attack followed the news of his gang involvement. He vowed to return for his grandfather when he finished school and could support the old man.

When sleep continued to elude him, Eduardo left for the airport and caught an earlier flight back to Los Angeles. At the airport, he called Perez to let him know he was on his way home. *Home*, he thought; the villa had become his home. He wished with all his heart that he could have brought his grandfather with him, but that would be imposing on the gracious hospitality of his mentor. If Uncle Philip suggested it once they had a chance to talk, well, that was a different matter. *One day*, he thought. *One day, I will bring Grandfather to be with me.*

Eduardo found his gate and took a seat. The picture was in his breast pocket. He slipped it from his jacket and studied the family. How remarkable. His parents looked just as he had always envisioned them. *They were in love, and they were happy*, he thought. *How would my life have been different*, he wondered, *if they had not died?* He closed his eyes and tried to imagine. The sleep that would not come in the night finally overtook him, and the picture slipped to the floor.

Eduardo was awakened by a hand on his shoulder. "Sir," the gate attendant said.

"You've been sleeping. You're about to miss your flight."

"Whaa?" Eduardo mumbled, waking with a start.

"We're getting ready to close the door," she said. "You need to hurry if you're going to Los Angeles."

"Eduardo grabbed his bag and ran to the gate. He handed over his boarding pass and hurried down the jet way. The door closed behind him. The plane was on the runway when he remembered the picture. Frantic, he looked first in his shirt pocket and then reached for his bag.

"Sir, you will have to stow your bag until we reach cruising altitude," a flight attendant warned him.

"Please," Eduardo said, "we've got to return to the gate. I left something where I was sitting, and I've got to get it."

"I'm sorry, sir," the attendant said, "but once the door is closed and we have backed away from the gate, we can't return."

"You've got to," he said. His desperation was evident to everyone around him, and a few passengers were getting nervous.

"What is it that you left?" the attendant asked.

"A photograph," he replied, "a photograph of my parents and me."

"I'm sure someone will pick it up and turn it in to security," she said. "This happens all the time. I'll give you the number for security, and you can call them as soon as we land."

It was as if Eduardo had lost his most prized possession; and indeed, he had, for back at the gate, a child awaiting the next flight, spilled a cup of orange juice where Eduardo had been sitting. The juice ran down the chair and soaked into paper and debris underneath the seat. A janitor was summoned; and the mess, including an orange juice soaked photograph, was cleared away.

*   *   *

As soon as the airplane landed in Los Angeles, Eduardo called security at the Guadalajara Airport. "Hundreds of things are turned in every day," the voice said on the other end of the phone. "I will look at the log for yesterday . . . you say it was on old photograph showing a man, a woman, and a baby?"

"No, not yesterday," Eduardo screamed into the phone. "Today, just a few hours ago." I lost it at gate 17. And yes, it was an old photograph of a man, a woman, and a baby."

"Well then," the voice said, "it most probably has not been logged in yet. Employees usually turn small items in at the end of their shift. Why don't you call back in three or four hours?" Eduardo hung up the phone, and as he hung it up, he felt he was hanging up on the only connection he had to his parents. In his gut, he knew the photograph was gone. He pulled the cross from his pocket, kissed it, and then went to meet Uncle Philip.

*   *   *

Though the picture was gone, its image was seared into Eduardo's mind; and he would never, as long as he lived, lose the mental image of his parents and himself upon that piece of paper. He forgave himself at length for his carelessness, and his thoughts eventually turned to other things. More precisely, his thoughts turned to a slender young blonde woman he last saw in Mexico City.

Eduardo felt some hesitancy calling Emily. He did not know whether it was the fear of being rebuffed or guilt for the way he had treated her over the years. Inner urgings finally took control, and he found himself dialing the Montoya house one evening in late September. He had no plan for what he would say. It seemed enough that he would hear Emily's voice. He hung up twice before putting the call completely through, asking himself, *What if Emily does not want to talk with me?* Taking a deep breath, he began dialing a third time and finished punching all the numbers. A thousand self-doubts raced through his mind from the time the phone stopped ringing until Mrs. Montoya's voice sounded on the other end.

"Mrs. Montoya? Hi, it's Eduardo Rodriguez."

"Eduardo, how nice to hear from you."

"I was hoping to talk with Emily. Is she at home?"

"No, dear. She left for school just yesterday, but she asked me to give you her number if you called."

*   *   *

CHAPTER TWENTY-FOUR

A Painful Diagnosis

Torrance, California
September 1989

At the beginning of Eduardo's junior year of college, Perez sat in the office of his old friend, John Montoya. It wasn't time for his annual physical, but Philip was troubled by persistent fatigue. "I've never felt so drained in my life," he told his friend. "I'm tired even when I get out of bed in the morning. We spent a couple of weeks at the lake, and I did nothing but sit and read, and even that seemed to tire me." The physical exam revealed nothing noteworthy other than some bruising on Philip's legs.

"Did you bump into something on vacation, Philip?" John asked.

"I'm always bumping in to things," he replied, "but not hard enough to create this kind of color."

"Has your lab work been drawn?"

"I had it done three days ago."

"Results should be in. I'll ask Betty to bring me a copy. Get dressed and meet me in my office." He had a worried look on his face as he left the exam room. Philip removed the gown, dressed, and walked down the hall where John sat studying a pile of papers on his desk. When he raised his head, the worried look had not left his face. "Sit down, Philip." He was about to perform the task he most despised in the practice of medicine. "It is not good news, Philip," he began. He was acutely aware that no one sat beside his friend. There was no family to help bear the stab of the diagnosis, no wife or child to lend strength, only he himself; and he would be the one to deliver the terrible blow.

Philip bowed his head. Though the details were lacking, the essence of the message was written in John's expression. "What is it?" he asked.

Montoya moved around the desk. No longer the doctor, he took the chair alongside his friend.

"What is it, John?" Phillip asked again.

Montoya bowed his head. "I believe you have leukemia."

"Leukemia," Perez repeated. "Not a diagnosis anyone wants to hear." Then looking into the face of his friend, he added, "Or a diagnosis anyone wants to give."

"Believe me, Philip," John said, "this is one of the hardest things I have ever had to say."

"Is there any effective treatment?"

"We have to confirm the diagnosis. I know an oncologist at UCLA—"

"Is there any effective treatment?"

John shrugged his shoulders. "It depends on the type, Philip. We will have to run some other tests. Then a course of chemo, possibly bone marrow transplant if we can find a compatible donor—"

"And if this treatment isn't effective?"

"A year, maybe two," the doctor said, studying his folded hands. "I will call my colleague at UCLA, but"—here his voice caught—"I just don't know."

"I will trust you to be honest with me as time progresses, my friend," Perez, now the comforter, said.

Montoya grasped Philip's hand. "We will do everything we can. New treatments are literally being discovered daily."

"You are a good doctor," Philip replied, "and an even better friend. And now I must decide how to tell Eduardo, Maria, and Tomas. I think the most difficult thing will be telling Eduardo. He has already lost so many—"

"If I can help in any way . . .," Montoya offered.

"Thanks, my friend, but this is something I must do myself."

That evening, following dinner, Phillip Perez called his family into his study. Eduardo, Maria, and Tomas looked from one to the other. They had felt something was amiss all through dinner, and now the assembling of the group bespoke a message they did not want to hear. Perez looked suddenly old and tired.

"Are you all right, Uncle?" Eduardo asked, unable to bear the suspense and fearing that something terrible was about to be revealed.

Philip raised his weary head. "No," he said. "I am ill, seriously ill." He looked at each of his companions to see the impact his words had on them. Maria quickly crossed herself and held her hands together as if in prayer. Tomas sat quietly, head bowed. Eduardo's hands clenched the arms of his chair as though he was ready to spring forward and accost some foe. "Dr. Montoya gave me news I suspected but did not want to hear," he continued. "I have been very tired of late, and now I know why." As he shared the details of his illness, only Tomas seemed unsurprised. He had watched Philip's strength wane and his appetite fail.

"What can we do?" Maria asked, unable to comprehend what life would be like if they lost their beloved friend.

"I will ask you to pray," Perez said simply. "And if God in His Providence chooses . . ." His words trailed off.

"There must be something we can do," Eduardo shouted. "In this age of modern medicine with all its technology, there must something we can do." *Please, God*, he prayed in his heart, *do not let me lose this man.*

There were many tests before a complete diagnosis was determined, and then the treatments began: rounds of chemotherapy followed by vomiting and weakness. There was concentrated prayer from the church family, and finally in March, there was a period of remission.

"We cannot say you are cured, Philip," John Mendoza cautioned, "but your blood work is normal. We will continue to check it every two months." Philip's strength and appetite returned with the remission. "Please ease back into your schedule," John cautioned. "You may feel your strength returning, but you have been through a lot. Go easy on yourself."

"Do you think it would be OK if Eduardo and I travel this summer?"

"Your immune system has been weakened by the disease as well as the treatment. You could pick up an infection so easily. I think you should stay close to home this summer."

"Well then, I think Eduardo will not mind since Emily will be home soon."

"She's arriving at the end of the May," John said, smiling for the first time. "We'll be glad to have her home from school. Tell Eduardo that her brother and sister have missed her too. He may have a fight on his hands for her time."

"As smitten as I think he is, he will probably put up a good fight."

"You know, I think she's had a crush on Eduardo since the day she met him," John said, laughing now.

That evening, Eduardo sat with Philip in his study. "I don't mind staying around home, Uncle Philip. I'm just relieved that you are cured."

"Not cured, Eduardo. I'm in remission. That is different from being cured, but we will take each day as a gift from God and make the most of it."

"There are a lot of things we can do around here," Eduardo said. "We can read and take walks, and I can help Tomas in the garden, and there's always swimming and tennis."

"Emily will be home in two months," Philip said.

"Yes, I know. We have been corresponding pretty regularly."

"She is a lovely girl, and I expect to see a lot of her this summer."

"Thanks, Uncle Philip." Eduardo smiled. "I'll make sure that expectation is met."

Philip had almost forgotten an appointment he'd made with his attorney until Martha reminded him as he was leaving work the following day. "It's so good to have you back at work, sir, even if it is only half days," Martha said. "I suppose you won't be in tomorrow, though."

"Why wouldn't I be in Martha?"

"You have an appointment with Mr. Lazlo at eight."

"I'd forgotten. Must be the chemo," he muttered to himself. "Thanks for reminding me. What would I do without you?"

Frank Lazlo worked for a large international law firm in downtown Los Angeles. Philip liked him because he was a man of integrity. His office handled every imaginable kind of law, which meant while Frank handled issues related to Philip's estate, one of his partners had been able to handle Eduardo's immigration issues. Philip parked in the garage and took the elevator to the thirtieth floor.

"Mr. Lazlo's assistant will be with you shortly," the receptionist told Philip.

A short young woman in a black business suit appeared two minutes later. "Hello, Dr. Perez. Come on back to Mr. Lazlo's office. He'll be with you in just a minute. Can I get you some coffee?"

"Coffee would be great." *It was nice to enjoy the simple things of life again*, Philip thought. During the chemotherapy, he had lost his appetite and his sense of taste; but things were slowly returning to normal, and a cup of coffee sounded very good indeed.

"Good morning, Philip," Frank said, entering the office like a gust of wind. Frank was a large man and would have been imposing in the courtroom if he had chosen to practice trial law. He grasped Philip's outstretched hand firmly and surveyed him from head to foot. "You're looking well. I thought Katy said—"

"I am in remission, Frank. I don't know for how long, but I will take whatever God allows me."

"I was so sorry to hear—"

"Thanks, my friend. Hopefully, I'm through with the worst of it."

"So you want to go over your trust?"

"That and something else. When you stare death in the face, the important issues really stand out. I have no heir, Frank, and I want to remedy that."

Frank stared at Philip over the top of his reading glasses. He was aware of the death of all of Philip's immediate family. He had drawn up Philip first trust, which provided generously for Tomas and Maria as well as Philip's church and various charities.

"I'm confused, Philip. Are you planning to remarry and start a family?"

"No, I want to adopt."

"Well, Philip, I'm sure your intentions are noble, but in your current state of health, I don't think an infant or even an older child for that matter would be placed in your home. I'm sorry, but—"

"The young man I plan to adopt will be twenty-one in seven months."

Frank studied his client for a long minute. He knew now who the prospective adoptee was because he had helped one of his partners wade through the red tape that had to be dealt with to keep Eduardo Rodriguez in the United States. "Philip, are you sure about this?"

"Believe me, Frank, I'm quite sure."

"I wish I was as confident about this as you are." Laying his arms on his desk, he leaned forward and held Philip's eyes. "This is hard for me to ask, but are you competent to make this type of decision? I mean it hasn't been that long since you were receiving huge doses of chemicals, has it?"

"Would you feel better doing this work for me if you could meet Eduardo again?"

"Perhaps," the attorney said. "The thing is, Philip, you can do whatever you like. I just, well, we've been such good friends—"

"I understand completely. Maybe you should become reacquainted with Eduardo. Why don't you join us for dinner at Angelini's this Friday, say seven thirty? You can get to know him a little better over a good meal. I want you to handle this for me, Frank, but I don't want you to do it unless you are comfortable with it." The men talked for another half hour, and Frank promised to meet them at his favorite restaurant that Friday evening. "Frank, I haven't mentioned this to Eduardo yet. I'm looking for the right words and the right time, so I'd appreciate it if you didn't say anything."

Frank shook his head and once again grasped Philip's hand. "You're a good man, Philip."

"I'm so glad you have an appetite again, Uncle Philip," Eduardo said when Philip told him about their dinner plans.

"It wasn't just the appetite," Philip told him. "Food tasted different while I was in treatment. My taste buds are slowly returning to normal, and I think I'll be putting on a little weight if I'm not careful."

"A few pounds wouldn't hurt you," Maria said, stepping into the room. "Here, I've prepared a flan. That should help start the process." She placed generous portions in front of Philip and Eduardo along with steaming cups of coffee. "Let me know if there's anything else you need," she said on her way out.

"I'll bring the dishes to the kitchen when we're done," Eduardo said. Turning to Philip, he asked, "Isn't Frank Lazlo the man who got me permanent residence and is working on my citizenship?"

"He's the man I called. One of his partners, a specialist in immigration and naturalization, is handling your case."

"Is there some kind of problem?" He had always secretly harbored fears that he might be deported.

Philip looked at Eduardo and realized the right time might have arrived for a discussion of his adoption plans. "No," he said. "No, there isn't any problem, I assure you." He rubbed his hand along the smooth leather arm of his chair. The two new leather wing back chairs Eduardo found had replaced the old couch whose upholstery had worn through to the stuffing. "These chairs are perfect," Philip said, sinking down further and stretching his legs. "The leather is so smooth. It reminds me of saddle leather, and saddle leather reminds me of my father." *Perhaps this is a start*, he thought.

Eduardo smiled. "I hope that is a good thing. Sometimes it's hard to be reminded of those we have lost."

"This is a good thing, Eduardo." He looked at the young man sitting next to him. "Are there things that make you think of your father?"

"No, I was too young when they died. I have no memory of my father at all. When I think of losing the photograph Grandfather gave me, I feel so bad I hate to be reminded of it."

Philip hung his head. This was not going well. He couldn't imagine having just one picture of his family and then losing it. "What do you know about your parents?"

"Grandfather never spoke much of them except to say that my father was a good man and my mother was a beautiful woman. He gave me my mother's cross, and thankfully, I have not lost that."

"What do you think they would have wanted for you?"

Eduardo sighed and repositioned himself in the ample chair. "I think they probably wanted the same things Grandfather wanted, a good education, good manners, happiness, and a strong faith in God." He looked at Philip. "All the things you have helped me acquire."

Philip shook his head in affirmation. "I believe so too. I am extremely proud of you, Eduardo, and I know they would be too."

The boy put his hand to his face, and Philip sensed he was near tears. "I've tried so hard since I've come to live with you. I do believe they would be proud of me now. If only I hadn't lost that picture," he said, choking back the sobs. "I don't know how I will ever tell Grandfather. It was the only one he had, and I know he cherished it."

"Are you sure there was no other picture?" Philip probed.

"Yes," Eduardo said. "Grandfather had kept it so carefully all these years, and then . . ." He choked again.

"I am truly sorry," Philip said, and he knew the right words would not come tonight.

The right words had not come by Friday evening, nor had another opportune time. Eduardo slipped into tan slacks and a blue plaid shirt with the sleeves rolled up. The arms of a navy sweater were loosely tied around his neck. "OK, Uncle Philip?" he asked.

"You look very preppy, Eduardo. How about me?"

"You always look good, Uncle."

Marco greeted the men at the door. "Buonasera," he said, shaking their hands. "Your table is ready, and Mr. Lazlo is already here." They were led to a corner at the back of the restaurant where the attorney waited. "Frank," Philip said. "You remember Eduardo?"

"Hi, Eduardo," Frank said rising. "I must admit I wouldn't have recognized you at all."

"Hello, Mr. Lazlo." Eduardo smiled. "I've changed a lot since our first meeting; in more ways than one."

"I'd love to hear about those changes," Frank said as they sat down.

"Well, let's take a look at the menu first," Philip suggested, "and then we have the rest of the night to talk." He picked up the wine list and called Gino over for a suggestion. "Can you bring us a nice bottle of Italian wine?"

"Red or white, dottore?"

"Red, I think. Is that OK with you, Frank?"

"Red is my choice."

"Then I suggest this nice bottle of Brunello," Gino said, pointing to an offering on the wine list.

"Very good. We'll have that."

"And for the young man, a soda perhaps?"

"Water, please," Eduardo said.

A waiter set an amuse bouche in front of the men and offered assistance with the menu. "Go ahead," Philip told Frank.

"I think I'll start with the beet salad, and then I'll have the lamb chops."

"The lamb is consistently good," Philip said, "but this evening, I think I'll have the muscles followed by gnocchi."

"I will have the tricolor salad and the lasagna," Eduardo said.

"Ah, our signature dish," the waiter replied. "You will not be disappointed."

"Philip tells me you're enrolled at UCLA," Frank said as they waited for their first course.

"That's correct," Eduardo replied, smiling. "It took a little work, but I made it."

"It had been a few years since I entered college," Frank said. "As I recall, there were applications, interviews, and forms for student loans that took up a lot of my time."

"It doesn't' sound like things have changed much, sir," Eduardo replied. "At first it seemed overwhelming, but I had a tutor who helped break things down into small steps for me. I got a small academic scholarship, and I applied for grants and loans."

Frank glanced at Philip. The attorney knew Perez had sufficient funds to pay for Eduardo's education.

"The whole process is an education in itself," Philip said, noting the question in Frank's eyes.

"I'm working hard to keep my GPA up," Eduardo interjected. "I'm going to be obligated to repay those loans, and the job market is pretty competitive."

"What's your GPA?" Frank asked.

"I'm heading into my senior year with a 3.79."

Frank raised his eyebrows appreciatively.

"What's your major?"

"Journalism. We have a friend who is doing freelance photography, and he just got an assignment for *National Geographic*. I might try some freelance writing and hope it works into a foreign correspondent position"—and here he glanced at Philip—"or I could possibly end up working on documentary films. I have a minor in film production."

"Impressive," the attorney said. "Well, I'm hoping you will graduate as a citizen. Things are looking good, my partner tells me."

The conversation was easy. An hour into the meal, Frank was convinced that Eduardo was not some slick gold digger drooling at a dying man's side. The young man had legitimately changed. He presented himself well without being overconfident or self-assertive. He held up his end of a conversation without dominating it. He was informed about local, national, and global affairs. *Yes*, he said to himself, *Philip has pulled it off, and this young man seems bright enough to get the job of his dreams.*

The following week in Frank's office, the men recounted the evening. "Philip, I am amazed," Frank admitted. "He's a wonderful young man. Do you want me to proceed?"

"Get things ready. I'll let you know when the time is right. He has very strong feelings for his parents, and I don't want to suggest anything that he might feel is disloyal to their memory."

"I understand," Frank said. "Let us know when you are ready. It won't take long to prepare the papers given his age."

"Thanks, Frank. Give my love to Shelly and the kids."

Philip's remission was short-lived. By the end of August, the lab reports confirmed he was out of remission.

"We have one last ace," John told him. "We'll check for a marrow donor. It would be easier if you had living relatives, but sometimes we find a compatible donor outside the family."

Philip's health continued to deteriorate. The decline was obvious to everyone, but Eduardo resolutely denied it. Although he would not openly admit Philip was dying, somewhere deep in his heart, Eduardo knew he was deluding himself. He began commuting to school just so he could spend every possible hour with Philip. Some nights he could not sleep; and at those times, he walked in the garden clutching his mother's cross, troubled and alone. Though he was alone, he was not unobserved, for in the apartment above the garage, an old man watched Eduardo leave the house, and he sat at the window until the young man returned. At first, the nocturnal walks occurred infrequently, but as Perez grew weaker, they increased.

"He cannot go on like this," Maria said one night as she peered over Tomas's shoulder. "Or he will get sick too."

The old man stood, took a light jacket from the closet, and descended the stairs to the patio. He lit a small candle on the table and sat waiting for Eduardo's return. The night breeze blew softly through the trees, and the scent of jasmine wafted through the garden. *If only life were as sweet*, Tomas thought. He did not know what he and Maria would do when the Philip was gone. Perhaps they would return to Mexico, but how they would miss this place and Philip and Eduardo. Philip was prepared to die; he had spoken of this to the couple. Tomas and Maria had accepted the inevitable, but Young Eduardo had not. Time was running out, and Tomas had decided to intercede.

It was nearly one o'clock when Eduardo returned to the patio. He was surprised to find Tomas sitting there. "Have you been here long?" he asked.

"Time is meaningless," Tomas replied. "Some events seem long, others short, even though they take exactly the same amount of space in the realm of time."

"I didn't know you were a philosopher, Tomas," the young man said.

"University of Mexico, class of 1951," Tomas replied.

Eduardo stared at the old man in astonishment.

"It is true," the old man said. "You can ask Maria if you don't believe me."

"But why—"

"Why am I gardening if I am a philosopher?"

"Yes," Eduardo said.

"I taught at the University of Mexico for many years," Tomas began. "That was where I met Philip. He came there to teach and conduct research in psychology. He was a man of integrity and old world manners, and I developed a high regard for him. We grew to be great friends, and then when he lost his family . . . Well, Maria and I tried to help as much as we could, but he seemed to descend deeper and deeper into despair. We finally suggested he move to a completely different place where he could build a new life. A year or so after the tragedy, he took a trip to California and secured a job with the school district. That's when he began talking to Maria and me about joining him. I took a sabbatical, and he put us in the apartment above the garage with a beautiful view of the ocean. Maria fell in love with it, and after a year, we did not want to leave. The grounds of the villa were nothing but dirt, and my fingers were itching to get in there and plant things and make the hillside bloom. I was near enough to retirement that we were able to stay. Maria enjoys managing the house, and I help Philip with his research." He looked up at the young man. "It is not just the garden that I tend, although that brings me great pleasure. I have my own little office over the garage."

"I did not know," Eduardo replied.

"Philip has been working on some important theories," Tomas continued.

"The work is nearly finished, and he asked me to promise that his work will be published." Here the old man lifted his eyes again and held Eduardo in his stare.

"He will publish his work, no doubt," Eduardo said.

"He knows he will not see this through to the end, but it is important to him, and he has asked for my promise that his work will be published," Tomas repeated.

"He will publish it," Eduardo said, rising to leave an encounter that was bringing him close to tears.

"There is very little in this life that we control," Tomas said softly, "We enter this world and we leave this world, but not at times of our own choosing."

"I don't want to talk about this," Eduardo said.

"It does not matter whether you want to talk of it or not. You do not have to talk of it, but you must face it, and talking makes the facing easier to bear."

Eduardo sat back down. "I cannot bear this," he said. "I cannot bear this. I have come to love him like my own father. My own father was taken from me. Now I am told I must prepare to say goodbye to Uncle Philip. Every night I walk in the garden and beg God to spare his life, but each day, he grows weaker and thinner. The nurses and doctors come and go. They treat him and go to their families and comfortable homes, but we sit here watching him grow weaker day by day, and there is nothing we can do. There is no escape for him or us. We are stuck in our own private hell. Some people fall asleep at night and dream bad dreams. We awaken to our nightmare each morning." Eduardo began sobbing. "Where is God?" he yelled. "Who hears my prayers?"

"Prayers are not magic," Tomas said, "though many approach prayer in that way. God knows our prayers and our hearts, and we must be prepared for His answers." He pulled a clean handkerchief from his pocket and handed it to Eduardo. "It is especially hard for you, my friend, but Philip is prepared for what will come, of this I am sure. His greatest concern now is for you." He paused and looked at the young man who had grown and matured so much since their first meeting. "Many young men would not have the courage to stay by his side as he faces this. You are here, as difficult as it has been, and you have not made excuses to leave, although we all would have understood if you had. I am very proud of you."

"First he taught me how to live with dignity, and now he is teaching me how to die with dignity. What will I do without him?" Eduardo cried.

"You will do what the rest of us do," Tomas said, grasping Eduardo's hand and holding tightly. "We will go on living, and we will do it together." In that moment, he knew his and Maria's lives would be incomplete without this young man. "We will keep his memory alive. We will never forget him."

"I do not want to lose you and Maria too," Eduardo said. "I do not think I could bear to be alone."

"We are family," Tomas said "And we will not leave you."

The sobs quieted and eventually subsided. "Thank you, Tomas," Eduardo said at last.

"Thank you for waiting for me here tonight."

"You are welcome, Eduardo." Then squeezing the young man's hand, he said, "You will be all right. We will all be all right."

That was the last of Eduardo's midnight walks for a very long time.

Eduardo's citizenship examination and ceremony came at the end of September, just before his twenty-first birthday. Though he was weak, Philip insisted on attending the ceremony. Tomas, Maria, and Emily sat with him, keeping him as comfortable as possible while cheering for Eduardo.

John Montoya was desolate at not being able to find a close-enough donor match for his friend to risk the procedure. Even with good a match, the procedure did not always work. "I will keep trying, Philip," he said. "I have even been tested myself."

CHAPTER TWENTY-FIVE

The Legacy

Palos Verdes Peninsula
October 12, 1990

"My story is finished, Eduardo. The rest, I think you know." The young man bowed his head in humility and anguish. He had grown to care very deeply for Philip over the years; but tonight, with the telling of his story, Eduardo felt a new bond with this man borne out of their tragic pasts. Each had suffered tragedy, and now another tragedy awaited them. Eduardo glanced at Philip in the dim firelight. The face was tired and etched with concern.

"What is it you would have me do for you?" he asked, hoping to relieve some of Philip's worry.

"I have no heir," Philip began. "When I lost my family, I not only lost my son, but I also lost the hope of children yet unborn . . ." Here he looked at Eduardo, and the consequences of the request he was about to make raced through his mind. Eduardo had every right to refuse the offer, and he might; but would he be angry? That was the reaction Philip feared most, for he would never ask a thing that might cause Eduardo anguish over loyalties to his own family. The strain showed clearly on Philip's face. He sat hunched over in his chair, drawing his breaths in short gasps.

Eduardo's stomach churned. He realized now that Philip's anguish was tied to the death of his son, but what could he do to lighten that pain? "I cannot imagine losing a child," he said. "He would have carried your name forward into future generations. That is something every man hopes for, but your name will not be forgotten, Uncle. Tomas has told me of your work. He will publish it, and that will be your legacy."

"Yes, my work. It seems so inconsequential now."

"It is not inconsequential to me," Eduardo said. "It is not inconsequential to Diego. Even though Matt did not read your papers, he read your life and provided the guidance Diego needed to set goals for his life. There will be others, Uncle. Your son may not be here to carry your name forward, but others will."

"Do you want to stay here, Eduardo?"

"Of course, I will stay here, Uncle Philip. I am a citizen now."

"Do you want to stay here, in this house?"

"It is home," Eduardo said sadly. "You have made it home, you and Tomas and Maria."

"I would have left this house and the ranch to my son," Philip said. Tears coursed down his cheeks.

"You are so tired, Uncle Philip. Can I please help you to bed?"

"I am tired," Philip agreed. "But this won't wait any longer. I have been waiting for the right time, the right words, but I haven't found them." He raised his head and looked Eduardo in the eyes.

"No one will ever replace Alejandro," Philip said softly, "but you have become like a son to me, Eduardo." He smiled, and his face relaxed. "In fact, Alejandro's middle name was Eduardo, Eduardo for my father, Victor Eduardo Perez, and Alejandro for Elena's father Pedro Alejandro Rodriguez."

Eduardo started. His grandfather was Pedro Rodriguez. It was a common name and an interesting coincidence. He reached into his pocket, withdrew his mother's cross, and began rubbing it with his thumb and forefinger.

Perez raised his head and nodded at the young man. "Yes, you are very much like my son would have been, I think."

"I owe you everything," Eduardo said softly. "I promise I will not let your family's memory . . ." The words trailed off. Eduardo could not meet Philip's eyes. The pain and sorrow of a lifetime of living without his own parents flooded his heart, and now he faced the loss of this man who had become both mother and father to him. His body shook gently with the sobs he refused to release in the presence of Philip.

Philip extended a frail hand and covered the boy's. He was happy knowing Eduardo would not allow his memory to be lost, but would the boy consent to adoption? As far as dying, he was at peace with God, and he looked forward to seeing his family once again. Oh, how he longed for them. His face though tired had taken on an ethereal glow in the firelight.

Eduardo turned his left palm up and gently interwove his fingers with Philip's. They sat, each lost in their own thoughts for a long time. Perez's thoughts eventually turned his attention to the room in which he and

Eduardo sat. Their story could have had a much different ending, he knew. There was something good that he had sensed in this young man. There was something he could not put his finger on, something that had drawn them together. He turned his gazed down at the strong hand enfolded in his own. It was a very masculine hand, though it was soft and uncalloused. There was a small amount of dark hair and large vessels on the back, and the fingers were long with neatly trimmed nails. "I have a request to make," Philip said.

"Anything," Eduardo replied.

"I have no. I, I," he stumbled.

Eduardo's grasp of Philip's hand tightened. "Yes, Uncle?"

Taking a deep breath, Philip started again. "I know you hold the memory of your parents very dear. I would never ask anything of you that might seem to diminish their memory, but . . ." His words failed him.

"What is it, Uncle Philip? Please just let me know what is on your heart. I can see that something is troubling you very much."

"Eduardo," he said, looking into the young man's eyes, "I wish to adopt you and make you my heir."

Eduardo stiffened. "Adopt me?" he asked. "I would take your name then and give up my own?"

"Yes," Philip answered. "That is usually how it is done." He studied Eduardo. "You do not wish to do this, I can see. I had no right to ask you." The disappointment in his voice was evident.

Eduardo laid his head back on the chair and closed his eyes. He had not released Philip's hand, and he felt tremors coursing through the man's palm and fingers. How could he deny this wonderful, gracious man his last request? But how could he give up the name his father had given him? He brought his mother's cross to his mouth and kissed it.

"What is that in your hand?" Philip asked.

Eduardo opened his hand and extended it to Philip. The dainty gold chain and simple cross gleamed in the firelight. "It was my mother's," he said. "My grandfather gave it to me when I left Mexico."

Philip took the small piece of jewelry and held it closer to his eyes.

"There is an inscription on the back," Eduardo said.

Philip's eyes narrowed as he turned the cross and tried to focus on the etching.

"You will not be able to see it in this light," Eduardo said, "and some of the lettering has worn away. It looks like ETR and underneath that P something."

But Philip was not listening. He had released Eduardo's hand and covered his eyes as sobs racked his frail frame.

"Uncle Philip?" Eduardo's eyes pled for an explanation of the man's sudden show of anguish. Philip extended his right arm and drew Eduardo to him. The sobs gave way to coughing, and Philip struggled for air. Eduardo knelt in front of the man and held his face, peering into the eyes now red and overflowing. "Tomas," he screamed, knowing Tomas and Maria were most likely sound asleep. He rose to call for help, but Philip grabbed his hand with what strength remained, and he would not let it go.

After a period of several minutes, Philip's breathing eased. "This is Elena's cross," he said, opening his hand and holding it aloft. "Elena Torrez Rodriguez."

Eduardo leaned close. "Uncle Philip, he said with great respect, "it cannot be your wife's cross. I did not take it from you." The words tumbled from Eduardo's mouth. "It was given to me by my grandfather. That and the picture were all I had in this world that belonged to my mother."

Philip shook his head almost imperceptibly. "Why," he said, "why, did I not see it? But how could it be?"

Eduardo was frantic. Thoughts raced through his head. *He thinks I have stolen this. He thinks I have betrayed him. Chemotherapy has affected his reasoning. He does not understand, and now as he faces the end of his life, he thinks I have wronged him.* A groan escaped the young man's lips as the agony of the thought tore at his soul. "Please," he said, "please understand. I love you. I owe everything to you. I would never take what is yours. Please . . ."

"Elena's Bible," Philip said, "may I see it?" Eduardo reached for the Bible that had been laid aside on the table. With some difficulty, Philip opened it and withdrew an old photograph. "This was my family," he said handing the picture to Eduardo.

Eduardo stared in disbelief. In his hand lay an old photograph, its edges tattered from frequent handling. Soft sepia tones had been muted by the passing of time, but the images were unmistakable. A beautiful young woman with a heart-shaped face and glistening black hair stood smiling the smile of one who holds a great secret. The woman was held in the protective embrace of a man whose eyes twinkled as he looked down at her and the infant held securely in her arms. A small cross lay against the woman's chest. Confusion swirled in Eduardo's mind. "These are my parents," he breathed. "This baby is me. Uncle, why did you not tell me that the photo had been returned?"

Philip motioned for Eduardo to turn the photo over. On the back, in feminine script, was a message. *My darling Philip, wherever we are, whether together or apart, know that Alejandro and I love you very much, your own Elena.* Eduardo looked at Philip.

"She set it on my desk before she left to visit her father. I never saw them again. This is not your picture, Eduardo. It is mine. You are the baby in this picture. You are Alejandro, Alejandro Eduardo Rodriguez Perez."

Eduardo rose and took a step back. "It can't be," he said. "This does not make any sense. My parents are dead. I have been told my whole life that my parents are dead. Why would I be told that if it is not true?"

"Your parents could not have both died in the accident," Philip said. "I did not go to San Jenaro. I was in Mexico City." He laid the Bible on the table and dropped the cross in its folds. With difficulty, he rose and held Eduardo's arm for support. "Tell me what you know of the accident," he said.

"My parents and my father's parents took me to see my grandfather." The pain of recounting the story was evident in his voice. "On the way there, a truck ran into my grandfather's car. The car caught fire. Someone rescued me just before it exploded. Everyone else was . . ." Here Eduardo's voice dropped off.

"Your mother was anxious to see her father," Philip said softly. "He had battled depression since the death of his wife, and from recent telephone calls, she could tell his depression was deepening. She felt a visit would lighten his mood. I was presenting at a conference at the university and could not leave, so my parents agreed to drive her and Alejandro. I planned to fly to Guadalajara in two days where my father would meet me and take me to see Uncle Pedro. We would stay a few more days and then drive back to Pachua together. On the way to San Jenaro, the car was hit by a truck. Just as you said, it exploded, and the passengers were all killed. I was told they were all killed." Philip choked and began to sob. "I did not know. I just did not know that you had survived. The shock of losing his daughter sent your grandfather into the hospital for months. When I travelled to Pachua to retrieve the ashes, I visited Uncle Pedro at the institution. I sat and held his hand for hours crying at our loss, but he did not even know I was there."

Eduardo still could not believe what he was hearing. "Why did he never tell you that I was alive? Why did he not tell me you were alive?" he asked.

"The accident happened on the way to see him. He must have thought I was in the car," Philip said. "He must have been told that only you had survived."

"But who took me?" Eduardo asked. "Who cared for me while Grandfather was sick?" And then he answered his own question, "Juanita."

"She hated us so much," Philip said. "But I never understood how much. She knew I was alive. She tried to stop me from visiting Uncle Pedro in the hospital. How clever she must think she is."

Eduardo stared at Philip in astonishment, and all he could say was, "Why?"

"Jealousy," Philip said, "selfish pride and jealousy." The realization of truth was dawning on Eduardo. Nervously, he rubbed the scar on his arm. Philip reached for the arm and tenderly turned it to reveal the old burn. He slowly brought the scar to his lips and kissed it. "That is what fathers do," he said, "to make it better."

"Father?" The dam that restrained all the pent-up pain of this young man's life burst, and sorrow flowed from his soul that night as he wept at his father's side.

EPILOGUE

Villa Perez
October 13, 1990

Dawn broke crisp and clear before father and son could bear to part for much-needed sleep. Eduardo helped his father climb the stairs to his bedroom. "You have become the parent," Philip said sadly. "And I never had a chance to show you how."

"Shhh," Eduardo soothed. "You've been showing me how a father cares for a son for the last seven years. Now sleep, because we have a lot of time to make up for when you've rested."

"I do not have a lot of time, my son," Philip reminded. "But I will die happy having spent even a few hours with you."

"Do not talk like that," Eduardo said. "I thought I had lost you once. I will not lose you again."

"This is not in our hands," Philip said.

"No," Eduardo replied. "It is in God's hands, and I don't believe He brought us together just to say goodbye. Now sleep, Father." He tucked the smooth sheet around Philip's shoulders and quietly closed the door.

Once downstairs, Eduardo reached for the telephone. "Dr. Montoya," he said breathlessly when the phone was answered. "We have found a relative. How soon can we test for donor compatibility?"

CPSIA information can be obtained at www.ICGtesting.com
Printed in the USA
BVOW07*0338290914

368552BV00001B/3/P